"They will hit the Croatian president at Vordjalik."

Gellar leaned closer, noting that the small village lay near the halfway point between Zdar and the Croatian capital. "It might be easier to take him there than in Zdar," he said, thinking aloud.

"But if we're wrong," Mack Bolan stated, "we blow our only chance."

That was the hell of it. Gellar couldn't be sure. The Nazi strike team—even if there was a strike team waiting for the president—might try to kill him in Zdar, or anywhere else along the two-hundred-mile route from the capital.

"Gerhard Steuben thrives on symbolism," Gellar said at last. "I think a hometown murder would appeal to him."

"Your call," Bolan said. "But if we miss, Steuben wins."

DON PENDLETON's
MACK BOLAN.

Power of the Lance

THE TYRANNY FILES
BOOK II

A GOLD EAGLE BOOK FROM
WORLDWIDE.

TORONTO • NEW YORK • LONDON
AMSTERDAM • PARIS • SYDNEY • HAMBURG
STOCKHOLM • ATHENS • TOKYO • MILAN
MADRID • WARSAW • BUDAPEST • AUCKLAND

First edition July 2001

ISBN 0-373-61479-9

Special thanks and acknowledgment to
Mike Newton for his contribution to this work.

POWER OF THE LANCE

Printed in U.S.A.

The pleasure of hating, like a poisonous mineral, eats into the heart of religion, and turns it to rankling spleen and bigotry; it makes patriotism an excuse for carrying fire, pestilence, and famine into other lands; it leaves to virtue nothing but the spirit of censoriousness.

—William Blake
The Plain Speaker, 1826

Professional haters understand nothing but hate. Terrorists understand nothing but violence and terror. It's time for me to speak the common language of my enemies again, and make them realize their day is done.

—Mack Bolan

For Simon Wiesenthal and Morris Dees

CHAPTER ONE

Germany

Thorsten Isaacson had wakened from a bad dream in the middle of the night, gripped by fear that some dark peril lay ahead for him and his loved ones. He wasn't psychic, and despite his strong religious faith, he put no stock in premonitions, ESP or any of the other New Age rubbish that appeared to be so popular with young people these days. Still, there had been times when his feelings had alerted him to some great trouble yet to come, and who was he, a humble pawnbroker, to say that there was no room in this troubled age for warnings from Almighty God?

And modern times *were* troubled in Berlin. There could be no doubt on that score. Newspapers were filled with stories of the thriving state economy since Germany had been reunified, but they downplayed the incidents of violence—and more particularly, the persistent omens that an ancient evil had been revived and was determined to reclaim its native land. Some three-quarters of a century before, that evil had encouraged Isaacson's grandparents to emigrate and try their luck in London, while most of their relatives remained behind and ultimately perished in the camps with names like Auschwitz, Buchenwald and Majdenek. Despite that evil, Isaacson's parents had returned in 1963, when he was barely six years old, expressing faith in Germany's concerted effort to atone, redeem itself, after the madness had subsided.

But he saw now that the madness still survived.

Isaacson had children of his own now—lovely daughters, in their teens—and he was gravely troubled by the turn that things had taken since The Wall came down in 1989 and the sundered halves of Germany were reunited a year later. His girls had still been small then, more or less oblivious to thoughtless comments from their schoolmates, but the evil had been growing, had become more brutally insistent with each passing year. The German state still banned open display of swastikas and other Nazi symbols, still proscribed the public praise of Adolf Hitler and his genocidal war against "inferiors," but racist skinhead gangs were everywhere, and they increasingly received support from older men—in politics, the media and, some insisted, the police force and the courts.

Sporadic racist violence was a fact of life in modern-day Berlin and in most other parts of Germany, where the Gestapo spirit still clung desperately to life. A wave of not so subtle Holocaust revisionism was in vogue: Hitler's slaughter of the Jews, Gypsies and others was "exaggerated" in the liberal—read Jewish—media; there had been concentration camps, of course, but they weren't specifically designed to kill, but were simply deficient—as was every German city during World War II—in food and medical supplies; the Nazis hated no one, rather "loving" Germans who were loyal to their blood and to the fatherland;

the true great enemy, since 1917, was communism, which, of course, had been the brainchild of a Jew.

It wasn't theory, though, that troubled Isaacson and woke him in the middle of the night; it wasn't simple propaganda that had him considering the installation of security devices that would let him lock the pawnshop even during business hours, buzzing in those customers whom he had scrutinized beforehand through a triple thickness of shatterproof glass. It was the daily evidence of mayhem in the streets: racist graffiti, cemetery desecration, beatings, arson, bombing, the occasional murder. Seven deaths within the past twelve months were publicly attributed to neo-Nazi skinhead gangs, and Isaacson took for granted that the tally was deliberately understated by police.

You didn't encourage tourism or capital investment, after all, by painting mental pictures of the führer and his brownshirts brawling in the streets of modern-day Berlin, Munich, Hanover, Düsseldorf.

Thus far, however, Isaacson hadn't purchased those new locks and windows for his shop, and so he was particularly nervous when the four skinheads passed by and glared at him.

There had been only one of them the first time. When the same youth passed again some twenty minutes later, he was joined by a companion, larger than himself, dull witted from the look of him. Both wore metal-studded leather jackets, denim pants, red laces in their high-topped boots. Another quarter of an hour passed before the two came back again, this time with yet another skinhead: stocky, this one, with a freckled scalp above a porcine face, an Iron Cross tattooed on the left side of his head. Now it was four of them, and Isaacson wondered as they passed his window, sneering at him, whether there would wind up being six or seven of the brutes before he closed the shop at half-past five, in honor of the Sabbath.

Would the young thugs wait for him outside, to waylay him as he walked home? Considering the possibility, Isaacson wished he had accepted the offer from one of his friends to help him purchase a black-market pistol, but he had never fired a gun in his life, and besides, it was too late to help him today. He would have to make do with his walking stick, its three-foot length of mahogany reinforced with a steel rod down the center, capped with a heavy pewter grip and a brass ferrule.

Distracted from the windows by his ledger of accounts, Isaacson was startled when the small bell mounted just above the door of his pawnshop jangled insistently. He glanced up from his work and found himself confronted by the skinheads. There were five now, with the new addition to their number hanging back as if to block the door.

"So," the seeming leader of the group addressed him with a sneer, "it's almost time for Sabbath, yes? Why don't you let us help you say your prayers?"

MACK BOLAN STOOD beneath the awning of a jewelry store on Lietzenburger Strasse, sheltered from a drizzling rain, and watched the skinheads pace outside the pawnshop opposite. They made a game of it, first one youth slouching past and peering through the glass, another stepping from the dark mouth of a nearby alleyway to join him on the second pass and so on. Bolan had been trailing them for close to an hour now, and it was almost with a sense of physical relief that he decided they were working up their nerve to strike.

He didn't wish the merchant ill, of course, and these particular skinheads meant no more to him than the thugs who made up any other two-bit street gang in the world...except that they were recognized associates of Manfred Roeder, German "bishop" of a global neo-Nazi cult and terrorist menagerie known as the Temple of the Nordic Covenant. That goose-stepping fraternity, together with its leaders lately vanished from the States, was Bolan's target, and an introduction to the Temple's shock troops on the street struck Bolan as a fair opening move against the sect's elusive leaders.

Anyway, it was something to do.

He could have picked off the skinheads from where he stood with the Beretta 93-R slung beneath his arm. The pistol had been fitted with a custom sound suppressor, though he would still be visible to passersby. He didn't necessarily desire to kill these sneering punks, however. Bolan would be just as happy if he simply put them in the hospital, providing he had time to question them about their leaders—more specifically, about the whereabouts of Manfred Roeder and the men he served.

There had been backup promised when he left the States, but his contact had yet to materialize. Still, it was only four hours since his flight had touched down at Berlin-Tempelhof Airport and Bolan had dropped his companion at the hotel on Kochstrasse. The contact would show when he showed. In the meantime, why wait?

Five skinheads now, and that appeared to be the lot. They loitered outside the pawnshop for a moment, butting one another with their leather-clad shoulders like nervous schoolboys or sloppy drunks, until one of them finally opened the door and they passed out of sight, single file.

Checking the traffic left and right, Bolan crossed the street to follow them, ignoring the raindrops that plastered his hair to his scalp. A police car rolled past on the nearest cross street, the uniformed passengers ignoring Bolan as he jaywalked in the middle of the block. No doubt they had more-pressing things to think about this afternoon than ticketing wayward pedestrians.

If not, he guessed, they soon would have.

The pawnshop had an awning of its own, and Bolan spent a moment on the outside, opening the buttons of his light raincoat and the jacket underneath so that the garments wouldn't stop him if he had to make a hasty grab for the Beretta. He was hoping that he wouldn't have to use the pistol, but with odds of five to one, nothing was guaranteed. The skinheads might have weapons of their own, and while he would have much preferred to pick one out and take him somewhere for a game of Twenty Questions, he wasn't prepared to sacrifice himself.

He checked the street again, both ways, relieved to note that the incessant drizzle had at least thinned out the normal sidewalk traffic. Those pedestrians who still remained were hunched beneath umbrellas, some of them with hats pulled low across their brows, most of them with their eyes downcast and staring at the pavement, as if worried it might turn to quicksand in the rain and suck them under.

That took care of witnesses.

He wished the shop were more old-fashioned,

maybe fitted out with roll-down blinds that he could draw after he stepped inside, thus simultaneously guaranteeing privacy and making a dramatic gesture that his adversaries—the survivors, anyway—might well appreciate when they reviewed the incident from a safe distance.

Never mind.

He would make do with the materials at hand and see what could be done.

A quick glance through the door's clean glass showed him the backs of five shaved heads, five leather jackets, one of them—the jackets, that was— decorated with a grinning skull that made the others seem unfortunately plain.

He couldn't hear what they were saying to the man at the register, likely wouldn't have understood it even if the words were audible. Bolan spoke very little German, which made grilling any prisoners he captured somewhat problematical, but he was counting on the fact that most Berliners seemed to know at least a little English, and the pawnbroker—assuming that he wasn't injured in the melee and didn't flee out the back—would probably be able to assist him with translations.

He thought of drawing the Beretta as he entered, just to chill things out, but was afraid that it might have the opposite effect.

Wearing a smile, he gave the door a shove and stepped into the shop.

FRANZ SPANGLER LIKED to see them squirm and sweat. The girls, especially, but he would make do with anyone in a pinch. A Jew in the hand was worth ten in the bush, more or less, and the main kick was seeing the fear in their eyes.

The fear, and the blood.

The man had a lesson coming. Not only because he was a Jew—though that was bad enough—but also for defying orders from the Thunderbolt Brigade, in which Franz Spangler held the rank of captain. As an adjunct to the Temple of the Nordic Covenant, the Thunderbolt Brigade was known to represent a cause that some Berliners would be happy to forget, but Spangler and his troops weren't about to let that happen.

More particularly, they weren't about to let the Jews forget.

Isaacson had been informed that he could stay in business for the moment, keep on swindling the Gentile idiots who traded with him in return for paying weekly taxes to the Thunderbolt Brigade. Instead of thanking Spangler for the privilege, as he should have, Isaacson had run to the police. The first time, a detective sympathetic to the movement had sidetracked the Jew's complaint and warned the boys to watch their step with Isaacson.

A warning had been chalked outside the pawnshop, on the pavement, but the guy never seemed to learn. Instead of paying up next time Spangler's collector came around, Isaacson pulled out a camera and started snapping photographs. That time, when he had called the police, he was referred to a detective who despised the skinheads, some Jew-lover who was pleased to take the case and file extortion charges. The collector, Willem Jödl, would be out of jail in six or seven months with any luck, and Spangler's charge had been dismissed when he produced five

witnesses to contradict the Jew's tale of their initial
meeting, the judge suggesting a case of mistaken
identity, since all skinheads resembled one another,
more or less.

Now it was payback time.

"Get out of here!" Isaacson said before Spangler
could even speak. "I will not pay you anything!"
Then, almost as an afterthought, he added, "I have
my camera!"

"He has his camera," Spangler repeated, while the
troops behind him laughed.

"We ought to take some pictures of him when
we're finished," Aldo said.

"Nice souvenirs," Drugi chimed in.

"We haven't come for money, Thorsten," Spangler stated, "though we'll take it when we're done
with you. You really should have paid the tax, you
know."

"I don't pay so-called tax to any Nazis. Not today,
not ever. You lot had your chance in Germany. Your
heroes are all dead."

"Perhaps we've learned from their mistakes,"
Spangler replied. And he couldn't help smiling as he
added, "This time, we do it right."

"This time the world!" Jurgen said from behind
and to his left.

"The world!" his comrades echoed.

"Tomorrow belongs to us, Thorsten," Spangler
taunted.

"Not while I'm alive."

"An oversight which we're about to remedy," the
jaunty captain of the Thunderbolt Brigade remarked.
"Unless, of course, you'd like to take my picture
first?"

The jangling of a bell behind him startled Spangler, brought him right around to face a total stranger, standing just inside the door. The man was roughly six feet tall, athletic looking, even with a suit and raincoat on. His eyes were hooded and dangerous, although he wore an edgy smile. Age indeterminate, the skinhead thought he still looked young and strong enough to kick some ass. At first, Spangler suspected that he might be a policeman, that the Jew might have set another trap, but then the stranger spoke.

In English.

"I was wondering," he said, "if one of you assholes could tell me where to find a walking sack of shit named Manfred Roeder."

Spangler had learned English in school, before he dropped out to fight full-time for the master race. Of his companions, only Drugi and Wilmot spoke no English at all.

"You are American," Jurgen said, speaking when he should have kept his mouth shut.

"Hey, you're not as stupid as you look," the well-dressed stranger said, before addressing all of them as one again. "So, how about Herr Roeder. Any thoughts, or am I giving you boys too much credit for intelligence?"

"You aren't in the United States, *scheisskopf*," Spangler reminded him, adding the "shithead" just in case the man spoke German.

"Score one for Einstein over here," the tall man answered, still with that infuriating smile. "He knows we're not in the United States. Is that an issue with you characters? I mean, the way our Immigration Service tries to keep out felons, junkies, trash like that?"

"You need to mind your business," Aldo cautioned the American.

"That's just exactly what I'm doing, boy. I'll ask again—can one of you sad-looking specimens tell me where Manfred Roeder hangs his pointy little hat when he's not busy terrorizing old ladies and children?"

"We'll be happy to discuss it with you," Spangler told him, "when we're finished with our business here."

"Oh, hey," the stranger said, "I didn't know you kids were working. Five on one? You must be braver than I gave you credit for. I would've thought you'd need at least eight cowards, maybe ten, to carry off a gig like this."

Spangler felt the hot blood rushing to his face, saw Aldo stepping off, his arm cocked to drive a fist into the stranger's face, and knew that he had to give the order swiftly or surrender all control of the event.

"Smash him!" he snapped in German. "Do it now!"

JACOB GELLAR HAD followed the American from his hotel, resisted the temptation to call out and stop him on the street. It wasn't perfect tradecraft, granted, but his curiosity had taken over. After coming all this way from the United States, what was so urgent that the tall man left his female comrade on her own at the hotel on Kochstrasse, to take off by himself?

Gellar hadn't been overly surprised when his unwitting quarry caught a taxi to the Kurfürstendamm district, disembarking on Uhlandstrasse, within a block of the Thunderbolt Brigade's run-down headquarters. There, he had loitered about, making it somewhat difficult for Gellar to conceal himself and watch, until a group of skinheads left the place and started walking north, ignoring the drizzle that beaded on their leather gear and shaved scalps. Nine blocks they hiked to Lietzenburger Strasse, the American trailing unnoticed behind them, with Gellar tracking *him* and offering a silent prayer that he, too, was unnoticed.

This one was supposed to be a nasty customer, by all accounts. Gellar wasn't afraid of him, but neither was he looking forward to a confrontation on the street. For one thing, it would get them both off on the wrong foot if they were supposed to be cooperating, and it might well ruin whatever idea the grim American was working on just now.

Skinheads.

They were the bottom of the heap as far as neo-Nazis went in Germany, but they were visible, violent and well connected to the more ''respectable'' members of the resurgent fascist movement. The American could have done worse for an unguided beginning, though what he hoped to achieve by trailing a handful of skinheads at random still eluded Gellar.

The pawnshop rang a bell, something about extortion charges, but there were so many race-related crimes in Germany these days that Gellar couldn't possibly keep track of all the details. Jews were often targeted, of course, but so were Turks and any nonwhite immigrants who dared to settle in the fatherland. Not even tourists were immune, and a white skin might not protect you from the roving wolf packs, if the skinheads had some reason to suspect you were a Jew, a Briton, or an American.

Gellar had watched the skinheads play their game

outside the pawnshop, finally going inside. His stomach gave a nervous little lurch when the American went in behind them, knowing that he would be forced to follow, now. It was the last thing Gellar wanted, at the moment, but the man he was supposed to meet had given him no choice.

He was assigned to do the damned job, after all, and reckoned that he might as well get on with it.

Before it was too late.

That would be all he needed, at the moment, for the stranger to be beaten, maybe stabbed or even killed, before they had a chance to talk about his mission in Berlin. It wasn't Gellar's fault, of course, if the American ran off in search of an adventure on his own, lacking the patience to await his guide and translator, but it would still go down as a strategic failure in the books.

Snugging the cap lower on his brow, Gellar stepped out from the sheltered doorway of the delicatessen that had sheltered him, making a perfunctory check for traffic before he jogged across the rain-slick street. He was intensely conscious of the Walther P-5 semiautomatic pistol holstered on his belt, well around toward the small of his back. Despite his rain slicker and sport coat, Gellar knew that he could draw and fire the double-action weapon in three seconds flat, if necessary.

Now, he only hoped that would be fast enough.

Reaching the north side of the street, he hurried east until he reached the pawnshop, slowing his pace, to make himself look casual, if one of the skinheads was watching the street. In fact, a quick glance through the shop's front window showed him all five youthful neo-Nazis facing his direction, but none of them were looking at Gellar. Their eyes were locked on the American, regarding him with various expressions ranging from amazement to pure hatred. Gellar couldn't hear what the man was saying, or what any of the skinheads answered back, but it was plain to him from the appearance of the youthful fascists that the confrontation was degenerating rapidly, with violence mere seconds away.

It always seemed to be that way with skinheads. They came out of the womb seeking trouble and weren't satisfied until they found it. Still, something told Jacob Gellar that his contact from the States had done his part, this time, to turn up the heat underneath the boiling pot.

He was still watching from the outside, rain dribbling from the bill of his cap, when one of the skinheads lunged forward, his lips drawn back from crooked teeth, throwing a hard, closed-fist blow at the American. Gellar was startled at the speed with tall man reacted, sidestepping the punch and taking the youth by his wrist, cranking it around at an obviously painful angle, while his free hand rose, the elbow lashing backward, into the young neo-Nazi's face.

Gellar imagined he could hear the snap of cartilage, the dull grunt of surprise and pain, as the skinhead lurched backward, arms windmilling for balance that he couldn't find, before he went down on his backside. The other four stood gaping at him for a moment, then they all rushed forward, raising a cry of fury that was audible in the street, even before Gellar pushed through the door to the shop.

THE FIRST SKINHEAD was easy, going from zero to frantic in two seconds flat, letting go at Bolan with a roundhouse swing he telegraphed almost before he raised his arm to strike. Rage ruled out any vestige of finesse, assuming that the young thug would have recognized the concept to begin with. Bolan stepped inside the punch and took advantage of it, cranking on the arm until he felt the pop and heard a squeal, his elbow whipping backward into contact with a magically collapsing nose.

The injuries weren't fatal, might not even be debilitating, but the punk was sidelined for the next few moments, anyway. Before he had a chance to crawl away, using his one good arm for leverage, the leader of the skinhead troop shouted something in German and threw himself at Bolan, the other three attacking simultaneously.

Four on one wasn't the best of odds for fighting hand to hand, but it was doable, assuming Bolan was resigned to take some hits. Obviously the skinheads weren't trained in any systematic way, but they were street fighters who had grown up on backyard brawls and kung fu movies, all of them displaying scars that testified to previous encounters, other enemies who may or may not have prevailed. On top of nerve, they all had weapons: one's fists glinted with the dull sheen of brass knuckles; two pulled switchblade knives; the fourth tugged loose a three-foot length of chain that had been serving as his belt a moment earlier.

Potential murder, now, and Bolan knew he could expect no mercy if they knocked him down. Steel-toed boots were a regular part of the skinhead uniform, initially adopted as a symbol of the working class, retained for their ability to shatter teeth and bones, rupture internal organs.

Time to shoot, he thought, but made no move for the Beretta yet. He had no doubt that he could drop the four young Nazis in their tracks, but killing them would move the Executioner no closer to his goal.

The skinhead with the chain reached Bolan first, his makeshift flail whipping overhead and downward, toward Bolan's face. The Executioner took it on the left forearm instead, ignoring the dull pain as he grabbed a handful of warm metal links, close to his assailant's knuckles, and pivoted to fling the punk over his head. An instant later, the skinhead was airborne, his chain bequeathed to Bolan as its former owner plunged headfirst into a glass display case.

Sorry, Bolan beamed out to the owner of the shop, but there was no time to observe the man's reaction as he turned to face the three remaining punks. He whipped the chain around as if he were a cowboy, preparing to lasso livestock, forcing the others back and creating a small comfort zone for himself. He saw it vanish as the skinhead with the knuckle dusters— the apparent leader—started scooping items off the nearby shelves at random, lobbing them at Bolan's head.

He dodged a flying crystal ashtray, used the chain to smash an antique lamp and took a solid hit to his already throbbing shoulder from an airborne saxophone. A few more inches, and the E-flat alto would have smashed into his face, stunning him, maybe breaking his jaw. It would be all the edge his adversaries needed to take him down, a faltering step, the dropping of his guard.

Time to attack.

One of the blade men lunged at Bolan, snarling like an animal and mouthing German phrases that could only be profanity or threats. He was surprised when Bolan's chain flicked out and stung his right eye, closing it immediately, as the cutter staggered backward, his free hand raised to shield his face.

Bolan went after him, whipping the chain to left and right as he advanced, holding the others back. The long blade feinted toward him, then came back for real to taste his blood. The chain lashed out to snare that arm and yank the skinhead closer, Bolan's left hand clamping tightly on the wrist behind the knife, his right letting the chain slip free and driving stiffened fingers deep into the neo-Nazi's throat.

The skinhead started choking, staggering. He let the knife drop into Bolan's waiting palm, and never missed the chain that suddenly released its grip on him and let him stumble off in the direction of the street. When Bolan turned to face the other thugs, he had the chain in his right hand, the open switchblade in his left.

"Hey, this is fun," he said. "Who's next?"

The jangling of the bell mounted above the door shouldn't have startled Bolan, but it did. He made the cardinal mistake of glancing toward the door to find out who was entering or leaving, and while Bolan didn't recognize the new arrival, he saw danger mirrored in the stranger's face.

"Look out!" the drop-in said, and moved past Bolan with surprising speed to intercept one of the charging skinheads. He took the one with the brass knuckles, ducking a left-hand swing and shrugging off a right that missed his face and caught him on the shoulder, wading in with what appeared to be a rapid series of karate blows.

There was no time to watch him work, as Bolan

spun to face the second blade, swinging the chain toward his opponent's face, then stepping closer, lunging with his captured knife. The blade sank home, piercing the skinhead's jacket sleeve, the flesh and biceps underneath. The neo-Nazi squealed and dropped his knife, thrashing away from Bolan and the penetrating blade with force enough to free himself, but at a greater cost in pain and blood.

Bolan stepped in to finish it, an elbow smash that dropped the wounded skinhead in his tracks, unconscious or the next thing to it by the time he hit the floor. Turning to see what had become of his unexpected ally, he found the stranger clutching his opponent's skull in a headlock, twisting with sufficient sudden force to snap his neck. That done, he let the lifeless body drop and stepped away, checking the others to make sure that none of them was any threat.

"You didn't have to do that," Bolan said.

"Perhaps not," the stranger replied, "but I don't like Nazis."

"I can see that."

Turning to the owner of the pawnshop, the stranger began speaking rapidly in a language that sounded like Yiddish. The dazed-looking man behind the counter nodded once and offered some affirmative reply.

"We need to leave now," the stranger said, once again addressing Bolan, "while he summons the police. His story is that this trash had a falling out when they came in to loot his shop."

"Will that stand up?"

The stranger smiled and shrugged. "It's not our problem," he replied. "We have more-pressing matters to discuss when we get back to your hotel."

CHAPTER TWO

They flagged a taxi on Uhlandstrasse, two blocks from the pawnshop, and were on their way back to Bolan's hotel when the first cruiser passed them, northbound with lights flashing and siren whooping, responding to Isaacson's call. Nothing had passed between them on the walk, beyond the briefest introductions and a code word that established Jacob Gellar as the contact Hal Brognola had arranged. Bolan had used the Mike Belasko alias that matched his paperwork.

"You think they'll buy pawnbroker's story?" Bolan asked.

Gellar responded with a shrug. "You never know about these things. Some of the powers that be favor the skinheads, though they won't admit it publicly. Others regard them as the scum they are. In any case, it will be one Jew's word against four skinheads, probably with what you call rap sheets for juvenile offenses, maybe violent crimes. They'll have some explaining to do before their friends can bail them out."

"How did you find me at the pawnshop?"

"It wasn't so difficult, considering that I had followed you from your hotel. I wasn't sure what you were doing, but it's good to see you don't waste any time.''

"For all the good it did," Bolan replied, "I may as well have waited in the room."

"It might have been a more relaxing way to pass the time," Gellar suggested with a crooked smile.

Bolan decided not to take it personally, even though the stranger obviously knew that he was traveling with a woman. How much had he been told about Marilyn Crouder's background, her involvement with the Temple of the Nordic Covenant as an undercover agent for the U.S. government? For that matter, how much did Hal Brognola himself know to pass along?

"When no one met us at the airport or at the hotel, I thought I might as well go out and see the sights," Bolan remarked.

"Beginning with the Thunderbolt Brigade? An interesting choice, my friend."

They weren't friends yet, but Bolan didn't call his new acquaintance on the obvious presumption. "I had skinheads on the menu, as a link to Manfred Roeder," he replied. "The one you took out seemed to be the leader of the group, but I suppose he won't be talking now."

"Franz Spangler," Gellar answered, putting a name with the dead punk's sneering face. "Last year, he was accused of firebombing a group home in the Turkish district, Kreuzberg. Two young children burned to death. Their parents and some six or seven other immigrants were injured."

"Since we met him on the street today, I'm guessing that the charges didn't stick."

"Indeed. He had an alibi, of course. Nine members

of the Thunderbolt Brigade swore on the very Bible they despise that he was drunk and whoring with them on Potsdamer Strasse all night long. The undercover officer who made the accusation got a reprimand for introducing hearsay testimony, and the case was dropped. It is among the many racial crimes that Germany's police work long and hard to solve, without result.''

It was impossible to miss the sarcasm in Gellar's tone. ''I take it that you don't have much faith in the local law,'' Bolan observed.

''I tell you something that you may already know,'' Gellar replied, glancing once more at the back of the cabdriver's head, as if to assure himself that the man wasn't eavesdropping. ''For close to twenty years after the war, much of the German government—West Germany, I mean—was run by so-called former Nazis. That included judges, legislators and the chancellor himself. Of course, the various police departments needed men trained for their work, which meant they either kept policemen from the Third Reich or hired new officers with military backgrounds—from the Wehrmacht, even the SS. Today, you understand, most of those men are dead or pensioned off. We have their sons and grandsons now, too often raised on stories of the good old days when Uncle Adolf made the railroads run on time. They won't have been informed that slaves laid down the tracks, or that the trains ran to the camps. *Some* of them won't, at any rate. Others, I think, wouldn't be sad to see the old days come again.''

''So, the condensed version is, don't trust the cops.''

"These days, in Germany, it's risky to trust anyone," Gellar informed him.

"Present company included?" Bolan asked.

His new acquaintance smiled. "One thing that you may take for granted, Mike—you don't mind if I call you Mike? —is that I'm not a Nazi."

"And I'm taking that on faith, because...?"

"Because I work for the Mossad," Gellar replied.

"Okay."

It was a safe bet, Bolan thought, that he would find no Nazi sympathizers on the payroll of the Israeli secret service. Mossad, in fact, had been instrumental in abducting or assassinating certain fugitives from Nuremberg and other war-crimes trials. There were fewer aging SS men to chase these days, more than a half century after the Third Reich's collapse, but Mossad still kept busy with Israel's Arab neighbors, and, it seemed, with the new crop of fascists that was springing up worldwide, from Hitler's old stomping ground to the American Midwest, Moscow, South Africa and parts of Latin America. The motto Never Again! took on a whole new meaning in a world where nuclear weapons could fit inside an average suitcase and fanatics still believed that Jews—or Mormons, blacks, Freemasons, Catholics, whatever—ruled the world in some bizarre, far-flung conspiracy.

"I'm guessing that you had a bone to pick with Spangler, then," Bolan remarked.

"A few bones, give or take," Gellar replied. "I'll lose no sleep about him, nor should you. He was a coward, like all Nazis, and we could have broken him with little difficulty, but it happens that you won't need Spangler or his playmates to provide Herr Roeder's whereabouts."

"You've got him spotted, then?"

"Indeed I do," the man from Tel Aviv replied. "We could go there directly, but there still remain some preparations to be made."

"I'll need equipment," Bolan told him.

"As will I."

"If you've got Roeder spotted, what about the others?"

Gellar frowned and shook his head. "Not yet," he said, "but they're in Germany. I have confirmed that much. The trick will be to root them out and— Ah! The rest can wait. It seems we have arrived."

He was correct, the taxi slowing to a halt outside Bolan's hotel on Kochstrasse. Before the solider could pay off the cabbie, Gellar raised a cautionary finger, examined the money in Bolan's hand and plucked one of the bills away.

"Too much," he said. "You spoil them if you tip like an American."

"I'll make a note."

As they approached the doorman, Gellar said, "I trust that your companion will not be disturbed by my arrival, unannounced."

"You're unannounced, not unexpected," Bolan said. "We've both been waiting for you. Anyway, it isn't like she had to cook or clean the place."

Gellar responded with a smile to that, and said, "You aren't very—what is the accepted term?—politically correct."

"You got that right," Bolan said as he led the way inside.

MARILYN CROUDER HAD been nervous from the moment that they landed in Berlin, her state exacerbated by the hours of waiting for some word from their elusive German contact, plus eight cups of strong black coffee. By the time she heard the soft knock on her door, she had a mighty caffeine buzz and precious little patience left.

Still, there was time to check the peephole, just in case.

Unarmed and virtually helpless in the eighth-floor hotel room, she still recalled her law-enforcement training and the common-sense rules of survival: look before you leap, whenever possible. Or, in this case, before you open the door.

Why bother? nagged a small voice from the back of her mind. If it was the bad guys, she was stuck just the same.

Or maybe not.

One thing was certain, after all that she had been through with the Temple of the Nordic Covenant in the past year and a half: Marilyn Crouder wasn't paranoid. People really were out to get her, had in fact tried to kill her several times, and they would keep on trying as long as the Temple and its leadership survived.

Neo-Nazis, she had learned early on in her infiltration of the fascist fringe, were the humanoid equivalent of elephants when it came to memory and bearing grudges over time. Some of the men who wanted to eliminate her had themselves been taken out along the way, of course—a few of them by Crouder herself, a somewhat larger number by her comrade, Mike Belasko—but the price on her head wouldn't be lifted as long as the cult's leadership remained intact.

And now, alone in the heart of enemy territory, she was answering a soft knock on her door.

The only person in Berlin who knew her true identity, at least in theory, was Mike Belasko himself. Crouder trusted him implicitly, but at the moment she couldn't help running down scenarios, some of them frankly bizarre, in which her mortal enemies managed to trace her, perhaps even waiting for Belasko to leave the hotel before they struck.

She was unarmed, since Belasko's pistol was the only weapon they had felt secure enough to smuggle in their check-through luggage. He was wearing that gun at the moment, traipsing around God knew where in the streets of Berlin, while she edged toward the door of her room on tiptoe, trying not to make a sound as she approached.

The peephole was always a giveaway, a shadow eclipsing the pinpoint of light from within, as someone leaned close to check out the callers through the fish-eye lens. There was no way to help that now, and even as she envisioned a killer poised outside her door, raising a sound-suppressed pistol to fire through the peephole the moment she betrayed her presence there, Crouder still had to look.

There was simply no choice.

She leaned toward the door, palms flat against the cool wood, and closed one eye while the other peered through the peephole's lens. Outside, Mike Belasko stood waiting with a man she didn't recognize, neither of them speaking, both facing directly toward the door. There were no guns in evidence, and Belasko didn't appear to be a prisoner. In any case, she didn't for one moment think that he would lead their enemies to her, no matter what the threat was to himself.

She released the security bolt and opened the door

a crack, shooting a quick glance toward Belasko's companion as she asked, "Is everything okay?"

"It's fine," Bolan replied, no wink or grimace to suggest he had been followed, much less captured, by the enemy. "May we come in?"

"Sure thing," she said, stepping aside, watching the stranger's hands as he passed. Still watching him, she double locked the door again, ensuring that a raiding party would at least be slowed for a moment, entering the room.

For all the good that that would do.

"So, who's your friend?"

Bolan made the introductions. "Jacob Gellar, this is Marilyn." Dropping her last name, as a matter of protection, leaving Crouder to share it if she wanted to. "Jacob's our contact. He's with Mossad."

"And you two met each other...where, again?" she pressed.

"An old pawnshop," Bolan stated. "Some skinheads wanted to redecorate the place. We talked them out of it."

She read between the lines, experienced enough at undercover work to know that Gellar—if, in fact, that was his name—had to have been trailing Belasko, keeping an eye on him, before it hit the fan. Hotel surveillance, possibly to verify that they were who and what they claimed to be?

That sounded like Mossad, all right. They were a suspicious lot, and with perfect reason. Part of it was Israel's half-century-plus as a target for terrorist fanatics, both left and right. Another part was Mossad's long-standing record of aggressive spying even on its friends, like the United States, which prompted said friends to return the favor. There were times, indeed, when she wondered if part of Israel's seeming isolation in the world should be blamed squarely on Tel Aviv.

"I thought we were supposed to hook up with a native," Crouder remarked.

"I'm all there is," Gellar replied. "If it is any consolation to you, my grandparents were German, three of them Jewish. They died in the camps, two at Sobibor, two at Treblinka. I'm not a friend of those you hunt."

"Talk's cheap," she told him, "and I don't know you from Adam. No offense."

"None taken. Shall I repeat the password once again?"

"Forget it," Bolan said. "We need to get busy."

"I'm just being careful."

"An admirable quality," the new arrival said. "No doubt, they taught you that at the academy. Was it FBI, perhaps? The Company?"

"ATF," she replied, "if you must know."

"Of course. The arms connection. Silly of me, that. I should have guessed."

"Nobody's perfect."

"Very true."

"If we're done fencing now, can we get down to business?" Bolan asked.

"Suits me," she told him. "Anyone for coffee?"

"Love some," Jacob Gellar said, her comrade-in-arms nodding in agreement as she went to turn on the coffeemaker again. She had already taken in enough caffeine to keep her up all night and part of the next day, but she needed an edge. Before much longer, Crouder hoped, it would be supplied in some form other than coffee.

Bolan and Gellar made small talk until she returned with the coffee, tiny hotel sugar packets, powdered "creamer" in small envelopes that would only tear at one unmarked corner. The room had two chairs, so she sat on the bed, making the third point of a triangle.

"So, what's the word?" she asked.

"Jacob has a line on Manfred Roeder," Mark replied.

"More than that," the Mossad agent said. "While I cannot prove it at the moment, I believe he may be with the others that you seek."

The room was silent for a moment, Bolan and Crouder giving Gellar their full attention, studying his face almost as if they thought more details might come seeping from his pores. He let the silence stretch between them for a time, until he started to experience uneasiness, beginning to suspect that they might sit and stare at him forever if he didn't speak. At last, he said, "You've come for Gerhard Steuben, yes?"

"That's what he likes to call himself," Crouder replied. "His real name's Gary Stevens."

Gellar was nodding as she spoke. "Of course. We have a file on him in Tel Aviv—I may say a substantial file. The Temple of the Nordic Covenant, despite the silly occult trappings, is a source of some concern to us, where acts of terrorism or potential terrorism are involved."

"So, you keep track of Stevens, then," Bolan said.

A shrug from Gellar. "We do what we can," he said. "There are, of course, restrictions placed upon us when it comes to keeping track of subjects, as you say, in foreign countries, most particularly when the

nations are our allies.'' Certain that the American got
the point, he forged ahead. ''We monitor the movements of suspected terrorists whenever possible, and
I can tell you that your subject is in fact in Germany.''

''It's good to have the confirmation,'' Bolan said.
''Can you narrow down the field a little bit?''

''He is, I think, still in Berlin,'' Gellar replied.

''Okay,'' Crouder said. ''So now, we only have to
check out, what, four million people in the city?''

''I'm thinking that you must have something better
than 'Berlin' to tell us, or you wouldn't be here,''
Bolan stated.

''There are certain leads and contacts that we may
pursue,'' Gellar said. ''You must understand, however, that Herr Steuben is a man with friends in the
united Germany. Some of them might surprise you,
if you knew their rank and names.''

''Not much surprises me these days,'' Bolan said.
''And I *will* need those names, no 'if' about it.''

''You know the most important one, already—
Manfred Roeder,'' Gellar said.

''The Nordic Temple's chief of staff in Germany,''
Crouder recited. ''Liaison with the Thunderbolt Brigade and maybe half a dozen other neo-Nazi skinhead
groups around the country.''

''You forget to mention his connections in the
world of German politics,'' Gellar replied, ''and not
only in Germany. The neofascist movement has revived in Austria, as well, electing various officials to
the legislature while the press was busy laughing.
Here in Germany, of course, the Nazis never really
left. Some took the time and trouble to disguise themselves, swallow their pride and make nice with America, with France and England, even with Israel, but

they have taught their children well. There have been stirrings since the 1960s, ultranationalists chosen for a minor office here and there, but only in the last decade, since they have managed to unite the fatherland again, have they truly begun to—what is it you say in the United States—come out of the closet.''

"That's what we say," Bolan confirmed. "So, you're telling me that Stevens has friends in high places?"

"Not too high, I hope," Gellar said. "We know of some policemen in Berlin and other cities who are sympathetic to the skinheads, slow to answer calls for help from immigrant communities, that sort of thing. Some judges—thankfully not many yet—give wrist-slap sentences for crimes that ought to put these thugs away for years. We see more neo-Nazis in the legislative branch of German government than anywhere. They vote to cut off immigration from the nonwhite countries, limit aid to children of the immigrants, restrict their housing. There are also certain businessmen who thrive on covert sales of weapons and technology to nations with a history of hating Israel. They are all the same at heart.''

"We can't do anything about the German government or the economy," Bolan said. "We need to focus on the Nordic Temple and its terrorist connections, operating on the premise that they may have one or more events scheduled for the immediate future.''

The Mossad agent frowned at that, arching one eyebrow in surprise. "You have, perhaps, details of these events?''

"I wish," Crouder said. "We could be out there

kicking ass instead of sitting here and making chit-chat.''

"I'm not sure how much you follow criminal activities in the United States," Bolan said.

"I know the Temple of the Nordic Covenant is thought to be responsible for the attack upon the Eli Sturnman Center in Los Angeles," Gellar replied.

"No 'thought' about it," Crouder informed him. "It's confirmed. They're also on the hook for what went down two days ago, at the civil-rights convention in Chicago."

"Ah." A sour churning had begun in Gellar's stomach. "You believe they may have something similar in mind for Germany?"

"At least," the woman said. "I spent the better part of eighteen months inside the Nordic Temple, feeding any information I could get my hands on to the Feds. They would have killed me three, four times within the past ten days if not for Mike. I promise you, their plans for bloodshed aren't in any sense restricted to the U.S.A.''

"We understand, of course, that groups like Steuben's would attack Israel if they possessed the resources."

"You're thinking small," Crouder said. "No offense intended, Jacob, but I have to tell you, Gary Stevens takes his buddy Adolf seriously when he says, 'Tomorrow the world.'"

"A madman's dream," Gellar replied, and silently cursed the feeling in his gut. "He doesn't have the manpower to seize an island, much less rule a nation."

"No one mentioned ruling anything," Bolan said. "Stevens has an apocalyptic vision. He apparently believes that Armageddon's just around the corner, and he wants to hurry up the timetable by any means available. It doesn't take an army to plant bombs, commit assassinations or conduct a sabotage campaign. One well-placed lunatic inside a nuclear facility can take out thousands, maybe millions.''

"Stevens doesn't want to rule the world, as is," Crouder explained. "He wants to burn it down and start from scratch. Get rid of all the Jews, 'mud people,' Communists. He has it in his mind that he'll survive the chaos and emerge to rule the new, improved reich.''

"And if he doesn't?" Gellar asked.

"No biggie. He's still got a first-class ticket to Valhalla waiting for him, either way it goes. He either wins the world or gets himself a ringside seat in Paradise. Some days, I wouldn't be surprised if he preferred to lose. You can't go wrong with Wotan and his buddies on cloud nine.''

"You're saying that he's certifiably insane?"

"No more so than the folks who buy airtime to talk about the rapture, how we'll all be driving down the freeway, sometime soon, and suddenly the Christian drivers will all vanish from their cars. No more than those who think they'll burn in Hell for eating pork or lobster, going to the movies, listening to rock and roll. He's certainly fanatical, no doubt about it, but religious quirks don't make the man unique. He's dangerous because he preaches violent activism in the here and now, because he's got a dedicated, well-armed following that wants to make his dreams come true.''

"What does he want in Germany?" Gellar asked.

Bolan glanced at Crouder, wearing a frown that

smacked of disappointment. "We were hoping you could answer that one, Jacob," he replied.

"Of course." His mind was racing now, in counterpoint to his unsettled stomach. "Please, forgive me. I was told that you pursued a fugitive who might be hiding in Berlin. There was no mention of a terrorist campaign about to break."

"Stevens is running, true enough," the woman said. "But he's got hidden charges planted everywhere the Temple's put down roots. My worry is that he's not running away so much as running toward the next explosion, racing to set it off, if you get my drift."

"I do indeed," Gellar replied. "We should begin with Manfred Roeder, by all means. Regrettably, his present whereabouts is vague, at best." He saw Belasko's frown edge toward a scowl, and quickly added, "But I do have contacts who can help us find him. I will have to make some calls, perhaps drop in on one or two of my informants, but it shouldn't take much time."

"How much?" Crouder asked.

"Two hours, maybe three," Gellar suggested, wishing he could pin it down with more precision.

"Try for two," Bolan suggested. "And while you're at it, I need some equipment."

Meaning weapons, Gellar thought. And he said, "I'm certain that can be arranged."

THE SHOP on Gutschmidstrasse, in the Neukölln district, was ostensibly devoted to antiques, some jewelry from estate sales, first editions of some classic texts. Bolan had parked his rented BMW across the street and three doors east, crossing to scrutinize the shop, up close and personal, before he went inside. The bell that jangled overhead reminded him of the pawnshop and his recent confrontation with the skinheads of the Thunderbolt Brigade, making him glance around in search of lurking thugs.

The only person he could see was an old man who stood beside the antique register, watching the new arrival with a bland expression on his weathered face. He said something in German as Bolan moved toward him.

"Do you speak English?" Bolan asked.

"But of course."

Bolan produced the business card he had received from Jacob Gellar. Something was written on the back of it in what he took for Hebrew.

The old man read both sides.

"I take it that you are not shopping for antiques," the merchant said.

"Something a bit more modern."

"And you have cash money?"

"But of course."

Cash was the least of Bolan's problems at the moment. He could get by with the single handgun for his personal defense, but he required offensive weapons to conduct his blitz against the Temple of the Nordic Covenant, and he hadn't been thrilled at leaving Crouder alone, unarmed, at the hotel. He would remember to include a weapon for her in his purchases, though he didn't anticipate her joining in the raids he planned to carry out, assuming Gellar came back with the goods.

Assuming he came back at all.

Bolan didn't believe the Mossad agent would desert them, but it still remained to be seen if he could actually lead them to their target, and if they would be in time to head off Stevens's next bloody event.

The old man pocketed the business card, moved at a brisk pace to the entrance of his shop to lock the door and turn the dangling cardboard sign printed in German on both sides, presumably announcing that the shop was closed.

"If you would kindly follow me," he said, leading the way into a kind of office-storeroom in the rear. It was sparsely furnished with a desk and swivel chair, a single battered filing cabinet, a calendar festooned with hand-scrawled messages the only decoration on the walls.

"This way," the old man said, opening what appeared to be a closet door and vanishing inside.

Bolan stood on the threshold, watched his host descend a flight of wooden stairs, using a handrail on his left, a dim light burning down below. He sensed no danger here, but kept his right hand close to the Beretta 93-R in its shoulder rig as he descended all the same. They had the claustrophobic basement to themselves, perhaps a hundred square feet, weapons mounted on the walls and racked in tidy rows, while stacks of wooden crates took up most of the floor space.

"This is what I have to sell," the old man said. "Some larger items I keep elsewhere, but I sense that you will not want armored vehicles or field artillery."

"You're right," Bolan agreed. He began reciting from his mental shopping list as he surveyed the mini-arms bazaar. "I need a good, compact assault rifle. A sniper's piece, with a suppressor if you have one. A machine pistol, smaller the better. A reliable side arm. Spare magazines and ammunition for all of the above, plus antipersonnel grenades. A dozen ought to be enough for now.''

''A man who knows his mind,'' the dealer said, and smiled, resembling a vaguely lethal Santa Claus. ''For your first choice, I recommend the Steyr AUG assault rifle, with an assortment of 30-round and 42-round magazines. Rifle grenades are optional. The launcher is built-in, and it requires a special cartridge, as you doubtless are aware.''

Bolan received the eight-pound weapon with approval, familiar with its capabilities, appreciating the compact bullpup design and factory-standard telescopic sight. ''Grenades might come in handy,'' he remarked. ''Why don't you put me down for half a dozen.''

''Very wise, I'm sure,'' the dealer said. ''I have several sniper rifles in stock. Do you prefer bolt action or semiautomatic?''

''Semiauto,'' Bolan said.

''May I assume concealment is a factor in your choice?''

''You may.''

''In that case, I would recommend either the Walther WA 2000 or the excellent Galil. The Walther is a slightly shorter weapon, at 905 millimeters, but the Galil's folding stock more than makes up the difference. The Galil is also lighter—about fourteen pounds, with bipod and sling, to the Walther's eighteen. And, of course, the Galil has a 20-round box magazine, compared to six rounds for the Walther.''

''I'll take the Galil,'' Bolan said. If necessary, in a crunch, the Israeli-manufactured sniper piece could double as a second assault rifle, thereby doubling his firepower—or arming Crouder, if worse came to worst.

"Machine pistols are no problem," the old man told him. "I discount the Skorpion for anything except close work in crowds, where accuracy is of minimal concern. The Italian Spectre is a good weapon, with first-shot double-action capability and superior ammunition capacity, at fifty rounds. I also have a mini-Uzi, the Beretta Model 12-S and the MP-5 K from Heckler & Koch."

"I'll take the Spectre," Bolan said, prepared to lug another pound or so of weight to gain the twenty extra Parabellum rounds.

"As for the side arm," the old man said, "since you have one at the moment, I assume you wish to find a smaller, secondary weapon."

Bolan gave him points for picking out the 93-R in its custom shoulder rig, despite the jacket worn a half-size larger to conceal it. In reply, he said, "The pistol's not for me."

"I see. A male or female shooter, if I may inquire?"

"Female."

"Of course. Revolver? Automatic?"

"Automatic."

"The Walther PPK is excellent," the old man said. "Heckler & Koch have several models—the P-7, P-9 S, USP 9—depending on your preference. Beretta's Model 92-F Compact might be suitable. If it were my woman, of course, the Glock 26, with 3.5-inch barrel and a 10-round magazine."

"Let's have the Glock, then," Bolan said.

"My stock of antipersonnel grenades is sadly limited. I have the Russian-manufactured RGD-5 model, or the American M-26. No French or British at the moment, I'm afraid.''

''A dozen of the Russian RGDs should do it,'' Bolan said. He didn't need to add that any fragments or discarded hand grenades discovered by police wouldn't suggest American involvement in their use.

''If you have luggage that is suitable...''

''Can you supply the necessary bags?''

''Of course. If you would be so kind as to assist me, we shall pack your purchases.''

The weapons, with spare magazines for each, filled up one duffel bag, the extra ammunition and grenades taking a second bag. The price wasn't unreasonable when he thought about the lethal firepower involved and added on the dealer's overhead, including bribes he had to have paid to stay in business. Thirty minutes after entering the shop, Bolan had loaded the two heavy duffels in the rented BMW's trunk and was en route to his hotel.

The best part of an hour gone, and he could only hope that Jacob Gellar would be quick coming back with his list of targets.

Sooner the better, Bolan thought, already looking forward to the showdown.

CHAPTER THREE

Washington, D.C.

It was six hours earlier in Washington, D.C., than in Berlin, and Hal Brognola hadn't gone to lunch yet, though he was already running late. His dining hour was flexible on workdays, sometimes overlooked entirely, and today the news from Germany had fairly killed his appetite.

He was concerned about Mack Bolan's mission to Berlin. There were so many wild cards in the game that it was well and truly up for grabs, a situation the big Fed didn't enjoy. He much preferred to have a battle plan drawn up beforehand and to stick with it whenever possible, making reasonable, well-thought-out allowances for changes in the situation as they came to pass.

This time, he had a niggling fear that they were in for major trouble, flying blind, below the radar.

It was difficult for him to prioritize his worries, but Marilyn Crouder ranked near the top of the list. An undercover spook for ATF—the federal Bureau of Alcohol, Tobacco and Firearms—she had spent a year and a half of her life inside the Temple of the Nordic

Covenant before she was exposed and marked for execution, rescued by Bolan at the penultimate moment. They had been traveling together, working together ever since, except for a brief period when Crouder had been recaptured by the cult—and, if he read between the lines of Bolan's terse reports, had been subjected to indignities that made her zeal for breaking up the neo-Nazi gang intensely personal. From talking to her closemouthed supervisor at ATF, Brognola couldn't tell if Crouder was still on the payroll or not. In any case, she was far outside her legal jurisdiction at the moment, apparently taking orders from Bolan...if, that is, could be trusted to follow instructions at all. She was a weak link in the warrior's armor, possibly unstable—and, if so, a mortal threat.

Brognola felt no greater confidence per se in Bolan's other ally, Jacob Gellar, presently on loan from Mossad. The big Fed took for granted that the man despised all Nazis, but he had no grasp of Gellar's skill, experience or training. Hedged around that void of information was Brognola's natural suspicion of Mossad, conditioned by exposure to the group's illegal spying in America, its use of covert execution squads around the world, amounting in some cases to state-sanctioned terrorist campaigns. Of course, he did much the same thing himself, through Stony Man Farm, when he dispatched Mack Bolan, Able Team or Phoenix Force to cope with problems that eluded settlement in courts of law. The difference, at least in his mind, was that Mossad's retaliation against sundry enemies sometimes involved displacement or destruction of the innocent, hapless noncombatants punished on a Biblical scale for the sins of their kinfolk or acquaintances. Above all else, in this specific case, he knew that Gellar would put Israel first, could do no more or less, and thus might reach a point where he decided Bolan had to be sacrificed to serve some higher good.

In contrast to his allies, Bolan's enemy was, if nothing else, at least a known commodity. The self-styled Gerhard Steuben was a racist head case who had wrapped up his morbid bigotry in religious trappings, seducing a motley collection of misfits, psychopaths, outcasts and sadists into signing on for the duration of his "racial holy war." The members of that crowd deserved one another, and Brognola would have left them to amuse themselves had they not been determined to involve the innocent and unsuspecting in their lethal dress rehearsals for the end of days. More important, perhaps, the other team enjoyed a home-court advantage in Berlin, while he was more or less out of his element, saddled with allies who required close scrutiny.

Distance was the crux of the problem, Brognola decided. In the United States, he had considerable weight to throw around, if circumstances called for him to intervene in Bolan's fight. As needed, on native soil he could unleash the FBI, the U.S. Marshals service, DEA and sundry other strike teams from the Justice Department. In a pinch, he could even prevail upon the White House for some hush-hush military assistance, though anything beyond routine transportation and arms deliveries required some explaining. Overseas, despite a trusted contact in the Company and situational liaisons with various foreign counterparts, however, Brognola's power was more limited. He could dispatch his other warriors, Phoenix Force and Able Team, in the direst of emergencies, but only then if their mobilization was likely to yield beneficial results.

A big part of the problem, he admitted to himself, was the chaos, the corruption and the criminality of reunited Germany. How much of that response was simply ingrained prejudice against the nation that had touched off two world wars? Brognola couldn't say and didn't care to speculate. He knew that virile strains of fascism and violence ran deep in Deutschland; he wasn't imagining that fact, nor did he think he was exaggerating Bolan's jeopardy. How many serious assaults on Jews, tourists and nonwhite immigrants had gone unsolved since communism folded like a cheap card table and the Berlin Wall came down? Some German cops and some elected politicians would have welcomed Adolf Hitler back with open arms, if given half a chance, and while Brognola judged their numbers to be small, it only took one traitor to disrupt a mission and get decent people killed.

The big Fed hadn't heard from Bolan since the brief check-in after they landed in Berlin. He knew the guy was busy—dammit, simple logic told him that—but Brognola was used to being in the loop. The worst thing about running Stony Man was that he did his watching from the sidelines ninety-nine percent of the time, while others put their courage and their futures on the line. That was part of getting old, he told himself, and liked it even less.

He could remember tracking Bolan back and forth across the country, jetting off to France and England when the Executioner went international with his one-man campaign against the Mafia. It didn't seem that long ago, viewed through the magnifying prism of his memory. Those were the bad old days, when Bolan had been hunted like a rabid animal, the law ironically enlisted to protect his targets, even though Brognola knew that they were guilty of a thousand heinous crimes for every one that Bolan had racked up. It had been dicey in those days, walking the razor's edge between collaboration with the world's most-wanted fugitive and following the orders handed down from Wonderland.

Brognola knew that he had failed in his official duty then, but he had never felt so free, so right, at any time before or since. Nowadays, he was more conscientious for the most part, though he still had certain latitude, a bit of wiggle room. As long as he achieved the ultimate results desired and left no tracks that led investigators back to Washington or Stony Man Farm, in Virginia, the big Fed was home and dry. Sometimes it felt like cheating, though, this arm-chair war he fought with enemies whom he would never see, whose throats would never feel his fingers tighten to the point where they were giddy, panicked, blacking out.

A damned old warhorse, Brognola rebuked himself.

He still had ample time before he reached the dead-line of retirement age and was required to take his ease, like it or not. Still, *ample* was a curious, subjective term. When you were in your teens and twenties, it was possible to cultivate a sense of immortality, regardless of the grim reminders that you saw in daily life or on the nightly news. Three decades later, and the time seemed fleeting, slipping through your fingers like quicksilver, there and gone before you had a chance to register the contact, savor the sensation of simply being alive.

That thought, in turn, caused him to think again of those who weren't alive, recalling orders he had given and would give again, perhaps that very afternoon, tomorrow or the next day at the latest, snuffing out more lives of people he would never meet, placing the souls he valued most, after his family, in mortal danger every time they followed through on his commands.

Brognola had helped devise the system, nurtured it from drawing board to flesh-and-blood reality. If there were flaws in it, then he had no one but himself to blame. Himself and life, which had been pitching curveballs at the human race since Man descended from the trees and started looking for a cave where he could hide from hungry predators.

Nowadays, the predators were mostly other people, cast in every shape and size and color of the human rainbow. They could never be wiped out, because they bred too rapidly, like roaches hiding in the dark, but they could be squashed when and where people got the chance.

This day, the opportunity had been presented in Berlin.

He wished that Bolan would call, update him on the progress of the mission, but sometimes no news was truly good news. Silence meant that Crouder and Bolan had connected with their contact from Mossad and were preparing for their next engagement with the enemy. With any luck, another day or two might see them safely home, their work complete.

With any luck.

Brognola wasn't counting on it, though.

There was a world of hurt between his suite of offices in the Justice building and what had once been the divided city of Berlin. That city in many ways was divided still, he knew, by race, religion, politics and brooding passions spanning generations.

Brognola only hoped that when those splintered portions of a modern European city came together, Bolan wouldn't find himself trapped hopelessly between them, maybe even crushed to death. The damned guy seemed immortal sometimes, but the fact remained that he was only flesh and blood.

This time, Brognola hoped, the blood that decorated Berlin's streets and gutters would belong to someone else.

Berlin, Germany

"EXPLAIN TO ME again what happened. Aldo, you go first this time."

There was no anger in the bald man's voice, not even any special note of urgency, but the four younger men who ringed his desk, bolt upright on their plain, uncomfortable wooden chairs, couldn't delude themselves into believing Manfred Roeder was relaxed. The firm set of his narrow lips, a bloodless razor slash across the lower portion of his oval face, beneath the wedge of nose, the piercing blue-gray eyes, the shiny dome of scalp, told them that Roeder was determined to find out what had gone wrong.

Aldo Gürlich was half Roeder's age, a burly skinhead dressed in standard leather gear, his bland face mottled by a bruise that bridged his flattened nose, between the purple stains that ringed his eyes and rusty-looking flakes of blood that marked his upper lip beneath his odd, pinched-looking nostrils. When he spoke, the voice wasn't familiar, seeming to emerge from the projector of a children's animated film, perhaps with talking ducks and geese.

"We went to sweat the Jew on Lietzenburger Strasse," he began, the second time this story had been told from the beginning, since they were conducted into Roeder's office. "Franz was talking to him, working up to it, when this American came in."

"Describe him."

"Six feet tall or so, maybe two hundred pounds," Gürlich replied. "He wore a raincoat and a suit."

"What color was the suit?"

"I didn't pay attention."

"No. Of course you didn't."

Roeder waited for the young man to continue, sketching out the brawl in much the same terms used by Jurgen Prosser, who had told the story first. If necessary, he would have each one of them repeat it, start to finish, until he learned something more about these men who had presumed to trifle with the Thunderbolt Brigade. Gürlich couldn't describe the second man, because he had had already been pummeled by the first—a broken nose, perhaps a mild concussion, still untreated; they had gone directly to Roeder's office, from the pawnshop—by the time the second man walked in and joined the fray.

"You didn't see him murder Franz," he said, referring to the second man. It hadn't been a question, but the young man answered him, regardless.

"No."

"No."

Almost unconsciously, Roeder began to stroke his shiny scalp. He was a skinhead by necessity, having adopted the extreme style years before it was politicized. At twenty-four, alarmed by the rapidity with which his blond hair was retreating from his forehead, Roeder had decided that he had a choice: shave now, or spend the next half century resembling a clown, wearing a circlet of pale fuzz above his small, flat ears. Roeder had shaved, and now applied a strong depilatory twice a week to keep the stubble down.

It was coincidence—a happy one, but still—that Roeder's shaved look had been adopted by the others like himself, who hated Jews and Asians, blacks and all the other branded peoples of the earth who had been made specifically to serve the master race. This way, it almost seemed as if he had anticipated the formation of the Thunderbolt Brigade, its later quasi-merger with the Temple of the Nordic Covenant. Manfred Roeder emerged as a minor prophet of sorts, prescient, a man who knew what was about to happen next and was prepared to meet events head-on.

Now, he was in the spotlight. Not a very large one yet, of course, but he could feel the heat already. With the boss in town, all kinds of trouble in the States, it stood to reason that the next front would be here, in Germany. Indeed, where better to begin rebuilding the Great Reich than in the fatherland itself?

He only hoped he would be equal to the task, and while self-confidence had never been a problem, it unnerved him that this problem with the Thunderbolt Brigade should plague him now.

"Two men in suits," he said to no one in particular. "Did they speak German?"

"English," Jurgen Prosser replied at once.

"English," Roeder repeated, frowning. "Was either one of them a Jew?"

No answer from the skinheads this time. They were glancing back and forth at one another, nervously, a shrug from Drugi Werner. Wilmot Bartsch made a face, some kind of grimace, and resumed twiddling his thumbs. For one long, painful moment, Manfred Roeder wondered whether this could truly be the master race.

"Was either one of them a Jew?" he repeated, and pinned Prosser with his eyes. "You, Jurgen! Let us have the benefit of your considered wisdom on the subject. Hurry up, now!"

"I couldn't tell," the youth replied. "They both were white, spoke English only. Neither one of them looked Jewish like the posters."

"But they asked for me by name," Roeder pressed, hoping that the answer might be different this time, wishing that the knowledge didn't raise a creeping tide of gooseflesh on his arms.

"The first one only," Gürlich said. "The second one came later, after we had started fighting."

"He asked where he could find you," Bartsch said. Adding, reluctantly, "And he insulted you, Herr Roeder."

"Ah. What else was said?"

"I don't—"

"What else?" His tone insistent now, brooking no insubordination.

"He called you a pile of shit, sir," Bartsch said.

"That's all?" Roeder inquired.

"I hit him then," Gürlich said.

"Hit his elbow with your face," Werner inserted. Wearing bruises of his own, he still found solace and amusement in his fellow warrior's greater injuries.

"You'll need a doctor to extract my boot from out your asshole, you—"

"Shut up, the two of you!" Roeder snapped. "One more word without a question being asked, and I will kill the one who speaks, you understand?"

To their credit, none of them replied aloud, their shaved heads bobbing like a row of Yankee dashboard ornaments.

"Now listen carefully," he said. "Which one of these two men killed Franz? Wilmot?"

"The second one," Barlich replied.

"You're sure of that?"

"Yes, sir. I was already down and saw him from...I saw him from...."

"You saw him from the floor?"

"Yes, sir."

"How did he do it, Wilmot? How did he kill Franz?"

"Grabbed him around the head like wrestling, sir, and gave a twist. I heard his neck snap."

"So. And then?"

"The first one looked a bit surprised. They left soon after."

"Why are you alive, then?" Roeder asked the group at large, but no one dared to answer him. It was rhetorical, in any case. If he wasn't mistaken, he already knew the answer to that question.

They were still alive because the men who sought him in Berlin had wanted witnesses to spread the word. They could have used the Jew in the pawnshop, but it wouldn't be the same. He had no daily contact with the Thunderbolt Brigade, or with the Temple of the Nordic Covenant.

The killers—one of them, at least—had wanted to

convey a message, letting Roeder know someone was after him, perhaps to make him frightened, spook him into some behavior whereby he would give himself away.

Was it coincidence that these English-speaking killers were looking for him so soon after Gerhard Steuben had arrived from the United States? Roeder didn't believe so. And no matter what it meant, he had a duty to his führer. He had to pass the word along as soon as possible, let Steuben think about it, work it out.

"I want the four of you to go see Dr. Kaltenbruner," Roeder said. "Mention my name, let him examine you. I need you fit and ready for whatever happens next. You understand?"

The four heads bobbed at him, mute.

"Well, then, go on! Get out of here!"

THE NEWS WAS BAD, of course. What other kind was there these days? Why should he have expected anything but trouble, with the last days coming toward him like a runaway express train carrying a load of nitroglycerine?

Calm down, for Wotan's sake!

The man who had been born as Gary Stevens, reborn in midlife as Gerhard Steuben, the self-styled reincarnation of an SS officer killed on the Russian front in World War II, to lead the Temple of the Nordic Covenant toward its apocalypse, knew that he should calm down, of course, but saying it was one thing; doing it was something else quite different, indeed.

"What did these men look like, who asked for you?" he said.

Sipping a mug of beer and frowning at his own lap, Manfred Roeder took a moment to collect his thoughts before responding. "They were white men, neither of them clearly Jewish, dressed in business suits and raincoats. Both of them spoke English only, in the presence of the soldiers they attacked."

"Soldiers?" In Steuben's mouth, speaking the German he had practiced from his high-school days, until it almost sounded like his native language, the word came out as a sneer. "Soldiers, you say? Five against two, our soldiers armed, and they are beaten down, one of them killed. If they're the best we have on hand, I tremble at the thought of our frustrated destiny, our prophecies denied."

"They're young men—little more than children, really. They were on a simple errand. Some Jew was holding out on them. The men they faced were obviously trained as fighters."

"I've been told that members of the Thunderbolt Brigade are trained as fighters, too. Was I misled, Manfred?"

"No, sir! By no means were you misinformed. They each attend a mandatory training session once a week, at least. I have instructors from the military, even one from GSG-9. They are schooled in unarmed combat and with firearms. As it happens, they were carrying no guns today and found themselves outmatched."

Steuben didn't pursue the matter. He had lost enough men in America, his former Navy SEAL chief of security among them, before he fled across the Atlantic to Berlin. It came as no surprise to him that he had enemies who could defeat a handful of young brawlers armed with knives and little else. It was a wonder, he supposed, that only one of the five skin-heads had been killed.

"They asked for *you*," he said to Roeder. "Not for me?"

"That's right, sir. From the insults that they offered, it may be some personal concern."

"What insults?" Steuben asked.

"Um…I believe one of them said I was a pile of shit, sir."

Steuben couldn't help but smile. "That's personal, all right. May we assume that you have enemies here in Berlin?"

"Oh, yes, sir. Thousands," Roeder answered, sounding proud of it. "There are the Jews, Turks, Communists, the homosexuals, the—"

Steuben interrupted him. "I think that very few of those would walk into a Berlin pawnshop, speaking English to a group of local boys. Do you, Manfred?"

"No, sir. Now that you put it that way, I suppose that they wouldn't."

"So, have you any enemies who speak primarily in English, then? The Brits or the Americans, perhaps?"

"We had some trouble during the Olympics," Roeder answered, "with the mud athletes from America."

"That's ancient history, Manfred. Something more recent, possibly?"

"Both countries still have soldiers here, of course, as part of NATO," Roeder said. "There have been certain incidents, with members of the Thunderbolt Brigade. Mud men approaching German women in the bars or on the streets, that sort of thing."

"You're not a member of the Thunderbolt Brigade," Steuben replied, knowing it was a specious argument before he spoke.

"No, sir. But I am known to be affiliated with it, through the Temple. That has never been a secret, sir. There have been stories in the press, as you're aware, and—"

"Very well. Should we suppose, then, that some British or American soldiers are looking for revenge against you, for these incidents, and furthermore that they are following skinheads around Berlin, to quiz them on your whereabouts? Before today, has there been anything at all to even hint at such a plot?"

"No, sir."

"I think we may discount it for the moment, then, although it still may prove to be correct. Are you a great believer in coincidence, Manfred?"

"I would suppose not, sir. I never really thought about it, but—"

"I share your view. Things happen for a reason, Manfred, either destiny or human agency, if there is truly any difference between the two."

"Yes, sir." The frown on Roeder's face told Steuben that he was confused.

"In other words," he said, spelling it out, "I find it curious that English-speaking killers should be asking after you, around Berlin, soon after my arrival in the city and this business in the States. It's odd, I think. Don't you?"

"Yes, sir."

"A bit too much of a coincidence, perhaps?"

"I see. Yes, sir."

"The question, then—how did they know, so quickly, where I would be found?"

Technology, Steuben thought, answering himself.

Agents of ZOG—the Zionist Occupational Government in Washington, D.C.—had toys for tracking human prey beyond his wildest fantasies. There were satellites orbiting earth, outside the stratosphere, that could read license plates and newspaper headlines on any street corner in the world, flashing the magnified, digitized images back to the top Jews in Washington, New York, Miami Beach or Tel Aviv. They had infrared detectors that could scan a skyscraper from miles away, count all the occupants and tell you whether they were working at their desks or having coffee in the lounge, perhaps a couple of them fucking in the basement when they thought no one was looking. There were microchips that could be surgically implanted in a person's body, sometimes done without his conscious knowledge, and—

"What's that?" Roeder was watching him, had asked him something, but the question had been lost. "Excuse me, Manfred. If you would repeat the question, please…?"

"Of course, sir. I was asking how we may identify the enemy and head them off before they do more damage here. We have a schedule to maintain, and—"

"I'm aware of that," Steuben replied. "You may remember that I wrote the schedule, yes?"

"Of course, sir. All I meant—"

"Your question is a good one, even so." The interruption showed who was boss, confirming his control over the situation. "We must certainly identify these bastards and destroy them all before they can do any further damage to the cause."

It felt strange, saying it. If victory was preordained by Wotan and the other ancient gods, how could it be derailed by mortal men? Of course, such logic had no place in a religious system of belief, where miracles were readily accepted as a fact of life, the supernatural admitted as mundane. Logic and religion were like oil and water: they would never mix, but to the detriment of both.

"We have a friend or two with immigration," Roeder said. "I can begin by asking them to check on new arrivals in Berlin. It's not entirely hopeless, sir. There may be something in the area of diplomatic passports. We can check the Brits and the Americans, first thing. Throw in Canadians, perhaps, for good measure."

"And Jews," Steuben reminded him. "Never forget the Jews."

"Of course not, sir. We don't get all that many visitors from Israel recently, I'm told." The smile was almost gloating now. "Apparently, they don't feel very welcome in the fatherland these days."

"A Zionist assassin wouldn't fly in from Jerusalem or Tel Aviv, Manfred. He will not wear a yarmulke or Star of David."

"No, sir." Humbled now, but only just. "It's difficult to spot the sneaky Jews sometimes, you understand. They dress and wear their hair like any normal person, have their noses bobbed, who knows what else? With circumcision so widespread among the Gentiles, it doesn't even help to take their pants down, half the time."

"Spare me the details, Manfred, if you please. I don't care *how* you find these men. Berlin is your domain. I leave it in your hands...for now." Reminding Roeder that if he wasn't successful, he could still lose everything. There was no guaranteed free pass into the Promised Land. Just ask the old Jew Moses, who had labored forty years and come up wanting in the end.

"I'll find them, sir."

"And soon, Manfred. As you so rightly pointed out, we have important things to do, schedules to keep. We must not fall behind. Our destiny depends on it."

CHAPTER FOUR

Gellar had come back from his scouting mission without any word on Manfred Roeder's whereabouts, but he had learned that members of the Thunderbolt Brigade had planned an "action" for that night, targeting Turkish immigrants in Kreuzberg, a mostly impoverished area of Berlin. They were coming out in force, Gellar reported: fifty young street fighters at the very least, perhaps as many as a hundred. They couldn't hope to wipe out the Turks, of course, but they would raise some hell—and maybe claim some lives—before the riot squad arrived. Police responses to that kind of call in Kreuzberg were often curiously sluggish, as if some of the police dispatchers or commanders weren't terribly concerned what happened to the Turks and other "undesirables."

There was no reason to believe that Manfred Roeder would be present to observe the raid, Gellar explained, but they could almost certainly pick up a skinhead who possessed at least a general idea of where the Nordic Temple's local honcho could be found at any given time. And if they had to squeeze the bird a bit to make him sing, so what?

Bolan had come prepared for trouble, the Beretta 93-R riding in its armpit holster, while the Spectre submachine gun he had recently acquired hung from a makeshift sling beneath his lightweight raincoat. Moving along Kottbusser Damm with Gellar at his side, he felt as if he had been dropped into the middle of a spy novel by Le Carré or Deighton, catching sidelong glances from the people who passed by him on the street. Unfortunately, this was real, and anyone who died this night wouldn't be magically rejuvenated for a sequel.

Dead was dead, in Bolan's world, the prime directive being that you did it to the other guy before he had a chance to take you down.

This night, though, they were looking for a prisoner.

"How long?" he asked Gellar as they approached the ruins of the Anhalter station, once the teeming equivalent of Grand Central Station in New York. It had been bombed out in World War II, leaving an urban wasteland that had never been rebuilt, a portion of the station's grand facade all that remained. Nearby, he knew, on Prinz-Albrecht-Strasse, the SS and Gestapo had maintained their headquarters, shining examples of the master race like Himmler, Heydrich and Eichmann toiling at their desks, keeping the books on genocide.

"It's difficult to say, precisely," Gellar answered. "These creatures we hunt tonight are not clockwatchers, as you might say in America. Sometime within the next half hour, we should see them starting to arrive."

"They just march in like it's a big parade, or what?"

"Too obvious," Gellar said, frowning at the very thought. "For raids like this they drive, sometimes steal cars or even rent a bus. It all depends how many will be coming to the party.''

"You know some of them, I take it," Bolan said.

"Oh, many of them, yes. You understand, tonight we may not have the greatest opportunity of all to pick and choose."

"So, you're thinking we should just grab one and bail, first chance we get?''

The frown hung on. "I'm not sure what is 'bail,'" the Mossad agent said.

"Bail out. Take off. Get lost. Split. Hit the bricks."

"Ah, yes. Your slang, I think, is one of the best things about America. And we should certainly expect to 'bail' without delay, as we shall be outnumbered."

"Just take off and let the rest of them raise hell?''

"It's what they do. Someone will ring up the police. The officers will come when they are ready.''

"In the meantime, though, these people could sustain a lot of damage.''

"You have something on your mind that I believe I don't like," Gellar replied.

"These skinheads coming in, should I assume that they'll be armed?''

"Of course. No self-respecting Nazi would go anywhere without a weapon.''

"So, it's more than fisticuffs and throwing rocks.''

"Murder isn't uncommon in these cases. Sadly, it's now almost routine.''

"Seems like we've got a chance to rain on their parade this time. I'd hate to pass an opportunity like that, because I'm in a hurry.''

"You propose we try to stop them? Fifty or one hundred skinheads against two?'' Gellar was smiling now. "It won't be like the pawnshop, I can promise you."

"I'm counting on it," Bolan said. He had the Mossad agent's full attention now. "It's what I do."

Gellar considered it, still walking. Finally, he said, "I think I need to have my brain investigated."

"Head examined," Bolan said, correcting him. "Is that a yes?"

"I told you once before," the Israeli said with a shrug, "I don't like Nazis."

"That makes two of us."

"In that case, we should probably split up. I see no point to giving them an easy target."

"Right. A cross fire works for me." That said, Bolan was moved to ask, "You're armed, right?"

"A Mossad agent in the German fatherland?" He smiled. "Weapons aren't unlike the American Express card. I do not leave home without them."

"Good. Where will you be?"

"Across the street, there." Gellar pointed toward what might have been a grand hotel or office building half a century before, no more than crumbling rubble now, ignored by various regimes with other, more significant priorities.

"The skinheads often gather here before their raids in Kreuzberg," Gellar said. "Aside from the proximity of targets, it reminds them of the Third Reich's loss and what they struggle to regain."

"They want to struggle," Bolan said, "I think we should accommodate them."

"So we shall."

He watched Gellar proceed across the street and merge with darkness on the other side before retreating toward the battered shell of the Anhalter station.

There, concealed within a shadowed doorway, Bolan stood and waited for the enemy.

Fifty, perhaps a hundred. Nazi skinheads, armed and aching for a fight, thirsty for blood. He reached inside his raincoat, double-checked the safety on his Spectre submachine gun, making sure that it was in the off position.

Ready.

All he needed now was targets, and a sudden flare of headlights in the distance told him they were on the way.

"THIS TIME, for Franz!" The beer gave Aldo Gürlich courage that he might have lacked without it, after seeing his own troop commander killed before his eyes that afternoon. Instead of begging off the Kreuzberg mission, though, he had been anxious to join in, lash out at someone—anyone—and thereby exorcise his rage.

Better than that, Gürlich had been selected to command one of the crews in this night's raid against the Turks. There were four crews in all, a dozen men in each, plus the crew leader. Seven of his men were packed into an old Volkswagen van, with the remainder trailing in a Volvo four-door they had stolen and would torch when they were finished, for the hell of it.

He had been chosen as a crew chief on the basis of seniority, and possibly—he couldn't rule it out, at least—because he bore the marks of his encounter with the strangers at the Jew's pawnshop, which had left Franz Spangler dead. Gürlich was thinking that they might drive past the pawnshop later and treat the Jew to a Molotov cocktail. It wasn't *his* fault Franz was dead, exactly, but he had described the situation to police and made them all the next-best thing to fugitives.

Besides, he was a Jew. What other reason was required to burn him out?

When they were close enough to smell the Turkish cooking from the tenements in front of them, he swiveled in his seat and found the others watching him, their eyes bright in the shadowed cavern of the van. The other bruised survivors of the pawnshop raid were there, as well, crouching beside the fresh troops who had seen no action yet today.

"This is for Franz!" he said again, and smiled to see the gleam of knives and razors, hear the meaty smack of pipes and truncheons striking open palms. Gürlich was carrying an Astra Falcon semiautomatic pistol, made in Spain, and his driver had a Llama Martial .38 revolver. There were two more firearms in the second car, another pistol and a sawed-off Franchi double-barreled shotgun. Altogether, in the striking force of fifty-two commandos, there were probably a dozen guns, perhaps fifteen.

This night wasn't supposed to be a massacre, of course—simply a lesson for the Turkish scum who had begun to think Berlin and all of Germany belonged to them. They came with nothing but the shabby clothing on their backs, stole jobs away from Aryans with families to feed, or else attached themselves like leeches to the body politic and made their living from the dole.

The cleansing fire would come, and sooner than the pigs suspected, but it wouldn't be this night.

This was a wake-up call.

"Two blocks," the driver said. "I see the station up ahead."

"The others?" Gürlich asked, already leaning forward, peering through the dirty windshield.

"Some of them are here."

He could see two vans already parked outside the shell of what had been Anhalter station, long before his time. Before his father's time, in fact, now that he thought about it, the old man just forty-something, born a few years after *his* father had come home broken, nearly crippled, from the Eastern Front. The bastard Soviets had nearly killed him during the retreat from Stalingrad, and it was sobering to think that if their aim had been a little better, there would be no Aldo Gürlich riding through the darkened streets of Kreuzberg, on his way to give the bastard Turks a whipping.

To Gürlich, it was simply one more bit of evidence that destiny had favored him from birth. A stranger might not recognize it, simply looking at him, studying his history in school or in the courts, but he had been born an Aryan, when billions more were not so blessed, and he had found the comrades who would stand behind him in the struggle to reclaim their birthright.

Starting now.

They pulled in close behind another van, more headlights flaring in the rearview mirror, even as his driver switched off the engine. Unloading from the van, his soldiers grouped together, closing ranks, while Gürlich moved to join another crew chief he had recognized, off to the side. A moment later, as the rest arrived, the other leaders joined them, huddling briefly while their soldiers massed along the curb, by squads. The overall commander of the action was a scarfaced twenty-four-year-old named Joachim Kroll who kept his orders terse and to the point.

"Our target is that rat's nest over there," he told them, pointing toward a block of tenements across the street and at an angle, fifty yards distant. "Shooters, cover the advance troops, but don't fire unless you have to, at the start. Don't throw the Molotovs until we have a chance to knock some heads. I don't want any of our people trapped inside there, when it starts to burn. We'll have them sleeping in the streets tonight, if they don't fry."

That had them laughing as the crew leaders dispersed and passed the orders to their men. The ranks formed up and started moving off across the street, behind their officers. Gürlich was sorry that he wouldn't be first among the fighters to make contact with the Turks and rout them from their filthy nests, but maybe he would have a chance to use the Falcon semiautomatic yet, before the night was over.

And if all else failed, he still had the Jew pawnbroker.

Crossing the street, his men around him, Aldo Gürlich saw a young boy standing on the front stoop of the tenement that was their target. He was small and dark, his clothes too large, most likely hand-me-downs. The boy was staring at them, wide-eyed. Gürlich wondered if he could drop him with a pistol shot from thirty yards, when the child bolted back inside, slamming the door behind him. The skinhead could imagine him as he raced through the halls, shouting his warning to the rest.

"They've seen us!" someone barked, away to Gürlich's left.

Another, closer shouted, "Hurry up, before they call the squealers!"

They sprinted across the pavement, Gürlich with the Falcon semiautomatic in his hand. The first sounds of gunfire startled him, knowing *he* hadn't fired, the weapon cold and silent in his fist. And these were automatic weapons, firing from a distance somewhere.

"Who's shooting?" Wilmot Bartsch asked, coming up beside him with a panicky expression on his face. He barely had time to ask the question before he was hit. Gasping, he tumbled to his knees, dropping his metal pipe to reach around and grope at something in the middle of his lower back. His fingers came back bloody, dark and dripping.

"Aldo?"

Gürlich lost it, and from what he saw around him, he wasn't alone. Other skinheads were dropping, some for cover, others obviously wounded, maybe dead or dying. And the strike force had begun to scatter, some redoubling their speed in the direction of the tenement, as if they would find shelter there. A larger group retreated toward their vehicles, still others taking off with no apparent goal in mind except to let the darkness hide them from their unknown enemies.

Gürlich was undecided, frozen in his tracks, until a bullet chipped the pavement near his feet and whistled off into the night, a ricochet. Cursing the sudden urge to void his bowels, he turned around and started sprinting toward the cars.

FISH IN A BARREL, Jacob Gellar thought as he lined up another target in the mini-Uzi's sights and triggered two quick rounds in semiauto fire. The lanky skinhead lurched and wobbled on his feet, not going down at first, and Gellar was about to let him have a third round when he buckled, sprawling facedown in the middle of the street.

Good riddance.

Gellar didn't know if he had killed the youth or not; in point of fact, he didn't even care. A crippled neo-Nazi in a wheelchair, spending the rest of his life with colostomy bags, would make a good cautionary tale for up-and-coming skinhead recruits.

The Mossad agent hadn't been entirely honest with Mike Belasko in telling the American that he didn't like neo-Nazis. In truth, he hated them. Gellar had studied their atrocities in school, when he was growing up in Israel, and his family still offered prayers for distant relatives who had gone up in smoke at Sobibor. Gellar supposed that history was part of what had prompted him to join Mossad after he finished military service. He wanted to wreak havoc with the enemies of Israel, and he still recalled the unofficial motto of Mossad's old breed, the ones who used to call themselves the Wrath of God.

All things being equal, never miss a chance to kill a Nazi.

This night, for the second time in less than twelve hours, Gellar had that chance, and he would make the most of it.

It made no difference that some of those who swarmed the street in front of him were in their teens, few of the others more than twenty-three or -four years old. Each one of them was old enough to rape and terrorize and loot and kill defenseless victims, chosen on the basis of their race, religion, politics or nationality. Young men like these had been the brawl-ers and assassins who put Adolf Hitler in control of Germany nearly three-quarters of a century ago.

Never again!

He kept the mini-Uzi set on semiautomatic fire, conserving rounds and minimizing muzzle-flash. Some of the skinheads he could see were armed with pistols, several more with what resembled sawed-off shotguns. In a panic, they had started to return fire without marking any targets, three or four unloading toward the nearest tenements, some others firing to-ward Anhalter station, where Belasko was presumably concealed.

Gellar didn't waste time trying to pick out the American's position by a muzzle-flash. He had too many targets, and so little time.

One of the skinhead shotgunners had fired both bar-rels into the yawning darkness, stopping like a moron to reload. He broke the stubby weapon, fumbled in the right-hand pocket of his leather jacket for more cartridges. Gellar squeezed off one Parabellum round and saw his target stagger, caught the skinhead as he dropped his weapon, clutching at his abdomen.

Too low.

He raised his sights an inch or so and fired another round. This time, the bald-headed neo-Nazi did an awkward little pirouette and crumpled to the asphalt.

Better.

Submachine guns weren't intended or designed for fancy target shooting; neither were they meant for killing at a distance, although most available nowa-days as had an effective range somewhere between 100 and 220 meters. All that meant, of course, was that a bullet fired from that extended range was capable of killing *if* it found a target, striking in a vital place. There was no calculation of the odds for making such a shot, which clearly would have been discouraging to sales.

As pleased as Gellar was to be engaged in shooting neo-Nazis—and, peripherally, with preventing injury or death to those the skinheads had been planning to attack—he hadn't lost sight of their mission to acquire a subject for interrogation. That meant breathing, and with all the necessary parts intact to let him speak coherently. What happened to the skinhead *after* they had had their little talk was something else entirely, and irrelevant to his immediate concern.

Scanning the shooting gallery in front of him, watching for any skinhead gunners on alert, Gellar emerged from cover, clinging to the shadows where he could, tracking the remnants of the strike force as it scattered. Chasing those who were retreating toward their vehicles meant barging out into the middle of the street, exposed and reasonably well lit, giving them a perfect target. On the other hand, from what Gellar surmised, the smaller group that seemed intent on seeking refuge in the nearby tenement could probably expect a warm reception from the Turks inside, and he wanted no part of that—except, perhaps, to watch them get their asses kicked.

Who else was there?

Gellar was quick to notice that a number of the skinheads, frightened and disoriented by the unexpected gunfire, simply scattered, moving neither toward the tenement nor back in the direction of their cars. He had already picked off two of them, but there were several left to choose from, ducking into shadows as he watched them, waiting for the gunfire to subside or else for someone to command them, tell them where to go and what to do.

It may as well be me, he thought, already moving toward the nearest of the skinheads he had spotted as the plan took shape.

In fact, there were two of them, huddled in the doorway of what once had been a shop, long closed, the windows painted over, milky white, with Turkish graffiti the icing on the cake. Gellar moved to overtake them, watching his flank the best he could, holding his fire now, to avoid giving himself away.

Two skinheads, and he only needed one. It might be possible to capture both of them, but what would be the point? His challenge, Gellar thought, would be to guess which of the neo-Nazis was most likely to possess information concerning Manfred Roeder's whereabouts, and cow the punk enough that he would talk—or would at least prove more susceptible to grilling when they found a safer place to question him.

No problem there, Gellar decided. He could soften one by taking out the other while his sidekick watched. He only hoped that he wouldn't be forced to kill them both and go in search of other prey. The final call, of course, was up to them.

Gunfire continued from the far side of the street—Belasko chasing the survivors—while Gellar advanced on his targets. One of the skinheads saw him coming when he was within fifteen or twenty feet. Both of them were clearly visible, although dark shadows masked their faces. Blurting an alarm, the neo-Nazi raised what appeared to be a short-barreled revolver, angling the weapon toward Gellar's face.

The Israeli was faster, squeezing off two quick

rounds from his machine pistol, their impact punching the human target backward and down to the pavement. The stricken youth's companion, standing with a baseball bat drawn back and cocked to swing, cursed Gellar in a voice that trembled on the edge of tears.

Advancing slowly, step by wary step, Gellar addressed him in a voice of stainless steel. "It's time to stop and think," he said, "if this is where and how you want to die."

BOLAN SWITCHED magazines on the Spectre SMG, reloading on the move from one sheltered alcove to the next. A couple of the skinheads had picked out his muzzle-flash, but those who spotted him were armed with bats or blades, forced to retreat before his fire while calling out in German to their comrades packing firearms. One skinhead had blazed away at Bolan with both barrels of a cut-down 12-gauge shotgun, but the shot had pattered harmlessly to earth before it reached him, wasted over distance that the stubby weapon couldn't bridge.

Bolan had killed the shooter anyway, no point in taking chances with him, no room in the circumstances for misguided mercy. The retreating neo-Nazis in his gun sights had come out this night expecting—hoping—to commit assault and arson, maybe rape and murder if they got the chance. The fact that politics or some religious tenet fired their savagery meant no more to the Executioner in Kreuzberg than it had in Southeast Asia, in the States or any other killing ground where he had placed himself between cruel human predators and their intended prey.

The skinheads had come armed, and they had come to play for keeps. Now that the game had gone against them, they were on their own, no quarter asked or offered.

Bolan raked the fleeing ranks with controlled 3- and 4-round bursts, watching leather-clad figures go down in slack heaps, combat boots drumming the pavement as life shivered out of them in feeble spasms. Dead or wounded, Bolan didn't care, as long as they were out of action, cutting down as many of them as he could before they reached their waiting vehicles.

Return fire, when it came, was scattered and disorganized. Only a handful of the raiders carried guns at all, and none appeared particularly skillful in their use. He wrote some of that off to panic, the surprise of being ambushed on what should have been a quick, head-knocking milk run, and was thankful for the tendency of his opponents to unload on shadows, silent structures, even one another as the grim, chaotic scene unfolded.

Two more targets ran across his field of fire, and Bolan chopped them down in tandem, mindful at the same time of his need to spare at least one of the raiders for interrogation if he had the chance. He wondered how Gellar was faring, noted the cessation of gunfire from across the street, hoping that none of the skinhead shooters had scored a lucky hit on his companion. He didn't know Jacob Gellar well enough to trust him fully yet, but it would only slow things if he was forced to call on Brognola again, in Washington, and try to make arrangements for another contact in Berlin.

Focus!

How many skinheads were still alive and on their feet where he could see them? Bolan gave up on the head count, settled for a ballpark estimate of twenty-five to thirty, which excluded those who'd made their break in the direction of the tenements, and several who had scattered aimlessly into the darkened Kreuzberg side streets. He could hear sufficient racket from the tenements to know that those skinheads already had their hands full, and he couldn't track the stragglers short of giving up on the majority contingent and allowing them to get away.

No sale.

He concentrated on the main group, saw that most of them had reached the line of waiting vans and cars some forty yards from the Anhalter station. He could hose them with the Spectre, take some of them down at least from where he was, but others would no doubt escape. Moving before he really had a chance to think it through, Bolan reminded himself that this action didn't need to be a clean sweep. Their primary objective was to bag a talkative skinhead—or, rather, one who could be made to talk. As for the rest, they had frustrated the attack against the Turkish housing project, left some neo-Nazis in the street. It was, in short, a good night's work.

But Bolan could not bring himself to let them go.

Not yet.

Concerned now by the absence of continuing gunfire from Gellar's position, Bolan put it out of mind and concentrated on the skinheads piling into vehicles ahead of him. He blanked out any thought of police cars racing toward the scene, no sound of sirens to announce them yet.

Choosing the nearest van, he strafed it front to rear

with Parabellum rounds, knocking out a fist-sized portion of the windshield and chipping shiny divots from the faded paint job, dropping three skinheads as they were jostling one another at the side door, struggling like some reenactment of an old Three Stooges skit. He dropped them all, their arms and legs still tangled as they hit the pavement, dying.

He swept on past the van, spraying the next vehicle in line, and the next, catching some of the would-be escapees on foot, nailing others in their seats, bullets and broken glass together scouring their flesh. He couldn't stop them all, of course, and he heard engines firing even as he raked the motorcade. A Volvo and a crowded BMW swung out of line, cutting dangerous U-turns and nearly sideswiping each other in their haste, burning rubber as they put the killing ground behind them. Bolan chased them with a burst to mark their bodywork, then let them go.

One of the vans, already pocked with bullet holes, lurched backward, grinding bumpers with a dark sedan behind it, then swung out from the curb, trying to follow the example of the smaller cars that had already fled. Bolan was ready this time, punching out the tinted side window with a short burst of automatic fire on the turn, stepping dangerously close to lob an RGD grenade inside the van.

Five seconds later, when it blew, the vehicle was halfway down the block and still accelerating. Was the rocking motion his imagination, or were skinheads in the van trying to scoop up the grenade, get rid of it before it blew? If so, they didn't make it. The explosion cleared the van's remaining windows, belching smoke and flame, its contained thunderclap less impressive than the Hollywood version. The van didn't flip or disintegrate, although the driver's door popped open to disgorge a smoking corpse. Without even a dead hand on the wheel, the van began to drift, decelerating, until it collided with a mailbox farther down and came to rest.

It was enough. The other skinheads were escaping, on wheels or on foot, and Bolan watched them go. It struck him that he had no prisoner to show for all the carnage and he turned to scan the killing ground, in search of anyone still showing signs of life.

"Lose something?" asked a gruff, familiar voice.

He spotted Gellar moving toward him from across the street. The Mossad agent had a frightened-looking skinhead with him, hands apparently secured somehow behind his back. The young apprentice Nazi had a gash along what should have been his hairline, and fresh blood streamed down the left side of his face.

"We had a bit of disagreement on the terms of our collaboration," Gellar told him, smiling, "but I think we've worked it out."

"I tell you nothing!" the bald captive said, but even he didn't appear convinced by his performance.

"We can work on that, my son," Gellar informed him.

Then, to Bolan he said, "I imagine we should leave, don't you? Even the slowest officers will have to show up sometime, yes?"

"The others?" Bolan asked him, glancing toward the tenements, where sounds of fighting still reverberated through the stricken night.

As Gellar turned in that direction, a battered, leather-clad form was ejected from the tenement doorway, bouncing down the steps and sprawling on the pavement, where it lay unmoving.

"Something tells me that our friends will get what's coming to them," Gellar said, and smiled again. "As for this one, I want to question him before that love tap on the head wipes out what little memory he may possess."

CHAPTER FIVE

The skinhead's name was Bruno. He was silent on the twenty-minute drive from Kreuzberg to a riverfront warehouse in the Treptow industrial district. Bolan drove while Gellar sat in back with Bruno, making comments now and then in German, while the youth didn't respond.

"This one," Gellar said, leaning forward and pointing through the windshield at the warehouse as it came up on their left. He got out of the car when Bolan stopped, unlocked the chain-link gate, waved Bolan through and locked the gate behind them once again when they were all inside. The fence, as Bolan saw, was topped with razor wire to keep out thieves and squatters.

"Park around in back," Gellar instructed, following the car on foot. There was a big, old-fashioned canvas-covered truck in back, reminding Bolan of something out of World War II. Two of the tires were nearly flat, while the accumulated dust and bird droppings confirmed that months—more likely years— had passed since this rig had been on the road.

Gellar produced another key, unlocked the back door of the warehouse, then returned to fetch their captive from the car. Bruno didn't resist, but he was sluggish on his feet, a slouching zombie—until Gellar took the mini-Uzi from underneath his raincoat, letting Bruno have another look at it. Whatever Gellar said this time, it got the skinhead moving briskly, up three concrete steps and through the open door.

When he had closed the door and bolted it against the night, Gellar switched on the overhead fluorescent lights, revealing that they stood in a wide, empty hallway. See-through office cubicles stood to their left, and a plastic tarp suspended like a giant shower curtain covered a broad door to their right. Gellar nudged Bruno in that direction, stepping past him to retract the tarp and clear their way into the warehouse proper.

It wasn't a truly large room, for a warehouse— Bolan made it roughly thirty feet across by fifty long, the metal roof and skylights twenty feet above their heads—but the stark gray emptiness, the echo of their footsteps on the concrete floor, somehow conspired to magnify it in his mind. A scream would echo here, he knew, but there was no one in the neighborhood to hear it, even if the voice was shrill enough to shatter glass.

A second look told Bolan that the place wasn't entirely empty. Planted at what seemed to be the perfect center of the room was a heavy, straight-backed wooden chair. It had no arms; the seat was broad enough to seat a fat man comfortably, which in turn meant that the square-cut legs were set too far apart to rock the chair without considerable effort. If the occupant was bound, Bolan suspected that the chair couldn't be moved at all.

A roll of silver duct tape waited for them on the

seat, the world's most awkward and uncomfortable Whoopee cushion.

"So, you plan ahead," Bolan remarked.

Gellar responded with a shrug. "Your famous Boy Scout motto, I believe, is Be Prepared."

He picked up the roll of duct tape and set it on the floor behind the chair. When Gellar spoke again, to Bruno, Bolan could interpret nothing but the young man's name. He watched as Gellar moved around behind the skinhead, thumbing through a ring of keys to find the one that fit handcuffs.

"I've told him that if he tries any foolish games, I'll shoot his kneecaps off and beat him to a bloody pulp his mother will not recognize. I have the feeling he believes me."

"That makes two of us," Bolan replied.

Gellar unlocked the cuffs from one of Bruno's wrists and motioned him to sit down in the chair, his arms bent behind his back. The skinhead hesitated, sizing up the two of them, but he clearly wasn't in any mood to die if he could possibly avoid it. He obeyed, sat still while Gellar locked the cuffs again and offered no resistance as the Mossad agent bound his legs with duct tape, to the front legs of the chair. A final loop around his chest and arms, resembling a curiously flattened python coiled about its prey, and he was perfectly secure.

"Our Bruno speaks no English, as you may have guessed by now," Gellar explained. "I will inquire first as to any knowledge he may have of Manfred Roeder's whereabouts, as well as links between the Nordic Temple and the Thunderbolt Brigade. If you have any special questions you would like for him to answer, I will translate them."

"It couldn't hurt to ask if he knows anything about the Nordic Temple's plans for action in Berlin, or anywhere in Germany, for that matter. He doesn't look like someone who'd be in the loop, but who knows what he's picked up from the rumor mill."

"Of course."

"I'm curious," the Executioner delayed him for another moment. "What's your plan if he decides he doesn't want to talk?"

The knife appeared in Gellar's hand as if by magic. It was a stiletto, activated by a button on one side, the six-inch blade shooting directly outward from the handle, then retracting with a snap. In out, in out.

"I'm confident Bruno will tell us what we want to know, assuming that he has the information in his rather ugly head," Gellar replied. "If not—" another shrug, as he went on "—that's why we have a drain beneath the chair."

And sure enough, there was.

Bolan wasn't a fan of torture. He had suffered it and seen it done to others, had applied strategic pain to certain human predators himself on past occasions, when he needed information in a hurry and their attitudes ruled out a quick response. He recognized the contradiction in his attitude—namely, that he would shoot Bruno without a second thought, if it was necessary, but he didn't care to see the neo-Nazi carved up like a Christmas roast.

Still, Bolan made his mind up that he wouldn't interfere, unless some still invisible, still undecided line was crossed. Sometimes, despite what pacifists and preachers said, when unknown lives were riding on the line, the ends did justify the means.

Gellar knelt beside the chair, leaned in toward

Bruno, almost kissing-close. When Gellar spoke again, his voice was low pitched, barely audible.

The skinhead listened for a moment, then responded in a pouting tone that verged on a sneer. Gellar stared at him, up close, his own face showing disappointment.

"You were right," he said to Bolan. "Bruno has decided that he doesn't want to talk to us." A few more words in German, Bruno frowning in confusion, making no response.

In English, Gellar said, "I've asked him if he saw Jack Nicholson in *Chinatown*. I think it was before his time. Still, even Nazis have been known to watch old movies on the television, yes?"

There was a blur of motion, the metallic snap of the stiletto, and almost before the gleaming blade was visible, its tip had disappeared inside Bruno's right nostril. With a twisting motion, still part of the lightning thrust, Gellar sheared through the fragile tube of flesh and ducked back as a jet of blood leaped from the skinhead's face, to spatter on the concrete floor.

That's why we have a drain beneath the chair.

Bruno let out a shriek that was still an octave short of turning crystal into dust. He thrashed against the tape and handcuffs, getting nowhere with it, finally subsiding into painful wheezing, blowing crimson bubbles from one nostril, while the other dribbled mucus.

"I've explained the situation to him," Gellar said, although in fact he had said nothing more to Bruno since the question about *Chinatown*. "I hope he has a better understanding now."

More German, rapid and angry sounding, but the skinhead was responding, fear and anger mingled in his tone. He spoke for several moments, answering more questions, snuffling blood between responses.

Gellar said, "He doesn't know where Roeder lives, but there's a place he always meets with members of the Thunderbolt Brigade. I have the address. It's the basement of a strip club near Potsdamer Strasse, if we can believe this one."

"You think he's lying to you?" Bolan asked.

"I doubt it. He appears to want his face left more or less intact. I'll ask about the Nordic Temple and their future plans, and see what he comes up with."

Gellar reeled off more rapid-fire German. The bloodied skinhead hesitated after Gellar finished speaking, frowning through his blood until the stained blade of the switchblade rose again and made a pass before his face. That seemed to do the trick, as he flinched and the verbal dam burst, pouring out a flood of words. From the look on Gellar's face, the way he snapped at their prisoner, making him repeat some of the spiel, it seemed that even his Mossad companion had some trouble keeping up.

At last, Gellar stood, stepped back and turned from the skinhead to face Bolan directly. Still frowning, he began to summarize what the young man had told him.

"It sounds like nonsense," Gellar said apologetically, "but I don't think he's lying to me. I suspect that he's repeating something he's been told, something he may even believe himself, though it's preposterous."

"I'm listening," the Executioner replied.

"You know the story of the Spear of Destiny?"

"Yeah. But you can refresh my memory in case I missed something."

"According to the early books of the New Testament, when Jesus Christ was crucified, a Roman soldier took his spear and stabbed Christ in the side. A legend has it that the spear—its tip, at least—has managed to survive across the centuries, a sacred relic now, because it has been stained by holy blood. Believers in the fable seem to think that anyone who owns the spear becomes invincible in battle, basically immortal. It's known that Hitler's SS tried to find the spear, apparently in vain.

"The irony," Gellar continued, smiling, "was that Hitler wasn't Christian. But he *was* a superstitious madman, and by late 1943 or early 1944, he was grasping at straws. Anything to help him stand against his enemies, hold conquered territory, win the war."

"Including magic spears."

"It's not the strangest scheme he hatched, I can assure you," Gellar said. "Hitler and several of his closest aides believed the earth was hollow, occupied by members of the original Aryan race, perhaps even by their Norse gods. He sent expeditions to the polar ice cap, looking for an entrance to the netherworld. Of course, they never found it. At the same time, Himmler and his master-race elite were trying to commune with dark powers at Wewelsburg castle, performing rites that may well have included human sacrifice."

Bolan had heard all of that before and was watching their captive while Gellar spoke, and he noted a sharp reaction, almost a grimace, at the mention of Wewelsburg. It could have been pain, and yet...

"I think you hit a nerve," he said. "Why don't you ask our little friend about Wewelsburg."

Another flinch, quickly suppressed this time, but

Gellar saw it, too. He knelt beside the chair once more, holding the crimson-stained stiletto in plain sight, and started speaking softly, earnestly, to their young prisoner.

THE STAFF and students of Humboldt University, on Unter den Linden, east of the national library, were barely stirring when Bolan and Gellar arrived on the campus. It was 8:13 a.m. on Bolan's second day in Germany, and he wasn't entirely easy with the course that his investigation of the Nordic Temple had begun to follow.

"Are you sure your friend will be at work this early?" he asked Gellar as they left his rental in the visitor's parking lot and began the hike across campus.

"Meir has never missed a day of work in thirty-seven years," Gellar replied. "I'm told that he was tardy once, twelve years ago—the day a taxi struck him on the walk from his apartment, knocking him unconscious in the street."

"That's dedication for you," Bolan said.

"More to the point, he has the knowledge we require. If anyone knows Wewelsburg castle, it is Meir Stern."

"I hope it's not a waste of time."

"We have to check out Bruno's story, yes? Although, admittedly, if he was lying, there is little we can do about it now."

Bolan hadn't asked him for details of the skinhead's fate. It had been obvious that their informant couldn't be released once they had questioned him, to spill to story and alert his comrades in the Thunderbolt Brigade, who would pass the story on to Manfred Roeder and the other Nordic Temple brass. When Gellar finished questioning the young neo-Nazi, he had requested privacy, asked Bolan to warm up the car, and when he left the warehouse moments later, he had been alone. There hadn't been a wealth of hiding places for a corpse inside the barnlike building, but disposal wasn't Bolan's problem at the moment. He was anxious to get on with the business of the Temple of the Nordic Covenant, conclude the mission and go home.

Wherever that was.

Gellar led him to an ancient-looking ivy-covered building that resembled any one of several dozen others they had passed so far on campus. There were newer buildings, to be sure, but Bolan had the sense that this was the university's heart, the old, established root from which the rest had grown. Inside, they mounted stairs worn shiny by generations of climbers, to reach the second floor. Meir Stern's office was located halfway down the dreary hall, on Bolan's left.

Gellar knocked on the door, waited for the summons from within, then pushed through with a broad smile on his face. Professor Stern rose from his desk to greet the Mossad agent, shaking Bolan's hand in turn, as he was introduced with the Belasko alias. The old man's grip was firm, his eyes bright beneath their bristling brows, his lower face and upper chest concealed by a thick gray beard, heavily shot through with white.

Gellar explained their errand, speaking English, and the professor answered in kind. "Wewelsburg," he said. "It is a place I wouldn't care to go myself, although I like to fancy that I'm not a superstitious man.''

"Why not, then?" Bolan said. "I mean, if you don't mind my asking."

"Not at all, young man." Professor Stern pinned Bolan with his clear gray eyes, a pale shade lighter than his beard and thinning hair. "Quite simply, this—while I am not a superstitious or religious man, I still believe in evil. And if evil ever had a seat on Earth in modern times—outside the Nazi camps, that is, or the gulag—that place is Wewelsburg.''

"And why is that?" Bolan asked.

"You're familiar with the racial and political aspects of the Third Reich, I would assume," Professor Stern replied, "but few alive today have studied the religious aspects of Hitler's regime. The Schutzstaffel was conceived as more than simply an elite bodyguard for the führer or a military spearhead for assaults in Europe. From the moment of its founding, Hitler openly described the SS as a cult, the hard core of his new racist religion, based on occult theories of the Thule Society and similar, like-minded groups. Wewelsburg castle, in turn, was the heart of Nazi paganism as administered by Heinrich Himmler, chief of that SS.

"He found the old, abandoned castle in Westphalia, during 1934, and bought it cheaply, with the story that he meant to build an SS fortress to withstand barbarian invasions from the east. In fact, over the next eleven years he spent no less than thirteen million marks on restoration of the castle, using slave labor for the grunt work, importing artisans for the details, using the finest materials at every turn. Each room was furnished in a different style, without so much as a desk or chair being duplicated. Himmler imported fine tapestries, solid oak furniture, wrought-iron handles for the doors, priceless carpets, heavy brocade curtains. The doors were hand carved, inlaid with precious metals and stones. Priceless works of art looted from the museums of occupied Europe were supplied as decorations. Rooms in the castle were dedicated to Germanic folk heroes—the Frederick Barbarossa suite, for instance, was reserved for Hitler himself, although he never visited the place. The central feature of the castle was the giant banquet hall, with thronelike chairs where Himmler and his closest aides—no more than twelve besides Reichsführer Himmler at any given time—would dine in luxury, with slaves on hand to serve their every whim.''

''And this continued until 1945, you said?''

''Almost until the very end.''

''Sounds like a massive waste of time,'' Bolan remarked, ''when Germany was fighting for her life against the Allies.''

''So one might assume,'' Professor Stern replied, ''if one wasn't aware that Himmler and his master meant Wewelsburg to be the very heart of Germany's defense. The spiritual heart, you understand?''

''Not quite.''

''The banquet hall was used for more than dining,'' Stern explained. ''Himmler and his appointed aides would sometimes sit for hours on end, in perfect silence, striving to perfect their bond with what they called the 'race soul.' Underneath the banquet chamber was a dungeon known as 'the realm of the dead,' excavated from the living rock by disposable lackeys. Within this crypt were twelve stone pillars, each surmounted by an empty urn. The urns were always ready to receive the ashes of Himmler's primary disciples, should they fall in battle or through any other means. Even in death, their essence would be used to serve the fatherland.''

''That's all the crypt was used for?'' Bolan asked him. ''Storing ashes?''

''At this point, who can say? There were reports—what you would call hearsay—of vile, malignant rituals conducted in the pit at Wewelsburg, but as far as we've been able to discover, no one who might actually have witnessed such an incident survived the spring of 1945.'' Professor Stern was frowning as he added, ''Perhaps it's just as well.''

''What interest would the castle have,'' Jacob Gellar asked, ''to a modern neo-Nazi group?''

Stern shrugged, the movement more a ducking of his head than any lifting of his rounded shoulders. ''It is difficult to say, Jacob. Of course, it would depend upon the group involved. If they were dedicated to the politics of fascism, it could be nothing more than a curiosity or minor shrine.'' He turned to Bolan once again, and smiled. ''In the United States, if I recall, you sometimes venerate old inns. George Washington slept here, that sort of thing.''

''And if the group involved was, say, the Temple of the Nordic Covenant?''

The old man's smile turned brittle, faded and was gone. ''Ah, well,'' he said, ''in that case, with a group devoted to the occult side of Nazism, I'm afraid the possibilities may be more sinister. They might wish to commemorate some of the rituals allegedly performed by Himmler and his cronies. Even if the early rituals weren't performed, in fact, you understand that modern-day fanatics often borrow their theology from sensational media accounts—your teenage satanists in the United States, for example. Someone of that bent conceivably might wish to emulate a ceremony without true historical precedent.''

''Including human sacrifice?'' Bolan asked.

''All I know about the Temple of the Nordic Covenant is what I read in newspapers and certain government reports,'' Professor Stern replied. ''But it would seem that they aren't averse to spilling blood. If those reports are accurate, well, then, I see no reason to assume that they would shy away from killing once again, particularly if the slaying was regarded as an article of faith.''

''They'd need a subject,'' Bolan said.

''Or subjects,'' Gellar added, ''all depending on the ritual.''

''Oh, my!'' Professor Stern was fairly scowling now. ''That *is* a most unpleasant prospect. Is there anything that you can do, Jacob?''

It was the Executioner who answered him.

''I have a few ideas,'' he said. ''The first one is to have a look around this castle, if we can.''

''That means we have a drive of some two hundred miles ahead of us,'' Gellar replied.

''Then I suggest we hit the road.''

THE HARD-ROCK MUSIC throbbing from upstairs was so familiar, it no longer bothered Manfred Roeder in the least, rarely distracting him from business at his weekly meetings with the leaders of the Thunderbolt Brigade. At any rate, it would take more than echoes and the thought of naked women dancing overhead to take his mind away from what had happened in Berlin this night.

It was a massacre. No other term applied.

Before him, standing at ease in a half circle, beyond his army-surplus desk, four grim survivors of the night had offered their report. Roeder had telephoned a contact on the police force, confirming that shots had been fired in the Kreuzberg district, possibly explosions. There were several dead—perhaps a dozen, maybe more—and others wounded, some of whom wouldn't survive. Aside from those who had been shot by unknown persons, several skinheads had been stabbed or beaten—one, according to reports, was even doused with boiling water—by the Turkish dwellers of a nearby tenement, apparently in self-defense. Detectives had no idea yet as to how many shooters were involved or what their motives might have been.

It was enough for Roeder to conclude that Gerhard Steuben's troubles had to have followed him across the water from America, and they were Roeder's troubles now. It was unfair, of course, but he was still a soldier, pledged to crush the enemies who threatened his comrades and his race.

The obvious dilemma was that he would have to find them first.

And what would he do then?

"You never saw the men who opened fire on you, I take it?" He addressed his question to the audience at large, the young men muttering, shaking their heads. "Did anyone return fire?"

"I saw Gunter firing with his shotgun, toward the station," one of them replied. "He got both barrels off before they cut him down."

"When you say 'they,'" Roeder pressed, "how many shooters did there seem to be?"

The skinheads spent a moment glancing back and forth at one another, as if beaming thoughts between them that would help to keep their stories straight. A twenty-year-old, Reinhardt, answered for the lot of them.

"We didn't get a chance to count them properly, you understand," he said. "It's definite that they had guns on both sides of the street—and automatic ones, at that. There's no mistaking them, when you've been under fire."

This youngster talked like a combat veteran of the Eastern Front, but he was right, of course. A group of pistols, for example, rapid-firing all at once, might sound a bit like automatic weapons for a moment, but they couldn't keep it up. It didn't take a great ballistics expert or lifelong military officer to tell the rattle of machine guns from the erratic noise of revolvers or semiautomatics.

Assuming that the shooters *had* pursued Steuben from the United States, would they have tried to bring an arsenal across the water with them? It was doubtful, even though they might get lucky with the check-through luggage, still a risk no true professional would take if he could possibly avoid it. That meant they would have to pick up hardware on arrival in the fatherland, which narrowed down the scope of possibilities a bit—but not enough to make the search an easy thing, by any means. Roeder had reason to be conscious of the fact that weapons and explosives disappeared from military bases every week, in Germany and all over the world. There weren't as many covert dealers in Berlin as in some stinking Third World rat hole, but enough to keep his people busy for a few days, anyhow.

And Roeder didn't have a few days he could spare.

Steuben had commanded that the Wewelsburg operation go ahead on schedule, and to hell with any risk. Their enemies weren't permitted to dictate the schedule of events that was decreed by prophecy.

He could, however, spare some members of the Thunderbolt Brigade. The ones who weren't wounded, dead or locked up in a cell.

"I want you to collect whatever troops are left," he told the young apprentice Nazis ranged before him. "I have reason to believe our enemies have armed themselves by dealing with a black-market purveyor of munitions in Berlin. You know these men?"

While he didn't address the query to any particular skinhead, Reinhardt responded once again, assuming honors as the leader of the pack. "We know who deals in weapons, sir," he said. "If there are any we have overlooked, we'll find them out."

"It must be done without delay," the German leader of the Nordic Temple said. "And yet you must accomplish it without attracting any more attention to yourselves, after this business tonight. Speed and discretion. Can you manage that?"

"We can, sir," Reinhardt promised him.

"I leave you to it, then. We need to know if anyone has entered into dealings very recently, the past two days or so, with any strangers, possibly American. I can't be sure about the nationality, of course. Any nonregulars, let's say, within the past two or three days."

"Yes, sir."

"Dismissed."

The skinheads left his basement office, and the pulsing of the music overhead intruded on his thoughts for the first time since they had straggled in to tell their tale of blood and woe. Roeder leaned back and put his booted feet up on the corner of his desk, stared at the ceiling for a moment, picturing the naked women writhing on the stage above him, almost close enough to touch. He felt himself responding, stiffening, and then remembered where he was, the grave responsibility he carried on his shoulders.

Suddenly, the weight of it was awesome, almost more than he could bear.

The wheels were already in motion for the action in Westphalia. The sacrifice had been prepared, its hour rapidly approaching. Roeder's ultimate commander in the Temple of the Nordic Covenant was adamant in his refusal to delay the ceremony, much less cancel it. Regardless of the risk, Steuben had said, in front of witnesses, the prophecy had to be fulfilled on time, and any man who tried to stop it was a traitor to his race, deserving of expulsion from the Temple and an agonizing death.

All right, Roeder thought. It would be all right.

Steuben knew that their enemies were drawing closer by the moment, but the ceremony, if successful, would imbue the führer and his warriors with new powers, granting them the wherewithal to crush those enemies like insects. In the meantime, when the skinheads found out who had armed their adversaries, he would slam that door, as well. They would be isolated and cut off, on hostile ground, with nothing left to do but die.

He wished that there was time to make them suffer, kill them slowly, one inch at a time, but there was still much to be done in preparation for the great apocalypse. Roeder had been preparing for that day for years on end.

He only hoped that he was worthy, that he passed the test.

And long before he reached the purifying fire, he knew that he would have to wade through blood.

CHAPTER SIX

Westphalia has been called "the forge of Germany," for it contains the industrial heart of the nation, the mighty Ruhr district, sandwiched between the Ruhr and Lippe Rivers. South of the Lippe lies the Sauerland and Siegerland, the heavily forested and ruggedly mountainous "land of a thousand hills." Between the Lippe and the Ems Rivers, the farmland dotted with ancient castles was known as Münsterland, after its primary city of Münster. To the northeast of Münsterland, the hilly Teutoburg Forest and Lippisches Bergland feature more woodland, with scattered health spas, between the upper courses of the Ems and Wesser Rivers.

They had their mark before they left Berlin, with Jacob Gellar driving the first leg while Bolan scanned the countryside. It had required a large-scale map of Westphalia to reveal the small village of Wewelsburg, and there was still no indication of a castle in the neighborhood, but Gellar had assured him they would have no trouble locating the castle, once they had reached the town.

"I made some calls before we left Berlin," Gellar told him after they were well out from the capital and westbound on the autobahn. "It seems the castle isn't one of those dilapidated ruins that the tourists love so much.''

"I don't suppose they've torn the damned thing down," Bolan remarked.

Gellar barked a laugh at that. "Tear down a castle in Westphalia? You must surely bite your tongue! Indeed, no," he continued, "I'm told Schloss Wewelsburg has been perfectly preserved.''

"Terrific.''

"And, in fact," the Mossad agent added, "it is occupied.''

"Say what?''

"They operate the usual obligatory gift shop and museum, of course, for tourist trade, but Wewelsburg castle has for some years now been used as a youth hostel. Young people—including students, backpackers, what have you—rent accommodations by the night, the week or longer, in some cases.''

"When you say young people…''

"For the students," Gellar said, "some may perhaps be twelve or thirteen years of age. The travelers, of course, are somewhat older. Twenty-one is meant to be the cutoff age, and there are laws forbidding Western tourists stopping at a youth hostel, presumably to make them use a more expensive inn. Of course, the rules are sometimes waived, if there is space available.''

Bolan was less concerned about the legal aspect of the youth hostel than by the prospect of their target— Gerhard Steuben's target—being occupied by teenage noncombatants.

"It wouldn't have a major skinhead clientele, this youth hostel?" he asked.

"I shouldn't think so," Gellar said. "Of course,

that's not to say that the proprietor checks his prospective lodgers for tattoos or quizzes them on their
political philosophy.''

''The more I hear about this place—particularly
with the talk about a human sacrifice—the less I like
it. Now, if we've got teenagers and children on the
scene, that spells a major problem, even if the Nordic
Temple goons don't intend to use the guest list as a
menu. On the flip side, if they *do*—''

''I see your point,'' Gellar replied. ''Of course, we
don't know what Herr Steuben and his lackeys have
in mind.'' He stopped short of suggesting that their
trip itself could be a waste of time, though Bolan
would have welcomed that solution, given the alternative.

He thought about the terrorist acts that the Temple
of the Nordic Covenant had already staged, including
paramilitary raids against a Holocaust memorial in
Los Angeles and a civil-rights convention in Chicago,
both involving dedicated do-or-die commandos, both
resulting in substantial loss of life. The Kreuzberg
fracas had been amateurish by comparison, most
likely dreamed up by the shaved numbskulls of the
Thunderbolt Brigade, with guidance from their older
contacts in the Nordic Temple. He had a sinking feeling, that for the Wewelsburg action, Stevens and his
goons would pull out all the stops, in terms of strategy
and hardware.

Would it be enough? Could he and Gellar stop
them from committing yet another massacre?

Or was the whole damned thing a wild-goose
chase?

It would be both good news and bad news if the
story they had gleaned from Bruno proved to be a lie.

The good news was that no one in the Wewelsburg youth hostel would be in any jeopardy. The downside was that while they traipsed around Westphalia chasing phantoms, Stevens and his storm troopers might well pull off another bloody coup, with no one there to interfere.

Turn back? Or go ahead?

The bottom line was he didn't think that Bruno had been lying when he spilled his limited knowledge of the upcoming Wewelsburg "event." His first reaction to the mention of the castle's name had been spontaneous, and he had been in too much pain to manufacture a convincing lie on the spur of the moment. If Bruno had been conning them, misdirecting them to a nontarget, Bolan would have expected more alluring details, something to sex it up a bit and set the hook.

And if the choice turned out to be a bad one, live with it.

An hour from Berlin they made a pit stop, Bolan driving on from there, while Gellar navigated. The Mossad agent had never toured this part of Germany himself, but he could read a map and translate road signs as they drove.

"How long to Wewelsburg?" Bolan asked a quarter of an hour later.

"At our present rate of travel, we should reach Westphalia proper in another thirty minutes, more or less. From there, perhaps another hour. The approach to Wewelsburg is a mountain road with many—what you call them?—zigzags."

"Close enough," Bolan said, cursing inwardly at the delay. Assuming that the Nordic Temple crowd was on its way, they could have reached the castle hours ago, or with the recent upsets in Berlin, they could well have postponed, even canceled, their plan.

That didn't sound like Gary Stevens, though, whacked-out fanatic that he was. He had pressed forward with the slaughter in Chicago, even after Bolan and Marilyn Crouder had interrupted the preliminary L.A. raid, knowing that it was possible—even probable—that enemies would try to foil the subsequent action.

That was the trouble with fanatic true believers, whether their faith lay in religion, politics or an unholy hodgepodge of both. Driven by hate and "destiny," Stevens would seem a traitor to himself and everything that he believed in if he backed off now.

Which simply left the question as to whether he was really sending soldiers to the Wewelsburg castle as predicted, and, if so, when they were scheduled to arrive.

It didn't take a psychic to pick up on Bolan's personal misgivings at the moment. "We are bound to try this," Gellar said after a silent mile or two had passed. "There's nothing else for it, as far as I can see."

"We could have gone for Roeder," Bolan said.

"This may still be our best chance to intercept him," Gellar said. "We could go on forever, chasing him around Berlin."

That much was true, of course, and while it left the flip side of the problem carefully unstated, Bolan understood the Mossad agent's reticence to focus on the negative. There was no percentage in it. From that point on, they would simply have to play the cards they held.

He only hoped that it wouldn't turn out to be a dead man's hand.

Between them, they were carrying sufficient hardware to interdict a small army. If the Temple of the Nordic Covenant was planning an assault on Wewelsburg castle, Bolan reckoned that they had a fair chance of aborting it, turning the game around.

Unless they were too late.

Unless the ball was already in play, and they weren't even on the field.

"I UNDERSTAND, sir," Manfred Roeder said. "I simply wondered if we have a confirmation that the spear is actually in the castle."

"Confirmation?" Gerhard Steuben, aka Gary Stevens, said, his tone somewhere between a question and a sneer. "You seek the confirmation of a prophecy before it is fulfilled? What sort of faith is this, Manfred? Have you become a doubter, too?"

"No, sir!" Instinctively, the leader of the Nordic Temple's German branch snapped to attention, heels clicking as his body stiffened, ramrod straight. "My faith is strong, sir!"

"You have no cause to worry, then," Stevens replied. As always, he felt more at home—more natural—when speaking German, than his native English. Every day he offered prayers of thanks to Wotan for the revelation of his true identity, the chance he had been given to play out a central role in the apocalyptic final days.

Of course, some players would not be so grateful in the end.

It always helped to know that victory was preordained.

"I was not worried," Roeder told him. "I was simply...curious."

"Of course. I understand, Manfred—and please, relax!" Smelling another private victory, he could afford to be magnanimous. "You've studied Himmler's diaries, have you not?"

"Yes, sir. I know the spear is mentioned, but, that is, I don't recall that its discovery is mentioned in the text."

"You're absolutely right, Manfred. Of course, the spear's discovery is not mentioned, since he never found it."

"Sir?" Now Roeder was confused, frowning, the bristling caterpillars of his eyebrows scrunched together into one dark hedge above the sharp hook of his nose. Stevens recalled that Manfred had been teased by some within the movement, long ago, suffering jokes about that nose, "Jew in the woodshed" gibes that ended only when he had begun to beat the comics down, and thus begin his own ascent to lead the pack.

"Schloss Wewelsburg is a place of power, Manfred. Himmler sensed that from the moment he laid eyes upon the place. It has a history of supernatural phenomena—strange lights, ghost stories, great black dogs that prowl the grounds and disappear if anyone gives chase. The explanation, I have reason to believe, is found below, where Himmler built his own ritual chamber."

"Yes, sir?" Roeder waited, still not grasping it. Not yet convinced.

"The spear was there *before* Himmler arrived, Manfred! You see it now?" Not waiting for an answer Steuben forged briskly ahead. "I now believe that it was captured during the Crusades, most likely in the thirteenth century. Knights Templar would have brought it back to Europe from the Holy Land. You know the Templars, certainly?''

"Yes, sir." Without conviction. Was he faking now? What difference did it make? Steuben enjoyed teaching his followers, could lecture by the hour and occasionally did so.

"The Knights Templar," he said, "more literally, 'knights of the temple.' They fought valiantly in the Crusades and were assigned to guard pilgrims on visits to Jerusalem, especially commissioned by the Pope. As prescient Aryans, they quickly saw the errors of Christianity and looked for answers elsewhere, on the darker side, although they wisely carried out their duties in the public sphere and thus maintained their subsidies from Rome. Years later, when they were betrayed by a defector, their grand master and the bulk of his initiates burned alive for heresy, their castles were seized, their treasure looted by the Vatican and local Christian noblemen.''

"Except the spear?" Roeder suggested, sounding hesitant.

"Precisely!" Steuben clapped his hands, had a mental image of the jerky little dance Hitler had done the afternoon that he accepted the surrender of the French armed forces, back in 1940. It was triumph. It was powerful.

"And it's been at Wewelsburg, undiscovered, all this time?"

"Yes! Yes! Himmler was close, but he was also constantly distracted by the war effort, the rigors of the Final Solution. His time at Wewelsburg was limited, mind you, and we must admit, in hindsight, that he made one critical mistake. Himmler believed that rituals performed at Wewelsburg would allow him to go out and find the Spear of Destiny at some unknown location in the conquered world. He didn't understand that the exact reverse, in fact, was true. The spear had drawn him to the castle, clamoring to be unleashed. In time, of course, he would have understood and turned his search inward. He would have claimed the prize. Sadly, the Allies did not give him time."

The frown was still in place on Roeder's visage. "Sir," he said, "if Himmler didn't know the spear was hidden in the castle, how—?"

"Do I know where to find it?" Steuben finished for him.

"Yes, sir."

"I do not know its precise location on the premises, of course," Stevens allowed. "If it were that simple, some idle treasure hunter would have found it long ago and turned himself into an emperor. My prayers and meditation, coupled with my study of the ancient Templar texts, reading between the lines, have told me how the spear may be revealed."

"The sacrifice." It came out almost as a whisper. Steuben couldn't say with any certainty if Roeder was expressing reverence or fear.

"Exactly! When the blood is spilled and the obligatory incantations are pronounced, the power of the spear will shine forth as a beacon in the darkness, plain for all to see. It will be ours. We will sweep our enemies aside the way a scythe cuts grain at harvest time. No force on earth can stand against the Spear of Destiny."

"You'll be there, sir?"

"As planned, I will be waiting for your signal that

Wewelsburg castle is secure. You have prepared your troops for the assault?''

"Yes, sir."

"There are no guards, per se, as you're aware. Local police should be no problem, in a village the size of Wewelsburg. Hold them at bay or kill them, as you wish. If they are frightened off, so much the better. We must be concerned primarily with those inside the castle, Manfred. You are clear on what will be required?''

"Yes, sir."

"They must be captured and controlled. Thirteen are needed for the sacrifice, essentially the youngest and the most attractive specimens. We cannot guarantee virginity, of course. It is beyond our power, in the circumstances.''

"Yes, sir." Still the brooding frown.

"When you've secured the castle, broadcast the alert, and I'll join you for the final ceremony. No one else must try to execute the sacrifice itself. That's critical. You understand, Manfred?''

"Yes, sir. I understand."

"You won't be cheated, though, I promise you. There will be blood and glory in this day, enough for all concerned. Your place in history will be assured.''

The corners of the frown turned upward slightly, almost microscopically, but Steuben caught the motion, understood that he was in control. Manfred was loyal, if not the most intelligent of men. He could be trusted to perform his role in the impending sacrifice, but certain doubts at this stage of the operation were anticipated. Men who pulled the trigger on adults without compunction still might balk at killing children, if they didn't grasp the need, see the larger picture. Himmler had encountered similar reluctance in his troops, at the onset of the Final Solution.

There was nothing new under the sun.

Not yet, the would-be führer thought. But soon, perhaps, there just may be.

SOME OF THE WEAPONS had been purchased from black-market dealers; others had been stolen from military bases and police arsenals throughout Germany. The stolen guns hadn't been taken in armed raids. Those days had passed with the destruction of the Baader-Meinhof and the Red Army Faction, ending divided Germany's equivalent of the American Wild West or Roaring Twenties. Rather, they were smuggled out—sometimes in the form of spare component parts—by insiders who either shared the world view of the Nordic Temple or were willing to accept its cash for services performed.

In either case, the guns all worked. Roeder and his commandos had already tested them.

The size of the Wewelsburg attack force had been earnestly debated prior to choosing members for the team. Steuben and Roeder had agreed that it would be a grave mistake to send too large a team; they had likewise concurred that if the strike force was too small, it would be doomed before the first shot had been fired. Agreeing on an ideal number had been something else, but Roeder was persuaded after some resistance that a crew of twenty-five would be sufficient for the task. Eighteen commandos would be led by Roeder himself to seize and occupy the castle. Four men would serve as Steuben's mobile bodyguards and escorts, and as backup, two of Roeder's finest marksmen, stationed at a distance and armed with sniper rifles, would support the penetration team and harry any opposition on the scene.

So twenty-five—and Steuben made it twenty-six, precisely twice the perfect number for a magic coven. Even if they met with armed resistance going in, which seemed unlikely to the point of being laughable, they should have men and guns enough to seize the castle and secure it for the length of time Steuben would need to carry out his ritual.

And after that, if he was right about the Spear of Destiny, then it would make no difference who or what was thrown against them. They would be invincible.

Roeder still had some difficulty buying that, the way that he imagined certain Catholics had to wink on hearing that their own communion wine and wafers were the selfsame blood and flesh of Christ. Still, if his faith was true and strong—as he believed it was, at least on good days—then he absolutely *needed* to believe. Who could predict what damage one man's doubt might cause, when Steuben started working magic in the castle's basement, spilling blood to satisfy Wotan and all the other thirsty gods?

Killing the children bothered Roeder more than he would ever dare admit, but he would do his duty in the end. He had no doubt of that. His ancestors had done no less in two world wars, had followed orders, killing anyone who stood between the fatherland and glory. How could he do any less today, when the ultimate prize of all human history hung in the balance?

The front-line assault weapons consisted of thirteen MP-5 submachine guns and ten G-41 assault rifles, all manufactured by Heckler & Koch, adopted as standard issue by the German military. The two sniper rifles were likewise H&K products, the supremely accurate Präzision Schützen Gewehr-1 model. The PSG-1s had been fitted with heavy barrels, chambered for the 7.62 mm NATO round, tricked out with adjustable butt and trigger, the otherwise noisy internal works silenced to help out with stealth. Each seated a 20-round box magazine, and while the PSGs were semiautomatic only, their six-power telescopic sights allowed them to drop man-size targets consistently at ranges of 700 meters or more.

His men were all assembled, checking out the hardware one more time, when Roeder entered the room, chose an MP-5 for himself and drifted toward the table where the loaded magazines and bandoliers were stacked. Side arms were optional, a private choice, but he knew most members of the strike force were carrying pistols in addition to the long arms they were issued. His own choice for backup was a Walther P-88 self-loader, initially designed during a competition to produce a new pistol for the American armed forces, replacing the venerable Colt .45 ACP. Walther had lost to the Beretta Model 92, but in the process had designed and marketed a high-quality double-action pistol in 9 mm Parabellum, with fifteen rounds in the staggered-box magazine.

Roeder had considered issuing body armor to his commandos for the assault on Schloss Wewelsburg, but had decided instead to take a leap of faith. The castle had no guards, and the surrounding village boasted two fat constables, neither of whom—at least, as far as Manfred Roeder could determine—was exactly a fighting man. They might have weapons in their office, dusty from disuse, but when it came to killing they would call for help, perhaps GSG-9, and by the time the specialists arrived, it would already be too late. The führer would have worked his magic, they would have the Spear of Destiny and no one, nothing, could defeat them.

He chose a double magazine, the two clipped end-to-end for quick reloading, and fed it into the MP-5's receiver, then picked up a web belt weighted with spare magazines slotted into canvas pouches. His thigh-length leather coat, Gestapo style, would hide the guns and ammunition easily. If they were stopped for any reason on their way to reach the target, by police or any others who might wish to interrupt the sacrificial ritual, the weapons would be close at hand, ready to clear the way.

"My warriors!" Roeder raised his voice, addressing the twenty assembled warriors. Steuben's bodyguards had already departed, covering the führer as he made his way toward Wewelsburg in a plain Volvo sedan.

When all of them were silent, facing him with weapons cradled in their arms, he said, "Today, we take a giant stride toward the fulfillment of our racial destiny! If we succeed, no enemy on Earth will have the strength to stand before us on the field of battle. If we fail, then we'll deserve no less than the contempt of every Aryan who follows after us."

He marked the scowling faces, lips pressed thin on mouths like bloodless wounds, and he was pleased. Soldiers were more efficient on the firing line when they believed their honor was at stake, against an enemy contemptible and vile.

"That said," Roeder pressed on, "I have the utmost confidence that none of you will fail me, fail your ancestors and future generations, in this hour when we stand so perilously at the crossroads. One way leads to victory and triumph, the annihilation of our godless, soulless enemies. The other leads to shame and death, not only for ourselves, but possibly for everything we cherish and believe in. Each of you has pledged his life, his blood and honor to the cause. Your race and nation should expect no less. If we are not victorious, let no man here return alive!" His arm snapped outward in the infamous, outlawed salute. Before him, twenty strong right arms did likewise, open hands like bristling spear points, aimed at Roeder's face.

"Sieg heil!" the warriors roared. *"Sieg heil!"*

"You make me proud," he told them as the echoes of their shouting died away. He was surprised by the emotion that he felt, the hard lump in his throat. "You make me proud to be a German and an Aryan!"

They passed before him, as if on review, leaving the weapons tables bare as they filed out. Roeder was last to leave the room, locking the door behind him, following his warriors to the waiting vehicles outside. It was already late, and dawn would break as they approached Schloss Wewelsburg.

It was the perfect time to catch their sacrificial lambs asleep and take them absolutely by surprise.

THE ROAD to Wewelsburg was a narrow, winding track that led through thick, forbidding forest all the way. After the high-speed autobahn, it seemed that they were creeping toward their destination now, managing little more than thirty miles per hour on the straightaways, before Gellar was forced to brake for yet another turn, always uncertain whether they would meet another vehicle approaching from the opposite direction and be forced to swerve aside, tree branches scraping needles on the passenger side of the car.

Watching the stout trees flicker past his window, Bolan found himself examining the German forest as a potential battleground, weighing advantages and obstacles that would confront each side if they were cast into a firefight here. There would be ample cover, which meant, in turn, that there were few clear fields of fire. It would be difficult to move with anything approaching silence on the forest floor that had been carpeted with fallen branches, leaves and needles. For a soldier unfamiliar with the killing ground, the danger would be magnified. Where could he turn for shelter? Who would be his ally if the battle went against him?

No one.

Bolan pushed the problem out of mind. He didn't plan on fighting in the forest, and if it came down to that—if they were ambushed on the final stretch of highway serving Wewelsburg, say, or if their exit from the village was somehow cut off—then he would simply have to wing it.

At the moment, he was more concerned about the fact that they had been unable to obtain a map of the village of Wewelsburg, much less anything resembling a floor plan of the castle. Tourist guidebooks had nothing to say about the place where Himmler and his ghouls once met to meditate and burn their candles, chant and carry on with God knew what sadistic rituals. Considering the various atrocities that Himmler's men had carried out in public, in the name of race and politics, who could imagine what they might have done when they were locked away from prying eyes, all in the name of their religious faith?

On second thought, Bolan was fairly sure he didn't even want to know. He had enough already on his mind, trying to think ahead of Gary Stevens, Manfred Roeder and the rest. He didn't know how many neo-Nazi troops were on their way to Wewelsburg, how they were armed or even when they were expected to arrive. In truth, he wasn't sure they were coming at all, but as Gellar pointed out, they had to be somewhere, try something, in lieu of drifting aimlessly around Berlin.

And he didn't believe that Bruno had been lying after Gellar slit his nose. He didn't think the skinhead had the courage to withstand that kind of pain, much less the brains to fabricate a complicated story on the spot.

So, here they were. Almost.

"A few more miles," Gellar said, once again as if reading his mind.

"Okay," Bolan replied. Despite a certain apprehension, Bolan longed to see the action joined and have what might turn out to be the final skirmish under way. If he could end the mission here, so much the better.

"Still nothing on the radio," Gellar informed him, summarizing the muted drone of voices from what seemed to be an all-news station, playing on the radio. "I think, if they had struck already, it would make the news. Someone would telephone. Reporters always know."

"No news is good news, then." Bolan drew little comfort from the old cliché. He knew that foreign antiterrorist police, especially in nations with a history of bowing to authority like Germany, often had better short-term luck in suppressing news items than their counterparts in the United States. He also knew that it was possible, at least in theory, for a strike team to take out a small town's two- or three-man police force and occupy a given target without raising any public outcry in the process. All it took was one or two effective sound suppressors, a willingness to kill on sight, a little luck.

And *he* would need the luck today.

"If they haven't reached Wewelsburg yet," the Mossad agent said, "you wish to wait?"

"Instead of turning right around and heading back?" Bolan replied.

"Of course. I mean to say, how long are you prepared to wait before we try another avenue?"

That was the question. Bruno had been convinced, or seemed convinced, that Roeder and his goons would make their move "this weekend," plainly meaning this day or the next. He hated marking time when he could feel the enemy so close but waiting was a skill that he had learned in battle, where it made the difference between success and bloody failure.

"I could let them have tonight," he told Gellar, "if we find someplace we can stay."

"They have a youth hostel," Gellar replied. "There's bound to be an inn or B and B for adults, even if they barely show up on the map."

"Terrific."

Staying over meant that one of them, at least, would have to be on watch all night, in case their enemies arrived under cover of darkness, to catch the town sleeping and thus minimize opposition. Again, it was nothing Bolan hadn't done before at least a thousand times.

What troubled him so much in this case, then?

He knew the answer to that question without even pausing to consider it: he didn't like the battleground. Sight unseen, he dreaded fighting Roeder's neo-Nazis in a German village where civilian noncombatants, some of them doubtless screaming for police, perhaps with children held as hostages by his opponents. One mistake, however trivial it seemed, could turn the village into a slaughter pen, especially given the Nordic Temple's demonstrated indifference to innocent bystanders.

Would it matter to the neo-Nazis that these villagers were their own flesh and blood, so to speak, the selfsame Aryans they were supposedly trying to exalt and defend? Would Roeder's men be more reserved in their bloodletting here, than their coreligionists had been in Los Angeles and Chicago?

Somehow, Bolan didn't think so.

The Nordic Temple goons were coming to Wewelsburg—if they came at all—with the specific intent of committing an atrocity, their very own blood sacrifice. Once they had steeled themselves for that, decided it was necessary for their holy cause, why should they shrink from turning their weapons on innocent strangers in the streets?

No reason at all.

The only way to frustrate their design, to head off the intended bloodbath, was to stop them in their tracks, as soon as he had target acquisition on the enemy. Shoot first, shoot straight and drop the enemy as cleanly as he could. The rest of it, in terms of judgment, rested with a higher power than himself.

The rule he had expounded in the first days of his private war against the Mafia held true in Germany, as well.

I'm not their judge, he told himself. *I am their judgment.*

Given any kind of chance at all, he meant to be their Executioner.

CHAPTER SEVEN

One of the vans had slowed them, a flat tire on the autobahn, but even so, the little caravan was still approaching Wewelsburg as the sun came up, its first gray light making the shadows of the forest seem even more menacing than in the dead of night.

Roeder was tired of driving—make that *riding*—and he wished that they could simply get on with the business of their mission, put the whole damned thing behind them. It wasn't the proper attitude for a religious ceremony, he suspected, but he couldn't help the way he felt. As long as he didn't say anything to Steuben that would give himself away, he thought he should be safe.

Wotan knew all, a voice inside his head reminded him.

Well, there was that, of course. But mighty Wotan, in his understanding of the matter, always showed more interest in the actions of his subjects than in what they thought or how they felt at any given time. He cherished fighters, those who gave their utmost, even laid their lives down for a cause, and Roeder didn't think Wotan would fault him for a bit of private doubt as long as he obeyed his orders and performed his given task as planned.

Strike one, as the Americans would say. He was already late, but not so terribly late that it should make a difference to the outcome of their mission. He couldn't have left the van and seven of his men behind, to catch up down the road, perhaps get lost and miss the winding forest highway altogether. Roeder had been forced to make a snap decision under pressure and he had directed that the flat tire be replaced as quickly as a dozen pairs of hands could do the job. In fact, at one point there had been too many soldiers helping, slowing the process, but they still made better time than any solo motorist could possibly have done.

Most of Wewelsburg village was asleep when they arrived, the huddled houses dark and silent. There were scattered lights, the early risers shaving, maybe fixing breakfast for themselves or for the husbands who would have to punch a time clock soon and earn their daily bread by...what? How did they live, these people of the forest? What did they do all day, before the sun went down and drove them back into the shelter of their modest homes?

"I still don't see the castle," Roeder's driver said.

"It's on the edge of town," Roeder reminded him. "Watch for the sign."

The words were barely out before he saw it on the left, ahead. Zum Schloss the sign proclaimed, its arrow pointing down what seemed to be an alley rather than a proper street. More twists and turns, with Roeder worried that the larger vans might not be able to proceed, but when he checked his mirror they were close behind the lead car, the reflected headlights fairly blinding him.

Next, Roeder thought that being trapped inside the

narrow, winding alley made them perfect targets, veritable sitting ducks. Two men could close the trap, one at each end, with automatic weapons or grenade launchers. His soldiers would fight back, of course, but in the narrow confines of the lane or alleyway it would be difficult for snipers not to cut most of them down. And if explosives were employed—

He stopped the morbid train of thought before the final massacre played out behind his drooping eyelids. If the alley was a trap, they would be under fire by now, his men already dying. As it was, he had seen nothing whatsoever to suggest they were expected in the village, much less that defensive preparations had been made.

"So, there it is!"

Small wonder that his driver was surprised. Wewelsburg castle was virtually hidden even from the little town that huddled in its shadow, screened by brooding forest and terrain. From what he saw of it as they approached, the outer walls bleached by their headlights, it appeared to be intact and well preserved. He wondered how young travelers enjoyed their stay there, whether they imagined ghosts in residence. How many of them knew the castle's relatively recent history, the rituals conducted here, the slaves who had been executed when they proved themselves too weak or ill to work?

After this day, there would be new souls for the grim menagerie.

The place was dark, though he imagined someone on the hostel staff had to be awake by now, perhaps already working in the kitchen, somewhere to the rear, where Roeder couldn't see the lights.

His men unloaded from the vehicles, the snipers

moving off without a word to find their vantage points. While Roeder knew that his troops wouldn't be enough to hold the castle in the face of a determined force, such a defense had never figured in his plans. He was required to seize the castle and corral its occupants, then call in Herr Steuben and hold the place just long enough for the climactic ritual to be performed, the Spear of Destiny revealed.

The major weak point of the plan was unavoidable, and it came down to architecture. When the castle was constructed, or perhaps when Himmler's slaves were busy renovating it, the ritual chamber—the Hall of the Dead—had been constructed directly below the north tower, but without an interior means of access. To enter the Hall of the Dead, one was required to step outside, walk around to the base of the tower, open a wooden door there and descend stone steps into the lower reaches of the castle. If the police or any other lurking enemy arrived after they had secured their hostages, it would be then and there, when Roeder's men were most exposed, that they would try to drop his troops.

Unless, that was, the enemy was there ahead of him, already watching from the darkness, sighting down the barrels of their weapons.

The notion made his skin crawl, raised the short hairs on his nape, and Roeder shook it off while stepping forward, stretching out an index finger toward the doorbell's brown, wall-mounted nipple, pressing it twice, a long buzz each time.

Gray dawn washed over him as someone fumbled with a heavy-sounding latch behind the door. Another moment, and the door eased open to reveal a man in tie and shirtsleeves, frowning through the aperture.

Roeder placed him somewhere beyond the hump of middle age and marked him down as something of a grump.

"What do you want?" the man behind the door demanded.

"We need a word with the proprietor," Roeder replied.

"The hour is unusual, to say the least. Is it some kind of an emergency?"

"You could say that." Roeder was smiling as he showed the pompous ass his MP-5. "In fact, it's life-and-death."

"WAKE UP! They're here!"

Bolan was on his feet a moment later, gray dawn leaking through the window of their smallish rented room, the feel of Gellar's hand still on his shoulder. He had lain down fully dressed, including shoes and shoulder holster, when his watch ended at two o'clock, and now he saw that it was 5:04 a.m.

"You're sure?" he asked Gellar, his voice clear, no cobwebs clinging to his brain.

"A dark Volvo sedan and two Volkswagen vans," Gellar replied. "They turned in at the sign. Who else, this early in the morning?"

There had been no lodging in the village that provided a direct view of the castle, so they'd settled on a clear shot at the only access road, in lieu of staying in the woods all night without a fire or any kind of camping gear. Now, it appeared, their adversaries had arrived.

Unless it was a false alarm, some kind of regular delivery involving food, linens, whatever else a youth hostel required to operate.

Three vehicles, led by a dark Volvo sedan? No way.

Most of their hardware had been left downstairs, locked in the car, but Bolan had the AUG, spare magazines, rifle grenades and the Beretta 93-R with its custom sound suppressor, snug in its armpit sheath. If it wasn't enough to deal with the opposing odds, then he would simply have to improvise.

Rushing downstairs, their rumbling passage sure to rouse the other tenants of the inn, he tried to calculate those hostile odds. Two vans and one sedan, presumably a four-door. If they were packed in like sardines, that could mean twenty-five or thirty guns against himself and Gellar. That was probably exaggerated, but he always liked to brace himself for the worst-case scenario when no precise statistics were available.

They exited the rooming house, passed by their car on foot and started down the winding access road or alleyway that led to Wewelsburg castle. It wasn't all that far, perhaps two hundred yards, and if they had to make a swift retreat, the car might actually slow them, traversing the narrow tracks twists and turns. Also, this way, there was no engine noise or headlights' glare to tip the enemy that they were on their way.

They had checked out the castle the previous day, taken the tour, as brief as it was, and dawdled in the gift shop. There had been no sign of skinheads or apparent neo-Nazis on the premises, but Bolan had glimpsed several of the youthful lodgers, passing on the stairs or peering from their upstairs windows. They were fresh faced, mostly smiling, and so very, very young.

He hoped that none of them would die this day.

As they drew closer to the castle, both men slowed, mindful of avoiding all unnecessary noise. The final thirty paces, they were almost creeping, weapons poised with fingers on the triggers, ready to respond with deadly fire if they were challenged by the enemy. In fact, their greatest peril at that moment seemed to emanate from overhead, encroaching daylight wiping out the shadows that would otherwise have helped them hide as they approached the castle.

A communal garbage bin saved them, set back in a niche to Bolan's left. He ducked behind it, Gellar on his heels, a slice of castle still visible from where they crouched.

And everything that he could see was bad.

The vehicles that Gellar had described were there, all right, parked out in front. The vans blocked Bolan's view of downstairs windows, but the open door was plainly visible, beyond the dark Volvo sedan. He watched the last few black-clad members of the strike team pass inside, all armed with automatic weapons, then the door swung shut.

"Too late," Gellar said. "Dammit!"

"They're inside. That doesn't mean they've got it made," Bolan replied.

"How are the two of us supposed to storm a castle?" the Mossad agent inquired.

"We can't," Bolan agreed. "But storming it and infiltrating it are two entirely different things."

"You have a plan, then," Gellar said. He wasn't asking, really; it was more like desperation talking, the Israeli hoping that his words, spoken aloud, would make the answer positive.

And so it was.

Part of their tour, the previous day, had been a quick look at the Hall of the Dead, downstairs, at the northern corner of the castle. They hadn't spent much time there, inside what Bolan took to be their adversaries' prime objective, but there had been time enough for him to rule out any other entrance to the chamber from the floors above.

"If they want to use the dungeon," Bolan told his ally, "they've got one way in and out. They aren't there yet, which means we have a chance to get inside before they do."

"One problem," Gellar said, reminding him. "The lock."

When it was first constructed, there had been a lock installed on the door to the Hall of the Dead, but it wasn't in use these days. Whether the keys were lost or rust had eaten out the mechanism, Bolan neither knew nor cared. A hasp and heavy padlock had been added sometime in the fairly recent past, its key residing with the tour guide who had shown them through the castle yesterday.

"I'm thinking one of us can pick it," Bolan said.

"And only one of us can safely go inside," Gellar replied.

He was correct, of course. If both of them went in, there would be no one left outside to close the padlock, and the fact that it was open would betray them to their enemies. The man who went inside would be locked in until the raiders came to join him, and if they were interrupted prior to reaching the Hall of the Dead—by the police, by villagers, by anything at all—there would be no escape for him, no way to join the fight outside, much less to get away.

It was a King Kong gamble, and there was no other way to go, as far as Bolan could determine.

"So," he said, "I'll go inside, you lock it up and cover me from here."

"If anything goes wrong—"

"Then I don't have to worry about getting shot," Bolan said.

"They may well be carrying explosives. We're only guessing that they mean to use the dungeon for their sacrifice."

"You have a better plan, let's hear it."

Gellar mulled it over for a moment, then he shook his head. "No, nothing. It appears to be the only way."

"Then let's get cracking," Bolan said, "before they beat us to the punch."

REPLACING THE padlock was easy, of course. It had been opening the thing that took time, almost two precious minutes crouching in the shadow of the castle's great north tower, while day broke around them and the village came to life. At any moment, Gellar had expected a policeman to come charging at them, brandishing a truncheon, maybe tweeting on a whistle as he came.

But they were left alone, Belasko standing guard, his weapon barely hidden underneath his coat, as Gellar picked the lock. When he was done, Belasko pulled a tiny flashlight from his pocket, snapped it on and started down the stairs leading to the Hall of the Dead. Without a backward glance or parting word, he went below, and Gellar closed the door behind him, replacing the padlock and snapping it shut.

Now there was nothing left to do but wait.

He had promised Belasko that he wouldn't try to storm the castle by himself, which would have been tantamount to suicide, in any case. If they were wrong about the significance of the ritual chamber in this latest scheme, then Belasko had entombed himself for no reason, and Gellar would be left to face the enemy alone.

Somehow, though, he didn't believe that they were wrong.

The whole thing had a ghoulish feel about it, so distinctly "Gerhard Steuben" that he couldn't doubt the madman would attempt a human sacrifice as one more symptom of his own degenerate insanity. As for precisely what he hoped to gain from it, that would be anybody's guess. Gellar was less concerned with motives than with crushing Steuben's dream once and for all.

One major problem was that he didn't know if Steuben was inside the castle or if he was even anywhere near Wewelsburg. And if they didn't crush the viper's head, Gellar had a sickly feeling that the struggle could go on and on, interminably, while they whittled down the Nordic Temple's ranks until some of the neo-Nazi scum got lucky, took them out and left the would-be führer to begin anew.

For that reason, if nothing else, he had already sent an urgent message back to Tel Aviv. If he wasn't successful in his mission, or if he lost contact with headquarters for a critical amount of time, his superiors should assume he was dead and retaliate accordingly, with all dispatch.

At least, that way, he could take the bastard with him, Gellar thought as he stood lurking in the alleyway directly opposite the entrance to the castle, feeling horrendously conspicuous as daylight probed the nooks and crannies of the village.

Already, workmen had begun to pass by on their way to early-morning jobs. They looked at him askance, a stranger in their midst, but didn't pause to challenge him. He feared that one of them would slip away to summon the police, and wondered what effect a flash of his Mossad ID would have upon a backwoods German constable.

Of one thing only was he certain: he wouldn't desert his post unless they killed him where he stood.

Desiring better range, control and stopping power than the mini-Uzi could provide, Gellar was carrying a Russian-made AKSU assault rifle under his coat. This stubby version of the classic AK-47 was barely eighteen inches long with the metal stock folded, but it retained the same grips, breech mechanism, magazine and firepower of the full-size original. Once a shooter made allowance for the loss of control on full-auto fire through the weapon's 7.5-inch barrel, he could learn to manage quite nicely with short bursts and semiautomatic fire. For close-in work, when it was now or never, the AKSU earned its awesome reputation as a point-blank "bullet hose."

Slumped against an old brick wall, right hand on the AKSU's pistol grip through the slit pocket of his raincoat, Gellar waited, checking his watch at fifteen- and twenty-second intervals. The tension made him grind his teeth, and he was conscious of a sudden need to urinate, but it would pass, he knew from prior experience, as soon as he went into action.

At that, preoccupied, he was startled when the first of the raiders emerged from the castle, taking little care to hide the weapon tucked beneath his leather jacket. Looking up and down the narrow street, he missed Gellar's retreat behind the garbage bin, turned and beckoned to his comrade, behind him.

They were coming now, and turning left to seek the northern tower and the door that granted access to the subterranean Hall of the Dead. Not only gunmen in the line, he saw, but hostages mixed in among them. Counting heads and faces, Gellar marked thirteen young people, all of them appearing frightened and confused, escorted by sixteen black-clad gunmen. Manfred Roeder was the last to exit, pausing in the doorway to speak with someone left behind, inside. A rear guard, then, to watch those tenants and staff members of the hostel who had not been chosen for the sacrifice.

The "lucky" ones.

There was no sign of Steuben, and while Gellar pondered his absence from such a critical event, he knew that they couldn't afford to wait around to see if any late arrivals were expected. His instructions were precise, and he meant to follow them exactly.

Let most of them get inside, then slam the door.

He shifted, opened up the AKSU's folding stock and braced the butt against his shoulder, sighting down the barrel. Gellar watched as one of the skinheads opened the new lock on the ancient door and stepped inside. He counted heads as others followed, letting all the hostages pass out of sight, waiting until the last three neo-Nazis stood upon the threshold, waiting to descend.

It was enough.

Their backs were to him, and he didn't care. He shot each of them once—two in the back, between their shoulder blades, clean kills; the third one through his rib cage as he was turning toward the unexpected sounds of gunfire. They were good shots, all of them, and while the third man kicked a little after crumpling to the ground, it only lasted for a moment, then he shivered and lay still.

The door was slammed.

ROEDER WAS ORDERING the special torches to be lighted when it happened. Miles above his head it seemed—much more than thirty feet, in any case— came the muffled popping sound of gunfire. Three shots, and that was all. They couldn't be mistaken for the backfire of a car engine, even though he favored wishful thinking at the moment.

No.

It was gunfire, but who had fired at whom, and why? What did it mean?

"Willem! Gunnar!" he barked, and jerked his head in the direction of the stairs. No other words were necessary, his two soldiers bolting up the steps into a spill of sunlight from the open doorway, where the last three should have entered by now, closing the portal behind them.

Willem edged forward, risking a peek around the doorjamb, and another shot rang out from the street. He slumped in the doorway, Gunnar recoiling, stopping short of firing off a burst at invisible targets.

They were trapped, and Roeder took for granted that his other three commandos were as dead as faceless Willem, or they would have been returning fire by now.

He couldn't summon Steuben now, dared not, at least until the opposition had been swept away. He *could* contact his snipers and the three men still remaining in the castle, with their hostages. Between them, those five should at least be able to report back what was happening outside and give him some idea of what had gone amiss, even if they couldn't provide relief.

Roeder was reaching for the two-way radio he wore clipped on his belt when gunfire suddenly erupted from *inside* the chamber where he stood. Up by the door, Gunnar recoiled, clutched his chest and plunged headfirst down the staircase, landing at the bottom in a boneless sprawl.

Spinning in his tracks, Roeder began to shout, "Cease fire! Cease fire!" But even as he spoke, another shot rang out and yet another of his soldiers crumpled to the floor. One of the girls whom they had brought downstairs to sacrifice began to scream, another and another swiftly joining in.

"Who's firing, dammit?"

Roeder's shout was battered back and forth by the peculiar acoustics of the chamber, seemingly designed to focus any sound, however slight, upon a central pit, near which he stood. Originally, he had planned to herd the thirteen sacrificial victims into that square-cut depression, prior to their execution, but now the plan was starting to unravel while he stood and watched.

In answer to his shouted question, there was yet another rifle shot, its echo deafening. Across the murky room, still lit primarily by flashlight beams, one of his soldiers—this one standing with his arm around a young girl's neck to use her as a human shield—lurched backward, reeling, as blood spouted from a hole between his eyes.

In less than thirty seconds, he had seen his force

of men reduced by almost fifty percent, and Roeder understood that none of them were firing in reaction to the gunshots from outside. Which meant that there was someone else inside the chamber, someone who had hidden there *before* they entered, and despite the padlock that secured the door above.

How was that possible?

No matter. It was true, and that was all that counted at the moment. What terrified him at the moment was the fact that all his men together couldn't seem to spot the lurking enemy.

"Watch out for muzzle-flashes!" Roeder bawled. "And get these children in the pit! Right now!"

If all else failed, he thought, at least he could still carry out the sacrifice. Common sense told Roeder that his führer would prefer to have it carried out by other hands than to forsake the opportunity and make it all a bloody waste of time. Indeed, it seemed to Manfred Roeder that he just might need the Spear of Destiny in order to escape from this predicament.

He had the radio in hand, was just about to transmit orders to his men outside the trap when he was stunned by the reverberation of another rifle shot. This one was even worse, complete with searing pain that lanced across his upper body, spinning Roeder like a dervish, ripping the small radio from his hand as he crashed to the floor.

Before his consciousness departed, Roeder realized that he was lying in the sacrificial pit and wondered if his blood would serve to summon up the Spear of Destiny.

THE MAN BOLAN had recognized as Manfred Roeder took a 5.56 mm round high in the chest, lurched through a jiggling little reel and plunged into a pit that had been excavated in the center of the floor. He didn't rise at once, and while he might still be alive, Bolan was more concerned with those targets still on their feet and clutching hostages.

Two of the neo-Nazi goons were firing blindly now, short bursts without a target, having failed to spot his muzzle-flashes yet. Their bullets ricocheted around the chamber, and one of their own went down squawking on the far side of the room, spitting out what had to be curses in German, as he wallowed around on the floor.

Stunned silence followed, every gunner frozen, echoes fading rapidly. The next sounds Bolan heard came from outside—or were they coming from directly overhead, heard through the castle's floor that served the hidden chamber as a roof?

Gunfire upstairs? Gunfire outside?

One could suggest that Roeder's men were killing hostages inside the castle, while the other might mean Jacob Gellar had engaged retreating enemies. Or the police, for that matter. There was no way he could interpret sounds of combat from an unknown source. Instead, he focused on the enemies before him, concentrated on eradicating them while time and opportunity remained.

Sheltered in a niche behind one of the chamber's thirteen carved pedestals, Bolan worked the room with his Steyr AUG, squeezing off head or chest shots as soon as he lined up each target in the rifle's optical sight. The chamber's weird acoustics helped confuse his enemies, preventing them from homing in on the reports, but Bolan knew it was inevitable that his muzzle-flashes would be spotted.

In fact, it happened even as the thought took shape in Bolan's mind. Off to his right, a shout and blaze of submachine-gun fire alerted him to danger, and he ducked beneath the probing spray of Parabellum rounds that sought to take off his head. The soldier rolled, keeping a firm grip on his weapon as he did so, triggering three rounds in rapid fire that stopped the shooter in his tracks and slammed him over backward in a heap.

The atmosphere inside the Hall of the Dead was thick with cordite now, that long familiar odor underlaid with the hot-copper smell of fresh blood. Out in the middle of the killing ground, he saw some of the young hostages lying prone, others scrambling around on hands and knees or duck-walking in search of cover, finding little as the bullets whistled overhead.

Uncertain as to whether any of them understood him, Bolan cried, "Stay down! Don't move! Get on the floor!" And even as he shouted out the warning, he was hunting, taking down another Nazi gunner on the far side of the room, a clean shot through the temple as the target tried to duck behind a pillar of his own.

He counted five of the gunners still on their feet, and they were breaking for the staircase in a flying-wedge formation, several of them milking cover fire from submachine guns and assault rifles. Bolan stayed low, knowing he was more likely to be drilled by ricochets than aimed fire. Working swiftly, urgently, he snapped the AUG's bolt open, chambering a blank round from his pocket, then reached out to fit a rifle grenade onto the built-in launcher that doubled as a small flash hider.

Bolan waited, praying that none of the young hostages would follow their abductors toward the open door and daylight. None did, and the shooters were all by themselves at the head of the stairs, pausing to survey the parking lot and street beyond the portal where their friends had died, as Bolan aimed and fired.

The high-explosive charge went off directly in their midst, its shrapnel joining shards of stone and concrete, shredding flesh and snapping bone. Two of the neo-Nazis vaulted from their high perch toward the stone floor of the chamber, splashing it with blood on impact. Two more tumbled down the stairs, all tangled up in a death embrace, while number five—the pointman—seemed to leap out through the doorway, somersaulting through a cloud of smoke and dust.

All done.

Or was it?

Bolan still heard gunfire overhead as he was moving toward the stairs. Still wondering if any of the children left behind were English-speakers, he called out to them in passing, "Stay down here until someone comes in to get you. The police, the fire department, somebody."

He had to watch his step on stairs that were blood slick and fouled with flesh, climbing toward daylight, finding that the stench of death and battle clung to him, pursued him. At the doorway, Bolan hesitated, then began to ease his way outside. He trusted Gellar not to shoot him, but he had no way of knowing who else might have zeroed in the aperture by now, whether surviving members of the neo-Nazi team, or even local cops.

He never knew if it was luck or skill that saved his

life. A flash of light, reflected from a telescopic lens, alerted Bolan to a sniper on a rooftop opposite and two doors farther north. He crouched and ducked back as a rifle bullet meant to pierce his skull sheared through the ancient wooden door instead.

He fed another blank into the Steyr's chamber, mounted a second rifle grenade. He was unable to identify the sniper, so wouldn't attempt to kill him with the HE round, but he would need a fair diversion, at the very least, if he was ever to escape from the Hall of the Dead.

Thought translated into action as Bolan made his move. He saw the wink of light again and aimed six feet or so below it, squeezing off the starter round that put the sleek grenade in flight. His adversary saw it coming, bolting to his feet, black clad like Roeder's other gunmen in the morning light. Bolan gave him three quick rounds across the chest as the grenade exploded underneath the eaves, his tumbling body vanished in a swirl of smoke.

Outside, he spotted Gellar, turned to face the street side entrance to the castle-cum-hotel, and found three more of Roeder's people crumpled on the pavement there, apparently cut down by Gellar's rifle fire. The man from Tel Aviv obviously hadn't been idle, and he covered Bolan now, as the soldier jogged across the parking lot and street to join him in the alleyway.

"The children?" Gellar asked.

"Downstairs and staying put, I hope," Bolan replied. "They're shaken up, but otherwise all right."

"Roeder?"

"I took him down. He's either dead or on the way. Stevens?"

"No sign of him," Gellar said. "He was either

never here at all, or Roeder somehow warned him off.''

Square one, Bolan thought as he followed Gellar back along the alley toward the inn, their vehicle, the only highway out of town. They were right back where they'd started.

''Well, we've learned two things, at least,'' Gellar remarked.

''Being?''

''They still don't have the Spear of Destiny.''

''That's one.''

The grim Israeli smiled. ''And they are still not bulletproof.''

CHAPTER EIGHT

Rolling along the autobahn at ninety-five kilometers per hour, Gerhard Steuben shrieked in rage until his voice gave out and he was left to hiss like some reptilian half human, wheezing in the back seat of the jet-black BMW and hammering the leather upholstery with his fists while his escorts stared out the windows, pretending not to notice.

They were halfway to Berlin and making decent time, when suddenly it hit him.

Destiny.

At first, he took the single word, repeating in his head, as a rebuke. It left him on the verge of tears, ashamed to weep before his men, uncertain as to whether he could stop himself. It took another six or seven kilometers for him to understand that it was meant to reassure him.

Destiny.

It was his destiny to rule a reich reborn. That much had come to him in prophecy, and he believed it to be preordained. Or had believed it, anyway, before the bloody setback at the castle. Yet, if he was truly destined to succeed and save the remnants of the master race from being smothered in a rising sea of yellow, black and brown, why was he frustrated at every turn, hamstrung by enemies whom he could not identify, much less defeat?

There was a plan.

It struck him then, full force. He hadn't found the Spear of Destiny at Wewelsburg because it wasn't there! Perhaps his calculations had been faulty, or the spear may have been moved at some point after the Crusades. So many things could happen in the course of seven hundred years. It was a residue of power from the spear that had enticed Reichsführer Himmler to the castle, and the same allure had drawn Steuben there, more than fifty years later.

But the Spear of Destiny itself was gone.

Gone where?

It was a problem he would have to solve, and soon, if he was going to succeed in his fulfillment of the ancient prophecies. This time, at least, he knew that he was close. His men had fought and shed their blood within the very chamber where the holy lance had once been kept.

That had to count for something, right?

The four men riding with him in the BMW were, at least as far as Steuben knew, the sole survivors of the twenty-five-man strike force that had left Berlin the previous night. He tried to crunch the numbers in his head and was chagrined to find that he couldn't recall the tally of his soldiers slaughtered in America and Germany since he was first bedeviled by these damned persistent enemies. At first, he had blamed Sean Fletcher, his American chief of security, but Fletcher was dead now, cut down with so many others in Chicago, and it was a hopeless stretch to blame him posthumously for the fatherland fiasco.

It was destiny.

And that made all the difference in the world.

Steuben now recognized that he was being challenged, tested, to determine whether he was fit to bear the spear and rule the globe-encircling reich that would be built upon the bones and ashes of decadent "civilization." He was being called upon to prove himself once more, and if he failed...well, then, he was the first one to admit that he didn't deserve to live, much less to reign.

His first order of business was selecting Manfred Roeder's replacement. Fortunately, that was easy, inasmuch as Roeder's second in command had been assigned to lead the bodyguard contingent in Wewelsburg. Karl Dengler was his name, and he was riding shotgun, up beside the driver, focusing his full attention on the highway in an effort to avoid embarrassing his leader with a sidelong, doubting glance.

Steuben leaned forward, placing a hand on his shoulder. "Karl?"

"*Jawohl, mein Führer!*"

"We have work to do."

"Of course." No trace of hesitation. Good.

"You will, of course, take Manfred's place."

"If you believe I'm worthy, sir."

"I have no doubt whatsoever." He watched Dengler swell with pride, the others listening, taking it in. The torch was being passed, and they were privileged to witness it. "There are three things that we must do."

"Yes, sir?"

"The first—avenge our losses from this morning. We must teach the Jews and all the other bastards who oppose us that there is a price attached to meddling with the master race."

"Yes, sir!"

"Second, we must take steps to single out the men responsible for the attack in Wewelsburg. A general response isn't enough. We must specifically eliminate these men before they trouble us again."

"Yes, sir!"

"And finally, we must continue with our efforts to retrieve the Spear of Destiny."

"The spear? But, sir…"

Steuben could read his mind. "My calculations were mistaken. I admit it. There! The spear has obviously been removed from the castle, or we would have it, even now. It is foretold. I must renew my research and discover where the spear was taken *after* Wewelsburg."

"Yes, sir."

"In the meantime, I was thinking that it might be only fair to give our enemies a small reminder of the way things used to be, and how they will be soon again."

Dengler was frowning. "Sir, I'm not sure that I—"

"Kristallnacht," Steuben whispered.

"The night of broken glass?"

"Precisely!"

Every neo-Nazi, young or old, remembered Kristallnacht. On the night of November 9, 1938, after a German diplomat in Paris was assassinated by a German-Jewish radical, Himmler and Goebbels had unleashed a reign of terror in Berlin, with the SA's brownshirts and black-shirted SS elitists rampaging through the streets, attacking any Jew, suspected Jew or Jewish-owned property they could find. The city's two main synagogues had been burned to the ground by Nazi rioters. The Kurfürstendamm and Tauentzien became a sea of shattered glass from Jewish shop windows and homes. Hundreds were injured, the final toll uncertain, since the ruling party and the press cared little for such things as counting wounded Jews.

A young SS officer named Gerhard Steuben had been in the thick of the action on Kristallnacht, raising hell with the Jews. Five years later, he had died fighting Communists on the Russian front. In America, four decades later, young Gary Stevens had taken the dead soldier's name, proclaiming himself the very reincarnation of Gerhard Steuben, and the Temple of the Nordic Covenant was born.

Back to his roots, he thought, smiling. Another Kristallnacht.

"You can arrange it with the young ones, I assume?" he said, referring to the eager skinheads of the Thunderbolt Brigade. "Draw up a list of proper targets and coordinate the strikes for...say...tomorrow night?"

"Of course, sir!"

He wasn't giving Dengler much time, Steuben realized, but how hard could it be to let his fingers do the walking through a telephone directory, draw up a list of synagogues, newspapers, shops and meeting halls owned by the Jews? How much time did it take to pass the list around and tell the street fighters to synchronize their watches?

"Do we still have friends on the police force, Karl?"

"We do, sir. But for something on this scale, they may be hesitant to help us. Even asking may be risky."

"Use your own best judgment, then," Steuben replied, settling back in his seat. "I'm more concerned

with ends than means just now. And keep a list of
those who stand against us, Karl. It will be useful later
on.''

KARL DENGLER FELT as if a great weight had been
lifted from his shoulders when Herr Steuben's driver
dropped him off a block from his apartment on Fritz-
Heckert Strasse. Dengler knew what he had to do, and
it would be a great deal easier without his führer
watching every move he made, suggesting possible
alternatives, exploding into rage the moment anything
appeared to go awry.

The fury that was manifest in Gerhard Steuben
went a long way in Karl Dengler's mind toward quell-
ing any latent doubts he may have had about the wild
American's legitimacy as the leader of the Nordic
Temple. It had seemed almost bizarre at first, a Yank
peddling his tales of mystical rebirth, claiming to
speak for Aryans around the world, but after seeing
him up close and watching him in action, Dengler
could have easily believed that Steuben was the reincarnation of Adolf Hitler himself, much less some
minor SS captain killed in Russia, fighting the Reds.

Steuben and Hitler shared a certain manic energy,
for one thing, coupled with a strong propensity toward temper tantrums if their slightest whims were
thwarted. Even some of Steuben's mannerisms reminded Dengler of the original führer, though that
wasn't especially unusual in the neo-Nazi movement.
Many would-be leaders studied German newsreels
and rehearsed with mirrors, practicing until they mas-
tered just the right jut of the chin, the proper cant of
head and shoulders, the dramatic hand gestures. Some
came off looking clownish, like most of the Elvis

Presley imitators in America; some others very nearly got it right, though a person could always tell that they were acting out a role.

Steuben, though, seemed born to it. A natural.

The Kristallnacht idea, for instance, was pure genius. In one stroke, they could light a candle to the Third Reich's sacred memory, damage the scheming Jews and send a message to their other lurking enemies that the fiasco at Schloss Wewelsburg hadn't been a fatal blow. Far from it. They were pressing on, as Steuben had explained in detail on the drive back from Westphalia to Berlin. The master schedule was still intact. All they required was courage and a bit of ingenuity.

The celebration for the following night wouldn't be difficult to organize, Dengler knew. There was no hiding for the Jews since Germany had been united once again, the cold war ended, at least on paper. All he had to do was scan the telephone directory, draw up a list of names and businesses, then divide it into sectors for the hunting parties. As far as troops, he still had men at his disposal from the Nordic Temple, though their number had been dwindling of late, and he could always count on skinheads from the Thunderbolt Brigade to help with any action that included violence. They thrived on bloodshed, although they were more adept at dishing out the mayhem than receiving it, as witnessed by their recent rout in Kreuzberg, when they moved against the Turks.

Dengler would spice his bid for their assistance with a claim that those responsible for the Kreuzberg had also sprung the ambush at Wewelsburg. That ought to set their tiny minds to working overtime, and Dengler thought that it might even be the truth.

How else could he explain so many deaths among the faithful in the span of just two days?

It struck him that the plague of blood had clearly chased Steuben from America to Germany, but Dengler didn't hold that fact against his führer. Every war required a starting point, a trigger incident. In 1939, the Nazi Party had grown tired of waiting for excuses to invade Poland, and so a border incident had been arranged to justify a blitzkrieg in the guise of self-defense.

And the rest, as someone said or wrote somewhere, was history.

Unfortunately, the Third Reich hadn't fulfilled its promise to survive a thousand years, but Dengler understood that certain prophecies hadn't been fulfilled in 1939-1945. The lack of certain mystic prime ingredients, together with a series of mistakes that wouldn't be repeated in the present day, had doomed Hitler to fail. But he had planted countless seeds, which were already bearing bloodred fruit around the globe. This time, the Jews and mud people wouldn't survive the coming tidal wave of ethnic cleansing.

Despite his racing thoughts and urgent plans, Karl Dengler stayed alert on the approach to his apartment. If their enemies were swift and smart enough to lay an ambush at Wewelsburg, there was at least an outside chance that they would also target the survivors of the raid. It seemed impossible that anyone could know he was replacing Manfred Roeder as the leader of the Nordic Temple in the fatherland, but paranoia was a die-hard neo-Nazi's stock-in-trade. There was no limit to the vast, complex conspiracies his adversaries might devise to foil his destiny and save themselves from righteous punishment.

But they were plotting all in vain.

Dengler had Gerhard Steuben and the weight of destiny behind him. He was living the fulfillment of an ancient prophecy.

How could he lose?

There was no evidence of any tampering with his apartment door, no strangers lurking in the neighborhood as far as he could see. Inside the flat, he checked the mute alarms that were supposed to warn him if the place was penetrated: here, a snip of thread draped at one corner of a slightly open drawer; there, a trace of talcum powder on a closet doorknob; in the tiny kitchen, cello tape fixed near the bottom edge of the refrigerator door, to tip him off if an intruder tried to poison him.

The basics of staying alive on the eve of Armageddon.

Having checked out the apartment, satisfied himself, Dengler immediately left once more, pockets jangling with spare change from his sock drawer, to find a public telephone. He didn't trust his own for calls of any consequence, and there was business to conduct.

This time the following day, storm clouds would be gathering over Berlin, and by the time the gale had run its course, the racial complexion of Berlin—and Germany at large—would never be the same.

Washington, D.C.

A SIX-HOUR time difference between Berlin and Washington, D.C., meant that Hal Brognola was scanning his later-afternoon paperwork when his private line shrilled, blessedly drawing his eyes and attention away from grisly photographs of mass graves in the mountains north of Medellín, Colombia. The skeletons and decomposed remains were those of children—dozens of them, from the look of it—and while the suspect now in custody insisted he had carried out the five-year slaughter on his own, rumors were circulating of at least peripheral involvement by a ring of narcoterrorists, perhaps a death squad using the worst form of violence to intimidate peasant families, keep them working for the local drug lords at bargain-basement prices.

The big Fed was wondering if Able Team should pay a visit to the region, when the phone rang and he seized the opportunity to push the photos out of conscious memory, closing the slim manila file.

"Hello?"

"It's me." Despite the transatlantic distance, Bolan's voice was crystal clear. "We'll want to scramble this," he said.

"Hold on." Brognola pressed a button on the telephone and waited all of half a second for the green light to come on. "Okay at this end," he pronounced.

There was no change in Bolan's voice when he resumed, but anyone eavesdropping on the call at any point between Brognola's office and the telephone the Executioner was using in Berlin would be awash in gibberish by now. They might as well be speaking Klingon, except that there were no nerd-friendly dictionaries on the market to decode their terse exchange of comments.

"Just an update," Bolan said, "before you start to pick up bits and pieces on the tube."

Brognola didn't like the sound of "bits and pieces," but he let it go. "Okay, what's up?"

"You've heard of Wewelsburg castle, here in Germany?"

"It isn't ringing any bells."

"All right. Long story short, it was a hangout for the Himmler crowd, where they apparently performed some kind of rituals from time to time. Some pilgrims from the Nordic Temple tried to reenact one of the ceremonies there, this morning, but they didn't fare so well."

"Civilian casualties?" Brognola asked.

"Right now, it sounds like they roughed up a couple members of the castle staff, but everyone's intact. The team went down, including Stevens's top man in Germany."

"But Stevens wasn't there." Not asking. Bolan would have said so, if their leading target had been numbered in the body count.

"I was expecting him," Bolan said, "but he didn't show. No telling whether he was hanging back until they nailed it down, or if he's hiding out and delegating the authority."

"Okay. What's next on the agenda?"

"We'll be playing it by ear," Bolan replied. "Our friend here has some contacts that he's reaching out to as we speak. If all else fails, he reckons we can always pick up someone from the Temple, maybe squeeze him till he pops."

"Okay, then. If you think of anything you need from this end…"

"What's been going on there, since Chicago?" Bolan asked, referring to the bloody raid that members of the Nordic Temple had staged in Chicago, against a convention held by members of a civil-rights group active in the 1960s.

"Well, you didn't leave us anybody to indict among the raiders," Brognola reminded him, "and dropping out of sight appears to be the latest fad among the Temple crowd. We have at least a partial list of members, maybe sixty-five percent of those who haven't gone to their reward, but overnight, it's like they're nowhere to be found."

"They're skipping, then."

"Looks like. The trouble is, we don't know where they're going. Marilyn's old boss at ATF appears to think they're going underground to plan some kind of 'general uprising.' That's his term, not mine. The FBI seems more inclined to think they may be slipping out of the United States, heading for parts unknown. A rendezvous with Stevens, maybe, for the final days and all."

A moment's silence on the other end told him that Bolan was considering the possibility of neo-Nazi reinforcements turning up in Germany. "If you could make that list available to immigration, over here," he said, "it couldn't hurt."

"Did that," Brognola reassured him. "Sent it off last night, in fact, and they've confirmed receipt, for all the good that it will do."

Both of them knew full well that fringe groups like the Temple of the Nordic Covenant were big on fake ID, disguises and safehouse networks. Computers had vastly enhanced the counterfeiter's art, where passports and similar documents were concerned, and transnational extremists cultivated allies who would gladly help them disappear without a trace, either for profit or as one more contribution to the cause. On top of that, there was a small but zealous minority in modern Germany that offered constant aid and comfort to far-right fanatics, even when their hands were crimson with the blood of innocents.

"You'd better watch your back," Brognola said unnecessarily, "in case familiar faces from the States start popping up at Checkpoint Charlie."

"No problem," Bolan replied. "The ones who've seen me won't be traveling, unless they go as freight."

"Okay. We'll keep on looking for them on this end," Brognola said, "and hope they're camped out in a basement somewhere, studying *Mein Kampf.*"

"In that case, watch for guys with bad toupees, whose lips move when they read," Bolan replied.

"It's good to see you've kept your sense of humor."

"No one else would take it. I'll be in touch, as soon as we nail something down on this end."

"Right. Stay frosty, guy."

"You, too."

The line went dead and Brognola replaced the handset in its cradle, watching as the scrambler's beacon light winked out. He rocked back in his chair, reviewing all that he had learned: Bolan had trashed a raiding party from the Temple of the Nordic Covenant, presumably assisted by his contact from Mossad, but Gary Stevens had slipped through the net. Again. The crazy bastard plainly had more luck than he deserved, and Brognola would happily have bet his next month's salary that each escape emboldened Stevens, even as it cost him soldiers on the street. Stevens was a fanatic who mixed far-out politics with even-further-out religion, seemingly convinced that he was on a "mission." Every time he wriggled through the net, therefore, it would confirm his view that he was somehow blessed, perhaps invincible.

The sooner he was disabused of that belief, the better. But the Executioner would have to find him first, and there appeared to be no rushing that event.

Brooding again, Brognola reached out for the folder on his desk and grudgingly returned to his perusal of the evidence that all was far from well on Mother Earth.

Berlin, Germany

THE AFTERNOON hadn't been kind to Jacob Gellar. He had touched base with his contacts in Berlin, employing every trick at his disposal in the quest to pick their brains. He flattered some and threatened others, called in favors where a debt was on the books and promised favors in return, where there was none.

But all in vain.

His contacts were familiar with the Temple of the Nordic Covenant and their skinhead compatriots of the Thunderbolt Brigade. Most were aware that something had befallen Manfred Roeder and a number of his men in Wewelsburg, though relatively few appeared to have full details yet. Gellar didn't enlighten them, unwilling to admit complicity in what would surely be regarded as mass murder, more intent on gaining information from his contacts than in sharing what he knew.

He had a possible solution to the problem, granted, but he wasn't sure that it was one which his American companion would approve.

In which case, Gellar thought, he would proceed alone. He had been born and raised in Israel, where occasional denunciations from the British and Americans were thought to be of no great consequence. Sometimes mistakes were made; more often, ruthless means were necessary to defend a tiny nation with its back to the sea, surrounded by a host of oil-rich enemies. Israelis did what was required to hold their promised land intact, to save themselves, their wives and children, from barbarians.

Never again!

The words were branded on his soul, and if he had to bruise or break a few more neo-Nazis to obtain the information he required, it was a small price to pay. More like a bonus, when he thought about it.

Returning to the small apartment he had rented shortly after his arrival in Berlin, Gellar rehearsed what he would say to Mike Belasko. He didn't require the tall American's approval for his plan, but mutual respect had grown between them—or, at least, it had on his part—and he didn't care to lose so competent an ally if the loss could be avoided via deft diplomacy.

In any case, you never knew unless you tried.

He found a parking space across the street from his apartment house, checked other cars along the curb, both sides, for loiterers who looked liked spies or members of a Nordic Temple ambush party, and came up with none. Still cautious, Gellar kept his right hand in the pocket of his topcoat, wrapped around the AKSU rifle's pistol grip, as he locked up the car and crossed the street.

Outside his door, he paused and knocked instead of fumbling with the key, letting Belasko scrutinize him through the peephole and release the dead bolt when he satisfied himself that Gellar was alone. The tall American stood back, let Gellar close and lock the door himself, when he was well inside.

"So, what's the word?" he asked.

"There is no word, as yet," Gellar replied. "Or none that my contacts would share, at any rate. No word on where Herr Steuben may be found, no word on any pending action by the Nordic Temple or the Thunderbolt Brigade. Not yet."

"Not yet," Bolan echoed. "Are we waiting, then?"

Gellar pretended to consider it, then shook his head. "I think not, in this case. My contacts either don't have access to the information we require, or they're too reluctant to disclose it. Either way, I feel the wait would be a waste of time."

"Okay." Just that. Bolan waited for the rest of it, not pressing him.

"There is, I think, another way," Gellar said.

"Something like with Bruno, that would be," Bolan replied, anticipating him.

"Something like that," Gellar agreed. "But not with children from the Thunderbolt Brigade."

"You want somebody from the Temple, then."

"Why not? I have a partial list of members in Berlin, with addresses for many. Even if they've gone to ground, we should be able to uncover one or two of them before the day is done."

He had expected more resistance from Belasko, but the man surprised him with a shrug. "All right," he said. "Suits me."

"You don't mind, then?"

"They're turning up the heat," Bolan stated. "This thing at Wewelsburg, and who knows what Stevens will dream up next? He made the rules. His goons are bought and paid for.''

"Very good." Gellar was gratified, though not without a trace of lingering suspicion. Belasko clearly wasn't squeamish when it came to spilling blood, but in their previous encounter with the skinhead, Bruno, he had seemed to show a righteous man's uneasiness with torture.

It was a debate that still divided Israel, in regard to the official handling of terrorists. The nation's highest court had officially acknowledged police torture for the first time in late 1999, denouncing the practice as unacceptable in a civilized society. Of course, the judges seemed to think that Israel's front-line fighters in the daily struggle for survival were confronting civilized opponents.

Jacob Gellar knew, from grim experience, that nothing could be further from the truth.

And he would do what had to be done, in order to complete his present task.

"We shall go hunting, then," he told Bolan. "I would like to pick up someone of sufficient rank within the Nordic Temple that has some knowledge of impending plans, but one whose disappearance will not be immediately noted with alarm. I have a few prospects in that regard."

"Let's hit the bricks," Bolan said. "The sooner we find out what's next up on the schedule, the sooner we can put an end to it. One thing you ought to know."

"What's that?"

"I spoke to my connection in the States," Bolan told him. "Members of the Nordic Temple over there are dropping out of sight like it's the rapture. There's at least an outside chance they may be headed this way, reinforcements for whatever's still to come."

"More reason to be quick about uncovering Herr Steuben, then," Gellar replied.

To which, Bolan said, "Your wheels or mine?"

CHAPTER NINE

Kurt Fraenkel didn't know if he should mourn or cel-
ebrate, and so he had decided to do some of each.
The news from Wewelsburg had been terrible, two of
his friends among the dead, and all of them acquaintances from working with the Temple of the Nordic
Covenant around Berlin. At the same time, of course,
came rage and the desire to lash out at the traitors,
still apparently unknown, who had disrupted what
was said to be a most important ceremony. Fraenkel
didn't have the details—it was strictly need-to-
know—but he accepted what he had been told, and
part of him was yearning for revenge.

The celebration side of it came from the knowledge
that he soon would have the very opportunity he
lusted for, to strike back at his enemies. This time
tomorrow, in fact, he would be leading one of
the strike teams Herr Steuben was unleashing on the
Jews. His rank of *oberleutenant* would finally mean
something, besides just leading protest marches
through the streets or counting cadence while the
skinheads drilled on vacant lots. He would be leading
troops in battle with the demon Jew.

And hopefully, he wouldn't fail.

Disgrace was one thing that Fraenkel knew about

firsthand. He had the kind of practical experience that started in a home with violent alcoholic parents and developed into school days when he was the smallest, weakest boy in class, the constant butt of cruel jokes. He had dropped out at age sixteen, forsaking education in his flight from daily punishment. Between his size and lack of a diploma, though, good jobs were virtually impossible to find. Fraenkel was on the dole, one more humiliation, when he walked into a public meeting of the Nordic Temple, hoping that they might be giving soup or sandwiches away.

And it had changed his life.

Before another week was out, he understood the pattern of his life and realized that none of the events that had conspired to make his life a veritable hell on earth had been his fault. It was the Jews and Communists—two labels so inextricably linked that some Temple members regarded them as synonyms, though Fraenkel recognized that some Communists clearly weren't Jews. They were tools of the Jews, still highly dangerous, but also pitiable in a sense.

Which wouldn't stop Fraenkel from destroying them to the last man, woman and child, on the coming day of retribution.

It was only fair, after all, considering what he had suffered at their hands.

The following night would be a start, and while anticipation put a new bounce in his step, Fraenkel acknowledged to himself that he was nervous, too. This reenactment of the great Kristallnacht pogrom would be his first major action, and he was going into it as a field commander, rather than simply as one of the troops. His personal responsibility was thus increased dramatically, along with the potential for disaster if he failed.

No failure. It wasn't an option.

Fraenkel had already resolved that he would die before he failed, if it should come to that. He owed it to himself, and to his race.

But first, he needed to relax.

There was a midnight meeting set, Karl Dengler having ordered all team leaders to report and draw assignments for the raids. It would enable them to stage coordinated strikes throughout the city, cause maximum damage to their enemies before police could intervene and hopefully thereby avoid arrests.

His destination at the moment was a club in the Tiergarten district, where the hostesses and dancers knew his name, his tastes and what he could afford. That spared him the embarrassment of having prices quoted that he couldn't meet, and Fraenkel also liked the fact that he had never seen another member of the Nordic Temple whom he recognized inside the club. For all it meant to him, for all the ways in which the group had changed his life, Fraenkel still enjoyed a bit of private time away from all the uniforms, the talk of guns and revolution and the final days.

If the apocalypse was coming—and he had no doubt of that—then who could tell when he might have another chance for down-and-dirty sex?

Fraenkel took no particular precautions on the drive from his apartment to the club. His ancient Fiat would be hopeless in a chase, and any ramming was more likely to destroy his vehicle than any he collided with, always excepting bicycles and scooters. He was armed, of course—the Temple's ranking officers were nearly always armed, unless they traveled with a bodyguard, but Fraenkel kept the Steyr GB semiautomatic pistol underneath the Fiat driver's seat and wouldn't take it with him when he went inside the club.

They didn't know him as a neo-Nazi there, and never would, if Fraenkel had his way. Unless, of course, he was required to come back at some future date and shut them down for crimes against the reich.

Until that day came, he was simply Kurt to the bartenders and young women who did everything within their power to satisfy his needs. Though not a wealthy man by any means, Fraenkel saved his money and was able to afford the trip to Tiergarten approximately twice each month. This trip would be a special treat. He meant to use his dusty credit card and make damned sure that he enjoyed himself the night before he went to war.

Fraenkel paid no attention to the Volvo sedan that followed him from his apartment into Tiergarten. It meant nothing to him, and despite the warning from Karl Dengler, Fraenkel had no reason to believe that anyone would target him in any way. Surveillance, possibly, but that would be police, and they would learn nothing from this excursion to the club. He would be more careful as he was leaving, certainly, and make sure no one trailed him to the meet with Dengler. As for whether someone saw him drinking or discovered that he had a yen for nude young women, sometimes tipping them for special favors in the nightclub's private dance rooms, they could put that in a file and mark it with a bright red flag for all he cared. It proved nothing, except that he had certain carnal needs, like any other man.

He saw the club's bright neon and pulled into the

parking lot. He still ignored the Volvo as it turned in after him, passed by him as he nosed the Fiat into the nearest open slot. He killed the lights and engine, checked his short hair in the rearview mirror, stepped out of the car and used his key to lock the driver's door. Fraenkel was turning toward the nightclub, pocketing his keys, when he was suddenly confronted by a stranger in the shadows.

"Kurt Fraenkel?"

The man was roughly Frawnkel size, possibly an inch or so taller, well dressed in a middle-income kind of way. The most arresting thing about the stranger was his eyes—and then, of course, the fact that he knew Fraenkel's name.

"I don't know you," the startled Nazi said.

"I hope to remedy that situation, *Oberleutenant*," the man replied, smiling without the slightest hint of mirth.

Fraenkel was suddenly reminded of the pistol hidden underneath the Fiat driver's seat. To reach it, he would have to take the keys out of his pocket, turn his back on the menacing stranger, unlock the door, then lean into the car and reach for it—by which time, if the stranger had a weapon or was skilled in any kind of martial arts, Fraenkel could be dead.

No good.

"What do you want?" he asked.

"Some information," the stranger said, "in the interest of peace and justice."

"I have no information that would interest you," Fraenkel replied.

"You're mistaken, I believe. Who knows what piece of trivia may interest me?"

There would be nothing for it but to fight, Fraenkel

realized, and that meant that his wisest course of action was to strike the first blow, if he could. Strike hard and fast, to knock down the grinning bastard with any luck at all, and finish him by any means available once he was on the ground.

"Well, since you put it that way," Fraenkel said—then he lashed out at the stranger with his fist, putting his weight behind it, aiming at the center of that smug, infuriating face.

What happened in the next split second was a blur, from Fraenkel's point of view. He saw a hand flash out to grip his wrist, the stranger ducking, pivoting, then he was airborne, whooping as he somersaulted through the darkness, gasping as he struck the pavement and the air was driven from his lungs.

Drowning, he thought. He was drowning on dry land!

Before he had a chance to panic, though, a fist came out of nowhere and obliterated conscious thought.

"WHO'S MISSING, then?"

Karl Dengler had just finished counting heads again, and had come up with seventeen. One short, again, and after counting three times over, there was no mistake.

The others looked around, some frowning, others silently mouthing the names of those they recognized. The basement room beneath the strip club smelled of tension and tobacco, aftershave and something else, akin to sex. Upstairs, the bass line of the music pulsed as if they had convened beneath a dragon's den, the giant reptile's heartbeat echoing.

"It's Fraenkel," someone said. "Kurt Fraenkel isn't here."

Now that he heard the name, it was an easy matter to confirm the statement. Fraenkel's ferret face was nowhere to be seen among the others, all turned back toward Dengler now.

"Has anybody spoken to him since this afternoon?"

Some shook their heads, some others muttered unintelligibly, most of them answering with stoic silence. Dengler turned to his assistant, Oscar Weingart. "Did he leave a message?"

"No, sir."

"Call his flat at once. If he's still there, tell him that he's relieved of duty until further notice."

"Yes, sir."

As Weingart left to run the errand, Dengler turned back to his team leaders, assembled to receive their marching orders. "Very well," he said. "If Fraenkel can't be troubled to attend this meeting, there's no reason to include him in our plans. I will be pleased to lead his team myself."

A hand went up in the back row.

"Yes, Axel?" Dengler said.

"Is it not possible that he has come to harm?" Axel Grubb asked.

"Fraenkel, you mean?"

Grubb nodded. "With the other troubles, first Berlin, and then at Wewelsburg…" He didn't finish, but there was no need to spell it out.

"If so," Dengler replied, "we have been fortunate. For, while we lose a comrade in the struggle, he wasn't yet privy to the list of targets chosen for the strike teams. He cannot betray us, even if he wished to do so."

"He knows there is an action scheduled for to-night," one of the others said. It was already after midnight now, the series of coordinated strikes planned to begin in less than twenty-two hours.

"No matter," Dengler said. "Who can protect all Jewish homes and shops within the city limits of Berlin? Not the police, assuming they should even care to try. At Wewelsburg, I'm told two men were seen. A sniper glimpsed them fleeing, but there was no time to make the shot. The same thing was reported by survivors from the shooting at Anhalter station, the night before last. Two guns, maybe three. There is no reason to believe we're up against an army here."

The pep talk didn't seem to reassure them much, but there were no more verbal protests from his audience. Dengler, for his part, masked the personal concern he felt, verging on fear. It was true, as he had told them, that the surviving sniper in Wewelsburg had glimpsed two men retreating from the castle, quickly lost to sight. And it was also true that those two men, apparently alone, had slaughtered twenty well-armed soldiers of the Nordic Temple in a stand-up fight.

So they were cool, efficient killers. And the worst part was, Dengler wouldn't have known them if they walked up to him on the street.

Projecting confidence that he didn't entirely feel, newly acquainted with his post as fatherland coordinator for the Temple of the Nordic Covenant and still a bit uncertain of his power, though he felt its weight upon his shoulders, Dengler managed to address his troops without a tremor in his voice.

"Two men," he said again. "Or let us say that there are double that, even five times that number. What have we to fear? It's obvious that they have no official standing, or else they would have come with lights and sirens and the television cameras, not as snipers lurking in the shadows."

"I prefer police to snipers," someone said from the back row, evoking nervous laughter from the rest.

Dengler allowed himself to join them with a smile, instead of flying off the handle, knowing that a tantrum now could lose them, even if it cowed them momentarily. He had to present himself as one who understood their personal concerns, perhaps shared them himself, and yet was able to control and subjugate his fears.

"I would prefer a jail cell to a table in the morgue myself," he said, "but once again I ask you, what have we to fear? Two men, even ten men, cannot protect the Jewish population of Berlin. It is a physical impossibility. And they cannot seek help from the authorities, since they are murderers themselves. Who would believe them? Who would even listen to them? They would be locked up before they could explain themselves, keys thrown away for good."

That seemed to change the mood a little, though the men who sat before him were still apprehensive. So much the better, Dengler thought. If they were too cocksure and overconfident, they would be courting disaster.

Weingart returned at that moment, leaning in to tell him, "There's no answer, sir. Not even a machine."

"So be it," Dengler said. "If Fraenkel has suffered a mishap on the way to this meeting, I'll expect to see him in a body cast."

Or in a body bag, he thought, and kept it to himself.

"Your targets, then," he said without further preamble. "Oscar has been kind enough to comb the various Berlin directories and list some juicy targets, broken down by districts of the city, for convenience and proximity. The major synagogues and Jewish centers are included, naturally. Also included are some forty Jew-owned shops and firms, identified by name or from personal knowledge of the proprietor's identity. To that list, we have added home addresses for three dozen of the city's richest and most influential Jews. When we are done this night, the fatherland and all the world at large will have no choice but to acknowledge what we have achieved."

"That means a crackdown," Axel Grubb observed.

"We may assume that's true," Karl Dengler said. "But they shouldn't assume that we'll sit idly by and let them herd us into cells. This time, my brother Aryans, our enemies are in for a surprise."

THEY WERE back in the riverfront warehouse. Same cold, dusty silence. Same plain wooden chair at the heart of the cavernous room. Same handcuffs and duct tape securing their second hostage in as many days.

Gellar had introduced the man to Bolan as Kurt Fraenkel, some kind of lieutenant in the Temple of the Nordic Covenant. He had been chosen from some mental hit list, on the theory that his rank was high enough to let him be aware of any major pending actions by the cult. If they were wrong, Gellar had noted with a kind of surgical disinterest in the captive's welfare, they could always try again with someone else.

From the expression on his face, the prisoner couldn't decide if he was furious or scared to death. In fact, Bolan suspected, it was some of both, the extreme emotions playing with his self-control, setting him up for a break despite his best efforts to appear stoic.

Research had shown that the subjects most likely to resist long-term interrogation were those who lacked imagination. Looking forward to the next pain, and the next, was part of what defeated those who spilled their guts. Bolan had seen some too-imaginative characters break down before inquisitors could lay a finger on them. Simply eying the array of instruments laid out in preparation for their own dissection did the trick.

Kurt Fraenkel wasn't that far gone, but he was on the way. His respiration rate had picked up since they strapped him to the chair, though he hadn't begun to hyperventilate. He was perspiring, even in the chilly warehouse atmosphere, and his eyes followed every move that Gellar made.

The chain saw was an interesting touch. Gellar had brought it from the warehouse office, with a propane torch, and set it off to the neo-Nazi's left, where Fraenkel had to strain his neck muscles to see it. One glimpse was enough to make the neo-Nazi swallow hard. He paled at first sight of the instrument, and his demeanor wasn't improved when Gellar made a second trip to the office, returning with a dolly and a hand-crank electric generator, jumper cables with big brass alligator clips slung around his neck like a sadomasochist's version of a feather boa.

Fraenkel said something in German, trying for a stiff-upper-lip tone and missing it by several degrees.

Gellar replied, "You will speak English only here. We ask the questions and you answer, promptly, truthfully. You are unable to deceive us, with your tiny German brain. If you attempt to do so, you will suffer consequences." Pausing, Gellar added, with a wicked smile, "As for myself, I hope you're stubborn."

"You are Jewish?" Fraenkel asked in English, glancing back and forth between them.

"I alone, among us, have that honor," Gellar said, bowing deeply from the waist. "I should inform you that your worthless ancestors assassinated mine during the Third Reich madness. It will be my endless pleasure to dissect you like a laboratory rat, if you don't provide the information we require."

That said, Gellar made one more quick trip to the warehouse office, coming back with two blue-denim jumpsuits, zippered in the front. Handing one suit to Bolan, he explained, "This will protect your clothing when I use the chain saw. It makes an atrocious mess."

The wink was just for Bolan, shielded from their prisoner as the Israeli turned his back and stepped into the jumpsuit. Bolan did likewise, thankful for the too large size Gellar had chosen. If it came to chain saws, though, he had decided that he would excuse himself and take a stroll around the block.

"Now, Herr Fraenkel," Gellar said, as he was zipping up his faded coveralls, "you are no doubt aware of what befell your comrades at the castle earlier today."

The neo-Nazi stiffened, unmistakable recognition showing in his eyes. "You are responsible," he answered, almost whispering.

"Correct, Herr Nazi scum. Your good friends died like squealing pigs, without a trace of courage, honor, dignity." Gellar allowed himself another smile, adding, "I shall expect no less from you."

Their captive raised his chin and said, "I will tell you nothing."

"On the contrary," Gellar replied. "You will tell me everything. Before we're finished here, you will be making up new tales to share. But not too soon, I trust. How will I have the fun of trying out my toys if you give in too quickly?"

"Nothing!" Fraenkel snapped.

"Perfect. I so admire a man of principle." Turning to Bolan, Gellar said, "The generator first, I think, don't you? It's my experience that when the muscles have been stimulated by sufficient voltage, they provide a measure of resistance to the saw. It is an interesting effect." He looked around at the display of torture implements and asked, "Have I forgotten anything?"

"I'd say the layout looks complete," Bolan replied, trying to stay in character.

"All right, then. It will only take a moment to prepare the subject for his treatment."

Turning back to Fraenkel, Gellar stepped in close to him and ripped the neo-Nazi's shirt wide open, scattered buttons rattling and rolling on the concrete floor. That done, he produced the familiar stiletto and snapped it open, crouching to slit the right leg of Fraenkel's slacks along the outer seam, from cuff to knee.

Speaking to Bolan as he worked, Gellar said, "The trick of using electricity, you know, is not to use too much. This generator, for example, can provide a lethal dose if handled carelessly, with contact too prolonged. I have no wish to let this Nazi bastard off so easily, of course, before he has a chance to suffer properly. Besides, if he dies now, he'll never feel the saw.''

"Our questions," Bolan said, reminding him.

"Questions?" Gellar seemed properly distracted. "Oh, yes, there'll be questions. Herr Fraenkel will divulge whatever secrets he possesses, even if I have to cut off his arms and legs first. Meanwhile..."

He laid out the jumper cables, keeping the alligator clamps at one end separated by a foot or so while he attached their mates to the generator. Their prisoner watched Gellar's every move with rapt attention, as if his life depended on it.

"What is it that you want to know?" the German blurted out.

"Not yet," Gellar replied, almost scolding. "I'll ask the questions when I'm ready. When we're both ready."

"But I know things!"

"In good time."

Addressing Bolan, Gellar said, "One clamp attaches to the ankle, thus." Their captive gave a little squeal as Gellar drew his slit pant leg aside and roughly fastened one alligator clamp to the back of his ankle, pinching the Achilles tendon.

"The other clamp, I think, should be positioned...here!"

Gellar held the alligator clip poised an inch or so from Fraenkel's right nipple, the pale flesh of the prisoner's chest already bristling with goose bumps in anticipation of the pain.

"No, wait!" Fraenkel cried out. "There is an action laid on for tonight, against the Jews!"

"ONE OF OUR team leaders is missing," Karl Dengler reported. "Otherwise, all is in readiness."

"Which one is missing?" Gerhard Steuben asked.

"Kurt Fraenkel, sir. Oberleutenant Fraenkel, that is. I will be leading his team personally."

"And you have tried to find him, I assume?"

"Yes, sir," Dengler replied. "There was no answer on his telephone, and so I sent two men to check his flat. He wasn't in, and there was no sign of his car around the neighborhood. There have been no reports of accidents involving Fraenkel or his vehicle, and he hasn't checked into any local hospital."

"Is this Fraenkel a coward?"

"I don't believe so, sir. Of course, he was promoted by Manfred Roeder. I've had little contact with him personally."

Shifting the responsibility onto a dead man. Steuben almost smiled at that, but caught himself in time. It was a fair enough defense.

"What other action have you taken in regard to Oberleutenant Fraenkel?"

"I've relieved him of authority, pending an explanation of his disappearance, sir. One of our friends on the police force has been asked to list his car as stolen, without calling any special notice to the case. If it is found, with or without Fraenkel, we'll be informed. I have men checking out the places where he likes to go. A few beer gardens and a strip club that he thinks nobody knows about."

"All right. You have done well." In fact, it was as much as anyone could do, without a firm location for the missing soldier. If this Fraenkel had deserted, he could certainly be far outside Berlin by now, perhaps already leaving Germany. And if he had been taken by the enemy, against his will...

"How much did Oberleutnant Fraenkel know about our plans?" Steuben inquired, keeping it casual, trying to make it sound like a stray afterthought.

"None of the details, sir. As I informed you, he was missing when the other team leaders received their orders and lists of targets."

"Surely he knew *something*, Karl." Using the Christian name made it seem more intimate.

"Well...yes, sir. Fraenkel knows we have an action scheduled for tonight, and that he was supposed to lead a team. He knew the hour and location of the meeting where the final orders were transmitted, but he never came. There were no strangers at the meeting, and we weren't interrupted. In accordance with Roeder's standard practice, the room was checked for listening devices before the meeting convened."

"Did Fraenkel know the other team leaders by name?" Steuben asked, falling naturally into the past tense when referring to his missing trooper.

Dengler thought about that for a moment, prior to answering. "None were identified to him by name, sir," he replied at last. "Of course, he knows that officers would lead the teams, and I assume that he knows most of them from meetings, training exercises and the like. We're using nearly all our captains and lieutenants, sir, because the action is...ambitious."

Dengler was hinting that his leader may have overreached himself, though he would never dare to speak the words aloud. No matter. Each man was allowed his private doubts, as long as they remained private and he followed every order without question. Obedience was paramount; commitment to victory was a given, once the battle had been joined.

"Given the thorough nature of your search," Steuben remarked, throwing the man a bone, "we must assume one of two possibilities to be the truth. Either Fraenkel has turned tail and run away from his responsibilities, in which case we may never find him, or he has been taken by the enemy—in which case we may logically assume that he won't survive captivity. The former circumstance may pose no threat to us, if Fraenkel is content to flee without contacting the authorities."

"I seriously doubt that he would do that, sir. Of course, I don't know him that well, as I explained."

"Of course. And if the enemy has taken him, as I suspect may be the case, we must assume that he will tell them anything and everything he knows. Regardless of his courage, after all, the man is only flesh and blood."

"Yes, sir." Dengler was glum. "Shall I abort the action, then?"

"Abort? By no means!" Steuben bristled at the notion. "You have just informed me that Fraenkel possessed no crucial details of the operation, that he didn't know the times or targets. Were you telling me the truth, Karl?"

"Certainly, sir!"

"Then what have we to fear?"

"Nothing?"

"Nothing. Precisely, Karl. The action will proceed as planned. The Jews who colonize Berlin will very shortly wish that they had fled to Palestine, to plague the Arabs as their aunts and uncles have. They'll wish they were as clever as they claim to be.''

''Just as you say, sir.''

''Now, if I am not mistaken, there are preparations you must make. For leading Oberleutenant Fraenkel's team in battle?''

''Yes, sir.'' Dengler clicked his heels and snapped his right arm out in the traditional salute. *''Sieg heil!''*

Steuben returned the crisp salute and watched his second in command for all of Germany depart. He now had misgivings about his plan to re-create the glory that was Kristallnacht, but he couldn't admit to weakness, much less to an error of judgment. If he scrubbed the operation now because one of his underlings may have been kidnapped by an unknown enemy, he would seem indecisive at best, cowardly at worst.

It simply wouldn't do.

Prophecy told him that the final days were fast approaching, when the Temple of the Nordic Covenant and Aryans around the world would be tested by fire. If he retreated from the first suggestion of a little heat, it would be proof that Gerhard Steuben was unfit to lead. Better to die, he thought, than to invite disgrace and compromise his destiny.

Better still for his enemies to die, and the sooner the better.

This night would be a start. The best was yet to come. His troops would do him proud, and Jews around the world, together with their lackeys on the left, their mud-race puppets, all the rest of those who stood beyond the pale, would know that something momentous had occurred. They would look up with dull, glazed eyes and see the writing on the wall.

If they mistook it for another empty threat, so much the better. That meant that his shock troops could expect to catch them napping on the day.

"Not long," he told himself, unaware that he spoke the words aloud. "Not long."

CHAPTER TEN

The list that Bolan had divided with his ally from Mossad included eighteen names, which came to nine apiece. They were the captains and lieutenants of the Temple of the Nordic Covenant within Berlin, plus one who had replaced the late, lamented Manfred Roeder as the second in command to would-be Führer Gary Stevens. They were scattered far and wide around the sprawling city, and the only way to tag them all, to even make a decent start on the job, had been for Bolan and Gellar to split up.

No problem, Bolan thought as he tooled his rented car along Greifswalder Strasse 2, in search of the first address on his half of the list. He simply had to watch his step, try not to draw attention to himself. Gellar had taught him several phrases rarely heard within polite society, which the Israeli judged would be enough, when coupled with Bolan's demeanor, to discourage most civilian challengers. They wouldn't work with the police, of course, nor could he engage the locals in even a casual conversation, to support his cover. That was why he had his targets marked on a detailed street map.

Unfortunately, while he had addresses, Bolan had no faces to go with them. Gellar had known three of the nineteen neo-Nazis by sight, which put them on his list when they made the split, Bolan getting by on the descriptions their late hostage had provided under threat of being boned and fricaseed.

He spied the first address and had to circle twice around the block before he found a parking space to suit his needs, including easy access and a speedy getaway. The place was an apartment house, and while he had the target's number memorized, there was no handy floor plan to advise him where Apartment G was found on the fourth floor. No sniping, then, since Bolan didn't know which window he should aim for, and he had no snapshot of the target to confirm.

That meant a trip inside, which Bolan didn't mind, as long as it paid off. He parked, got out of the car and left the Galil sniper rifle on the floorboard in back, snug inside its OD duffel bag. For what he had in mind, the Beretta 93-R should be adequate, and he had pocketed a Russian frag grenade, just in case things got rough.

Midmorning traffic was fairly light in this mostly residential neighborhood. Everyone with a job was already at work, and most of the kids were in school. He waited for a bus to pass before he crossed the street and was relieved to find that the apartment house had no doorman, no apparent security devices in place.

A passing glance at 4G's mailbox showed him the name B. Koettler. That was *B* for Bernard, and Bolan's information was that the Nazi crew leader lived alone, no bedmates or bodyguards in residence. The elevator door was standing open, but he took the stairs, eight zigzag flights before he reached the fourth floor and was forcibly reminded of the European system, wherein—unlike the numbering of floors in the United States—the ground floor doesn't count. Two more flights, and he found the floor marked 4.

Although his target was supposed to have no roomies, they were only twelve or thirteen hours from a major operation in the city, and it wouldn't have surprised him to find Koettler huddled with a number of his men, discussing details of the targets they had been assigned. There was at least a fifty-fifty chance, he knew, that Koettler wouldn't be at home, or that he might have company. Perhaps the kind that carried guns.

Hence, the grenade in Bolan's pocket.

Just in case.

The stairs put Bolan in a corner on his target floor, Apartment 4C to his left, a door marked Privat to his right. Passing 4C, he came to A and B, facing each other from across the dingy hallway, and he turned back in the opposite direction, homing on his mark.

The whole place smelled of cabbage, grease and something else that Bolan couldn't quite identify. To him, it smelled like disappointment, with a dash if disillusionment—or was that resignation?—added to the mix. This was a place, he realized, for people who had mostly settled for their lot in life, whether they liked it or not. Upward mobility had no place here, though it was always possible to backslide, be demoted, miss the cut. In which case, if their luck went south, some might be forced to look for smaller, even less inviting digs.

One of their number, though, didn't intend to stagnate in a dead-end job, much less to hit the skids. Bernard Koettler had dreams and aspirations that incorporated visions of a global holocaust. When the smoke cleared, Koettler imagined, he and his Aryan brothers would be on top of the heap, commanding the survivors in a slaughterhouse about to blossom into Paradise.

Koettler was in for a surprise.

Assuming he was home, of course.

4D...4E...4F...4G.

He stood before the door with its fish-eye lens installed around chin height. His jacket was already unbuttoned, Bolan drawing the Beretta and thumbing back its hammer, holding it down and out of sight from the peephole, slightly behind his thigh. He reached out with his left hand, knocked lightly and waited for the sound of footsteps from within.

They came at last, after what seemed a long delay. Koettler deciding whether he should answer? Maybe going for a weapon? Bolan saw a shadow move behind the peephole's lens, facing it squarely, no attempt to look away.

A man's voice issued from behind the door, asking him, *"Ja?"*

Bolan could easily have shot him through the door, but he wouldn't have known for sure who he was killing. It was unacceptable.

"Herr Koettler?" Maybe mispronouncing it. A hazard, there.

"Vas ist?" No confirmation, still.

Gellar had taught him one more phrase, not rude, for situations such as this, if they arose. He leaned a little closer to the door, painfully aware that Koettler would be hard-pressed to miss him from that range, concentrating on the German words that meant, "I have a message from Herr Dengler."

Muted grumbling behind the door, before a bolt was thrown and it opened perhaps three inches, still on a chain. A slice of Aryan visage was revealed, one eye regarding him suspiciously.

"Vas ist?"

"Herr Koettler?" Bolan repeated.

"Ja, ja!" Impatient now. "Vas—"

The Beretta's muffled sneeze cut him off in midsentence, its single Parabellum round taking out the suspicious eye, knocking its one-time owner backward, out of frame. Bolan waited for a heartbeat, listening for any clamor of reaction from other occupants, then reached out and pulled the door shut.

One down, and he was on his way.

AXEL GRUBB LOVED beer the way some men profess to love their wives and children, with a passion that ran second to his hatred of the Jews and mud races, while tying with his love of cracking heads. Whenever he could put the three together, as he planned to do that very night, he felt as if he might be favored with a preview of Valhalla. All he needed for complete perfection were some naked dancing girls along the sidelines, standing by to service him in style when he was finished spilling blood.

There were no naked dancing girls available just now, of course, but that was for the best. They always managed to distract him, and he needed all his wits about him at the moment, for the final planning of tonight's festivities.

The city map was spread before him, weighted down with beer mugs at the corners, red ink from a chunky felt-tipped marker indicating targets in the zone that he and his shock troops had been assigned.

They had Neukölln, in the southeastern quarter of the city, easily Berlin's most populous district, with more than three hundred thousand mostly working-class inhabitants. In the early days of the neighborhood, notorious tenements had been erected there that prompted graphic artist Heinrich Zille to comment that it was easy to "kill a man as well with an apartment as with an axe."

Much had improved since those days in the nineteenth century, of course, and Neuköllners were now justly proud of certain historic and cultural monuments, although most tourist routes still bypassed the district. Axel Grubb had no interest in culture, and little knowledge of history beyond that of Adolf Hitler's glorious reich. He knew, though, that the Neukölln district harbored Jews aplenty, including both shops and home.

In the interest of efficiency and security, Grubb had summoned half a dozen members of his strike team to the small machine shop that he managed for an absentee owner in suburban Treptow. The mechanics were busy as usual, but Grubb had other fish to fry this morning.

Gefilte fish, he thought, and almost giggled, childlike in his glee.

This evening's targets weren't only marked on the large-scale map to single them out, but they were also connected by arrows drawn in red, suggesting the quickest, most efficient route from one point to the next. If Grubb's raiders were able to follow the plan, remain at least one jump ahead of the police, they should be able to strike all fourteen targets within the allotted time, leaving ruin and bitter grief in their wake.

No more or less than the scheming Jew traitors deserved.

"Once again," Grubb informed them, "we start here." His blunt index finger stabbed at a fat red dot drawn on Skalitzer Strasse, in the northwest corner of the Neukölln district, where an old Jew and his grown-up daughter ran a modest jewelry store.

"From there," he continued, tracing the route southward, "we proceed along Kottbusser Damm to the second target." That being a successful haberdashery and millinery shop, much envied and despised by Aryan competitors.

He continued, following the red-ink trail of carnage to be along Karl-Marx Strasse then east on Granzallee, circling ever farther east- and northward, toward Treptower Park. By the time they completed the circuit and exited Neukölln on Skalitzer Strasse, in the district's northern quadrant, police should be scrambling to keep up, tripping over themselves, perhaps strategically distracted by certain allies within the department.

Some of the other strike teams would have fewer targets in their districts; some had more. Grubb knew that there were richer districts to be plundered, finer shops and homes than Neukölnn offered to his soldiers, but the job was his, and he would see it carried out to the best of his ability.

This was a chance for Grubb to prove himself, perhaps move another rung or two up the ladder of rank, particularly if one or another of the competing teams suffered misfortune. He would never wish them ill, of course, but if *his* men managed to sack more targets than another team, if they were able to avoid police entirely while some others went to jail—well, it wasn't his fault that certain brother officers who sometimes sneered at him behind his back now failed to make the grade.

Grubb had considered calling the police himself, and tipping them to certain targets outside Neukölln, thereby hobbling the competition even as he gave himself an edge, but he had finally discarded the idea, feeling vaguely traitorous for having thought it up in the first place. After all, this night wasn't about personal glory; it was all for the advancement of the Temple and the master race.

"I need a drink," he told his three companions, seeing smiles bloom on their faces as he folded up the map and put it in the top drawer of his desk, locking the drawer and pocketing the key. "Who else wants beer?"

Of course, they all did, laughing at his little joke as they filed out of the office, through the workshop's racket, to the street outside.

Grubb was turning toward Rudolf, asking, "Do you have your van?" when something wet and warm splashed the left side of his face. He blinked, blind in one eye, the other seeing Rudolf's nearly headless body dance an awkward two-step on the sidewalk, then collapse as it ran out of steam.

"*Mein gott!*" one of the others blurted, Grubb still trying to determine what could—

Sniper!

Even as it came to him, he heard a meaty smack behind him, and another of his friends was down, half of Gunther's face sheared away, as if by an ax or cleaver.

Grubb spun back toward the safety of the machine shop, leaving Roy to look after himself. A grunt and thud of impact on the sidewalk told him that his final comrade hadn't been successful in securing cover.

He ran with everything he had, and knew it wasn't good enough. Two long strides short of safety, Grubb felt the stunning impact, low down in his back. It picked him off his feet and slammed him facefirst through the plate-glass door of the machine shop, jagged lancets ripping through his face, neck, scalp and outflung palms. He struck the floor facedown, sliding in blood and shattered glass, vaguely aware that he had no sensation in his lower body.

It seemed to Grubb then that the floor opened beneath him, sloping sharply downward like a garbage chute, no bottom visible.

And he was gone.

JACOB GELLAR PARKED across the street and three doors down from the garage where several members of the Thunderbolt Brigade were known to be employed. In fact, he knew from research he had done on local neo-Nazi groups, the owner of the place was himself a one-time skinhead street fighter who had graduated to a low-ranking post in the Temple of the Nordic Covenant, suspected of at least peripheral involvement in a string of violent crimes involving nonwhite immigrants.

It came as no surprise to Gellar, then, when the Mercedes-Benz that he was following pulled into the garage's parking lot and coasted to a halt at the north end of the rundown-looking structure. Gellar watched as Ludwig Eberhard emerged from the passenger side, his driver stepping out a moment later, falling into step behind him as they entered the garage.

How many men and guns inside?

There were no customers in evidence, which was a bonus, but Gellar had no way of making an accurate long-distance estimate of the hostile odds inside. He was already pushing it, trailing Eberhard to the shop in Schöneberg instead of taking him down on his own doorstep, twenty minutes earlier. Instead, he had gambled that Eberhard might lead him to a fatter target, and now he had gotten his wish.

How many men? How many guns?

The garage proprietor, Meinke Finster, kept anywhere from three to half a dozen skinheads on his payroll at any given time. To be on the safe side, prepared for the worst, Gellar took the maximum number, added Eberhard and his driver, then rounded the total up to ten.

Those were the kind of odds that got men killed.

He checked the mini-Uzi one more time, its L-shaped double magazine in place, a live round in the chamber. The Walther P-5 pistol, nestled in its fast-draw holster on his belt, was also fully loaded, ready when he needed it. He took a look around the neighborhood, its other shops fairly busy at that hour, and retrieved a suppressor from beneath the driver's seat, quickly threading it onto the mini-Uzi's muzzle. Finally, in blatant defiance of the need for stealth, he reached into the glove compartment, palmed the antipersonnel grenade he found there and slipped it into the left-hand pocket of his raincoat.

Not that it was raining now, but he would need the lightweight garment to conceal his submachine gun as he crossed the street. From that point on, he thought, it might not matter much what happened next.

Ludwig Eberhard was marked as a potential team

leader for the still unidentified action that Gerhard Steuben had planned for that night, in Berlin. Gellar had taken out one other Nordic Temple officer already, a simple drive-by dust-off in a sidewalk telephone kiosk, and now he meant to make a larger score—take some of the foot soldiers down, perhaps, along with their field commander.

Gellar stepped out of the car and locked the driver's door behind him. There was no point in taking chances, and the battery-powered key fob would unlock the door with the touch of a button at any distance up to fifty feet away.

Assuming he made it back.

Approaching the garage, Gellar heard none of the usual sounds that normally accompany automotive repair. There was no clank of wrenches, no whine and whir of power tools, no off-color banter from mechanics with grease on their faces and hands. From all appearances, Eberhard's arrival had suspended normal activity for the duration, all present retiring for a private talk.

Gerhard breezed into the glass-walled reception area and heard a buzzer going off somewhere in the back to announce his arrival. Seconds later, a strapping young skinhead emerged from a doorway behind the cash register and display counter, holding in both hands one of the largest wrenches Gellar had been privileged to see.

"We're closed," he said without preamble. "Come back later, if you want."

"I need a word with Ludwig," Gellar said.

"And who are you?" the skinhead asked.

"Mossad," Gellar replied, and wiped the startled look from the young neo-Nazi's face with a 3-round burst to the chest. Blood sprinkled the display case as he toppled over backward, huge wrench clanging on the floor, his impact with stacked shelves of motor oil cans completing the effect of an alarm bell's clamor.

Gellar vaulted the counter, one gloved hand sliding in the blood spatter, nearly spilling him on his rump before he caught himself. No time to stop and wipe his palm now, as he passed the leaking corpse, tracking the sound of voices toward another room, in back of the garage.

The mini-Uzi's sound suppressor was fairly effective, but his targets had clearly heard their boy go down, taking the shelves of motor oil with him. They were on their feet and drawing weapons, two of them advancing toward the doorway just as Gellar cleared it. He had time to count six men, six guns, before all hell broke loose.

The two advance men raised their pistols, firing at him without taking time to aim. It cost them, bullets chewing up the door frame to his left and right, spraying Gellar's face with wooden splinters but missing the mark. Even squinting to protect his eyes, there was no way to miss them with the submachine gun, when they stood no more than four or five yards distant.

Gellar stitched them both, a sweeping burst from left to right, and watched them fall, thrashing in blood, one of them triggering another wasted round into the ceiling, taking out a long fluorescent light fixture. Gellar kept firing, emptying the mini-Uzi's magazine, but his other targets, the four survivors, were scrambling and diving for cover now, two dropping out of sight behind a metal desk, another throwing himself behind a pair of filing cabinets.

Retreating under fire, Gellar swiftly reversed the magazines, priming his SMG, but caution made him hesitate rushing the meeting room again. His enemies were still taking pot shots through the open doorway, and their weapons were unsilenced, the reports echoing loudly through the garage, into the street beyond.

How long before some frightened neighbor summoned the police? Were they already on the way?

No time to waste.

He fished inside his raincoat pocket, palmed the frag grenade he found there and released the safety pin. A sidearm pitch put it through the door, and Gellar heard the lethal egg strike something hard, metallic, bouncing once before the Nazis started shouting in alarm.

Four seconds…three…

He fired a short burst through the doorway, pinning them down, then recoiled into a crouch as the grenade exploded, spewing smoke and shrapnel through the open portal.

Gellar followed through, his ears ringing from the blast, and started mopping up. One of the shooters was already gone, his face in shreds, his brains protruding from the gashes in his skull like cotton wadding from a punctured sofa. Gellar moved among the others, found them stunned and wounded, finishing each one in turn with short precision bursts. When it was done, he turned away and took himself outside.

It had begun to rain again, and Gellar blessed the drizzle, raising one arm as if to shield his eyes, obscuring his face from any lurking witnesses in the process. Someone still might note the number of his rental car's license plate, but there was nothing he could do about that at the moment.

The Israeli still had work to do. Places to go, people to kill.

And he was running late.

KARL DENGLER'S business, when he wasn't plotting murder for the master race, involved the operation of a print shop in the Spandau district, on Zeppelinstrasse. The shop, Gellar informed Bolan, had produced much of the Nordic Temple's literature in recent years, along with various pamphlets and posters for the closely allied Thunderbolt Brigade. Having discovered that Manfred Roeder's replacement wasn't at home in his apartment, Bolan drove by the shop and found it open for business, a familiar-looking face behind the counter.

Bolan knew what Dengler looked like because he was one of the half-dozen local neo-Nazis whose photos Jacob Gellar had managed to provide. Of the others, Roeder had died in Wewelsburg, and the rest weren't on Bolan's hit list of team leaders for the action planned that night.

No matter.

At the moment, Dengler's likeness was the only one required.

On Bolan's second pass, he concentrated on the buildings facing Dengler's shop. He found one three doors up the street that suited him, three stories tall, with a flat roof, apartments stacked atop a beauty parlor and a ground-floor bakery. If he could find a way up to that roof, it would be perfect.

He drove around the block once more, picked out the alley as he passed and parked his rental car on a smaller side street, feeding coins into the meter until it would swallow no more. He had already stopped along the way and changed into the denim coveralls that he had worn in the warehouse, while Kurt Fraenkel was spilling his guts. It gave him the appearance of a workman, more or less, and matched the duffel bag he lifted from the rental better than his suit or any sports clothes would have done. No one appeared to notice Bolan as he locked his car and walked back to the alley, ducked inside and disappeared.

He counted back doors, found the building that he wanted and was gratified to see the fire escape attached to its back wall. Checking both ways, he drew down the folding ladder, was rewarded with a squeal of rust and paused to see if anyone would venture to respond. When no one did, he started climbing, kept it casual, not rushing past the windows in a manner that would make a stranger's presence on the fire escape seem any more suspicious than need be.

The roof was pooled with water here and there, small ponds where drainage to the rain gutters was less than complete. The day-long drizzle had subsided temporarily at least, and Bolan took advantage of the moment, moving toward the street side of the roof and peering down at Dengler's print shop, to the east.

Inside the shop, he had a clear view of Dengler speaking with what appeared to be a customer. From the expression on the neo-Nazi's face and his animated gestures, Bolan couldn't tell if he was angry, excited or maybe in the middle of a racy joke. Whatever, he was visible, and that was all that mattered at the moment.

Bolan set down the duffel bag and unzipped it, removing the Galil sniper rifle. Step one was unfolding the stock, its butt pad and cheek rest already adjusted for maximum comfort. There had been no time or opportunity to practice with the weapon, but he trusted the Nimrod six-power telescopic sight to do its job at that distance, amounting to something like sixty yards. He could have made the shot with open sights, but why take chances when he had the telescopic sight available?

He attached the suppressor, slipping it over the Galil's factory-standard flash hider and tightening the screw that would hold it in place. He couldn't expect Hollywood-style results from the "silencer," given the fact that supersonic bullets produced their own sound in flight, distinct and separate from the original gunshot, like a tiny sonic boom, but the suppressor would help confuse passersby and witnesses for the short amount of time his strike here would involve.

Loading the rifle came last, the 20-round box magazine snapped into place, the bolt hauled back and released with a metallic click-clack sound to chamber a live one. That done, Bolan sat on the roof, taking advantage of his own knees as a bench rest, sitting far enough back from the edge that his rifle barrel wasn't readily visible to pedestrians on the street below. With any luck, by the time one of them looked in his direction for the source of gunfire, Bolan would be finished and away.

In field tests, the Galil sniper rifle had been known to group rounds within a 30 cm circle at six hundred meters, more than adequate for most sniping missions. Bolan's shot that afternoon was barely one-eighth that distance, the only obstacle a plate-glass window fronting Dengler's print shop. Through the Nimrod scope, he saw none of the distortion or blurring typical of heavy-duty bulletproof glass, and he had no reason to believe the print shop had been fortified to that extent, at great expense. Still, his first round through the window might be deflected enough to result in a nonfatal wound, perhaps a clean miss, and he had to be ready for the follow-up, as soon as it was breached.

Bolan centered his scope on the print shop's glass facade. He framed the customer first, an older man than Dengler, studying a piece of paper on the counter between them and nodding now, as if some formerly obscure point had been clarified. Shifting slightly to the left, he acquired Dengler's face and pinned its smile in the crosshairs. If there had been a disagreement here, it was apparently resolved.

Which meant the customer could leave now.

Bolan wanted him out of the way, in case the first round through the plate-glass window was deflected more than he anticipated. At the same time, though, he knew that Dengler was unlikely to remain in sight for long, without a customer to keep him there. How many printers lounged around the cash register in an empty shop when there was work to be done with the machines in back?

Bolan caught a break as the customer left, though he didn't recognize it instantly. First thing, his target ducked out of sight behind the counter, then reappeared a moment later, with two reams of paper tucked under one arm. Instead of making a beeline toward the rear of the shop and rushing the shot, as Bolan had feared, Dengler moved around the counter toward the front, approaching one of three copy machines near the windows, apparently provided so that patrons could make photocopies for themselves.

Bolan watched Dengler crouch behind the large copy machine, all but the curve of one shoulder concealed as he loaded the machine's paper tray. It only took a moment, though, and then he rose back into view, crumpling the wrappers in his hands, turning back toward the register and whatever task next awaited him.

Now!

The Executioner released a portion of the breath he had been holding, taking up the trigger slack with something close to loving care. The rifle bucked against his shoulder, but he was prepared for that, riding it out. No matter if it kicked, in any case. The bullet was already gone, well on its way to the target at a muzzle velocity of 2,649 feet per second.

Downrange, the plate-glass window rippled, sprouting cracks in a spiderweb pattern, then collapsed with a crash. Bolan had been correct on the deflection problem, though he didn't miss his mark completely. Instead of striking Dengler in the face, the 7.62 mm NATO round tore into his upper chest, snapped his left clavicle, and pitched him back against the counter where the cash register sat. He had a stunned expression on his face, unmoving for the moment Bolan needed to line up his second shot and put round two between the neo-Nazi's eyes.

It was that simple. The Temple of the Nordic Covenant in Germany was leaderless. Again.

Bolan repacked the sniper rifle swiftly, retracing his path to the car without incident. The hit on Dengler was a major blow against his enemies, but he still wasn't finished with his list of targets. If he wanted to derail that evening's action, he had to try for a clean sweep.

He hoped that Jacob Gellar was on schedule, mopping up the targets he had drawn. In any case, the Executioner was on a roll.

And he was blitzing on.

CHAPTER ELEVEN

"This should have stitches, sir," the would-be medic told him as he swabbed the wounds with hydrogen peroxide, pink foam spilling from the gashes onto newspapers that had been spread across the tabletop to soak up blood.

"No stitches," Gerhard Steuben said, speaking through teeth clenched against the pain. "I won't be cornered in a hospital."

He wasn't saying that he was afraid to go; instead he made it sound as if he had devised some great stratagem, sitting there and leaking blood onto a Formica-topped dining table in a four-room Templehof apartment. Steuben almost had to laugh at that, the foolish notion that he had control of anything that had been happening since he arrived in Germany.

He had gashed his palm and fingers on a water glass, crushing it in his fist when he heard that Dengler had been killed. At first, his own strength had surprised him. It looked like a Hollywood stunt, and felt that way, too—at least, until the first rush of fury had passed and the pain kicked in, his bright blood spilling from the wounds that ached and burned bone-deep.

"There is a doctor we can call," his host informed

him. "He's one of us, a member of the Temple. If he's at home, he could be here in ten or fifteen minutes."

"Very well. Call him, then."

It was a small concession, even though he hated needles, both the hypodermic and the stitching kind. It made a bad impression on the troops, those who survived, to see their leader sitting in a daze and bleeding out on old newspapers.

Now the telephone was ringing—more bad news, no doubt—and Steuben waited, grinding teeth against the pain that radiated from his self-inflicted wounds until his aide, a stout Berliner named Josef, signed off and cradled the receiver.

"It is definite on Dengler, I'm afraid, sir," Josef said as he approached the bloodstained table. Hesitating for a heartbeat, he pressed on. "And we have also lost two more field officers since the last call. Kessler and Grimm."

The names meant nothing to Steuben. They were soldiers he had never met, and he had missed his chance. How many dead now in this latest series of attacks? Thirteen? Fourteen?

"All officers," he muttered.

"Sorry, sir?"

"Nothing. Just call the doctor and be done with it!"

But it was something, Steuben realized. Attacking members of the Temple or the Thunderbolt Brigade was one thing. Singling out the officers assigned to lead strike teams in a specific action, mere hours before it was scheduled to begin...that was something else entirely. It meant that he had been betrayed by someone close enough to know his plans.

Or Dengler's.

Steuben, in fact, hadn't handled the operational side of the plans for the new Kristallnacht. He hadn't chosen leaders, didn't even know the officers, in fact, despite brief introductions to a handful of them shortly after his arrival. No one in his U.S. entourage could have betrayed the latest victims, even if he wanted to, since none of them possessed the names, addresses, any of the information that a hunter would require.

But someone clearly did.

"Treason," he said, not muttering this time.

"Sir?" Josef's thick brow was furrowed by confusion and alarm, his small eyes darting around the apartment as if in search of trespassers who had escaped his notice.

"Someone has betrayed us from within," Steuben replied to the room at large, including all of them in his revelation. "How else could the enemy target our officers so precisely? How else would they know where to go and who to kill?"

Josef appeared relieved that he wouldn't be called on to repel invaders anytime within the next few minutes. "The police have lists, sir," he reminded his leader. "It is known they watch our every movement in the city. To compile a list would not be difficult."

"Our enemies aren't police!" Steuben snapped. "The police don't sit on a roof and shoot an unarmed merchant in his shop across the street. Police don't run away from their killings. They plant weapons and plead self-defense. They hire lawyers and public-relations consultants to make excuses. If police had killed these men, there would be nothing else on television anywhere in Germany!"

"Of course, sir," Josef said to placate him. "I didn't understand."

One of the others came back from the telephone and said, to no one in particular, "The doctor's on his way."

"This smacks of Jews," Steuben declared.

"No, sir, I promise," the younger man said. "This doctor is a loyal—"

"The killings, idiot!" Infuriated, Steuben raised his hand as if to slap the soldier, his sudden movement spattering those around him with blood and peroxide foam. Some grimaced, but none dared to speak.

"Forgive me, sir," the young man pleaded, retreating toward the small living room.

"We must get out of here," Steuben announced. "*I* must get out of Germany!"

"But, sir," Josef began, "the doctor—"

"After that!" the leader of the Temple of the Nordic Covenant fairly snarled.

The bodyguards who had accompanied him from the United States were seated in the living room, watching television with weapons close at hand, awaiting their orders. They would go where he told them to go, and do what he told them to do. These, at least, he could trust. If they had been corrupted by the enemy, he would be dead.

"I need a charter pilot I can trust," Steuben said. "If not a member of the movement, then at least a man whose temporary loyalty, once purchased, is secure. You know of such a man?"

"There are two men we use primarily," Josef replied.

"Call both of them at once," Steuben instructed. "Tell them to be ready, that they may be needed on

short notice. Do not under *any* circumstances mention
me or the attacks we have sustained.''

"Yes, sir, I'll—''

"Wait!'' Steuben had seen the flaw in his design,
the loophole in his plan. "You must not call them on
the telephone. Do you know where these pilots live?''

"Yes, sir.''

"Send people out to find them, then. Give them the
orders face-to-face and stay with them until they're
needed. Every move they make must be observed. I'll
take no chance with either of them tipping off our
enemies.''

"I'll give the orders now, sir,'' Josef said. "If you
could give me some idea of where you're going…''

"That can wait. I'll tell the pilot when we're on
the runway. Not before.''

"Sir, as you know, the law requires a flight plan
to be filed before—''

"Say anything, for God's sake!'' Sudden cunning
sparkled in the great man's eyes. "Tell one of them
to file a flight plan to Zurich, the other one to Warsaw.
That should keep the bastards guessing for a while.''

"And fuel, sir?'' Josef asked.

"Take on as much as they can carry and prepare
to stop as needed,'' Steuben said. "They should expect to fly at least five hundred miles.''

"Yes, sir.''

"How long before the doctor gets here?'' Steuben
asked the room at large.

"It won't be long now, sir,'' the makeshift medic
said, still dabbing bloody freckles from his cheeks
with tissue.

"Good,'' the leader of the Temple of the Nordic
Covenant said. "I have no time to waste.''

He had a destination fixed in mind now, but he wouldn't share it with these men who had already seen their comrades slaughtered, their ranks decimated. Steuben didn't know which of them he could trust, but he was making do with what he had. If all else failed, his American bodyguards would lay down their lives to protect him, to buy him some time. They had been trained for that. He would expect no less.

But it shouldn't be necessary if his plan worked out. A few more hours, and he would be on his way, beyond the reach of those who had pursued him from Chicago to Berlin. There had been losses, grievous disappointments in the meantime, but he wasn't beaten yet. The cause wasn't defeated yet. In fact, adversity only increased his personal commitment to succeed.

Where they were going next, the locals had a taste for blood surpassing even that of loyalists in the fatherland.

And they were still in practice, too.

"EIGHTY PERCENT'S not bad," Bolan remarked. "It has to slow them down, at least."

"I want them all," Jacob Gellar said, crumpling up the hit list in his fist and firing it across the hotel room, missing the trash can by at least a foot.

Of eighteen Nordic Temple officers they had gone hunting for five hours earlier, fourteen were dead, along with sundry hangers-on. The other four had slipped past them somehow, by dumb luck or coincidence. The news reports on radio, as translated by Gellar, had been claiming anywhere from twenty-one to twenty-five dead neo-Nazis in what the reporters called "apparent fratricide within the neofascist movement."

Bolan didn't know where they had come up with that notion, and he didn't care. If the police believed it, it would make a nice diversion, keep the heat on members of the Nordic Temple and the Thunderbolt Brigade, instead of kicking off a hunt for foreign shooters in Berlin.

"Whatever they had laid on for tonight," he told Gellar, "I think we can assume we've screwed up their plans. Even if they try to go ahead, they'll need to start from scratch."

"There's no predicting what they'll do, as long as Steuben is at large," Gellar replied. "As long as he's alive, the Temple of the Nordic Covenant remains a threat."

"Agreed," Bolan said. "But we still don't have a line on where he's hiding out, or if he's even still around Berlin."

"I may be able to find out."

"I think we've worn out our welcome at the warehouse," Bolan said, not looking forward to a third interrogation. "Anyway, smart money says the Nazis who know anything have gone to ground by now."

"There is more than one national socialist faction in modern Berlin," Gellar replied. "Herr Steuben's people and their juvenile delinquents in the Thunderbolt Brigade are one part of the problem, perhaps the most dangerous part. But they aren't alone."

"I'm listening."

"The neo-Nazi movement in united Germany isn't so much an octopus," Gellar said, "as it is a nest of snakes. The fascists share a common list of enemies, with Jews on top, and they all wish to rule the fatherland, but there are monster egos in the master race. Greed and jealousy have divided the movement since the old Odessa days, in the late 1940s. Today, the German Nazis are fragmented, much like your Ku Klux Klan in the United States, and there is no love lost between the rival leaders.''

"So?"

"So," Gellar continued, "I've cultivated some of them—'kissed up,' I think you call it in America—until they see me as a friend. They think I come from Austria or Latvia, whatever suits my purpose at the moment. I wasn't successful with the Nordic Temple, but I have contacts in three other groups, specifically the National Vanguard, the New German Order and the Teutonic Legionnaires.''

"Which helps us how, again?" Bolan asked.

"All three groups are on record as preferring open politics to violence. Of course, that's merely window dressing for their racism, and sour grapes besides. Their leaders hate Gerhard Steuben because he has been more successful in recruiting the young, militant Nazis for himself. They would be pleased to see him taken out of circulation, even dead.''

That came as no great shock to Bolan. Human predators were always quick to turn on one another, fighting bitterly among themselves as "lower" species rarely did. With men, it didn't have to be a matter of survival. They would lie, cheat and betray each other over ego strokes and childish arguments. They would kill each other to resolve the question of how many angels could dance on the head of a pin.

"You're thinking one of these competitors can put us onto Steuben's trail?"

A shrug from Gellar. "It's a possibility, at least.

For all of their division at the top, the lowly followers of different Nazi groups are more inclined to get along. They drink together in the same nightclubs, fraternize at the same athletic clubs. Secrets have a way of migrating from one group to another and making their way around Berlin, sometimes around the country.''

It was worth a try, Bolan admitted to himself. The bad news was that he would be sidelined while Gellar pulled his strings and stroked his contacts. *Kissing up.* It had to be a most distasteful duty for a dedicated agent of Mossad and an Israeli, listening and laughing while a bunch of would-be Hitlers told their racist jokes and spewed their venom, looking forward to another, more efficient Holocaust. The role-playing went far beyond simple surveillance, and it had to cost Gellar accordingly.

''Well, if you want to go that route,'' Bolan remarked, ''we may as well get started. Our boy has a history of taking off when things get rough. I wouldn't want to lose him.''

''I'll make some calls,'' said Gellar, ''and arrange for meetings if I can. This type always has more to say in person. They're afraid of telephones, and with good reason. Fortunately, they're not smart enough to spot a Jew unless he wears a yarmulke or yellow star.''

The bitterness was audible in Gellar's voice, despite the smile that showed a set of nearly perfect teeth. Bolan had heard that tone before, from deep-cover agents disgusted with themselves for the things they had to do on the job, seeking absolution—or at least approval—from a stranger they had barely met, trust forged in battle, tempered by fire.

"I'm guessing that there's nothing I can do to help," Bolan said.

"Nothing at the moment," Gellar replied. "I would imagine you could use some rest."

Sleep was the furthest thing from Bolan's mind. He felt a certain measure of fatigue, but was conditioned to adapt, suck it up and move on. If nothing else, he would take time to clean and oil his weapons, reload magazines, take stock of the surviving targets he would strike, if all else failed.

But first, he had another job to do.

"Fact is," he said, "I need to make a call or two myself."

It had been hours since he'd been in touch with Marilyn Crouder, and Bolan knew she had to be worried, isolated from the action in a city where she didn't speak the language and her only friend was constantly in motion, following the enemy. And there was Hal...

"Make them from here," Gellar suggested. "I must go out, anyway, to reach the men I need to see."

"Okay, then, if you're sure," Bolan replied. "But watch your back."

"It is my specialty," Gellar replied, with more warmth in his smile this time. "I'll be in touch as soon as I have any news."

"I'll be here," Bolan said, already reaching for the telephone as Gellar left and locked the door behind himself.

ROTISLAV CHALOUPEK wasn't a man easily surprised, but the sound of Gerhard Steuben's voice on the telephone line achieved that result, while his leader's message nearly floored him. Still, Chaloupek was a man who took pride in his swift response to crises, and he was relieved to hear no tremor in his voice that would betray him.

"By all means," Chaloupek said, "I shall look forward to receiving you." No names or titles bandied about on the open line in this day and age, when electronic eavesdroppers were everywhere, their pernicious influence omnipresent.

"The same airfield as last time, then?" Gerhard Steuben asked.

"Yes, sir. I'll be there personally, with a small security detachment."

"Not too small," Steuben said, surprising Chaloupek again. "You are aware of what has happened in Berlin?"

Chaloupek wasn't a great reader, shunning books and most newspapers as propaganda rags controlled by scheming Jews and Communists. When he turned on the radio, he wanted music. Television was, except on those occasions when he feared pending indictment of himself or his associates, reserved for pornographic videocassettes and tapes made from old newsreels of the glory days, in World War II.

"I'm sorry, sir," he hedged, "but circumstances here—"

"I speak of treason," Steuben interrupted him, oblivious to the fumbled excuse. "There have been casualties. I will explain more when I see you. In the meanwhile, though, be watchful on your own account."

"Yes, sir."

"I'll be in touch at least an hour before we land," Steuben concluded.

"Yes, sir. Everything will be arranged."

The line went dead without goodbyes. Chaloupek checked his Rolex watch and discovered that Steuben had been on the line less than sixty seconds, apparently mindful of a possible trace. It was a wise precaution, all the more so when calling internationally, and Chaloupek was more concerned with his leader's comments than the brusque termination of the call.

"I speak of treason," the führer had said. "There have been casualties."

What casualties? What treason?

"Be watchful on your own account."

That much, at least, was unnecessary advice for Rotislav Chaloupek, national director of the Temple of the Nordic Covenant in the Republic of Croatia. Active in his homeland's civil war and ethnic-cleansing campaigns of the early 1990s, Chaloupek had once been indicted for war crimes, the epic list of charges dismissed when prosecution witnesses began to die or disappear, affidavits of the missing destroyed in an incendiary fire in March 1996. Since that time, he had immersed himself in the black market—weapons primarily, with a profitable sideline in drugs—and had missed no opportunity to punish Jews and any other undesirables he found within his reach. There was a reason why his enemies called him the "Butcher of Zdar."

Considering the source, Chaloupek took it as a compliment.

Distracted by the warning from his leader, still he started making calls and getting ready for the drive north to the secret, unpaved airstrip sixty-five kilometers southwest of Zagreb. The last time he had made that trip to meet Steuben had been almost two years earlier, when the führer embarked on a whirlwind tour of his European territories, laying early groundwork for their coordinated actions in the final days. Now, it was almost time to light that fuse, and Steuben was returning—but not in triumph, as a conqueror. Rather, he was slipping into Croatia as a fugitive, muttering darkly of treason and unexplained losses.

It was troubling, but Chaloupek was determined not to falter, not to fail. Whatever had happened in Berlin to trouble his führer so, the Butcher of Zdar would make it right.

And if that meant spilling blood, so much the better.

Killing was what Chaloupek did best.

The führer's words came back to him again: "Be watchful on your own account." If there were German traitors in the Temple of the Nordic Covenant, did that mean that there were Croat traitors, too? Chaloupek didn't want to think so, but he knew enough of human nature to expect the worst from everyone. With that philosophy of life, he found that he was seldom disappointed, and those rare disappointments always came as a pleasant surprise.

How many soldiers would he need for the security detachment? "Not too small," Steuben had said, meaning that trouble was anticipated on the ground. He would send ten or fifteen shooters to the airfield from Zagreb, and take another dozen with him from Zdar. Chaloupek—who was satisfied with one bodyguard himself, a pair for special occasions—couldn't visualize a situation in modern-day Croatia that required more than twenty-odd guns. Whatever had transpired in Germany, the führer had survived and he was getting out. There was no reason to believe the troubles there would follow him across three borders and five hundred miles.

No time to waste.

Chaloupek found a scratch pad near the telephone and ripped off the top sheet before he started writing a list of names, the soldiers he would summon to accompany him on his journey north. Using a single sheet of paper on the countertop prevented spies from creeping in and reading the impression of the names from "blank" sheets on the pad. And while Chaloupek realized that he was taking unnecessary precautions, that the chance of a prowler breaking in to read his private notes was slim to none, he had seen the technique used in an American crime movie, once, years ago. Employing it now made him feel clever, in tune with a broader underground society where subterfuge was second nature and sudden death was the coin of the realm.

When he was finished with his list making, Chaloupek reached for the nearby telephone and started making calls. He brooked no arguments and no excuses from the men who answered, spitting orders at them and abruptly hanging up before they could ask any questions or complain.

Whatever had gone wrong in Germany, Gerhard Steuben wouldn't find a weakling at the Nordic Temple's tiller in Croatia. They would face tomorrow's risks together, side by side.

And when the smoke cleared, Rotislav Chaloupek thought he might just rate promotion to the führer's second in command.

"THANK GOD you're all right!"

A warm sense of relief enveloped Marilyn Crouder,

nearly eclipsing the mixture of anxiety and anger that she had nursed for the past few hours, waiting for Mike Belasko to make contact, ultimately fuming when he failed to do so. While she spoke no German, she could still interpret the breaking news on local television, listening to excited newscasters jabber their voice-overs while video cameras captured scenes of sheet-draped or rubber-bagged bodies on stretchers being carried or wheeled out of various shops, offices and apartment houses scattered around Berlin.

The shit was coming down, and that chafed on her nerves for two reasons. First, because she was excluded from the action by Belasko's order. And second, because she feared that one of those bagged or shrouded corpses might be his.

"I'm fine," Bolan reassured her, sounding far away, although she knew it couldn't be that far. A few miles at the most, if he was still inside the city limits of Berlin.

"Where are you?" she asked him, suddenly suspicious.

"Here with Jacob," he replied, not telling her a thing. "We're working on some leads and trying to find out what happens next."

"I don't suppose there's any way that I could help you?" Feeling stupid even as she asked the question. What could *she* do in a city where she didn't know the players or the layout, didn't even speak the language? It would be a travesty.

"I think we've got it covered pretty well," Bolan said. "Truth is, I'm sitting on my hands while Jacob works his contacts." He was careful to avoid last names on open lines.

"Well, then, if you're not doing anything," she

said, "we could do it together." Blushing furiously, even as the comment echoed in her ears, her free hand rising to a cheek that radiated sudden heat.

"That's very tempting," he replied, ever the gentleman. "But I should really hang in here in case we have to jump on something in a hurry."

Jump on me, she almost said, shameless.

"Okay, then, I'll just hang out here and wait." She tried to keep it cheery, shied away from telling him it was his loss. He already knew that, and a damned sight more about loss, she suspected, than he would ever share.

"It shouldn't be much longer," he assured her.

"Right," she said. A sudden nagging thought took hold and worried at a corner of her mind. "You wouldn't ditch a girl, would you?" she asked him, cringing yet again but needing a response.

"Nobody's ditching you," he said. "But when we have to move, it may be in a hurry."

"Great," she told him, trying hard for bright and sparkly. "I'm already packed. Just give the word."

"And there's no telling where we might end up."

"It's not a job, it's an adventure. Right?"

"I thought that was the Navy," Bolan replied.

"So, what's the difference? I'm being all that I can be," she told him. "Looking for a few good men. Bring on that wild blue yonder, guy, and make it snappy."

It was good to hear his laughter on the other end, a measure of connection, although less intense than that which they had shared before they left the States. No follow-up on that, so far, and she admitted to a trace of disappointment, a dark cloud to go with the afterglow. If forced to wager, Marilyn Crouder would probably have said that Mike Belasko was concerned about her safety—and his own, hell yes, if they were bantering in the middle of a job that called for wet work on the scale the TV news revealed—but she couldn't entirely mute the small voice in her head.

There was something wrong, it said. Maybe she didn't please. Maybe she wasn't good enough.

"Yeah, right!"

"Excuse me?" Bolan said.

Blushing furiously, she replied, "Nothing. Forget it. I'm just getting senile here. Ignore me."

"Okay." He sounded hesitant. Concerned? "Well, I should go and see what Jacob's got. I'll be in touch as soon as we know anything for sure."

"I'll be here," she assured him. "With my knitting."

"Right. So long, then."

"Bye."

She beat him to the hangup, and so what if it was only by a fraction of a second? It was lame, but it was still the only victory she had to show, so far, for their sojourn in Germany.

Without Belasko's voice to interrupt her stream of consciousness, she started worrying again. Okay, he *said* he wouldn't ditch her and run off to parts unknown, but did he really mean it? Was there not at least an outside chance Belasko would decide that leaving her behind was in her own best interest? And if he made that chauvinistic choice, what could she do about it?

Squat.

She didn't know where he and Jacob Gellar were, and she had no means to trace his call. She wouldn't know if he left town—or left the country, for that matter—unless Belasko himself decided to enlighten her. Which he could do by calling her from anywhere on Earth, of course.

What did he think of her by now? There had been angry sparks when they first met, despite the fact that he had saved her from certain death, and it wasn't the last time he had stepped in at the crucial moment, when her life was on the line. So far, she had repaid the favor by defying his request that she refrain from mixing in the action, in Chicago and Los Angeles. Each time, her interference had increased Belasko's risk of getting wasted, but he didn't seem to bear a grudge. In bed, the one time they had coupled, he had seemed to like her very much indeed.

And nothing since.

She understood the cutoff; she had verbally agreed to it, in fact, in order to persuade him that her presence on the jaunt to Germany wouldn't be a colossal error. Now, her damned feelings were getting in the way again, but she was more afraid that Belasko and Gellar would abandon her, go off to finish the assignment on their own, when she had started it some eighteen months ago and half a world away.

For all that was worth, she thought, and recognized the pent-up bitterness inside herself. So far, her rough-and-ready approach to the job had gotten her bounced, for all intents and purposes, from her job at ATF, and now she had a sneaking hunch that her clandestine alliance with Mike Belasko, representing God knew what or whom, was on the verge of breaking up.

It made her want to cry—and that, in turn, immediately angered her.

"You try and ditch me, mister," she advised the empty hotel room, "and you'll regret it. Yes, you will. Hell hath no fury, Mr. B. You'd best remember that."

CHAPTER TWELVE

Meeting with neo-Nazis in Berlin—even the self-proclaimed "nonviolent" ones—was always hazardous. For starters, neo-Nazis weren't renowned for their stability; they were paranoid by definition, and many, perhaps most, were given to sudden, unpredictable tantrums. Paranoia aside, they also had enemies who might pop up at any time, on recognizing a prominent fascist, and try to initiate a violent confrontation, with bystanders caught in the cross fire. Finally, whenever Jacob Gellar met with neo-Nazis under cover, it was the ultimate test of his own self-control.

All things being equal, never miss a chance to kill a Nazi.

And the problem was, of course, that when he wanted information from a fascist source, when he was posing as a neo-Nazi himself, then Gellar had to put his guiding rule of life aside and listen to the venom spewing from his contacts, smile and pretend agreement with their hatred of Jews and all other minorities, join in the banter about looting, rape and murder.

Still, it was a small price to pay, he calculated, if it would allow him to destroy them in the end.

His meeting for that evening, so hastily arranged, was with a subcommander of the National Vanguard, one Ubel Finster. A short, wiry ferret of a man, Gellar reflected, Finster was notable at first glance for the dueling scar on his left cheek and the heavy sheen of oil that kept his dark hair slicked back, flat against his skull. He also dressed in black habitually, the only color in his wardrobe being pastel shirts.

If Finster had been taller, with a cloak perhaps, he could have passed for Dracula.

It was a challenge not to laugh at him, sometimes, but Gellar felt no mirth, as Finster stepped out of his car. The vehicle moved on, at least two other men inside it, checking Gellar out as Finster made his way across the grass, all smiles.

"Mr. Dortmunder!" he said, using the pseudonym Gellar assumed when he was posing as a neo-Nazi from Vienna. "How good it is to see you again, and in such marvelous surroundings."

Gellar had chosen the vast Tiergarten park as neutral ground, unclaimed by any neo-Nazi faction, with sufficient open space that he could spot any lurkers before the trap was sprung. He expected no trouble from Finster, but the neo-Nazi runt had enemies, including members of the rival Nordic Temple, who would gladly kill him if a risk-free opportunity presented itself.

"And you, Mr. Finster," Gellar offered in response. "I'm glad to see you still in fighting trim."

"I watch my diet," Finster told him. "Stay away from kosher foods, you can't go wrong."

They shared a laugh at that, Finster interrupting it to ask, "So, tell me, friend, what brings you to Berlin this time?"

"There have been threats against the party in Vienna from an unknown source," Gellar said, reciting the tale he had rehearsed on the drive over. "When we heard about the troubles in Berlin of late, it was decided I should come and look for any possible connection, maybe head the problem off before it spreads to Austria."

"About your threats, I couldn't say," Finster replied. "But as for troubles in Berlin, so far the only ones to suffer are the poseurs from the Temple of the Nordic Covenant. If you ask me, they have brought this down upon themselves. It's known the trouble started in America, where Gerhard Steuben hails from."

"Perhaps I ought to speak with Steuben, then," Gellar remarked.

"Good luck," Finster said, snorting out a kind of laugh. "He's hiding like a mouse and won't be here much longer, if my information is correct."

"He's leaving Berlin?"

"Leaving Germany, my friend," Finster corrected him. "No spirit for a fight, that one. Of course, what can you expect from an American? He's already let these bastards run him out of his own country, and now he runs from Germany. Our savior! What a hero! I've suspected for some time now that he may have Jewish blood, you know."

"I've never met the man," Gellar said noncommittally, "but I should try to get in touch with him. If nothing else, to satisfy Vienna that I've left no stone unturned."

"That's where you'll find Steuben, right enough," Finster said, grinning. "Under a rock."

"But if he's leaving," Gellar pressed, "where would he go?"

Gellar's companion shrugged at that. "Who knows? Who even cares? The man's more trouble than he's worth, if you want my opinion on the matter."

"Probably," Gellar agreed. "But I was thinking that if I can't see him in Berlin, perhaps I could catch up with him at his next stop."

"You're a detective now, I take it," Finster joked. "Well, if you must know, he approached a friend of mine—a private pilot, friendly to the cause—and tried to book a charter flight to Warsaw. Think of it! He wants to hide among the Polacks now, as if they cherish any love for Aryans. It's really too hysterical!"

"Warsaw, you say. When does he leave?"

"Who knows? Our friend the pilot had another job to do and couldn't take him on. For all I know, Steuben will be thumbing rides along the autobahn. Perhaps he'll hop a freight train. It would suit him well enough."

"Or, possibly your friend took sympathy on him, and recommended someone else? Another pilot?"

Finster shrugged. "It's possible, of course. I didn't ask, myself. I find pleasure enough in knowing that this fraud from the United States who calls himself an Aryan is running for his life. He's lost whatever little credibility he may have had in Germany, I promise you."

"It's just as well," Gellar replied, "a man like that. Still, I should talk to him, if possible. I have my orders, after all."

"Good luck to you, in that case," Finster said

again. "I'd help you if I could, of course, but with a coward like this one, who knows where he might be."

"If I could have a brief word with this pilot who rejected him, perhaps I might learn something," Gellar said.

"Of course, my friend, of course. His name is Waldo Rahn. He has a small place near the airport. I don't know the address or his phone number offhand, but he's in the directory."

"Waldo Rahn." Gellar repeated it to fix the name in his memory. "You have my thanks, Mr. Finster."

"Ubel, please! We're all friends here."

The car was coming back for Finster now as they shook hands and parted in the dusk, Gellar retreating toward his own vehicle on the far side of the park. The brisk walk gave him time to think.

He had a pilot to interrogate, and he could only hope that Waldo Rahn knew something, anything, that might prove useful.

In the meantime, fouled by Ubel Finster's touch, he would be stopping at the public men's room first, to wash his hands.

WALDO RAHN WAS RUNNING through the last-minute checkup on his twin-engine Mitsubishi MU2 Marquise when the stranger approached him on foot, coming out of the early-evening darkness and called him by name.

"Waldo Rahn?"

The pilot didn't answer immediately, sizing up the stranger who stood before him. The man was average height and weight, dressed stylishly enough, but without the flash of a big spender. Rahn judged his age somewhere in the mid to late thirties, but that was a guess. The two words he had thus far spoken betrayed no obvious accent, and there was nothing in the stranger's face that offered any clue to his nationality.

"Who looks for Waldo Rahn?" the pilot asked.

"Fritz Dortmunder," the stranger said, introducing himself without the offer of a handshake. "I'm a friend of Ubel Finster and the Vanguard. In fact, he told me where to find you."

"Ah." It wasn't quite a magic word, but it was close enough. "In that case, comrade, how may I help you?"

"As I told Ubel, earlier this evening, I'm trying to make contact with a man named Gerhard Steuben. He's the leader of—"

"I know who Gerhard Steuben is," Rahn interrupted him. "Why come to me?"

"I understand he sought your services," Dortmunder said. "A charter flight to Warsaw, I believe it was. You were unable to accommodate his needs."

"That's right," Rahn said. "Which means that you shouldn't expect to find him here."

"Quite so." There *was* a hint of accent to the stranger's German, after all. Was this how Austrians sounded? "I was hoping that you might have referred him to another pilot, someone with an open schedule."

"Oh? What if I did?"

"Then I would go and pester someone else with questions you can't answer—after paying for your time and help, of course."

"Paying how much?" the pilot asked.

"Perhaps a hundred marks," Dortmunder said.

"Make it two hundred, and you have a deal."

"Two hundred, then."

Dortmunder fished a hand inside his pocket, came out with a roll of notes and peeled off several, handing them to Rahn. The pilot was already wishing he had asked for more.

"The name?" Dortmunder prodded him.

"Ah, yes. I recommended that Mr. Steuben try his luck with Berdy Braun. Of course, I cannot guarantee he followed my advice, or that a deal was made."

"Of course not." Dortmunder was reasonable, sounded satisfied. "One other question, if I may?"

"What's that?"

"I'm simply curious...do you *believe* the master-race nonsense, or do you simply smile and take their money when it's offered to you for a job?"

Rahn felt the short hairs bristling on his nape, aware that something was terribly wrong. No Aryan would ponder such a sacrilegious question, much less utter it aloud. Who was this person, then? Whom did he represent?

Rahn had a wrench and a screwdriver in the right hip pocket of his denim coveralls. Holding Dortmunder's gaze, he let his hand slip backward toward the tools that could suffice as weapons in a pinch.

"You're not a friend of Ubel Finster," he accused.

"Oh, but I am," Dortmunder said. "I tell him what he wants to hear, and he gives me the information I require. You mustn't blame the man for being stupid, Waldo. Inside every Nazi is a moron, struggling to emerge."

"Are you a Jew, then?" Throwing out the worst insult that he could think of, almost close enough to tough the handle of his screwdriver.

"You're smarter than you look, Rahn," Dortmunder said. "Or, should I say, this time your paranoia has presented you with a correct interpretation of the facts. How does it feel, to know you're right for once? It can't be something you're accustomed to.''

Rahn's fingers closed around the plastic handle of the screwdriver. His enemy still had no weapons showing, but the pilot sensed that he would have to do it right the first time, that he might not get a second chance. As for the body, where to hide it, he could think about that later.

''I have no more time to bandy words with kikes,'' Rahn said with a sneer, and drew the eight-inch weapon from his pocket, lunging toward Dortmunder's face and throat. It didn't matter to him if he pierced the stranger's eye, nostril or larynx. What he needed was a killing—or, at least, a crippling—blow, to make the cleanup easier.

It was incredible, how swiftly his opponent moved, the hands a blur. One of them locked around Rahn's wrist and twisted, levering his elbow out and down in a direction it couldn't accommodate, the joint snapping loudly as pain flared through his arm and shoulder, on across his chest. Rahn tried to scream, but it was cut off, an abortive yelp, as Dortmunder's elbow smashed into his throat.

Gagging, unable to breathe, Rahn collapsed to the tarmac beside his airplane. The world was spinning, dark flecks swarming in his field of vision, as if his head were a spotlight and thousands of insects were drawn to its glare. His good arm fanned the air in front of him, met no resistance, and he knew the jiggling specks were on the inside of his eyes, somehow.

The good news was, they disappeared within a few short seconds, as the darkness stole in from his blind side, swallowed him, eclipsing sight and sound and smell, to leave him numb and drifting in the silent void.

THE KNOCK WAS soft, insistent. They hadn't worked out a code beforehand, leaving Bolan to approach the door with caution, the Beretta 93-R weighting his right hand. He had the pistol set for 3-round bursts and knew its Parabellum rounds would easily pierce the door if he had to open fire.

He leaned in toward the peephole cautiously, aware that bullets fly both ways, and was relieved to see Jacob Gellar standing outside in the hall, all alone. He had a key, of course, but would have courted death by using it without a warning knock. That much they *had* agreed upon before he left to mine his sources in Berlin.

Bolan unlocked the door and opened it, stepped back to let the Mossad agent pass, and double locked the door again once he was safe inside. Gone for nearly five hours, Gellar now crossed the room and sat down in the same chair he had occupied before he left, as if no time at all had passed. Instead of prodding him, Bolan sat down, relaxed and let him tell the story in his own way and his own good time.

"Steuben is gone," the Mossad agent said at last. "I'm afraid we've missed our opportunity to stop him in Berlin."

"Where did he go?"

Gellar seemed not to have heard the question. "You remember that I told you I would meet with Ubel Finster, an officer of the National Vanguard."

"Right," Bolan said, playing along.

"The Vanguard is Herr Steuben's primary rival for members in the German neo-Nazi movement, though its leaders outwardly disavow violence and concentrate their public efforts on elective politics. Of course, the Vanguard keeps tabs on the Nordic Temple as opportunity permits."

"Makes sense," Bolan replied.

"Herr Finster had already heard that Steuben planned to flee the city. He gave me the name of a charter pilot sympathetic to the neo-Nazi movement, whom Steuben had approached about a flight to Warsaw."

"He's going to Poland?" Bolan had no luck concealing his surprise.

"It was a ruse," Gellar replied. "The pilot, being unable to help Herr Steuben with his problem, in turn recommended a colleague for the job. It would appear the second pilot had an open schedule. When I checked, he had already left, four passengers on board."

"To Warsaw," Bolan said.

"Zurich," Gellar corrected him. "At least, that was the destination listed on his flight plan."

"Let me guess. It's bogus?"

"As you say. That information was a bit more difficult to come by, and accounts for the delay in my return," Gellar explained. "I had to spin a tale for one of Herr Braun's friends—the pilot's name is Berdy Braun—and thereby make connections with his woman."

Bolan smiled. "A pilot named Berdy? You're serious?"

The Mossad agent spelled it for him, then pressed on. "Herr Braun's young woman—and I do mean young—was most concerned to hear that he had left without one of his passengers, namely myself. As luck would have it, he had violated every known rule of security by giving her a number where he could be reached on landing, at the other end."

"But not in Zurich," Bolan guessed, "and not in Warsaw."

"In Zagreb," Gellar replied.

"Croatia?"

Nodding, Gellar said, "I should have guessed it, I suppose. The region was a stronghold of Nazi sympathy during World War II, with the Iron Guard eagerly assisting the SS in genocidal exercises, and it remains a hotbed of anti-Semitism today. The Temple of the Nordic Covenant has an active branch in Croatia, albeit smaller than the German and American chapters. The leader in Croatia, if I'm not mistaken, is a war criminal named Rotislav Chaloupek."

"Birds of a feather," Bolan said.

"But this one has experience with mass murder, from the civil war and ethnic cleansing days," Gellar observed. "While Steuben's lackeys in America and Germany talk a good game, beating up on Jewish shopkeepers and vandalizing synagogues, Chaloupek and his thugs have real blood on their hands. They've slaughtered Muslims, Jews, you name it. They have also been linked to drug-dealing by Interpol, thus far without indictments or prosecutions."

"A little profiteering to support the reich?" Bolan surmised.

"Or on their own behalf," Gellar said. "We know that few regimes in history have been more corrupt than Hitler's Third Reich, looting Europe at large for personal profit. As for drugs, Hermann Göring himself was a heroin addict, and he wasn't alone in his vice, by any means."

"So, we've got Nazi pushers in Croatia, and Stevens is going to ground in their backyard. Whatever he's got cooking as a backup plan, Chaloupek and his men sound like the types to help him pull it off."

"You'll wish to follow, then." It didn't come out sounding like a question. Gellar knew the answer, going in.

"As soon as possible," Bolan replied. "About that charter pilot you interviewed, the first one—"

"He won't be flying anymore," Gellar said. "His health took a sudden turn for the worse."

"But you can line up an alternative?"

"No problem. All it takes is money."

"Then we're cool," Bolan replied.

"It will be just the two of us?" Gellar asked, plainly hoping that the answer would come back affirmative.

"Give me an hour," Bolan said, thinking of Marilyn Crouder, "and I'll get back to you on that."

"CROATIA?" Crouder was startled at first, but she recovered quickly, putting a lid on the mental images of mass graves and bombed-out villages with starving children screaming in the rubble of their former homes. That was ancient history, she told herself. Five years ago, at least. Now, she thought, Zagreb was probably a safer place to window-shop than New York City or Los Angeles.

"Croatia," Bolan repeated, confirming it. "I've got an hour, give or take, before Gellar reports on the flight arrangements. He's working on some kind of charter."

"And?" She had a hunch as to what was coming

next, but didn't want to blow it, put any negative thoughts in his mind, in case she was wrong.

"And, since we're several light-years out of U.S. jurisdiction, I was thinking this would be as good a time as any for the ATF to disengage."

So, there it was.

"Sounds good to me," she said. "When do you plan to tell the ATF?"

"Look, Marilyn—"

"Because, as I recall," she interrupted him, "*they* disengaged from *me* before we left the States. They busted me, remember? Is that ringing any kind of bell at all?"

The sat facing each other in her hotel room, the suite they had rented together shortly after their arrival in Berlin. It was the first time Belasko had crossed that threshold since he had left with Jacob Gellar, almost forty-eight hours ago, and he was only there now in an attempt to blow her off, send her packing with a wink and a handshake.

"Okay," he said, "I think it's time for *you* to disengage. From this point on, it will be dangerous."

She almost laughed aloud at that. "I see. Is it more dangerous than home, where they tried to kill me four times? Where I was raped and tortured? Is it more dangerous than here, where you've already killed, what is it, forty, fifty men these past two days? What kind of danger did you have in mind, Mike? Make it good, because I've basically been there and done that, where the mighty *danger* is concerned."

"The Nazis we've been dealing with in Germany are amateurs, compared to those we may find waiting for us in Croatia, Marilyn. They're not just trigger-happy bookworms with a yen to reenact the Third

Reich's good old days. They've been there, very recently, with civil war, mass murder, ethnic cleansing, concentration camps. This isn't jumping from the frying pan into the fire," he said. "We're jumping into a volcano."

"Then it makes no sense for you to go at all," she said, "but if you're going, you need all the help that you can get."

"What help?" he asked her. "You have no Croat contacts, you don't speak the language—"

"And you do?" she challenged him. "Let's hear you ask directions to the washroom in Croatian."

"Marilyn, that's—"

"Different?" she interrupted him. "And why is that, pray tell? Because I'm Barbie, and you're G.I. Joe, the one-man army? Wake up and smell the new millennium, my friend. The old-boys' club is closed for renovations, and it's not a man's world anymore."

"This has nothing to do with gender," Bolan replied.

"Oh, no? What is it, then?"

"The sad fact is that when the heat's on, I can't trust you."

The pronouncement hit her like a sucker punch to the stomach. Crouder could feel the angry color draining from her face.

"You broke your word," Bolan told her, forging on before she had a chance to speak. "First, you agree to stay out of the line of fire, but when I turn around, you're in the middle of it. In Los Angeles, it almost got you killed and may have been responsible for Fletcher slipping through the net."

"Oh, please!" The heat and color coming back. "You know as well as I do—"

"In Chicago, you were looking for revenge," Bolan pressed on, talking over her. "I can't fault you for that, but you still broke your word—the second time—and people died."

"The bad guys died!" she snapped. "And while we're on the subject of Chicago, don't forget who saved your ass from—"

Suddenly, she caught herself, blinking. It was as if someone had switched the burner off beneath the cauldron of her rage, or maybe killed the pilot light itself.

"I see," she told him in a softer, calmer voice. "So, this is how you do it, then?"

"Do what?" Bolan asked.

"Dispose of obstacles, particularly clinging vines. You piss them off so badly that they storm out in a snit and let you go about your merry way? Forget it, pal. It isn't working."

"I meant what I said," he told her.

"Which?" she asked. "About the danger, or my breaking promises?"

"Both parts."

"All right, how's this—the danger is a given, and I'm used to it. Not in Croatia, granted, but I spent the better part of eighteen months inside the Nordic Temple, and I haven't done so badly since you bailed me out. I *did* drop Fletcher when he was about to serve you up with salad on the side."

"There's still—"

"The promises, I know," she said. "I'm not excusing what I did in L.A. or Chicago, but you can't claim I've pulled any stunts in Germany. I've been the perfect little hausfrau, sitting on my butt and waiting for the menfolk to come home. Two days without a peek at you, and barely any word, but you'll recall I didn't strafe the Reichstag or go hunting skinheads at the local beer garden."

"Gellar thinks it's a bad idea to bring you in," Bolan said.

"So, he can keep ignoring me," she said. "He's done a good job of it, so far. And I am in, just in case you hadn't noticed. I was in before you ever heard of Gary Stevens and the Temple of the Nordic Covenant. It's my fight more than yours. I'm claiming it." She hesitated, wondering if she should voice the rest, then went ahead. "I need it, Mike."

"You could be killed," he said.

"You say that like it's news."

"It won't be pretty, and you absolutely, positively cannot be involved."

She smiled and said, "When do we leave?"

"CROATIA?"

There was nothing wrong with the transatlantic telephone line, but Hal Brognola still had trouble believing his ears. If Bolan had said he was flying off to Tomboctou or Oz, it would hardly have been more surprising.

"Zagreb, specifically," Bolan replied. "I wouldn't go so far as to assign that as our final destination, though."

"Whatever." Brognola dismissed the fine point of geography, fanning the air with one hand as if Bolan could see it. Swiftly, silently, he ran down what he knew about the relatively new Republic of Croatia. A contested, often occupied battleground since medieval times, it had become a part of Yugoslavia after World War II. Independence had finally come in 1991, followed immediately by brutal conflict between ethnic Serbs and Croats. A 1992 cease-fire had collapsed the following year, Serbs declaring a makeshift Republic of Krajina in 1994, only to see it overrun by Croat government troops in 1995. Peace accords had been signed with neighboring Bosnia and Serbia by year's end, and President Franjo Tudjman had been reelected in 1997, the climax of a contest which international monitors deemed "free but not fair." The last Serb-held enclave had surrendered to Croat troops in January 1998, theoretically ending the carnage.

Brognola wasn't precisely sure where the Nazis fit in, but they were past masters at ethnic cleansing on an epic scale, and he seemed to recall something about Nazi sympathizers running amok in Croatia during World War II. Whatever, it was one of the more treacherous places on earth, scarcely better than the slaughterhouse of Bosnia and Herzegovina, right next door.

And now, Bolan was plunging into that benighted morass, accompanied by a Mossad agent and a woman with no official standing whatsoever.

"Tell me again why you're taking the lady," he said.

"It was her case to start with," Bolan replied. "She knows the Nordic Temple inside out. She may be some help."

"Or she may get you killed."

"I'm not worried."

"You should be," Brognola told him. "Croatia's a grade-A disaster area, no matter what they put on the tourist brochures. Bosnians get the headlines, but their neighbors are every bit as rowdy. You're going in with an Israeli and a female civilian, to try to clean house. Do you even have a phrase book for the local lingo?''

"Gellar has some contacts in Zagreb. He tells me they're reliable.''

"Is that 'Mossad reliable'? Because we've had some problems there, in case you haven't heard.''

"I've heard,'' Bolan replied. "If you've got someone better we can hook up with, I'm listening.''

"You want to know the truth,'' Brognola said, "there aren't a lot of people east of Paris that I trust right now. None of them fit the bill for this job. Not a one.''

"Okay. That narrows down the field.''

"I can't help thinking that it's hard enough to swim in quicksand, and the woman's only bound to weigh you down.''

"If we don't follow through, then Stevens gets away,'' Bolan reminded him. "That's still the bottom line. And from the samples of his work I've seen the past few days, I can't imagine that he's going to retire and disappear. He's not just looking forward to the last days, Hal, he's got himself convinced that it's his job to bring the whole thing down.''

"Well—''

"As for Marilyn,'' the Executioner continued, "she may be a help or she may not. The bottom line is that I can't afford to ditch her here. She'd hop the next flight out and follow us, which means a wild card in the game, just when we need to concentrate.''

"Nobody said you had to leave her on the loose,'' Brognola said.

There was a momentary silence on the other end. "I didn't hear that,'' Bolan told him, sounding grim.

"I didn't mean— Oh, hell, you know me better

than that!'' The intimation needled him. ''One way
to go, you drop her at the U.S. Embassy and let the
FBI or the Marines sit on her for a while, then ship
her stateside, under guard, if necessary.''

''Where her first stop is the newsroom of the *New
York Times*,'' Bolan suggested. ''Are you ready for
that kind of ink?''

Brognola thought about it. Crouder knew nothing
about Stony Man, had never heard his name, could
offer nothing but an alias and police sketch artist's
rendering of Bolan's face to document reports of an
elaborate clandestine agency devoted to eradicating
neo-Nazi scum around the world. In fact, her worm's-
eye view of what the Farm and its field agents really
did was so restricted, so distorted, her documentation
so ephemeral, the big Fed doubted that the story
would ever run at all.

Still...

''What if she pulls another fast one where you're
going?'' he asked Bolan. ''I don't know the lady, but
so far, she doesn't strike me as a poster child for
Promise Keepers.''

''We've already had that talk,'' Bolan replied.
''Whatever happens, if she goes back on her word
again, I'm ready to take care of it.''

Whatever *that* meant. Bolan wasn't just the Executioner; at the same time, inside, he was the soldier
who had once been labeled Sergeant Mercy in the
Asian killing fields. And sometimes, Hal Brognola
thought, the two diverse personae weren't compatible.

''All right,'' he said at last. ''I don't like second-
guessing agents on the line. That doesn't mean I buy
your argument,'' he added. ''I assume we're clear on
that.''

"We're clear," Bolan replied. "And you're absolved."

"Too late for that," the man from Justice said. "You watch yourself in there, all right?"

"Sounds like a plan. I'll be in touch."

"You'd better be," Brognola said. But he was talking to dead air.

CHAPTER THIRTEEN

Croatia

"You're sure about this target?" Bolan asked his two companions, leaning forward in the back seat of the moving compact car.

"I sure," the driver said, shifting his gaze as he spoke to make brief eye contact with Bolan in the drooping rearview mirror. "No mistake, okay."

The driver's name was Agoston Domokos. He was thirty-something, a Croat known to Jacob Gellar by some means that the Israeli agent hadn't bothered to explain. Presumably, Mossad had eyes and ears throughout the region, including splintered Yugoslavia, and the rise of anti-Semitism, coupled with proliferating arms deals and heightened potential for mercenary terrorism, would have maintained Tel Aviv's interest in news from the former Warsaw Pact nations. As far as trusting Domokos, Bolan had pretty much placed his life in Gellar's hands from the moment they boarded the charter flight in Berlin. The best that he could do now was to stay alert, keep his fingers crossed and sell his life dearly if anything went wrong, taking any traitors with him when he bought the farm.

In the meantime, they had places to go and Nazis to kill.

"He knows about the Nordic Temple, right?" Bolan addressed his question to Gellar, riding up front in the shotgun seat.

But it was Agoston Domokos who replied. "Temple of Nordic Covenant, Iron Cross, is all the same," he said. "They all like this." To demonstrate, he lifted both hands from the compact's steering wheel and clasped them tightly, knuckles blanching with the force of his grip. The car began to drift and nearly flattened two squealing pedestrians before Domokos took control and veered back toward the center of the street, heedless of blaring horns behind them.

They were navigating through the narrow, crowded streets of Zagreb, a city that—at least to Bolan's eyes—lacked even the superficial charm of most European capitals. The classic architecture was there, of course—or, rather, that which had survived the country's brutal civil war was still intact, more or less—but everywhere he looked, Bolan beheld a city mired in poverty, untended and unloved, beset by apathy at best and brooding grief at worst. The clothing sported by pedestrians was almost uniformly drab, conservative, almost funereal. Small wonder, Bolan thought, that you could search in vain for tourist handbooks on the wonders of Croatia beckoning to foreign visitors.

Who, in his right mind, wanted to vacation at a wake?

"The Iron Cross are the skinheads, right?" Bolan said, making conversation as they sped along one teeming street after another, a mobile accident waiting to happen.

"That's correct," Gellar replied. "They occupy the same position as the Thunderbolt Brigade in Germany and have the same affiliation with the Nordic Temple. All unofficial, of course. If there's a major difference, besides the language, it would be that members of the Iron Cross are more violent than their German counterparts."

"We should expect a warm reception, then," Bolan commented.

"I believe that they will not anticipate us," Gellar said. "We should have time to damage them a bit before they organize a good defense. If we are lucky, one of them may know Gerhard Steuben's whereabouts."

"We could be asking someone from the Nordic Temple that," Bolan reminded him.

"And so we shall," Gellar replied. "The Temple has an office in Zagreb, although its headquarters is situated in Zdar, about 250 kilometers due south, on the Adriatic coast. I thought you would prefer to see some action right away. How do you say it in America—get in some licks?"

"That's what we say."

He thought of Marilyn Crouder, waiting in yet another hotel room, sidelined from the action by her promise to remain in place and out of sight. Bolan had less concern for her safety in Zagreb than he had in the States, or even in Berlin, since language posed a more formidable barrier. If she tried to take off on her own, she would be lucky to find a cabdriver who spoke rudimentary English, and she had to understand that prowling Zagreb without a trustworthy interpreter would be tantamount to suicide. That was enough to keep her safe and sound...or so he hoped.

They had been on the ground for ninety minutes, give or take. Domokos had met their charter flight at a rural airstrip outside Zagreb, thus circumventing Customs and avoiding any troublesome inspection of their weapons-laden luggage. He had driven them directly from the plane to their hotel, where three rooms were reserved and waiting. Bolan gave the place two stars, although Domokos confidently told them it was one of Zagreb's best. All things considered, and from what he'd seen so far, the Executioner suspected that was no exaggeration.

"How much farther?" Gellar asked their guide.

"Not far," Domokos said, bobbing his head as if the question had required a yes-or-no response. "Perhaps one mile."

Their destination, as he understood it, was a kind of social club that members of the Iron Cross patronized exclusively. Perhaps they owned it outright; he couldn't pretend to understand completely everything Domokos said, so far. Their guard had promised several nice, ripe targets in Zagreb, and would convey them to Zdar, he said, if such a trip proved necessary to complete their mission.

Bolan hoped that it wouldn't, but he was ready for the worst. As always, right.

Despite the weary, rundown look of nearly everything in sight, Bolan could detect a not so subtle change for the worse in real estate as they continued on their way. Buildings were smaller here, their sooty facades even less imposing than those at the heart of downtown Zagreb, some shops closed with the windows whitewashed or boarded over. Here and there, gutted storefronts bore mute witness to raging fires; whether accidental or intentional, Bolan couldn't guess. Zagreb wasn't as bad as the unreconstructed district of Berlin, where he and Gellar had ambushed the Thunderbolt Brigade a few days earlier, but it still had the blighted look of war zones the world over, its populace composed of walking wounded whose worst wounds bled out through the eyes.

Without a clear view of the compact car's odometer, Bolan had to guesstimate the distance they had traveled, since their driver had pegged the remaining trip at one mile. He was about to ask how distance was measured in Croatia, when Domokos eased down on the brake and declared, "This is the place."

The social club was nothing to write home about. It had no windows facing on the street, its once red door had faded to a washed-out pink and spray-painted graffiti scarred the walls. Bolan couldn't come close to reading it, but from the look, there were no compliments included in the jet-black scrawl.

"What's that about?" he asked their driver, nodding toward the paint-daubed building as they passed.

"Someone challenges the Iron Cross to fight," Domokos told him. "Most probably, they are dead now."

"And the skinheads leave the challenge painted on their clubhouse?"

"If the fate of those who painted it be known," Domokos said, "the challenge is a warning in itself."

He had a point, and Bolan concentrated on a quick scan of the block as they rolled past. It wouldn't do to circle endlessly, alerting any hidden lookouts. He saw no hidden sentries, but there could be peepholes, maybe spotters in some other building on the block, peering through curtained windows, automatic weapons ready to unload on any interlopers.

No.

If they had that kind of security around the club, no tagger could have sprayed his challenge on the wall to start with.

Then again, perhaps the hidden guards—if they existed—were a relatively new addition, their assignment prompted by the vandalism itself.

"How do you know if anyone's inside?" he asked.

"Some of them always there," Domokos said. "Some live there."

"You wouldn't know how many, I suppose?"

The driver shook his head at that. "Is never twice the same," he said. "Some go, more come. Is not hotel, with registry for the police to check."

"I recommend we go in through the back," Gellar remarked. "There is an alley, yes?"

"Sure, alley. Car not fit," Domokos said, "but I drive back around and watch the front, stop any Iron Cross coming out that way."

So saying, Domokos leaned forward, shoving one hand underneath the driver's seat, and came out with a sawed-off double-barreled shotgun. Bolan couldn't make out the model, but it was old, the twin external hammers making it resemble something that a stagecoach guard might once have carried to defend Wells Fargo's mail on the American frontier.

"I'd say we're covered, then," Gellar remarked, and turned to flash a mirthless smile at Bolan. "Are you ready?"

"Ready as I'll ever be," the Executioner replied, easing his Spectre submachine gun from the duffel bag that rested at his feet. He slipped spare magazines into the outer pockets of his coat, adding two Russian frag grenades for backup, just in case.

"Let's do this thing," he said.

THE BACK DOOR to the social club was locked, of course. They stood in darkness, breathing the odor of rancid garbage, while Jacob Gellar crouched before the door, a penlight clenched in his teeth, and plied his metal picks on the first of two locks he would have to defeat.

So far, it wasn't going well.

"It's taking too long," Belasko said.

"I'll get it," Gellar said, forcing more confidence into his voice than he felt.

"We don't have time," the tall American replied. "Step back."

Belasko had a pistol in his hand, its muzzle bulky with a sound suppressor that still seemed smaller than normal. Some kind of custom job, Gellar decided, courtesy of the CIA or whomever the man worked for.

"If there are guards inside—"

"We'll have to take them down before they tip off the others," Bolan said, completing his thought with a whole different twist.

Gellar dropped the picks into his pocket and drew the mini-Uzi from under his raincoat. It was fitted with a suppressor, too, in a concession to the neighborhood and basic stealth. They didn't know how many members of the Iron Cross were inside the clubhouse, or how well they might be armed. The longer they could put off rousing active opposition, Gellar thought, the safer they would be.

And he was all for safety at the moment, even

though he stood in peril of an imminent and bloody death.

Belasko took a long step backward, away from the door, and sighted down the slide of his pistol. It was a Beretta, Gellar saw now, one of the selective-fire 93-Rs. He braced himself, prepared for all hell to break loose, as his companion fired one muffled round into the dead bolt and another at the doorknob, fairly blowing it away.

The shots were muffled, but the impact of those bullets sounded like a hammer clanging on the metal door and locking mechanism. Gellar couldn't help but grimace, but then he had no time for further thought. Belasko stepped forward, leg raised for a flying kick that flung the door back into murky half light, opening their way into a kind of storeroom with a corridor directly opposite.

The next time Gellar glanced at Belasko, the American had stashed his pistol out of sight and held the Spectre submachine gun ready, close against his side, where he would have no problem with the recoil. The SMG, like his own weapon, had been fitted with a sound suppressor, this one conventional in profile, adding eight or nine inches to the Spectre's compact length.

Checking the empty storeroom took only a moment. As they moved into the corridor together, following the distant sounds of music, it occurred to Gellar that they might just pull it off. From all appearances, the Iron Cross skinheads they were hunting hadn't heard them breach the door, and there was no alarm to bring them running with their weapons.

That was careless. It would soon prove fatal.

Doors opened off the corridor to either side, Gellar

and Bolan quickly checking each in turn, finding only dark and silent rest rooms, a janitorial closet, a squalid kitchen, an untenanted office that reeked of cigar smoke. Moving on, they homed in on what seemed to be the main room of the social club, separated from the hallway by a swing door that had a porthole window set about chest level for a man of average height.

"The master race must come a little shorter in Croatia," Gellar said, keeping his voice down as they neared the door, light showing through its porthole from the room beyond.

"People keep telling me size doesn't matter," Bolan said, smiling thinly as he raised his submachine gun, ready to open fire at the first sign of active resistance.

Gellar leaned close to peer through the Plexiglas window, scanning the club room as best he could without revealing himself to his foes. The part of it that he could see was roughly thirty feet by fifteen or twenty, with small, round wooden tables spotted around the floor at irregular intervals, as if they were shoved around often and rarely put back in their original places. There were two horseshoe booths to his left, one empty, the other occupied by four skinheads sharing a pitcher of stout. Of twenty tables he could see, approximately half were occupied by two or three skinheads each. One table boasted four young neo-Nazis, jammed so close together that they kept knocking elbows. Off to Gellar's right, there was a wet bar, but he couldn't see if it was manned, or whether anyone was drinking there. The music, with a vaguely martial air, came from a set of ceiling-mounted speakers, situated in the corners of the room.

"It's bad," he told Bolan. "There's some kind of

party going on. I make it close to fifty targets, and I still can't see the north end of the room."

Bolan took his place before the porthole, craned his head in both directions, counting silently. When he stepped back again, he had a grim expression on his face.

"No weapons showing, but we have to figure most of them are packing side arms, anyway," he said. "Close range, that many guns unloading, even if they're drunk, they could get lucky."

"You want to leave?" Gellar asked. He was shamed by the idea, more so by his own undeniable urge to cut and run.

"I didn't say that."

The American released his submachine gun to hang by its shoulder strap, against his flank, and he plunged both hands into the pockets of his overcoat, coming out with two apple-green fragmentation grenades.

"I'm thinking we should crank the party up another notch," Bolan said, "and make our entrance with a bang."

So much for stealth.

Gellar accepted one of the grenades from his companion, held it in his right hand and pulled the pin with his left, careful to maintain his grip on the spoon. The grenade's four-second fuse wouldn't be activated until he released the spring-loaded lever to begin the deadly countdown.

When he glanced up again, Gellar saw that his companion had primed his own grenade, holding it cupped in his left hand, the fingers of his right clutching the Spectre's pistol grip.

"On three?" he asked.

"On three," Gellar agreed.

AGOSTON DOMOKOS TOOK a long drag on his cigarette and waited for the killing to begin. His nervous eyes flicked constantly between the rearview mirror and the windshield of his battered, aging Yugo compact, checking out the street in both directions for a hint of any hostile presence. In his lap, the Bernardelli Italia 12-gauge shotgun was ready to rip, its original thirty-inch barrel sawed off within a half inch of the forearm, its walnut stock truncated to a crude pistol grip swathed in black friction tape. Beside him, on the hump next to the driver's seat, a grease-stained paper bag held extra shotgun shells, a hasty mix of bird- and buckshot, with perhaps a few rifled slugs thrown in by mistake.

Domokos lit a fresh cigarette from the stub of his last one and pitched the butt into the gutter. An ardent smoker at the best of times, the Croat chain-smoked when his nerves threatened to get the better of him, as they were just now.

There had been few such moments lately, he reflected, but they couldn't be avoided altogether in the life that he had chosen for himself. Surviving chiefly on the proceeds from assorted petty crimes—blackmarketing, smuggling, commercial theft, the occasional burglary—Domokos had contrived to supplement his income by dabbling in the cloak-and-dagger world of espionage. It was a risky sideline, but Croatia was ripe for such business since independence, with clandestine services from Russia, Britain, United States and half a dozen other nations clamoring for fresh intelligence on war crimes, political trends and the potential for a Communist revival in the area. Contrary to the slurs about Jews being tight with money, Agoston Domokos found Mossad to be most generous in paying for the kind of information he was able to provide, via his contacts in the underworld and sundry political fringe groups. Of course, there was a downside, as well. The occasional risk to life and limb.

Like this night.

Domokos had no grudge against the Iron Cross personally, but he wouldn't hesitate to shoot a skinhead, either, if it meant his life—or if it meant another juicy payday from the man he knew as Lazarus. The tall man who accompanied his contact this time was a stranger, an American by the sound of him, and he held no interest for Domokos beyond the fact that he was clearly friends with Lazarus—and thus, perhaps, a source of cash or other favors sometime in the future. It was best, therefore, to help both of his recent passengers remain alive, if possible.

Domokos checked his watch and grimaced when he saw that Lazarus and the American had been inside the Iron Cross clubhouse for the better part of five minutes, already. Unless, of course, they had been waylaid and disposed of in the alley, before they could gain entry to the building. In which case, Domokos thought, he should be on his way to safer streets before—

The two explosions came so close together that the second could have been an echo of the first. Despite the muffling walls, it sounded to Domokos as if someone had just fired the largest double-barreled shotgun in creation, squeezing off one barrel right behind the other.

Time to play.

He spit his half-smoked cigarette through the driver's window, took the Bernardelli shotgun from its place across his lap and thumbed the hammers back, left-right. He braced an elbow on the padded windowsill of the driver's door, shifting slightly to obtain a better field of fire. His first and second fingers found the Bernardelli's twin triggers, resting lightly against the curved tongues of steel as he waited for targets to surface.

If he was lucky, Domokos thought, there would be none. Lazarus and the American would find a few skinheads inside and kill them there, without allowing any to escape through the front door and onto the street. It was their plan, and he wished them luck, preferring to do as little work as possible for his money. Driving was one thing, but killing...

He debated charging extra for the mission, but imagined that Lazarus might take it badly. In which case, there could be hell to pay.

If he offended Lazarus too badly, at the very least he could expect Mossad to find a more agreeable contact to take their money in the future. There were doubtless more of Domokos's countrymen on the Israeli payroll even now. He was expendable, at best.

At worst, they might decide to silence him forever, to make sure he couldn't finger Lazarus or run and sell his meager knowledge of their operations to the state police. That notion, more than any other, helped him focus on the door in front of him and hold the Bernardelli shotgun steady while he waited for his human targets to emerge, still hoping none of them would reach the sidewalk.

He heard the sound of gunfire now, coming from somewhere in the building he had covered with his shotgun. Pistols, from the sound of it, and no small number of them, either. Lazarus and the American were armed with automatic weapons, he recalled, both fitted with suppressors, but that was wasted effort if the enemy made no attempt to mute its own gunfire.

The nervous eyes began to shift again, scanning the block to left and right, seeking pedestrians or sudden lights that would suggest a shopkeeper or tenant roused from sleep, perhaps considering if it was wise to summon the authorities. In this part of Zagreb, Domokos knew, the first instinct was to ignore any disturbance that didn't immediately threaten life or limb. Wife beaters, rowdy drunkards, teenage vandals and the like were more or less ignored whenever possible, unless there was some kind of personal relationship involved, a bond of duty. Even then, it would be even money as to whether someone from the neighborhood would call police or grab a piece of metal pipe and try to solve the problem on his own.

With gunfire and explosions, though, it was a different game. Someone would surely hear the racket and alert police, even if they remained anonymous. How long before the sirens started wailing and patrol cars filled with men in uniform, with automatic weapons of their own, converged upon the scene?

As if in answer to his thought, the front door of the club burst open, spilling light and shadows on the pavement. Three men piled out, with others close behind. Domokos didn't try to count them, didn't check to see if they were armed. He had his orders, and he knew what he had to do.

He squeezed one of the Bernardelli's triggers, braced against the recoil, then unloaded with the second barrel half a second later. Buckshot pellets, spreading rapidly from the abbreviated muzzle of his weapon, struck the startled skinheads like a storm of shrapnel, dropping them amid a cloud of plaster dust from the clubhouse facade.

Domokos broke open the shotgun, heard the empty casings strike the roof behind him, rattling as they dropped back to the floorboard. He reloaded swiftly from the paper bag, snapped shut his weapon, covering the door again, where other men were crouching now, afraid to show themselves.

"Come on to Papa," Domokos whispered to them in the smoky night. "Come out and play."

THE DOUBLE BLAST of the grenades gave Bolan the advantage he desired, shrapnel still slicing through the air and gouging divots in the walls as he pushed through the swing door with Jacob Gellar close behind him. It was chaos in the club room, several of the wooden tables capsized, chairs and prostrate bodies scattered, other targets lurching to their feet or scrabbling around the floor on hands and knees, groping for weapons, trying to decipher what had happened to their party.

Off to Bolan's right, he saw another six or seven skinheads at the bar, one of them leaking crimson from a scalp wound, all stunned into fleeting immobility. Behind the bar, a fat man with a tattoo of a reptile on his round, bald head was stooping, reaching down around his knees for what had to be a weapon of his own.

It was a place to start, and Bolan hit him with a short burst from the Spectre, stitching him across the broad expanse of chest, slamming him backward, down and out of sight. Unless some of the barkeep's bulk was Kevlar, worn beneath a sweat-stained denim shirt, that made it one more down, with thirty-five or forty left to go.

He swept on with his submachine gun, raked the skinheads at the bar, and caught them frozen somewhere between shock and outrage. Bolan's Parabellum manglers tore through flesh and fabric, shattered beer mugs into foaming geysers, spilling blood and lager on the bar.

Behind him, Jacob Gellar was engaging dazed survivors of the twin explosions, with return fire coming in from skinheads crouched behind upturned tables or huddled in booths along the southern wall. Dodging a stray round from some unseen handgun, Bolan ducked behind a nearby table, tipped it on its side and peered around it as he started seeking targets in the smoky room.

There was a movement toward the exit, something like a dozen skinheads disengaging, breaking toward the street, and Bolan let them go. Gellar's Croat sidekick was waiting outside to receive them, and even if they got past him, their exodus could only shave the hostile odds. For Bolan's money, if a few of the Iron Cross commandos got away, the tales they spread by word of mouth could only help demoralize his future targets in Zagreb.

Two burly shooters rose as if on cue, sighting in Gellar with their pistols, squeezing off wild rounds before they made target acquisition. Gellar spun to face them, taking one down with a burst from his mini-Uzi, and Bolan surprised the other, stitching him beneath his left arm with a zigzag from the Spectre. Both fell thrashing to the blood-slick floor and didn't rise again.

There was no time for thanks or high signs as the

firefight continued, skinheads dodging and sprawling around the club room, Bolan and Gellar tracking them with automatic fire, reloading as they emptied one magazine after another. Spent brass rolled and clattered on the linoleum floor, making footing treacherous in places.

Even with the crackle of gunfire in the club room, Bolan heard the louder, heavier sound of shotgun blasts from outside, as the skinhead refugees made it to the sidewalk. He wished Domokos well, then put the problem out of mind and focused on survival for himself and Jacob Gellar, still confronted with the bulk of the Iron Cross survivors.

A lanky youth with tattoos twined around both skinny arms came out of nowhere, rushing Bolan from his blind side, firing wildly with twin chrome-plated revolvers. Fear or excitement spoiled his aim at first, but he was getting closer by the heartbeat, and Bolan knew he had no time to waste.

Pivoting in a crouch, he cut the tattooed gunner's legs from under him, then met him with a rising burst that opened up his scrawny chest and knocked his lower jaw askew before he hit the floor. A shiver racked the dying skinhead's form, then he lay still.

Too close, Bolan thought as he checked the room behind him, seeing no more signs of life back there. Granted, it didn't mean that some of those he had already shot were not still breathing, maybe waiting for a chance to shoot him in the back, but he couldn't afford the time required to visit each of them in turn and make sure with a point-blank coup de grâce. The more-obvious living opponents took priority, with their hardware and potential for inflicting lethal damage.

And there were fewer live opponents now, he saw, as Gellar sprayed the horseshoe booths at the south end of the room with his mini-Uzi, toppling bodies from the vinyl-covered seats, pinning others beneath the tables and finishing them there. What had been temporary refuge for the neo-Nazi skinheads thus became a slaughter pen.

More shotgun blasts echoed from the street, and Bolan saw a backwash of survivors from the exodus lurching into the club room, some of them bloodied, others looking dazed. He met them with automatic fire and chopped them down like targets in a shooting gallery, before they had a chance to recover from their initial shock outside.

So much for word of mouth.

The last survivors of the skinhead drinking party had been driven toward the middle of the room for cover, tipping over tables as they went, pegging wild shots at one or the other of their assailants. Bolan was briefly reminded of paintings from American West, with wagons drawn up in a circle, pilgrims making their last-ditch stand against bandits or painted tribesmen. There was no such romance or adventure in the present scene, however. It was simply butcher's work, the challenge being to annihilate the enemy before one of them scored a hit by skill or pure dumb luck.

Wishing for another frag grenade, Bolan could only make do with the arms at his disposal, and he signaled Gellar with a lifted arm, catching the Israeli's attention for a moment as he paused to reload his mini-Uzi.

"On three!" Bolan called to his comrade, trusting that the young skinheads huddled in their makeshift fortress at the center of the club room spoke no English, or at least wouldn't divine his meaning. Gellar nodded in response, snapping a fresh magazine into the Uzi's pistol grip, and Bolan braced himself, the muscles bunching in his calves and thighs.

"One!" Bolan shouted.

"Two!" Gellar answered.

"Three!" the two of them said together, bursting from cover and rushing their handful of surviving adversaries from opposite directions, firing as they ran, bullets ripping into tables, bodies, floor and walls.

Some of the skinheads died on their knees, trying to line up a shot that would save them, cut down before they could accomplish it. Others bolted toward the exit, unaware of the shotgunner waiting outside or willing to risk him in lieu of the devils they faced where they were. In either case, they were too late, a storm of automatic fire strafing them from the rear and flanks, taking them down in a tangle of twisted arms and legs.

When it was done, and ringing silence had descended on the slaughterhouse, Bolan met Gellar's eyes and knew that it was time to go. "You want to warn our friend out front to hold his fire?" he asked.

Nodding, the Mossad agent led the way past crumpled bodies, stepping gingerly through slicks of blood.

It was a start, Bolan thought, hardening his heart to so much death. But they were still a long way from the finish line.

CHAPTER FOURTEEN

"And that is all we know at the moment," Rotislav Chaloupek said, ending his grim narrative as he paused to light another black cheroot, expelling acrid smoke in twin streams through his round, hairy nostrils.

Gerhard Steuben felt the too familiar pressure building up inside his body, threatening to blow at any moment. He could hear and feel his own pulse throbbing in his ears, a cadence that seemed to increase in both volume and velocity with each beat of his heart.

"Tell me again," he said, somewhat surprised that he could still control his voice. "How many died?"

"Forty or fifty," Chaloupek replied. "They aren't sure yet about the numbers. No list of the dead has been released by the authorities. They like to notify the families before they publish names. These things, sometimes it takes a week or more."

"But were they all from the Iron Cross?"

Chaloupek shrugged. "It was the group's headquarters. Who else should be there?"

Steuben thought he saw a sudden gleam of hope— or maybe he was simply clutching straws to keep himself from going under in a sick whirlpool of fear.

"What I am saying is, it could be that not all the victims found were members of the Iron Cross, true? Perhaps they finished off the raiders, too."

"I don't think so," Chaloupek told him, drawing deeply on the miniature cigar. "Men were apparently seen running from the building afterward. They jumped into a car and drove away."

"All right," Steuben replied. "Perhaps they killed one of the raiders, then. We need only one name, in order to identify our enemies, find out who they are working for, which nationality they represent."

"You told me they were Jews," Chaloupek said, sounding confused.

"It's not enough," Steuben reminded him. "The world is full of Jews. We need to know who sent them, what they want."

"They want to kill us," Chaloupek said, as if the answer should be obvious to anyone with eyes.

"I understand that," Steuben said, wishing that he could reach across the desk and slap Chaloupek's sallow face. He made no move, however, since the Croat was rather unpredictable—perhaps the most unstable of his chief lieutenants, when he thought about it. He didn't think Chaloupek would attack him physically, but you could never tell for sure. Of all the Nordic Temple's foreign leaders, Rotislav Chaloupek had the most impeccable credentials when it came to spilling blood.

Instead of slapping him, therefore, Steuben maintained his cool—or what was left of it—and told his host, "I know they want to kill me, Rotislav. They have been chasing me halfway around the world. They have already killed more than a hundred of our soldiers and associates."

"That many?" Now Chaloupek *was* surprised.

"At least that many," Steuben said. "In Germany, within the past few days, they murdered close to fifty friends and members of the Temple. Now, we have this slaughter of the Iron Cross in Zagreb. Before last week, there was a string of killings in America."

"It's you they want, then," Chaloupek said, and the way he said it sent a shiver down the would-be führer's spine.

"I am a symbol of the movement and its founding father. They focus upon me, of course, but it's the Temple of the Nordic Covenant and all we've struggled for that they are trying to destroy. They have a traitor, a defector from the Temple in America, who has informed them of our plans."

Chaloupek frowned at that. "How did this traitor know the plans?" he asked. A simple question, cutting to the heart of it.

"She was a spy who—"

"*She?*" Audaciously, Chaloupek interrupted him. "This traitor that you speak of is a woman?"

"Yes!" Steuben snapped, biting back on rage that threatened to engulf and overpower him. "We have both men and women in the Temple, as you know quite well. In the United States, especially, they have been helpful to the movement, in recruiting and—"

"And spying out your plans," Chaloupek said. He stopped just short of sneering. "Who was sleeping with this bitch and telling secrets while he poked her, eh?"

"No one that I'm aware of," Steuben said. "She was apparently a spy implanted in the Temple by the U.S. government. We still don't know which agency."

"Excuse me, sir." Was there just a hint of sarcasm behind Chaloupek's words? Was it enough to call him on right here and now? "This does not sound like something Washington would do, if you'll excuse me saying so. Not even in the old days, when the CIA still had its balls, were killers sent around the world to do such things. Your government taps phones and bugs hotel rooms, sometimes opens mail. It questions friends and neighbors. When it kills, there is publicity. We see it all on CNN. After the killing, then the government investigates itself and publishes a million copies of the findings. This," the Croat said at last, "is clearly something else."

"All the more reason for us to identify the men responsible."

"Or women, as the case may be." Chaloupek's smile was sly, disgusting. Steuben longed to rip it from his face. Already, in his head, he was considering replacements for his soon-to-be ex-chief lieutenant in Croatia.

Soon, but not just yet. They had a deadly problem to resolve before he started making any major changes in the local hierarchy.

And beyond the phantom threat, they still had other work to do, as well.

"How are the plans proceeding for our project?" Steuben asked.

"We are on schedule," Chaloupek said. "Or were, at any rate. Of course, some of the men who were supposed to help us on the target date are dead, now."

"You can find replacements if you need to?"

"Probably," the Croat said. "But it would help if we could find out who is killing them and put a stop to it, without delay."

"You must have other contacts in Zagreb."

"Of course," Chaloupek said, each syllable accompanied by little puffs of smoke from his cheroot.

"Contacts with the authorities?" Steuben asked.

"Ah. That's not so easy in the present climate, when they know we hate the government. Few office holders will collaborate in anything that leads to loss of power for themselves, much less a loss of life."

"You told me once that you had friends with the police."

"A friend," the Croat said, correcting him. "We're still in touch from time to time. I use him sparingly, to minimize the risk that he will be exposed. I try to save him for emergencies."

"I think this qualifies as an emergency," Steuben replied. "Don't you?"

"Of course. And I *have* been in touch with him, concerning what's become of the Iron Cross. He's not assigned to homicide, of course, and must be circumspect in asking questions. He dares not expose himself."

"Keep after him, regardless. If there is a lead of any kind that helps identify our enemies, then we must find out what it is and follow it. Meanwhile, the other operation must proceed."

"Of course. Our plan is presently on schedule, as I said."

"I need a victory. The movement needs a victory! Defeat, if unreversed, becomes a habit and a state of mind. It is a cancer, gnawing from within."

"Your enemies were lucky in Zagreb," Chaloupek said. "They caught some young men with their guard down, drinking beer, with no real weapons handy.

The Iron Cross survivors learn from their mistakes, and so do I.''

"I hope so, Rotislav. The final days are coming, as predicted, and we can't afford to be caught napping. We will only have one chance to win the world for Wotan's sake. You understand?"

"Of course, sir," Rotislav Chaloupek said. "So let it be.''

WHEN HE HAD GATHERED his lieutenants at the normal meeting place, outside Zdar, with sentries covering approaches to the farmhouse, Rotislav Chaloupek felt more confident. He was relieved to be away from Gerhard Steuben for the moment, and while it occurred to him that such a thought should probably inspire guilt feelings, he could conjure none for the occasion. As it was, he couldn't stop himself from wondering if Steuben might have lost his grip.

There was no doubt that someone—Jew or not, Chaloupek couldn't say with any certainty—was following the man as he made his way from the United States, through Europe, to Croatia. There had been too many violent deaths, most recently the slaughter in Zagreb, for any sane man to deny the fact of a conspiracy against Steuben and the Temple of the Nordic Covenant.

The point wasn't whether those enemies existed, but rather how Steuben responded to the threat. It seemed to Chaloupek that his "fearless" leader had been on the run for weeks now, hiding like a rabbit when it hears the hounds approaching, sacrificing soldiers in a vain attempt to save himself.

It was a leader's job to stay alive and lead. Chaloupek didn't question that imperative. The leaders of the

Third Reich had done no less in 1945, and when they were defeated, they had either killed themselves or tried to flee like common criminals. Chaloupek would have liked it better, though, if Gerhard Steuben had adopted a more manly attitude. If nothing else, he could revere the memory of those who gave their lives to save him from the unknown enemy.

Chaloupek's problem now was threefold. He had to protect his leader, find and stop his tormentors, while still proceeding with the plan that they had hatched together, months before, as part of the on-going preparation for the final days. Already, major damage had been suffered by the plotters in America and Germany. Chaloupek frankly doubted that the chain reaction planned in the beginning was still viable. Instead of rapid-fire explosions that would set the world ablaze, it seemed as if they might be left with wet firecrackers, sputtering in vain.

He could be wrong, of course. America, though it was Steuben's home, had never really been the centerpiece of the plan. Even Germany, where the Great Reich had its roots, was of secondary importance to the führer's scheme. America was too Jew ridden for resounding victory. The German fatherland was tired, still wallowing in guilt about events that should have made its people proud. The actions scheduled for those countries had been mere preliminary sparks to light the Armageddon fuse.

The real explosive charges lay elsewhere, and Rotislav Chaloupek knew that he was sitting right on top of one. If he could carry out his mission for the Temple and the führer, there was still a chance...

Chaloupek pulled himself out of his reverie and found his soldiers watching him expectantly. He cleared his throat, refusing to be hurried by subordinates, and waited yet another moment to begin.

"By now," he said at last, "you've heard about the killings in Zagreb. Someone—we don't know who, as yet—attacked a group of Iron Cross members when their guard was down and slaughtered them like sheep. There is a lesson in this for the rest of us."

Chaloupek paused, waiting for questions. Hearing none, he forged ahead. "It is my duty to inform you that the men who did this are apparently outsiders, possibly with the assistance of some Jew or Communist who is a native of Croatia."

"Jew or Communist," one of his people said. "Is there a difference?"

He gave the rest of them a chance to laugh at the familiar joke before continuing. "I must inform you also that Gerhard Steuben is among us, even now."

"No! Where?"

"If he decides to show himself," Chaloupek said, "you'll be among the first to know. Meanwhile, you should be conscious of the fact that the Zagreb incident was most likely committed by men who have been stalking our leader for several weeks. They made their first attacks in the United States. More recently, they were responsible for certain losses suffered by the Temple in Germany. They have followed him here, to play in our backyard."

"Where are they?" one of his lieutenants challenged.

"Show them to us!" another demanded.

"We'll kill them!" a third soldier vowed.

"I regret to inform you that we have no clue as yet to the identity of those responsible. Gerhard Steuben is convinced they are Americans who may have infiltrated the Temple there. Because there have been no indictments or arrests, only attacks that violate the law of every jurisdiction where they have occurred, we still don't know which agency may be responsible. In fact, we have no proof the killers are American, or that their orders come from Washington. So far, it is a theory, nothing more.''

''It sounds more like Mossad,'' one of his people offered.

''Right! The Jews behave that way,'' another said. ''They always have.''

''In any case,'' Chaloupek said, ''it is our duty to protect our leader while he shares our hospitality. If we are able to identify and stop his enemies, it is our job to do so. And,'' he added with the bare hint of a smile, ''it wouldn't harm a soldier's prospect of promotion, either, I might add.''

Some of his soldiers chuckled knowingly at that, while others sat grim faced, already skulling out some strategy for tracking down the unknown enemy.

''Let us remember also,'' Chaloupek added, ''that the new task we've inherited does not in any way absolve us of our previous responsibilities. We have a mission that is critical, as you all know, not only to the resolution of the last-days prophecy, but to survival of the master race and the future of the Croat people under Wotan's cosmic plan. One task doesn't replace the other, my loyal comrades. Is this understood?''

''How will we know the men who hunt our leader?'' one of his lieutenants asked.

''We hope that they will come to us, and so expose themselves,'' Chaloupek said. ''If not, we will find other methods of discovery, even if it means squeezing every Jew in the republic.''

Laughter was followed by another question. ''And when we find them, sir, will there be any special orders for their handling?''

''When you find them, there will be but one instruction—kill them. Slaughter them. Destroy them, root and branch. No mercy and no quarter.'' Chaloupek paused and smiled, before adding, ''In other words, the usual.''

''You spoke of traitors in the Temple, sir,'' another one of his lieutenants said.

''That was in the United States,'' Chaloupek said, reminding them, ''but we cannot rule out the possibility that one or more among us may be vulnerable to the Jewish purse. There have been traitors to their race and blood in every era, every nation. It should come as no surprise to anyone.''

That left them silent, watching him—and one another—with varying expressions of concern, suspicion, outright paranoia. Chaloupek was content with the effect his words had had.

''And to the traitors in our midst,'' he said, ''if there be any, I say this—you will be hunted down and punished for your crimes against the master race. Your fate will be appropriate, but it will not be merciful.

''Now, on a lighter note,'' he said, and cracked a beaming smile, ''I want to hear how preparations for our grand surprise have been progressing. Who goes first?''

ISTVAN DKANY KNEW that his survival hinged upon a twist of fate, and he wasn't amused by the idea. A punctured tire on his Fiat had made him tardy for the meeting with his Iron Cross brothers at the clubhouse in Zagreb, and by the time he had arrived, having concocted a delicious lie about a female hitchhiker who had demanded sex, he found the neighborhood crawling with uniforms, policemen and ambulance attendants scurrying in and out of the club, bending over several crumpled bodies on the sidewalk, out in front.

As late as he was, Istvan Dkany had smelled cordite in the air.

The long, dark night had passed now, and he knew the worst. Thirty-nine of his brothers were dead, four others clinging to a frayed thread of life in the hospital, their prospects "guarded," in the weasel dialect that let physicians hedge their bets. Dkany had no reasonable hope that any of the four would manage to survive, much less identify the enemies responsible for the attack.

He couldn't visit them in the hospital, of course. The warrants still outstanding from his last brush with the law—a trifling matter that involved some Jewish shops, a little spray paint and some broken glass—prevented him from surfacing where the police might see and recognize his face. Another time, they might have overlooked him, but the massacre made grilling any known or speculative Iron Cross member top priority for homicide investigators in Zagreb, and all the more so, since the group was out of favor with the ruling government.

Given sufficient time, Istvan Dkany thought, the pigs in uniform would probably devise some means to call the slaughter a mass suicide and blame it all on him.

The young men who had died in the attack had been as brothers to Dkany. They were also his soldiers and subordinates, of course, since he was founder and reigning warlord of the Iron Cross itself. For that reason, if nothing else, Dkany automatically suspected that the raid had been an effort to kill *him* with any collateral damage to his troops a mere bonus in the eyes of the attackers. And his question now was, did the bastards think they had succeeded? Had they taken time to scrutinize the bodies and determine that he wasn't found among the dead?

Dkany didn't stop to consider whether it was pride or paranoia that made him automatically regard himself as the primary target of the Zagreb massacre. He had been told by Rotislav Chaloupek that the raid was seemingly connected to a visit by the leader of the Temple of the Nordic Covenant, some kind of plot to chase him all around the world and make him look a fool even if he wasn't assassinated, but the story lacked something in terms of common sense.

Why would a group of international assassins targeting the Nordic Temple strike against the Iron Cross clubhouse in Zagreb? Granted, it was a kind of common knowledge that the two groups were affiliated, friendly, even formally allied when it came down to certain instances of raking Jews over the coals. Still, there was no good reason to assume that Gerhard Steuben would be wounded, psychologically or otherwise, at hearing that a group of Croat skinheads had been killed in a city some 250 kilometers from where he was presently hiding.

Dkany hadn't been entrusted with Steuben's specific whereabouts, of course. That was need-to-know information, and his present duties required no such knowledge on his part. Rather, he was charged with pushing on despite his recent losses, acting out the role that he had been assigned before the massacre, before Steuben took it in his head to visit the Republic of Croatia. It was an important job, part of an even more important mission for the master race, but there would still be time within his busy schedule for Istvan Dkany to pursue a sideline of his own.

That sideline was revenge.

A group of his surviving soldiers had assembled in a warehouse on the outskirts of Zagreb. There were perhaps a hundred skinheads present, excluding the dozen guards he had posted outside and on the warehouse roof, armed with shotguns and automatic rifles stolen from the military. The assembled group represented just under fifty percent of his surviving troops. Twelve hours earlier, the Iron Cross had boasted some 250 members in Zagreb, but nearly one in five of those had died in the assault by gunmen he had yet to name, much less track down.

Not decimated yet, Dkany thought, but close enough.

He could expect desertions, too, after the massacre. Some of the weaker members who talked tough and did their part all right when they were beating up on helpless, unarmed Jews or Muslims would undoubtedly rethink their role in the Iron Cross, now that there was a lethal risk attached to membership. Scanning the faces ranged before him, skinheads perched on metal folding chairs or plastic crates, some of them leaning up against the nearby wall, Dkany missed a few already. Only three or four, perhaps, but it was starting—the attrition every army suffered when the training and the lectures ended, giving way to mortal combat with determined enemies.

"My brothers," he began, "by this time you are all aware of what befell our order last night, in Zagreb. So far, my best efforts haven't managed to identify the men responsible. We know that there were three of them involved, at least, but as to who they were or why they chose this moment to attack, I can't say with any certainty."

"The fucking Jews!" one of his soldiers called out from the crowd.

"Muslims!" another said. "The bastards!"

"Communists!" a third proclaimed.

"I have been asked to tell you that the raid may be connected to a visit by the leader of the Nordic Temple, who is presently conferring with his people at a top-secret location in Croatia, which I'm not at liberty to name." There was no need to mention that Dkany hadn't been entrusted with the information; let them think that he was in the know. "There have been similar attacks at other points on his itinerary, and the murder of our brothers may be linked to his arrival in the country, but we can't rule out the possibility that evil forces wish to stop us from fulfilling our responsibilities the day after tomorrow."

"They won't stop us!" one young soldier shouted.

Yet another asked, more meekly, "How can we go on?"

"Shut up!" another cautioned him. "Don't be a woman all your life!"

The two of them were on their feet and squaring off, chairs grating on concrete, before Dkany raised his voice to calm them. "Peace, my brothers!" he called out, the hard edge of his voice—and the appearance of armed bodyguards beside him—letting the would-be combatants know that they would pay a price for breaking up the meeting with a private brawl.

When they had finished muttering and pulled their crooked chairs back into line, Dkany picked up where his pep talk had been interrupted. "We have work to do, my brothers, with the day so close at hand. We must not be deterred or sidetracked. That which is prepared must still be carried out. And yet—"

He left them hanging for a moment, letting tension mount.

"And yet," he continued, "there may be time and opportunity for us to punish those who defy our order and assassinated our kinsmen when their backs were turned." Again, no need to mention that some of them had apparently been running for their lives when they were shot. "Who here among us thinks that he can carry out two jobs at the same time?"

A hundred hands stabbed skyward, angry voices raised in cries of, "Me! I do! Annihilate the bastard scum!"

Istvan Dkany smiled.

ANOTHER HOTEL ROOM, another cheap TV set beaming images she didn't want to see, with voice-over commentary that she couldn't understand. It was enough to make a lady climb the walls, and Marilyn Crouder was feeling less like a lady with each passing moment.

The slaughter had resumed, as she had known it had to, after the brief respite while they were airborne out of Germany, winging toward the next in a seemingly endless series of killing fields. Just when she thought that she was used to it, new images of carnage flashed across the television screen, and Crouder was once again astounded. So much damage, so much bloodshed, all of it inflicted by the two men who had come to share her life.

There was a certain measure of hypocrisy in her reaction. She herself had killed several men since the night Mike Belasko had rescued her from certain death at the hands of Nordic Temple executioners. Crouder took comfort from the fact that all those she had shot and killed were engaged in violent acts at the time, directly threatening her life or that of someone else—including her savior Belasko—but at the same time, she couldn't deny taking a certain satisfaction from the violence, feeling a certain rush.

Particularly when she killed Sean Fletcher, after he had—

That's enough!

It didn't pay to dredge up *those* emotions, here and now, when they were better left interred. She could exhume them later for postmortem study, after she achieved some distance from the incident—and if she lived that long herself.

For now, she understood that any bridge between the present and her old life as an agent for the U.S. federal government was well and truly burned, the ashes scattered far and wide. Crouder didn't know if she was still on salary with ATF, or if she had already been cut from the rolls for going AWOL, traipsing off to Europe with Belasko on a personal mission that had turned into a marathon of blood. There was an outside chance that warrants had been issued for her apprehension, but she doubted it. The brass in Washington were more than likely glad to see her go, taking with her a whole list of troublesome questions and their equally disturbing answers.

She still believed the Temple of the Nordic Covenant had to be destroyed, or, at the very least, emasculated, permanently robbed of its ability to terrorize and kill. Belasko and his friend from the Mossad had proved adept at dishing out the kind of punishment that Nazis understood, but there appeared to be no end in sight. The viper's head, personified by Gary Stevens, still continued to elude them, even as they hacked the writhing body into grisly pieces.

And the odds, she realized, weren't with Gellar and Belasko. They could win only so many battles, face so many foes, before the sheer weight of statistical probability rolled over and crushed them flat. Every soldier took hits if he stayed on the line long enough. Every active-duty lawman suffered damage, both physical and psychological, before he pulled the pin and took retirement, assuming he lasted that long. And those were situations when the odds, more often than not, were fairly well balanced, even weighted in favor of the good guys.

How long could Belasko and Gellar hurl themselves headlong against forces of superior size and yet emerge intact? How long before their luck ran out and one of them was badly injured, maybe even killed?

The sudden tears that filled her eyes infuriated Crouder. She was supposed to be beyond such sentiment. She was a trained professional, dammit, or, she had been, anyway, when she was still on salary with Uncle Sam.

What was she now?

Before she had a chance to ponder that, much less

come up with a definitive response, the jangling of the telephone surprised her, made her jump. The television had no remote control, but she lunged for the set, turning down the sound before she grabbed the telephone receiver on its second jarring ring.

"Hello!"

"Back at you," Bolan said.

"Are you all right?" She closed her eyes, silently curing the impulse that had made her ask the question, coming off more like a wimpy girlfriend or camp follower than a seasoned comrade in arms.

"I'm fine," he told her. "It may be a while before I check back in, though. We've got leads we have to follow, one thing and another."

"Well, you know where to find me," she said, and could have slapped herself for using the cliché. Could she be any more pathetic if she tried?

"Just don't go out, all right?"

"Don't worry, Mom." She regretted the words before she even finished speaking them, but they were gone, away down the wire, beyond recall.

"Okay," Bolan said. "I'll be in touch."

The line went dead, and Crouder couldn't hold back the tears. "You idiot!" she blurted out, unsure if she was talking to the soldier in harm's way or to herself.

CHAPTER FIFTEEN

Agoston Domokos lit his fourth cigarette in fifteen minutes, dragging heavily on it as soon as it sparked, hoping that this one, finally, would help him calm down. His nerves were twanging, making him jumpy, and he knew the wrong mood—even the wrong attitude—could get him killed this night.

The alley was a pigsty, reeking with human and animal waste, littered with garbage that rotted where it fell, the odor one more reason to keep smoking while he was compelled to linger in this equivalent of an open-air gas chamber. Zagreb had limited sanitation services, and they were reserved for high-priority areas: government buildings, the major stores downtown and residential neighborhoods whose occupants had money and power. In poorer neighborhoods, like this one, on the city's east side, merchants and residents shoveled and hauled their own refuse or let it pile up, spreading stench and disease.

The neighbors of this reeking alley had clearly chosen the second option, using the fifty-foot stretch of shadowed pavement as a combination garbage dump and lavatory. Mangy-looking rats bustled through the heaps of once edible refuse, while clouds of shiny flies drifted and hummed, feeding, mating, laying eggs and dying, all within their small, malignant universe of filth.

Disgusted with the fact that he would have to wash his clothes now—maybe even burn them—Domokos still reflected that the stinking alley made an almost perfect meeting place. Only the most disoriented of the district's homeless alcoholics would be dumb or crazed enough to drop their threadbare trousers here. Their more sophisticated brethren had moved on to other alleys, where the air was fresh as springtime in comparison to this miasma.

Just the place to meet a neo-Nazi, Domokos thought, breathing through his mouth as he picked his way between the septic rivulets and mounds of rotting trash. The sawed-off shotgun wedged beneath his right arm would have made him feel lopsided if he hadn't stuffed the left-hand pockets of his slacks and jackets with a dozen extra 12-gauge cartridges.

With neo-Nazis, it was always better safe than sorry.

Domokos was reaching for another cigarette, distraught to find it was the last one in the last pack he was carrying, when someone hailed him from the far end of the alleyway. He recognized his contact, even with a shimmering veil of blowflies between them. He wore the same leather as always—God help him getting the stink out of *that*—and had the same shaved head, eyebrows sacrificed with the rest, until he looked like something from an old Madonna video. The ones where she resembled an escapee from a concentration camp.

The irony of that struck Domokos, and he might have laughed out loud if he weren't so busy making certain that he and his contact were alone. There was a chance, however small, that this one could have sold him out after the massacre, or that some other member of the Iron Cross might have grown suspicious, deciding to tag along at a distance.

Ready, then. His right hand slipped into the side pocket of his long coat, where the lining had been slit to let him reach and fire the shotgun with a minimum of interference.

"Janos, you look well," he told the twenty-something neo-Nazi skinhead, lying through his teeth.

"I do not have much time," the leather-clad zombie informed him.

"Straight to it, then," Domokos said. "What can you tell me about any new developments within the unit?"

"There is danger now, you know?" Janos replied. "Last night we lost—"

"I have the money we agreed on when we spoke," Domokos interrupted him. "Two thousand *kuna*, here and now. That's all there is. If you have changed your mind and want for more, you should have told me on the telephone."

"My risk—"

"Was known to you when you made the appointment, Janos. And you also know I never carry extra cash. Do you have something for me now, or have we tramped around in all this shit and stink for nothing?"

Janos frowned and muttered, "Let me have the money, then."

Domokos drew it from the left-hand pocket of his coat, stepped forward with his arm extended, while the fingers of his right hand curled around the Bernardelli shotgun's triggers. One false move from

Janos—grabbing for him, reaching for a weapon, calling out for backup—and the neo-Nazi's entrails would be spread out for the hungry flies. Whatever happened after that…well, Domokos would simply have to wait and see.

The money changed hands without incident, Janos riffling through the bills and quickly counting them before he made them disappear inside his leather jacket. "You already know about the killings at the club last night?" he asked.

"Old news," Domokos said. "The television speaks of nothing else. Is that the best you've got?"

"There was a meeting last night," Janos said. "Or, I suppose you'd say this morning. Istvan gave one of his talks designed to raise morale, reminding us of all the work we have to do."

"Go on."

"Two thousand *kuna* really isn't—"

"Bad," Domokos finished for him, "since you set the price yourself."

"All right, damn you! Sometimes I think you must have Jew blood in your veins, the way you squeeze the money."

"You were saying…?"

"Some of us have been assigned to search Zagreb until we find the men responsible for last night's killings," Janos said. "The rest are going with Dkany, later on this afternoon, down to Zdar."

"What's in Zdar?"

"The Temple of the Nordic Covenant, for one thing," Janos said. "Their leader is supposed to be in town. Also, if what I'm told is accurate, our president is visiting Zdar to make one of his thrilling speeches. Possibly the residents are short on sleeping powder and they want to try the next best thing.''

''What has the president to do with the Nordic Temple—or the Iron Cross, for that matter?''

Janos shrugged, but he was smiling now. ''There comes a time when revolutionaries must decide if they are good for anything but talk, eh, Agoston? Sometimes a movement has to prove itself, before it can attract the masses it requires for final victory.'' The narrow smile became a grin. ''Who knows? This time next month, we may be meeting in a nice, big office, one that doesn't smell like shit. Next time, maybe I'll be the one who asks the questions, eh, Domokos?''

''I don't think so, Janos.''

At the first glimpse of the sawed-off shotgun's double barrels, Janos blanched and raised both empty hands in front of him, the fingers splayed, palms offered as a flimsy shield.

''Wait, Agoston!''

The buckshot charge ripped through his outstretched hands, arms and the leather that he wore, lifting the neo-Nazi off his feet and dropping him atop a dung heap that was partly canine, partly human. Domokos thought about the money in his pocket, maybe stained with blood by now, and chalked it up to operating costs. Dortmunder would reimburse him, possibly. If not, there was a chance Domokos wouldn't need the money, anyway.

If they were going to Zdar, there was a fair chance that he would be dead before the sun came up tomorrow.

''YOU'RE SAYING that they plan to kill the president of the republic?'' Bolan asked.

"It wasn't stated in so many words," Agoston Domokos said. "There was mention of a revolution and a movement that must prove itself before it claims the victory. I could be wrong, but I do not believe they want the presidential autograph."

Bolan nodded amiably as he said, "I see your point. And then, after he told you that—"

"I shot him dead," Domokos said.

"And you did that, because...?"

"He made some threats," the Croat replied. "I feared that if I let him go back to his friends in the Iron Cross, he might disclose that we had spoken. They are looking for you now—for *us*—to seek revenge for last night's killing."

"That's not a problem," Gellar said, "as long as they have nothing to work with. Gerhard Steuben will undoubtedly connect last night's events to the unpleasantness in Germany, but his men couldn't find us in Berlin. They won't find us here."

"They won't find you, perhaps," Domokos said, "because you fly away when you are finished. I still live here after, which is why I shot the Nazi."

"Never mind that, now," Gellar replied. "We need to think about Zdar."

"You think they're trying for the president?" Bolan asked.

"I can't come up with any logical alternative," Gellar replied.

He turned to Agoston Domokos. "There was no hint of any plan from this skinhead," he asked, "before you shot him?"

"No." Domokos shook his head while firing up another cigarette, the combined effect striking Gellar as almost comical. "He said, 'Sometimes a movement must prove itself.' Something like that. I had no doubt as to his meaning.''

"Fair enough,'' Gellar said. "Do we know anything at all about the presidential visit to Zdar?''

"They've had some kind of trouble there,'' Domokos said. "A shipyard strike or something similar, I think it is. Some people have been killed. There was a bombing, maybe more than one. I don't pay much attention to such things.''

"Perhaps he wants to mediate,'' Gellar suggested.

Domokos shrugged. "Or maybe get his face on television, eh? Our politicians here are not so different from those in the United States. They live for cameras and microphones. It's all about appearances and how much you can make the people swallow.''

"I'm guessing that the guy in office didn't get your vote,'' Bolan said.

Another shrug. "I have not voted since the mandatory-suffrage law was scrapped in 1991,'' Domokos said. "The Communists forced everyone to vote, but offered no real choices. I believe that freedom to choose includes a right not to choose anyone.''

"Well, I can't fault you there,'' Bolan said.

"The point,'' Gellar reminded them, "is not the popularity of a particular official. If the Temple of the Nordic Covenant intends to kill this president, with or without assistance from the Iron Cross, Herr Steuben must believe his cause will benefit from the murder.''

"Unfortunately,'' Bolan said, "in his state of mind, that benefit could be anything from a Nazi successor waiting in the wings to causing chaos for the sheer hell of it.''

"In any case, we have to stop him,'' Gellar stated.

"The easy way," Domokos said, through drifting clouds of smoke, "would be to get in touch with the security police. They don't need much excuse to crack down on dissenters. Give them names and let them do the dirty work."

"There are two problems with that method," Gellar told Domokos. "First, I don't know whether we can trust the officers of the security police. There may be Nazi infiltrators in the ranks, or even in the leadership. Second, there's no way they could round up everyone associated with the Nordic Temple and the Iron Cross—even if they wanted to—before the president flies to Zdar this afternoon."

"He isn't flying," Domokos said.

"Excuse me?"

"What?" Domokos frowned. "I thought you'd know. It's been in all the newspapers."

"We must have missed it in Berlin," Bolan said wryly.

"What are you saying?" Gellar pressed him.

"Simply that the president is driving from Zagreb, down to Zdar. It isn't far, less than two hundred miles. He plans to stop in his hometown along the way and have what the Americans would call a photo opportunity."

"And where is his hometown?" Gellar asked, swallowing the sudden sense of urgency that made him want to shout the question out.

"Some village on the way to Zdar," Domokos said. "Let me think a moment. Verdolak? I think that's it. Perhaps, if I could see a map…"

Gellar produced one from his travel bag—the one without the weapons—and unfolded it for Domokos. The Croat seemed to take an endless time examining the map, running one nicotine-stained finger along the narrow thread of highway linking Zagreb to Zdar on the Adriatic Sea, but finally he smiled and tapped his square-cut fingernail on the paper.

"Here," he said, self-satisfied. "Vordjalik. I was close, at least."

Gellar leaned closer, noting that the village—small, even on his large-scale map—lay near the halfway point between Zdar and Zagreb. "It might be easier to take him there than in Zdar," he said, thinking aloud. "Fewer police and soldiers, much less traffic to obstruct the getaway."

"But if we're wrong," Bolan said, reminding him, "we blow our only chance."

That was the hell of it. Gellar couldn't be sure. The strike team—if there even was a strike team waiting for the president—might try to kill him in Zdar, or anywhere along the route that he would follow from the capital. Less than two hundred miles, indeed! That was no consolation, when an ambush could be laid at any point along the way.

"Gerhard Steuben thrives on symbolism," Gellar said at last. "I think a hometown murder would appeal to him."

"Your call," Bolan said. "The only thing I know for sure right now is that we need to hit the road."

"THE PREPARATIONS ARE completed, then?" Gerhard Steuben asked. He had entered silently, his one good eye fixed steadily on Rotislav Chaloupek, seeming to ignore the three lieutenants who were with him, ringed about the table where the topographic map was spread.

"They are proceeding well, sir," Chaloupek replied. He thought it should be obvious that nothing was complete, since he was still at headquarters, the strike force hadn't been assembled yet and their target had only left Zagreb some twenty minutes earlier.

Instead of belaboring the obvious, though, Chaloupek continued, "Our trackers have confirmed the target's departure from Zagreb. The motorcade is on its way and presently on schedule, sir."

"How many cars?"

"The presidential limousine and three escort sedans," Chaloupek said. "A pair of motorcycle officers ride point, a mile or so ahead of the main body, watching for any hazards on the way. Besides the target, that makes twenty men."

"All armed, I would assume."

"We take that for granted, sir."

"It will be small arms only, I suppose?"

"The presidential guards are known to have Kalashnikovs. Most likely, for convenience, the AKSU models. Their standard-issue side arm is the CZ-75 automatic. We believe the motorcycle escorts carry pistols only, but they could have machine pistols in their saddlebags. Perhaps Skorpions, or the Finnish Jatimatics."

"We have them outgunned, then," Steuben said with a sense of satisfaction.

"Outgunned and outnumbered," Chaloupek assured him. "Our men and the Iron Cross auxiliary commandos have a more diverse arsenal, including assault rifles, shotguns and submachine guns. We also have a Barrett Model 90 sniper's rifle—a bolt-action .50-caliber weapon with an effective range of 1,800 meters. With armor-piercing ammunition, it should help us crack the limousine. If all else fails, we have two RPG-18 antitank weapons, roughly equivalent to your own LAW rocket launchers in America.''

"You must not think of me as an American, today,'' Steuben replied. "We've moved beyond the bounds of nationality.''

"Yes, sir.'' Chaloupek bobbed his head obediently, thinking to himself that Steuben would start to believe that he was truly German after all.

Of course, the point was that Steuben *did* believe precisely that. The first time Rotislav Chaloupek had heard the tale of "Gerhard Steuben's'' reincarnation, he had nearly laughed out loud, although he caught himself before he made that critical—possibly fatal—mistake. In time, he had come to believe that it made no difference who Stevens or "Steuben'' thought he was, as long as the man otherwise kept his wits about him and was capable of leading his troops to victory. The road had been rocky of late, with grim setbacks in America and Germany, but they weren't defeated yet, by any means.

The strike they were preparing for that very afternoon would go a long way toward reversing the defeats Steuben and his other troops had suffered recently, assuming that they were successful, of course. If they weren't...

Then, Chaloupek thought, it might be time to see about a change of leadership, discard some of the gothic ritual that seemed to yield no concrete benefits and focus on a more practical approach to victory. Armies won wars by killing or capturing their enemies, and Chaloupek, as demonstrated by his record from the early 1990s, had never been one for taking prisoners.

"How long before the ambush will be ready?" Steuben asked.

"Our comrades from the Iron Cross left Zagreb an hour ago," Chaloupek said. "I will be leading the contingent from Zdar within another ten or fifteen minutes, maximum. The vans are being loaded as we speak."

"How many men will be involved, again?"

"Fifty, sir. We have the presidential guard outnumbered more than two to one."

"Assuming that they don't have any unexpected help, that is."

Chaloupek heard the tremor in his leader's voice, not quite concealed. It was a sad and shameful thing to see the man whom he had once admired wholeheartedly now reduced to such a state of apprehension when he should be looking forward to a stunning victory. Steuben was frightened that the hunters who had tracked him from America would somehow find him once again, or else devise some way to foil the latest battle plan.

The recognition of that human weakness was another nail in Steuben's coffin, driven home with silent strokes.

ISTVAN DKANY WATCHED the countryside unfold along the highway leading southward from Zagreb. He occupied the front seat of an aging bus, which one of his light-fingered troops had stolen two weeks earlier. Concealed inside a rented warehouse, it had been repainted and bore the logo of a nonexistent charter firm along each side, beneath the rows of windows. While the bus accommodated sixty passengers, this day it carried less than half that many: twenty-six in all, counting Dkany.

On a number of the other seats, in place of passengers, sat heavy duffel bags containing arms and ammunition. On the floor, away in back, two wooden crates designed for wine bottles were filled with homemade Molotov cocktails, gasoline mixed with powdered laundry soap to make it gel and stick, the fuses made of rags soaked overnight in lighter fluid.

Istvan Dkany thought his soldiers were prepared for anything that might await them at their journey's end.

"A question, sir," one of the skinheads piped up from behind him, his hand raised like a child in school.

"What is it?" Dkany asked, half turned in his seat to face the youth and those around him.

"How many civilians in this town again, sir?"

"It's more a village, really," Dkany reminded them. "Five or six hundred, perhaps, if you count the outlying farmers. Of course, they may have visitors this afternoon, to see their favorite son."

"And watch him bleed!" another of the skinheads hooted, speaking up from somewhere farther back.

"You will recall that local residents aren't our target," Dkany said, putting on a stern face for the younger members of his team. "Of course, they cannot be allowed to interfere with us or shield the target. Let the wise ones run away. No mercy, though, for any fools who would resist."

"No mercy!" came an echo from a youthful voice, picked up at once by others on the bus.

"No mercy!"

"Just be sure to remember who your targets are," Dkany said, a father chiding his rambunctious sons as they embarked on a hunting expedition. "It would be a critical mistake to let the goose escape while shooting sparrows."

None of them mistook his meaning. It was plain enough for even the most thick skulled of his followers to grasp. If they got busy sniping villagers and let the big fish wriggle through their net, there would be bloody hell to pay.

And some of them wouldn't survive the aftermath.

"I never heard of Vorkulak before," one of the skinheads said.

"It's *Vordjalik*," Istvan corrected him. "And there's no reason you should know of it. The only contribution it has made to history, so far, has been the birth of him who dies today. We finish him exactly where he started, and the world will know of Vordjalik. They'll see our work on CNN tonight."

"Film at eleven!" someone blurted out.

"News on the hour, every hour!" someone else replied, laughing.

Dkany was relieved to find his soldiers in good spirits. They were young, most of them, and still relatively inexperienced. A handful of the older ones had seen their share of bloodshed in Croatia's civil war, but most could only brag of fighting in the streets with the security police or trashing Jewish shops, staging the robberies that kept the Iron Cross in the black.

This day would be a breakthrough for them—or, at least, for those who managed to survive.

Istvan Dkany wasn't stupid. He didn't delude himself into believing that his troops would leave the battlefield unscathed. They would be facing trained professionals—hired killers, in effect—and even though they had their targets heavily outnumbered, with the strike team from the Nordic Temple, they were bound to suffer causalities. It was the way of war, the way of life and death.

Dkany had been scrupulously honest with his team of volunteers. Some of them almost certainly would suffer wounds, he had explained; some of them might be killed. The mission wasn't suicidal, but it *was* high risk, and anyone who placed his life above the cause should quietly withdraw, no questions asked. It was a point of pride that none had scrambled for that exit hatch. In fact, a dozen more than he could use had volunteered to join the mission, fistfights breaking out among those chosen and troops who were passed over for one reason or another.

It was that kind of zeal that guaranteed the cause would never die, whatever happened to Istvan Dkany and his men. It didn't really matter if they failed today, if they were killed to the last man, because the master race would always be the master race. As long as one pair of Aryan breeders survived in the world, possessed of the mandatory racial consciousness, there would be someone left to fight against the Jews and Communists and mud people who soiled the planet with their very presence.

Of course, in that case, Dkany wouldn't be around to see the fight, much less participate or triumph, and he didn't really care for that idea, at all. The notion of a dead winner was oxymoronic, somehow. What good was winning, if you didn't live to toast your fallen comrades and enjoy the fruits of victory yourself?

That was the reason why the leader of the Iron Cross had already hedged his bets. If anything went wrong this afternoon, he had a secret plan worked out, whereby he might escape and live to fight another day. His soldiers didn't know it—would have raged against him, maybe physically attacked him, if they knew—but he didn't intend to sacrifice himself if there was any viable alternative.

Dkany had a contact in the village of Vordjalik. There would be a motorcycle waiting on a certain side street at a certain hour, its rider tinkering with an apparently stalled engine, ready to step aside and give up his helmet on hearing a certain password. Dkany could be on the bike and out of town in minutes flat, leaving chaos and carnage behind.

Assuming there was any need to cut and run.

If they should be victorious, of course, then it would be a very different story. He would gladly linger with his troops and reap his share of praise for changing history.

It was a no-lose situation for Istvan Dkany.

Which explained the neo-Nazi's smile as he and his companions rode on toward a rendezvous with Death.

"YOU'RE WORRIED, yes?"

Gellar's question seemed to come from far away, but Bolan heard him, snapping back to here and now in a heartbeat. "Not worried," he answered. "Concerned."

"Because you think we're wrong about the target?"

Bolan shrugged. "It's just about two hundred kilometers from Zagreb and Zdar," he replied. "If someone's gunning for the president, his stop-off in Vordjalik may be handy for an ambush. It may even be symbolic. But they could wait for him in Zdar instead. They could ambush his motorcade at any point along the way, or even mine the highway. Pack a culvert with your basic fertilizer charge, and it's the big bang all over again.''

''All right,'' the man from Tel Aviv responded. ''First, there is no culvert bomb. The president knows he is vulnerable, and his men from the security police spent all last night and this morning on the route of travel, looking into culverts, under bridges, beating bushes. There will be no mines or other booby traps. If he is ambushed on the highway, it will need a mobile team to overtake the motorcade and force it to a halt.''

''Could happen,'' Bolan said. ''It wouldn't be the first time.''

''Which is why the president has helicopters standing by for an emergency response,'' Gellar pressed on. ''I checked. He has two waiting in Zagreb and two more in Zdar, to cut reaction time. One signal from the motorcade, and all four take the air with rockets, 20 mm cannon and assault troops.''

''Great,'' the Executioner replied. ''Except that's no advance deterrent if the shooters on the ground don't know about it.''

''You're correct, of course. The preparations have been broadcast in a string of media reports, most recently last night.''

That ought to help, Bolan thought, unless they were dealing with a group of suicidal zealots. If the neo-Nazis wanted to come out of it alive, they had to plan their ambush for a killing zone where helicopter gunships would have less chance of employing airborne firepower. That meant civilians in the way, to serve as human shields, and that, in turn, meant striking in a populated area.

In terms of population, Bolan knew, Zdar would be a better bet than some small village, but Vordjalik still might serve the Nordic Temple's purpose.

And if they were wrong, they would have blown their one and only chance to save the day.

Bolan wasn't egotistical enough to believe that the Croatian president's survival depended on him or his two mismatched companions. Far from it, in fact. His mission, bottom line, was not to save anyone, but rather to destroy Gary Stevens and, as far as possible, the Temple of the Nordic Covenant. In regard to the cult, Bolan knew he could never hope to wipe out every member, much less retrieve the hundreds of thousands of pamphlets and propaganda sheets Stevens and his goons had distributed over the years. The plague of racism and anti-Semitism could only be eradicated through education, starting from the cradle up, but he could damned well try to stop the present crop of neo-Nazi fanatics from setting the world on fire.

And for that, he knew that he would need a little combat stretch.

The president's security precautions were a case of good news, bad news. The support troops took a load off Bolan and Gellar, relieving them of a potentially lethal distraction, but they also posed a deadly threat. The presidential bodyguards, the pilots in those helicopter gunships and the shock troops that they carried into battle would have no idea who Bolan and his comrades were once battle was joined. Anyone with a gun who wasn't part of the home team when the shooting started would be fair game. If Bolan judged the presidential elite guard correctly, they would shoot first and ask questions later, assuming they ever got around to asking questions at all.

Which meant, of course, that Bolan, Gellar and Domokos weren't simply up against neo-Nazis, arrayed in unknown numbers, armed with unknown weapons, plotting to assassinate the president of the Republic of Croatia at some unknown point between Zagreb and Zdar. They were also up against the full machinery of the state, with no defense beyond their own speed, skill and wits.

And they were gambling everything they had on one specific ambush point that might still prove to be a bust.

Bolan pictured his little trio, loitering around Vordjalik while the president delivered his speech, shook some hands, kissed some babies, then climbed back into his limo and went on his way. What would they do—what could they do—if the attack didn't take place in his hometown?

Their only option, then, would be to chase the motorcade, a course of action fraught with peril, which might well result in their being stopped by police, disarmed and arrested, while the president went on to Zdar.

Good news, bad news.

The bad—they had one chance to do this properly, and if they had already blown their choice, it was too late to turn the game around.

The good—with that in mind, there was no point in worrying. The hit would either come or it would not, and there was nothing he could do about it now.

Relax, then, Bolan told himself. Enjoy the ride.

Just like a turkey on its last ride to the slaughterhouse.

CHAPTER SIXTEEN

"Your men are in position, then?" Rotislav Chaloupek asked. He was standing in the shadow of a monument whose subject he couldn't identify, some peasant who had once performed some service long since erased from the memory of anyone outside this small Croat village.

"They are ready," Istvan Dkany assured him. "And yours?"

"In place and anxious to begin," Chaloupek said. "The Temple of the Nordic Brotherhood will make its mark today."

"With help from the Iron Cross, of course," Dkany said.

"Of course."

The men weren't precisely rivals, more like allies with a friendly sense of competition between them that sometimes went to extremes. Despite their common purpose, Rotislav Chaloupek knew that Dkany was hoping one of his skinheads would score the killing shot on their primary target, thus ensuring a heightened measure of respect for the Iron Cross at large. The triggerman himself, if he could be identified—and if he managed to survive the firefight—

would receive some personal reward, as yet unspecified.

Chaloupek hoped that he might do the job himself, instead of leaving it to one of his subordinates.

He was aware of all the risks involved, of course. Besides the normal presidential guard, there were the helicopters standing by in Zagreb and Zdar. The good news was that with Vordjalik situated almost equidistant between the two cities, roughly one hundred kilometers from either, an ambush, well planned and skillfully executed, could be carried out and the assault team safely scattered before reinforcements arrived.

But if it blew up in their faces...

"Your team's radios are tuned to the proper frequency?" Chaloupek asked, feeling a sudden pang of anxiety, imagining a last-second mix-up that would leave their attack hopelessly uncoordinated.

"Channel 9," Dkany replied, with a not quite mocking smile. "Relax, Rotislav."

"I am relaxed."

"Of course you are. In that case," Dkany said, "I will go and join my soldiers."

Dkany left the shadow of the monument, which was positioned at the northwest corner of Vordjalik's combination village square and marketplace. In truth, it wasn't much of either, there being precious little village to serve. No matter how he racked his memory, Chaloupek could not think of anything significant that had transpired in this vicinity throughout Croat history. He could be wrong, of course—the knowledge reaped from books had never been his strong suit, if the truth be told—but he was reasonably certain no great battles had been fought here, no momentous proclamations issued, no great treaties signed.

This afternoon, he meant to change all that.

Forever afterward, Vordjalik would be known as the flash point of Croatia's modern revolution, the place where members of the master race struck first to reclaim their birthright. All the other skirmishes with Jews and Muslims had been mere rehearsals for this moment, sparks and sputterings along the powder train that led to this inevitable, inescapable detonation of Aryan wrath.

And when the smoke cleared, days or weeks from now, Chaloupek would be standing at the apex of a whole new world.

He shifted slightly as he leaned against the statue of the nameless peasant hero, feeling the AKSU assault weapon shift against his hip, suspended from a makeshift shoulder sling beneath his overcoat. The short Kalashnikov's truncated barrel reduced effective range, but Chaloupek had positioned himself in a ring-side vantage point for the day's festivities. When the presidential motorcade entered Vordjalik, it would surely park in the village square, to avoid the trap of short, narrow side streets. If the president was going to address his native villagers as planned, he would be forced to do it here.

And Rotislav Chaloupek would be waiting for him. Not to mention fifty other dedicated Aryans, all armed and itching for a chance to kill.

It was Chaloupek's job to give the signal that would start the bloodbath. He was carrying a compact two-way radio in the breast pocket of his shirt, its small microphone clipped to the lapel of his coat, where he could key the button with his left hand and give the order to his soldiers even while his right hand raised and aimed his own AKSU.

The rub would come if anybody jumped the gun. It was entirely possible, he realized, with fifty nervous shooters spread around the village square, some of the Iron Cross gunners little more than schoolboys with a yen for action. If that happened, if Chaloupek missed his killing shot, then it would be up to others. If Chaloupek was cheated of a personal kill, the overall action was still his brainchild. He was still in command.

Raising a hand to his lapel, he keyed the tiny microphone and spoke to it, his lips barely moving, so that he wouldn't appear to be a crazy man, talking to himself.

"Report by number," he commanded.

One by one, the soldiers did as they were told, small voices carried through the plastic earpiece that he wore in his left ear. Chaloupek himself was Number One, and the others sounded off in order until each member of the strike team, whether from the Nordic Temple or the Iron Cross, had confirmed his readiness to fight.

And they were just in time.

Chaloupek had raised his left arm for a glance at his watch, when two motorcycle patrolmen roared into the village, circling twice around the square and speaking into their own microphones before they parked directly opposite Chaloupek's statue. They remained astride their machines, hands resting on their holstered side arms, as the presidential motorcade approached.

The assembled peasant crowd began to cheer, some of them waving small Croat flags—a copy of the Yugoslav red, white and blue, with a crowned shield squarely in the middle of the field, displaying a red-and-gray-checkerboard pattern. Others brandished homemade signs of welcome or tossed bouquets into the square, where they were quickly ground to tatters by the long limousine and its escort sedans.

Chaloupek could imagine armed men crouched behind the tinted windows of the four vehicles, clutching automatic weapons, scanning the crowd for targets, ready to open fire at the least provocation.

Not yet, he thought, willing the command to his soldiers. Not yet.

They waited, while the cheering redoubled, more bouquets airborne from the assembled crowd. The AKSU underneath Chaloupek's coat seemed to gain weight by the second, threatening to drag him down. He shrugged the feeling off, squaring his shoulders, and took control of himself by sheer force of will.

This moment was his destiny.

He wouldn't fail.

BOLAN WAS on the roof of a two-story building on the east side of the square when the presidential motorcade arrived. It had been no great trick to slip inside the empty shop downstairs, its back door unlocked in this trusting small-town atmosphere, the shop itself unoccupied as everyone in town turned out to greet Vordjalik's favorite son. A flight of wooden stairs took Bolan to the second floor, from which he climbed an old wall-mounted ladder to a simple trapdoor, opening onto the roof.

Someone else had been there ahead of him, a young man with his hair buzzed down to stubble and a lightning-bolt tattoo behind one ear. He was surprised at the intrusion, saying something Bolan couldn't understand as he turned toward the opening trapdoor, a submachine gun clutched in his hands.

The Beretta 93-R met him halfway, with a silent Parabellum round that opened a keyhole between his dark eyes, punching the skinhead onto his back in a lifeless sprawl. A bit more force of impact, and the dead man might have tumbled off the roof into the square.

He would have ruined everything.

As it was, the corpse kept Bolan company as he moved into position, noting the make of automatic weapon—a Beretta Model 12-S submachine gun— and the walkie-talkie lying on the flat, tiled roof, beside the skinhead's outflung arm. The radio was silent, no lights showing to suggest it was transmitting, but he checked it anyway, to satisfy himself that no one on the street below was eavesdropping on Death.

All clear.

There could be trouble if the neo-Nazi fire-control officer tried to check in with his rooftop sniper, but the motorcade's noisy arrival precluded any sort of long-winded consultation. Shooters in the village square would try to avoid tipping their hands with any peculiar, surreptitious movements, he reasoned, and there was nothing more to be gained from conversation, anyway, beyond transmission of the ultimate command to open fire.

Freeing the Steyr AUG assault rifle from the confines of his raincoat, Bolan knelt beside the bald corpse to scan the other rooftops circling the square. On three of them—no, four—he spotted furtive movement, hunched shapes seeking cover behind cornice molding or the occasional ancient swamp cooler, trying to stay out of sight.

Snipers.

He couldn't pick out any obvious assailants in the cheering crowd below, but reckoned they would show themselves plainly enough when the shooting started. In the meantime, he would leave them to Gellar and Domokos, concentrating on the gunmen he could see, preparing to take them out of action as quickly and efficiently as possible.

It wouldn't be long now.

He sighted on the targets, one by one, tracking them with the AUG's optical sight, aware that all of them would be more clearly visible when they rose up to fire on their targets in the square, below. Bolan couldn't afford to wait, though, since four gunners firing simultaneously could wreak havoc on the crowd before he nailed them down.

Better to get a jump on the festivities, he thought, than to risk falling behind with deadly results.

The AUG was fitted with a foot-long suppressor, the weapon loaded with slightly underpowered rounds to reduce noise and minimize any risk to innocent bystanders from through-and-through shots once the real action started. As it was, with the cheering and shouting from below, Bolan imagined he could do his work undetected, unless one of his targets tumbled to the game and opened up prematurely with an unsilenced weapon.

Then again, he didn't really have a clue what *prematurely* meant, since the signal to fire en masse could be relayed at any moment from the neo-Nazi officer in charge.

No time to waste.

He chose the farthest sniper from him to begin with, sighting on a shoulder and the upper portion of a blond-haired visage, raised above the cornice of a shop whose signs Bolan couldn't interpret. Lining up the shot, he fixed the crosshairs of the Steyr's sight upon the neo-Nazi's hairline, held his breath and stroked the trigger once.

Downrange, he saw the impact as a spurt of red, the target slumping backward, out of sight. There was no way to tell if he had scored a fatal hit, but any head wound with the 5.56 mm tumbling projectile would be serious, debilitating, if not instantly lethal. Trusting ballistics, he moved on to his second target, the next farthest from his own sniper's nest.

Another skinhead, this one, wearing shooter's glasses with pale amber lenses. The sniper seemed almost relaxed, resting with his back against an old swamp cooler that was silent on this crisp, clear day, no artificial breeze required inside the shop it served. The structure in question was one story tall, giving Bolan a better view of this shooter, squatting with an automatic rifle braced across his knees, one arm extended and braced against the rooftop for better balance.

Bolan shot him in the face, below one eye, and followed with a second round when the young man still clutched at his weapon, thrashing about as if he meant to fire a warning shot, perhaps defend himself against the unseen foe who had already claimed his life. The second shot sprayed blood and brains across the cooler's faded paint job, and the dead man crumpled in a heap.

Two down, two left to go.

Bolan tracked on, caught the third neo-Nazi rising

from a crouch, tugging at his pants as if to give his genitals more room. A shot behind the ear drilled through his skull and opened a silver-dollar-sized exit wound above the opposite eye, spilling gray and crimson as the dead man went down on his face.

And that left one.

As Bolan found the final sniper, though, the man was already on his feet, staring in the direction of the last sniper to go down. He had seen something, clearly, and alarm was written on his brutish face as he swung back toward the main square below, lunging toward the parapet with his Kalashnikov at high port.

Whatever he had seen or thought that he had seen, the final sniper wasn't waiting for a signal from the street. He stood above the drop, his rifle shouldered now, his index finger on the trigger.

Bolan shot him in the shoulder, throat and face. Three quick rounds, the rag-doll figure lurching backward, legs turning to rubber as he fell. His trigger finger still had spring steel in it, though, and he unleashed a long burst of automatic fire as he slumped to the roof, his dead man's grip maintaining pressure on the trigger for two or three seconds, until the bucking AK kicked free of his grasp.

And that was all it took.

Down below, in the village square, it all went to hell.

JACOB GELLAR WAS working the crowd, flicking glances back and forth between the presidential party and the crush of cheering villagers, when the first burst of gunfire sounded to his left and above him, emanating from one of the rooftops on the south side of the village square.

The cheering faltered, faded, was transmuted into shouts and screams as sudden panic swept through the crowd, replacing pride, excitement, the enjoyment of an unfamiliar holiday.

A visual sweep of the rooftops showed him nothing, no snipers visible from where he stood on the west side of the square, and Gellar instantly refocused on the motorcade. He was in time to see the president's bodyguards drawing weapons, still uncertain where to aim them, as they tried to cover everyone at once. Two of them literally had the big man covered, shielding him with their bodies as they hustled him back toward the open rear door of his black limousine.

And suddenly, the world seemed to explode.

The gunfire seemed to come from everywhere at once, on all sides of the village square. There was no way for him to count the guns, or even spot them in the early moments of the firefight, as the unarmed members of the crowd began to mill about in confusion spiced with sudden terror, looking desperately for cover, someplace to hide. The scene reminded Gellar of some West Bank actions he had been involved with during his military service, before he joined the Mossad.

Clearing hostile villages was always dirty, bloody work. Sparing the innocent, when gunmen lurked among them, was even more difficult, and sometimes impossible. There were kill-or-be-killed situations that the drill instructors never talked about in basic training, where you did what had to be done to save yourself and your comrades, and destroy the enemy before he could inflict more damage on the friendly side.

The presidential cars were taking hits, he saw, and so were members of the entourage. One of the motorcycle officers was first to fall, shot through the neck or lower jaw, his baby-blue crash helmet helpless to protect him from a well-aimed bullet. Clutching at his wound, the dying trooper dropped his pistol, tumbled backward from the saddle of his bike and took the machine down with him, its weight pinning him to the ground.

Not that it mattered, in his present state. The shot had clipped his jugular, perhaps the carotid artery. He would be dead in minutes.

Even as he scanned the milling, shoving crowd for shooters, one fact registered on Jacob Gellar's mind: the presidential limousine was bulletproof, but the three escort vehicles weren't. Already, in the first few seconds of the battle, one sedan had lost its windshield, pebbled safety glass glittering like faux diamonds on the dashboard, where a burst of gunfire had punched through. The paint on all four cars was marked by shiny divots, bullet scars, but while the limousine was dinged, the three sedans were ventilated, sometimes through-and-through. One of them had a flat tire on the driver's side, leaning drunkenly to port, and another was dribbling gasoline from a newly punctured fuel tank. It would take only a spark to light that liquid fuse, Gellar knew, and the bloody chaos in the square would be amplified tenfold.

So far, most of the casualties were noncombatants from the village, caught in a vicious cross fire as the presidential guards began defending themselves and their charge. If any of the soldiers had their wits together, Gellar thought, the helicopter gunships from Zagreb and Zdar would already be scrambling skyward, but that presupposed presence of mind under fire—and, in any case, the choppers still had a hundred kilometers, some sixty-five or seventy miles, to travel before they reached Vordjalik. That wasn't far, in terms of travel by air, but he estimated that most military helicopters would need twenty or thirty minutes to cover that distance at normal cruising speed.

And that could be a lifetime under fire.

Gellar spotted his first neo-Nazi shooter while those grim numbers were still rattling around inside his skull. The target was a young man, twenty-something, in a long gray overcoat, with mostly denim underneath. He had a folding-stock Kalashnikov and he was firing short, controlled bursts toward presidential vehicles, unmindful of the scattered, so far ineffectual return fire from his enemies.

He never saw Gellar coming, had no warning of the 3-round Parabellum burst from Gellar's mini-Uzi that tore through his rib cage and dropped him like a broken mannequin, his rifle clattering beside him on the pavement. Gellar brushed aside two screaming women, stooped to pick up the rifle and fished beneath the dead man's coat to find a hidden cache of extra magazines.

Better, he thought, and went in search of other prey.

ISTVAN DKANY FIRED another short burst from his AKSU rifle toward the presidential vehicles, cursing as a peasant woman ran across his line of fire and took most of the bullets herself.

"Stupid cow!" he shouted at her prostrate body, twitching on the pavement.

It was her own damned fault for being careless, and he couldn't care less if she lived or died. It was the wasted ammunition that infuriated him, the fact that now his original targets—two blue-suited members of the president's security detachment—had ducked behind their car, no longer in his line of sight.

"Goddammit!"

From all around him, gunfire echoed in Dkany's ears—well, in the one without the plastic earpiece, anyway. And the receiver had been strangely silent since the shooting started prematurely, with a long, apparently aimless burst from one of the rooftops where he had a sniper stationed. Bela, that would be, if he wasn't mistaken, and what had become of him? Why had he jumped the signal?

The only broadcast since their countdown had been Rotislav Chaloupek's frantic command to fire after the first, unexpected shots had spoiled his surprise. Since then, it was all crackling chaos, the occasional burst of raw static in Dkany's left ear, while automatic weapons popped and sputtered all around him, in the village square.

At the moment, in all the confusion, Dkany had no clear idea of which—if either—side was winning the battle. Aside from one of the outriders, sprawled beneath his toppled motorcycle, all the dead or wounded he could see were villagers. Dkany estimated there had been at least a thousand people in the square before the shooting started, roughly twice the population of the village stated in the pregame briefings, and those still on their feet, uninjured, were scrambling madly for safety now, jostling one another like drunken teenagers at a rock-and-roll concert with festival seating. They didn't seem to care if women, children or old people were knocked down and trampled.

Neither did Istvan Dkany, for that matter, as long as the stupid bastards cleared his line of fire.

He could have cleared a fire lane fast enough, by emptying his magazine into the crowd, killing indiscriminately until the peasants got the message and sought cover elsewhere. The idea appealed to him, in fact, except that it would be a waste of precious ammunition, and of time that he couldn't regain. Each second counted now, with helicopter gunships on the way, perhaps already airborne, bearing reinforcements that would pen them up inside the village, kill them all, if they didn't escape before the aircraft found their mark.

Where were Chaloupek's soldiers with the RPG-18s? Dkany wondered. In his estimation, one or both of them should have fired by now, disabling the presidential limousine, adding its flame and shrapnel to the general chaos of the shooting gallery. Bulling his way through the mob scene, slashing with the muzzle of his AKSU at those who blocked his path, Dkany tugged his walkie-talkie from a pocket and keyed the button to transmit. He meant to ask Chaloupek what in hell was going on, but all he got for his trouble was a high-pitched squeal of feedback, prompting reactive screams from two nearby girls.

Dkany flashed them a withering smile and swung the short Kalashnikov in their direction, making childlike gunfire noises as he did so. The girls managed another scream in unison, before they turned and bolted headlong through the crush of bodies milling in the square.

So much for fun and games.

He pocketed the useless radio and swung back toward the bullet-scarred vehicles that had brought his enemies to Vordjalik. First thing, Dkany saw that the second motorcycle was down, collapsed into a spreading pool of gasoline that burbled from its punctured fuel tank, but there was no sign of the driver, presumably crouched behind one of the cars. For the sheer hell of it, Dkany fired a short burst at the bike, striking sparks, and watched the fire catch, flames spreading as if by magic to envelop the machine.

When the gas tank blew seconds later, it sent another shock wave of panic through the already hysterical crowd, bodies surging away from the gout of smoke and flame as if God's hand had dropped a stone from heaven and created instant ripples in the pond of sentient flesh. Istvan Dkany cursed and staggered as an unseen elbow jabbed his ribs, then almost fell as some unwieldy peasant struck him from the opposite direction, running blindly, head down, like a football player racing for the goal.

"Goddammit!" he bellowed, and fired off a short burst at no one in particular, rewarded with screams and the dull thud of at least one body striking pavement.

Better.

They could show him some respect, or they could all go straight to hell.

A bullet whispered past his face, but Dkany was unclear on which direction it had come from, much less who had fired the shot. In any case, he ducked his head lower, using the peasants for cover, struggling against the tide to find a better view of the stalled motorcade. The ultimate humiliation now would be death by what Americans called "friendly fire," shot by one of his own men or Chaloupek's. Not that anyone would be able to tell the difference, when the smoke cleared.

He thought about the waiting motorcycle and his plan to slip away if things went sour on the ambush. It wasn't that bad, so far, but he was counting off the seconds in his mind, grimly aware of fleeting time. A few more minutes, even if they scored the kill, and it would be high time to flee the scene.

Dkany hadn't signed on for a suicide mission, and he didn't intend to throw his life away. Dying for a cause was one thing; flushing your life down the toilet in vain was the height—or nadir—of stupidity.

He found himself a clear view of the limousine, surprised to see it suddenly appear in front of him and raised his AKSU for another burst.

"Come on and show yourselves," he whispered to his hidden enemies. "One little peek. What could it hurt?"

THE CHAOS in the village square made Bolan's task of choosing targets, much less sniping them, more difficult than if his enemies had been alone and had him zeroed in, returning fire en masse. That way, at least, he could have hit them back with everything he had, no worries about ricochets or stray rounds clipping innocent bystanders on the street.

The way it was, he had to find his target first—no easy job, with better than a thousand frantic bodies jostling and stampeding down below—then line up the shot and deliver the payload before some terrified

civilian ran across his line of fire. In fact, there was
no guarantee that he could pull it off at all, but he
was bound to try, since the alternative meant sitting
on his hands, leaving Gellar and Domokos to take the
heat alone.

He wondered where his comrades were, and just as
quickly pushed the thought away. There was no time
to look for them when he was busy tracking hostile
shooters in the crush, daylight preventing him from
even using muzzle-flashes as a guide.

The one good thing about guns firing in a panicked
crowd of noncombatants was that you could often
place the shooters by their impact on the innocents
around them. Look for fallen bodies first, and look
for guns in the immediate vicinity. If that failed, take
the broad view and keep track as the unfortunates
below recoiled from each new burst of fire that tore
into their ranks. You couldn't necessarily see the
shooter, at first, but it was easier to spot the villagers
as they reacted, reeling and stumbling away from a
new, unexpected source of peril.

His first ground-level mark in Vordjalik was
crouched behind a heavy bench that faced the square.
He had some kind of compact submachine gun and
was firing measured bursts at the presidential cars,
raking them without inflicting any clear damage on
the guards crouched behind them.

Still, he was an enemy, a target.

Bolan lined him up in the AUG's optical sight and
shot him once, in the back of the head. The impact
kicked him forward, slammed his chest into the
bench, before he toppled over on his back, blood
spilling on the pavement from his shattered skull. In
seconds flat, a troop of running feet had spread it up

and down the sidewalk, as if manic children had gone racing through a pool of crimson paint.

That made five down by his personal count, and how many remained of the original hit team? He had no way of knowing, but the sheer volume of gunfire from the village square told Bolan that the presidential guards had to be outnumbered at least two to one.

Which meant the Executioner had more work left to do.

He marked another shooter, this one on the move and shoving through the crowd, like a commuter late to catch his train and damned if he would miss it for the sake of simple courtesy. Bolan was lining up his shot when the young man collided with a woman, lashing out to strike her with his weapon, following the backhand with a burst that took her down and out.

"Bastard!"

He shot the callous gunner twice—once in the chest, and once more in his mouth as it fell open, the cliché expression of surprise. The neo-Nazi staggered, legs turned to rubber as his heart and brain shut down together, dropping on his backside with a jolt before he slowly toppled over on his side.

He still had more than twenty rounds left in the Steyr's transparent plastic magazine, easily confirmed at a glance. So far, thanks to the sound suppressor and the confusion down below, none of his enemies had spotted Bolan or attempted to return his fire. They focused on the presidential vehicles, one of the motorcycles burning now, its fuel tank detonating seconds later with a sound approximating that of a grenade.

The blast produced new eddies in the swirling human pond below, and Bolan had to wait another moment while smoke from the blazing two-wheeler briefly obscured his field of vision. One of the chase cars would be next to go, he suspected, its tank already pumping gas from several bullet holes, a pinkish river burbling over cobblestones to meet the crackling lake of fire, some thirty-five or forty feet away. When they met…

No time to waste, then.

Bolan swept the teeming crowd below, in search of targets, his index finger curled around the Steyr's trigger, taking up the slack.

CHAPTER SEVENTEEN

Agoston Domokos took a last drag on his Turkish cigarette before he spit it out, the sweet, familiar rush of nicotine reviving him somewhat. He wasn't tired exactly, but the nervous strain of so much violence in the past twenty-four hours was starting to wear on him, beating him down. He would be glad when it was finished.

As long as he came out alive.

Domokos had exchanged his sawed-off Bernardelli shotgun for an AK-47 with a folding metal stock, mindful of risk to civilians if he sprayed the village square with buckshot. Crouched in an alleyway between two shops, he had the weapon set for semiautomatic fire, another concession to innocent bystanders as he scanned the killing ground for legitimate targets.

He had shot three neo-Nazis already, two of them surely dead, considering the way they dropped and didn't rise again. Domokos wasn't sure about the third one. It was a definite hit, but the skinhead had fallen and rolled out of sight, behind some kind of statue situated at the northwest corner of the village square. He had no fear that the young man had spotted him, or that he could approach the alleyway—much less retaliate—without Domokos seeing him well in advance, but he preferred a job well done and didn't like loose ends.

A wild burst of automatic fire raked the wall above his head, and a group of women ran screaming into the alleyway, stopping short at the sight of Domokos and his rifle, reversing themselves in a panic and plunging back into the square. Domokos, for his part, didn't look after them to see if they would make it. He had grown to manhood in a nation subjugated by Communist secret police, had fought in and survived Croatia's recent civil war, and so considered himself immune to suffering—at least, on behalf of others.

But why, then, was he here?

The question nagged him, and because he had no ready answer, Domokos forced it from his mind, concentrating on the fact that it was time for him to move. He could see no more targets from his present haven, and the acrid smoke from burning vehicles nearby was threatening to gas him out, besides obscuring his vision in a way that could prove fatal.

Go, then!

He had two routes to choose from: straight ahead, into the square, or out the back way and around behind the shops, to find another street or alleyway, another angle of attack. The second way was safer and would shield him from the threat of sniper fire, but Domokos wasn't in a mood to play it safe. For some reason he couldn't quite explain, he had a yearning to engage the enemy, destroy those who would drag his homeland kicking and screaming back to the bad old days of the German reich. If they weren't stopped here and now, who could predict when they would rise again?

Stepping from the alleyway, onto the crude sidewalk that lined the west side of Vordjalik's central plaza, he collided with a fat woman who trailed two screaming children by their scrawny arms, nearly toppling Domokos as she ran past. There was no backward glance and no apology from that one, desperate as she was to save her children and herself.

Domokos wished them well and went in search of human prey.

The crowd was thinning out a bit, its original mass bleeding off into side streets and alleys, ducking into shops for cover, anywhere the threat of being shot by total strangers was decreased. Of the original thousand or so civilians in the square, perhaps one-third were still visible, some crouched in the meager shelter of doorways, others wailing over bodies in the middle of the killing ground, refusing to leave their beloved dead and maimed. A few, including some walking wounded, still drifted about the smoky square, looking dazed and disoriented. They didn't rush around as before, but seemed to have lost direction, perhaps even their will to survive.

The thinning of the crowd made targets easier to spot. It also made Domokos an easier target. Mere seconds after stepping from the alley and colliding with the woman, he came under fire, rifle slugs raising brick dust from the wall close beside him. He dived for cover, found it underneath a sturdy bench that sheltered him from the incoming fire, while still allowing him to see a portion of the village square.

Unfortunately, his assailant wasn't visible from where he lay.

Instead of giving up or cursing fate, Domokos started scanning the plaza for fresh meat, targets he could engage without revealing himself to the still unseen sniper. There was no prayer involved—had long since given up on faith of any kind—but he was wishing hard enough, as fervently as any Western child at Christmas, whispering his need aloud.

"One target. Just one target. One is all I ask."

Instead, Fate gave him two.

The skinheads, armed with submachine guns, were emerging from another alley, thirty yards or so beyond the one where Domokos had been sheltered moments earlier. He watched as they moved closer, lining up the shot, his adversaries focused singlemindedly upon the presidential vehicles. If they had any clue that there were *other* enemies abroad in Vordjalik, besides the official bodyguards, the skinheads gave no sign of it.

When they were close enough that Domokos judged he couldn't miss, he shot the gunman on his right, a double tap aimed at the center of mass, his 7.62 mm rounds ripping into the skinhead's chest and putting him down. Dead or dying, the man thrashed briefly on the pavement, flailing feet in polished combat boots, and then lay still.

It was an easy shift, mere inches, to acquire the second target in his sights. The skinhead was recoiling, looking for the shooter who had nailed his comrade, realizing for the first time that there was another player in the game. His eyes met Domokos's just as he squeezed the trigger of his AK-47 one more time and shot him through the Adam's apple from a range of thirty feet.

Blood spouted from a blow hole in the dying neo-Nazi's throat as he collapsed, first to his knees, then sprawling over on his side. The bullet had to have clipped his spine, judging from how he slumped into a flaccid heap, as if he had no bones.

Life was incredible, Domokos thought. It could be there and gone, within the time it took to blink—or pull a trigger.

The unseen sniper had observed his execution of the skinheads, firing down upon his shelter once again, slugs chipping at the heavy wooden bench that sat on legs of stone. The bullets had not penetrated, so far, but Domokos knew that it was only a matter of time. There was no wood on earth that could withstand rifle fire indefinitely.

And it was time to move. Again.

Domokos had already braced himself to make the run and take his chances, when another loud explosion rocked the square, smoke rising in a ratty kind of mushroom cloud. The Croat knew he would never have a better chance to make it. He rolled out from underneath the bench and sprinted for the alleyway that had concealed his last two victims, conscious of the rifle bullets snapping at his heels.

THE ROCKET SEEMED to come from nowhere, flashing across the periphery of Bolan's vision, striking one of the presidential escort cars broadside and exploding in a smoky thunderclap. The car's fuel tank went off a heartbeat later, adding more smoke and flame to the square that could already pass as a preview of Hell.

He was looking for the source of the rocket, wondering why it hadn't been used on the president's armored limousine, when he saw Agoston Domokos break from cover down below, sprinting from the shadow of a heavy-duty bench toward the mouth of an alley several yards away. It wasn't a great distance, but someone obviously had the Croat zeroed in, rifle bullets chipping at the pavement right behind him, coming closer all the time.

Bolan backtracked, working from the angle of the ricochets, and spied the sniper perched on a second-floor balcony overlooking the square, almost directly opposite Bolan's position. He hadn't been there when the Executioner was clearing the rooftops, but now was what mattered, taking him out before his aim got any better and he brought Domokos down.

Bolan lined up the shot in an instant and triggered two quick rounds from the Steyr, their explosive impact pitching the neo-Nazi gunner backward, away from the balcony railing and through the open window that had been his access to the sniper's perch. Below, Domokos made the alley without knowing who had saved him—or even, perhaps, that he *had* been saved.

No matter. With the odds still ranged against them and the numbers falling until airborne reinforcements reached Vordjalik, the salvation was likely to be transitory, at best.

Another rocket streaked across the village square, this one striking the front end of the armored limousine before it blew, punching the vehicle around through a ninety-degree arc. There was no fire to speak of, yet, but men were spilling from the car like popcorn, scrambling to retrieve weapons they had dropped during the hasty exit, doubling back to shield the one man all of them were paid to protect with their lives, if need be. The president himself appeared disheveled, his gray hair standing up in spikes, blood trickling from a cut beside one eye. He seemed to grapple with his guards, as if reluctant to abandon the damaged vehicle that had brought him back to visit his hometown.

Some welcome party, Bolan thought.

He had the rocketeers, this time, two shooters crouching on the west side of the plaza, discarded launcher tubes on the pavement beside them, their arms now cradling stubby AKSU assault rifles. They had apparently exhausted their artillery, and were preparing to mop up with small arms. Triangulated fire from other snipers was chipping away at the crippled limousine, forcing the guards and their client to duck low, preventing them from breaking toward the nearest open shop.

One thing at a time.

Bolan sighted on the nearer of the neo-Nazis who had fired the RPGs, slamming a 5.56 mm tumbler through the right hinge of his jaw and out the other side, nearly decapitating him. The guy went limp on impact, folding like a dishrag as he crumpled to the pavement, his companion sprayed with blood and mutilated flesh.

The second thug was gaping at the ruin of his comrade's face, recoiling from the sight, his AKSU raised before him almost as a shield, when Bolan placed the crosshairs on his forehead and closed the space between them with a bullet traveling 3,185 feet per second. It struck the target above his left eye and snapped his head backward with the force of a hammer blow, taking him down before he had a chance to realize he had been shot.

Bolan checked the AUG's transparent magazine again—still nine rounds left—and started looking for another target. He was there and ready when a shooter burst out of a shop behind the presidential party, having evidently run around behind the buildings to gain access from the rear. He was firing as he came, a submachine gun braced against his hip, one of the security officers stitched from chest to groin as he shielded his master.

Bolan shot the gunner, one-two-three in rapid fire, and plugged him once more in the back as he spun away, falling, already the next thing to dead. As Bolan shifted the Steyr's scope, he saw the other members of the presidential team rubber-necking, looking for the sniper who had taken down their enemy.

One of them spotted Bolan, pointing toward his rooftop aerie, his lips moving as he announced his discovery. Instinctively, Bolan ducked backward, dropping behind the building's cornice, as a storm of automatic fire sprayed overhead.

"A simple thank-you would have been enough," he muttered, jogging in a crouch toward the hatch and ladder that would take him to the ground floor and the street outside. The roof had just become untenable, and he would have to find another way to reach surviving members of the neo-Nazi ambush team.

Which ought to be no problem, he decided. From the sound of things down in the plaza, there were still more than enough of them to go around.

JACOB GELLAR TRIGGERED a burst from his captured AK-74, watching the skinhead dance a jerky little reel, the bullets slamming into his back, propelling him across the blood-streaked pavement. When he fell with arms outflung, Christlike, his face struck concrete with a sound of snapping cartilage.

Good riddance, Gellar thought, resisting an urge to

spit on the corpse as he moved past it, searching for more targets.

The Israeli had no idea if the president was still alive and well; there was no way for him to check, since any direct approach to the battered vehicles and their remaining guards would be a suicidal act. He checked his watch, surprised to see that barely five minutes had elapsed since the first shots were fired in the plaza. There was still time to spare, before the helicopters arrived, though any escape would be dicey, in the face of airborne pursuit.

Gellar had been circling the square, keeping his distance from the president's embattled bodyguards and tagging neo-Nazis where he found them. He had taken seven out so far, but time was slipping through his fingers, and the impasse that remained was seemingly beyond his power to dissolve. He couldn't join the presidential guard without Domokos to interpret for him, and he frankly doubted whether they would have lived long enough to make their point in any case, once they were glimpsed with weapons in their hands.

Where was Belasko now? The tall American had spoken a desire to find high ground before they separated, but from Gellar's vantage point, the village rooftops were invisible, no snipers readily apparent. If Belasko—

Suddenly, a concentrated storm of automatic fire erupted from around the presidential limousine. Gellar glanced in that direction and saw four or five bodyguards firing diagonally across the plaza, hosing a particular rooftop with their Kalashnikovs and submachine guns. He followed their lead, saw nothing but the drab shopfront, its cornice being ripped apart by bullets fired in vain.

Gellar almost felt sorry for the poor bastard on the receiving end of all that fire, until he recalled that it was just another neo-Nazi, the scum of the earth.

"Rot in hell," he suggested, moving on in his own search for targets.

As it was, he caught a break. Four skinheads, huddled in the doorway of a shop just up ahead, were distracted by some urgent conversation, two of them reloading automatic weapons while they scanned the plaza for potential enemies.

Not well enough.

Gellar was smiling as he shouldered the Kalashnikov and shot the nearest of them in the back, squarely between the shoulder blades. The bullet kicked the skinhead forward, lurching into one of his companions, as the other two reacted, swinging their weapons around toward the source of the shot.

They were quick. Gellar gave them that, as the bullets started whispering around him, forcing him to duck inside another doorway, separated from his enemies by two small shops. He knew they couldn't see him now, but they kept firing anyway, peppering the wall that shielded Gellar from their incoming rounds.

Stalemate, he thought.

Unless…

It was a deadly gamble, but he seemed to have no real alternative. Remaining where he was, pinned down, was an infuriating waste of precious time at best; at worst, it could be fatal if he loitered too long and the helicopter gunships blocked his getaway. The time to make his move was now, when they were least expecting it. All that the move required was courage, and an understanding of the fact that these could be the final moments of his life.

A momentary lull in firing from the enemy gave Gellar the opening he needed. Diving from the doorway's cover, tumbling through a painful shoulder roll, the Israeli wound up prone on the sidewalk, facing his enemies down the barrel of his liberated AK-74.

And found two of them standing firm, while the third broke ranks and took off running for his life.

Something about the runner, as he glanced back briefly, elbows pumping. What was it?

No time for riddles, as the two skinheads remaining opened fire on him from forty feet away. A common failing of those relatively inexperienced with automatic weapons was the reflexive habit of firing too high, and his assailants fell into that trap, hosing the air where Gellar would have been if he were standing, maybe even kneeling on the pavement. He could hear the bullets rattling overhead, could almost feel the hot wind of their passage, and it was enough to hasten his reaction, get him off the dime before the skinheads found their mark.

Gellar had switched his rifle to full-auto mode before he made his headlong dive from cover, and he only had to stroke the trigger now, raking his enemies from left to right and back again. The upward angle of his 5.45 mm rounds lifted both skinheads off their feet, as if a set of ropes had yanked them from behind. They fell almost on top of each other, one young neo-Nazi thrashing for a moment on the pavement, while the other was already deathly still.

Gellar scrambled to his feet and hurdled their bodies, dashing in pursuit of number four. Something about that face, even distorted by a look of panic—

Yes! He had it, now. Domokos, while no great photographer, had managed to produce snapshots of the major neo-Nazi leaders in Croatia, and one of them—Istvan Dkany, leader of the Iron Cross skinhead clique—was just about to slip through Gellar's grasp.

A left turn down the first side street he came to, lurching on the uneven sidewalk, and he was in time to see Dkany mounting a small motorcycle, taking a helmet with a tinted plastic visor from another young man who had obviously waited for him there. Gellar called out to them in Yiddish, never dreaming either one of them would answer him, hoping surprise would slow Dkany enough to let him take a shot.

Instead, Dkany pulled on the helmet and kicked the motorcycle into whining life. Beside him, his companion drew a pistol, pointing it at Gellar, squeezing off a hasty shot that missed him by at least two yards. Gellar's return fire was more accurate, spinning the shooter and dumping him facedown on the cobbled street.

Dkany was rolling now, racing through the gears as he accelerated. Gellar dropped to one knee, held the Kalashnikov steady as he aimed, squeezed the trigger, held it down until the AK's magazine was empty, nothing left to give.

It seemed that he had missed, until the bike began to drift, then skipped the curb and slammed broadside into a stucco wall. It wobbled back across the sidewalk, out into the middle of the narrow street, and there fell over on its side, spilling the rider in a flaccid heap.

Gellar discarded the AK's empty magazine, drawing a fresh one from his pocket and reloading as he paced off the block and a half to his fallen enemy.

All things being equal, never miss a chance to kill a Nazi.

And always, *always* make damned sure they're dead.

ROTISLAV CHALOUPEK'S Rolex Oyster wristwatch—stolen from the limp wrist of a Muslim he had murdered eight years earlier, still keeping perfect time—told him the airborne reinforcements from Zdar could be arriving in Vordjalik any time within the next ten or fifteen minutes. They were running out of time, and still Chaloupek couldn't tell if they had wounded, much less killed, their primary target.

It was no good judging by the presidential bodyguards, he knew. They were fanatics, chosen for their willingness to die in combat, men without families—essentially without lives—who would keep fighting even if their charge was killed before their very eyes. They would expect no quarter from their enemies, and they would offer none to any member of the ambush party who might fall into their hands.

Chaloupek knew that he had lost some men, though he couldn't have said how many. His own plan to score the kill shot on the president had gone awry with the first sound of premature, undisciplined gunfire. He had managed to wing one of the bodyguards, a trivial wound from the look of it, and then he had been driven under cover by return fire from the presidential limousine. From where he sheltered now, he could see five...six...seven members of the raiding party down, unmoving where they lay, some of them sprawled in creeping pools of blood. As for the rooftop snipers, none of them had managed to accomplish anything at all, and he couldn't make out a single one of them engaging the defenders crouched behind the bullet-riddled cars.

Where were they? Could they *all* be dead? If so, how had it happened?

Fruitless questions, Chaloupek realized. Even if he could answer them—which he couldn't, without a cease-fire and a search of every rooftop fronting on the plaza—it would still do nothing to resolve the present stalemate. With the snipers, they had lost at least one-quarter of their starting number, and both rockets had been fired without demolishing the presidential limousine. It was disabled, true enough, but it hadn't caught fire, and it still offered shelter to the gunmen who defended it, still hid their master from the bullets meant to bring him down.

Chaloupek had decided it was time to mount an all-out charge against the enemy, overwhelm him with numbers while the numbers still existed, and wrap up the job that should have been finished by now. The first thing he had to do, quite obviously, was to find out exactly how many soldiers he had left.

Fumbling with the lapel-mounted microphone of his two-way radio, Chaloupek managed to activate it on his second try. He cursed his hands for trembling, telling himself that it had to be a combination of tension and battle fatigue—anything, in fact, except fear.

"Report by numbers," he commanded, waiting a moment, answered only by static and the echoes of continued gunfire from around the plaza. When no one had responded after thirty seconds, Chaloupek tried again, more forcefully, this time. "I said report by numbers, damn you! Do it now!"

Another brief, infuriating delay, and then they started talking back to him, more or less in numerical order, almost every second number missing from the lineup. By the time they finished, Chaloupek understood that the problem was worse than he had thought: nearly one-half of his initial force was silent now, the soldiers dead or wounded, some of them perhaps deserters under fire.

Istvan Dkany's voice wasn't among those who had answered him. Somehow, somewhere, his number two was lost.

He had begun with fifty men, himself aside, and now only twenty-nine answered his call. There was a chance that others were alive and well, their walkie-talkies either lost or damaged, but Chaloupek couldn't count on it. He had to work with the known quantity, make no allowances for phantoms who might—or might not—heed his coming call to action.

"Listen carefully," he told the tiny microphone, rewarded with an abrupt cessation of gunfire around the village square. "Our time is running out, and we haven't yet achieved our objective. On my order, every man will rush the enemy together, overwhelm them and annihilate them all. Questions?"

No answer from the unseen soldiers this time. Chaloupek couldn't say with any certainty if silence meant acceptance of his order, or if some of them were even now retreating, running for their lives. He would find out soon enough.

"Make ready!" he commanded, his furtive eyes darting here and there around the plaza, trying to locate his soldiers, ready to fire on anyone he caught retreating in that crucial moment. "Watch your fields of fire! And…charge!"

Chaloupek, for his part, stayed where he was, as figures rose from cover here and there around the square and started rushing toward the battered, bullet-scarred vehicles of the presidential motorcade. He tried to count them—twelve, thirteen, fourteen—but it was too confusing with his men all firing as they ran, and the defenders instantly returning fire. Within the next few moments, he would know if—

There! He saw the first of his attack force struck down, tumbling backward, shot in the chest. Almost immediately, he saw a second raider, one of Dkany's Iron Cross skinheads, pitched *forward,* his arms out-flung, his weapon spinning free of lifeless fingers.

Shot in the back? How was that possible, un-less—?

Chaloupek heard the sharp, staccato sound of a Ka-lashnikov, much closer than the others, somewhere away to his right. He turned in that direction, and he glimpsed a man he didn't recognize, leaning from the mouth of a narrow alley between two village shops, firing the automatic rifle from his shoulder.

Firing at Chaloupek's men!

The gunman wasn't dressed in navy blue, no but-ton-down white shirt and tie, which meant he wasn't part of the security detachment riding with the pres-ident. Who was he, then?

It hit Chaloupek like a stinging slap across the face. One of Steuben's faceless nemeses!

Chaloupek had a chance to do what no one else in the United States or Germany had managed since the series of attacks had started nearly two weeks earlier. With just a bit of luck and courage, he could be the first to bag one of the hunters who had tracked his leader from the West Coast of America to Vordjalik, killing scores of loyal Aryans along the way. And once the man was dead, he could go through the corpse's pockets, possibly identify him, maybe even find out who had launched him on his long vendetta.

Go!

Chaloupek cast another glance after his soldiers, the thinning ranks still rushing toward the wall of bullet-scarred steel that shielded their enemies, shouting, firing, falling in their mad rush toward the goal. He left them to it, drifting out of cover and maneuvering to take the mystery sniper from his blind side, by surprise.

A few more steps, and—

He would never know what tipped off the shooter, but suddenly the smoking muzzle of that AK swung around to face him, spitting death. Chaloupek felt the bullets rip into his abdomen—a dull pain to begin with, more like solid body blows than any kind of piercing wound—and in another moment he was falling.

There was time enough to curse his fate and Gerhard Steuben's enemies before the sidewalk rose and struck him squarely in the face.

IT WAS THE BANZAI CHARGE that broke them finally. Bolan assumed it had been ordered by some officer he never saw, since the climactic rush was more or less coordinated, the neo-Nazis racing forward all at once, albeit without anything resembling discipline or strategy.

It was a turkey shoot.

The presidential guard—or what was left of it—began unloading with Kalashnikovs and submachine guns as a single unit, a determined firing squad, their bullets winnowing the skinhead ranks and dropping neo-Nazis in midstride. He joined in with the silent

Steyr AUG, taking his targets from behind, shooting them in the back without compunction. On a real-world battleground, vastly removed from Hollywood, fair play came down to anything that let you walk away from an engagement with the enemy.

A moment later, it was finished, though sporadic gunfire still crackled from the defending position, presidential guards firing on prostrate enemies to make sure they stayed down, the bodies jerking rest-lessly with each new impact. Bolan checked his watch again and saw that they were nearly out of time.

He palmed his two-way radio and told the air, "It's time to go. Who reads me?"

"I do," Gellar's voice came back. "I'm on my way."

"And I," Domokos chimed in, sounding slightly winded.

Bolan kept a low profile, retreating toward the ve-hicle that they had stashed three blocks from the cen-tral plaza of Vordjalik, arriving just as Domokos slid behind the steering wheel. Gellar showed up seconds later, lugging a Kalashnikov he had picked up some-where along the way. With nine minutes and counting before the cavalry arrived, they were rolling out of town, northbound along the highway leading to Zagreb.

They met the helicopters three or four miles out of town. There were two of them, as predicted—a Mil Mi-8 Hip model carrying the troops to battle, while a Mil Mi-24 Hind gunship rode shotgun, its weapons pylons loaded with air-to-ground rockets. Bolan braced himself as the two choppers roared overhead, following the highway southward. He half expected the Hind to circle back and blow them off the pavement, better safe than sorry, but the great insectile shapes continued on their way, distorted shadows racing out ahead of them, flickering across the rough terrain.

"That was a bit close for my taste," Gellar said once the choppers had receded in the rearview mirror, fading out of sight.

"It could be worse," Bolan reminded him.

"You mean to say, we could be dead."

Bolan shrugged. "Any day above ground's a good day," he replied.

"Perhaps," Gellar allowed. "You realize, of course, that we've missed Gerhard Steuben again."

"It didn't figure that he'd join the strike team," Bolan said. "He's more the armchair-warrior type. You saw how it went down at Wewelsburg."

"Woolsburg?" Domokos asked.

"Bygones," said Bolan. "What we need to do right now is find out if he's left Croatia yet. We may still have a chance to catch him on the ground before he slips away."

"And if we don't?" the Mossad agent asked.

"No choice, at least for me. I follow where he leads."

CHAPTER EIGHTEEN

Running again.

The prospect made Gerhard Steuben feel physically ill. His stomach churned as if devouring itself, and a throbbing ache had started behind his good eye, while the false one, immune to normal suffering, simply felt like a leaden weight implanted in the left side of his face.

Small favors, Steuben thought, considering where he should go to try to hide this time.

The number of prospective shelters he could count on had been radically reduced within the past two weeks, but Steuben wasn't cornered yet. As long as he could still gain access to an airplane and a pilot, he had friends and allies who would help him activate his master plan.

The parts of it that hadn't been derailed.

So many dead.

Rage mixed with fear to generate the sense of near-debilitating sickness that he felt inside, but that abiding fury also gave him strength, however marginal, to persevere. Steuben was clear on what he had to do, and he would have to do it soon, before the bastards who had killed Chaloupek and the rest managed to track him down somehow.

They would be coming for him; he was certain of it.

Steuben had to make sure he was gone when they arrived—or else he would be dead. Like so many of his disciples in recent days, from Los Angeles to Vordjalik.

There was only one hour's time difference, some six hundred miles give or take. Once he secured the necessary airborne transportation, greased the wheels with money from his ever-dwindling supply, he should be safe and sound at the other end within three or four hours, tops.

Steuben sat and watched, his face impassive, as two of his counterfeit passports were devoured by fire in a large ceramic ashtray shaped like some kind of gourd or squash that he couldn't identify. The false identities that had seen him through transit from the States to Germany and on from there to Croatia had ceased to exist. The trail ended here, on a cheap Formica-topped table in some anonymous stranger's apartment, with a pile of gray, crumbling ash. The smell of melted plastic stung his nostrils, bringing tears to his one good eye.

To follow him beyond Zdar, his enemies would need more than a slim paper trail. His new disguise was more radical than the last one, makeup and prosthetics taking him further from his original self with each successive incarnation. It would match his passport photo perfectly, of course, and he could speak the language well enough to pass for a bumbling professor of archaeology. They wouldn't double-check, because security was always lax except in times of national emergency, and what harm could there be in a frail academic from Vienna, pushing sixty years of age?

As covers went, it was no more than average, but Steuben only had to use it once before it was consigned to ash and ancient history. As soon as he cleared customs, the professor would evaporate as if he had never existed—which, of course, he hadn't.

Another stumbling block for anyone who sought to trace or follow him beyond Zdar. This time, with luck, the dodge would be successful.

Still, Steuben would have felt better, more secure, if he had known how his still nameless enemies had tracked him to Germany and Croatia, disrupting critical plans that had been a year and more in the making. If they could do it twice—*four* times, counting Chicago and Los Angeles—what would prevent them doing it again?

He had no answer to that question, only faith in his personal destiny and that of the movement he led. Granted, that faith had been shaken of late, a major portion his end-time prophecy had been derailed and the movement itself had been severely whittled down by battlefield losses. Still, despite one near miss in the States, before he fled to Germany, Steuben had managed to remain one step ahead of his pursuers.

Now, if he could only gain a bit more time...

His bodyguards from the United States were restive, feeling out of place and cast adrift among foreigners who, despite their shared ideology and racial background, spoke relatively little English and were plainly suspicious of outsiders.

Who could blame them? Steuben wondered, with the havoc that had followed him from Germany, into their own backyard. He was supposed to be their führer, leading them to victory, instead of bringing hell-fire down upon their heads. As for his escorts from America, how could they feel at ease when they were harried and hunted halfway around the globe?

It was time for him to turn the tables and regain the upper hand, inaugurate a brisk offensive on another front, before his unknown adversaries had a chance to track him down and interfere. To show what he was made of, proving to his enemies that he wasn't a beaten cur.

And step one of that plan meant reaching out to touch his allies on the new frontier, alerting them to his arrival and to the acceleration of the plan they had been working on for months.

He should have used a public telephone, to minimize the risk of taps or traces, but his instinct told him that if anyone outside the Nordic Temple knew where he was hiding, he would already have been surrounded, more than likely killed. Steuben didn't believe his present hideout would be traced, but if and when it was, he would be long gone, spreading death and devastation in his wake.

He used the telephone located in his Spartan bedroom, while his escorts smoked and stared at television programs they couldn't translate, muttering darkly among themselves from time to time. He wondered briefly, waiting while another telephone began to ring six hundred miles away, if they would stand behind him to the end or try to cut and run. There was a fleeting moment of anxiety before he steeled himself, remembering that he had chosen them himself, from the elite guard of the Nordic Temple. If he couldn't trust these few when times were hard, then there was no one he could trust.

A gruff voice answered on the telephone's fourth ring, speaking a language Steuben didn't understand. With no interpreter, he did the best he could, announcing his code name in German, then repeating it in English. There was nothing more that he could do.

"A moment," said the stranger on the other end, and Steuben heard the handset clatter on a tabletop or something similar. Steuben was left alone, thankfully without insipid background music to distract him from the tick-tock-tick of passing time. His watch told him that forty-seven seconds had elapsed before another voice came on the line, speaking in English, more or less.

"Hallo?"

"You recognize my voice?" he asked.

"Of course, sir."

"Verify the code, please."

"Yes, sir. My blood is my nation."

"My race is my religion," Steuben answered, completing the exchange.

"I trust that you are well, sir." Sounding just the least bit hesitant about it, though it may have been the language.

"I'm alive," Steuben replied. "Others are not, our comrade in Zdar among them."

"That is grim news. I will miss him."

"Miss him later," Steuben said. "The fight goes on. I have need of your services today."

"You will be coming here?" If he objected to the plan, no reservations were expressed.

"As soon as possible. I'll call with details when a flight has been arranged."

"You will be met, of course. The same place as last time?"

"Provided it is safe," Steuben replied. "Our enemies have been...persistent."

"All will be prepared."

"I'm counting on you. I'll be in touch."

IT HAD OCCURRED to Agoston Domokos that he use
a different method to obtain the information he required this time. There was a possibility, however
slight, that someone else in the Iron Cross knew of
his meeting with late and unlamented Janos. If they
did, and if the skinhead's death had been discovered
in the meantime, then someone on the wrong side
might put two and two together. Scholarship of any
sort wasn't a skinhead strong point, but the goons
could count that high, and with the recent bloodshed
in Zdar, they would be total idiots if certain links
weren't at least hypothesized.

Another angle of attack, then. He wouldn't arrange
the meeting in advance, and he wouldn't waste time
with the Iron Cross. If Gerhard Steuben still remained
within the borders of Croatia, or if he had lately fled
and left a forwarding address, Domokos needed
someone well placed in the Temple of the Nordic
Covenant to fill him in.

The first problem was that the Croat leader of the
Temple, Rotislav Chaloupek, was already dead, killed
in Zdar. Domokos knew a few of the dead man's
lieutenants and assistants, but they weren't friends of
his. He didn't know which of them had been slaughtered with their chief, and if they were alive, he still
couldn't call up and ask them to drop everything, desert their posts in such a time of crisis, for a cup of
coffee and some conversation with a stranger.

What he could do, though, was check around their

haunts and see if he could spot someone he recognized. Someone with rank, if he was given any kind of choice at all. Someone who might have certain basic information and a willingness to share it, once he fully understood the price of standing mute.

And he had to do it soon, his two companions visibly uneasy at the thought of wasting hours, much less days, while their primary target used the time to slip away.

The first two addresses he tried were swarming with police. He didn't linger, staying only long enough to watch a file of uniforms and suits move in and out, some of them bearing weapons, others weighted down with boxes full of God knew what—papers, perhaps, or ammunition, possibly explosives.

Raiding parties meant the Nordic Temple members had been singled out, identified, and the authorities were cleaning up behind them. Domokos couldn't swear to it, but he would happily have bet his monthly earnings that the two whose homes were being ransacked would be found among those slaughtered in Zdar. His first thought was good riddance, then he cursed them for the inconvenience they had put him to by dying, forcing him to go in search of someone else, pursuing what might prove to be a squad of ghosts.

The third stop looked more promising. There were no squad cars, flashing lights or uniforms, at least. Domokos drove past the apartment house one time, and then again, checking the street to make sure that he hadn't overlooked lurking surveillance teams. When it appeared that all was clear, he found a place to park the taxi he had stolen for the expedition, left it at the curb and made his way inside.

It could mean nothing, he admitted to himself, that there were no police or soldiers on the premises. Perhaps they had already been there, though he doubted it. From what he had already seen at his first stops, it seemed unlikely that the searchers would be finished yet, when they could just as easily take time and tear the place apart.

Another possibility that came to mind was that the raids weren't coordinated perfectly and raiders could be on the way, approaching even as he cleared the threshold, crossed the lobby, searching small mailboxes for a name to match with the apartment number. Why should anyone be in a hurry, after all, if the inhabitants of all the homes they meant to search were dead?

Again, Domokos doubted that his idle supposition was correct. The man he'd come to see—and to abduct, if all went well—was ranked among the second tier of leaders for the Temple of the Nordic Covenant in the Republic of Croatia. He wasn't some teenage hooligan whose name would show up near the bottom of the roll, if it appeared at all. He was—had been—among the chosen few whom Chaloupek had regarded as his right-hand men.

And why should he be dead, a lump of meat and bone bagged in Zdar? Would any sane commander risk all of his chief lieutenants into the same engagement, when he recognized the hostile odds?

The neo-Nazi's name was Soma Boldizsar. His flat was on the second floor, two flights of stairs that smelled like cabbage, beets and urine. When Domokos knocked, there was a long delay, and he was just about to try again, when he heard footsteps moving toward the door.

"Who's that?" a male voice asked him, from behind the door.

"A friend," Domokos said, not daring to make up a name. "The Temple needs you, Captain Boldizsar."

He had the well-worn Tokarev TT-33 automatic pistol in his hand as he heard the latches start to open, one by one.

GELLAR WOULDN'T DENY that he had been concerned when Agoston Domokos left to scour Zagreb for leads all by himself. It was a risky plan, but there was more to his concern than simple fear that they might lose their translator and guide.

What would Domokos say if he were taken by police? Would he betray them if it came down to the question of his freedom, even a reduced sentence for his role in what police would certainly describe as two mass murders? More important, what incentive would he have not to betray them?

Still, those weren't the foremost questions nagging at the Mossad agent's mind. He knew Domokos had a lifetime of experience at dodging the police, staying one jump ahead of the corrupt and often inefficient justice system in Zagreb. More dangerous, by far, were those Domokos hunted through the nighttime streets. Survivors of the Nordic Temple and the Iron Cross would be on their guard tonight, well armed and in no mood for trifling with strangers. Those who hadn't made the one-way journey to Zdar would know about its bloody outcome from the media by this time. They would probably go into hiding, or at least make ready to defend themselves from any follow-up assaults by the authorities or foes as yet unknown. If they were wise, they would shoot first and let the questions slide.

That meant Domokos was at risk, but Gellar made no effort to restrain him when the Croat had suggested finding out what could be learned from any stray survivors of the Nordic Temple in Zagreb. They had no other leads, and Gellar would be no help on that quest, unable as he was to even speak the language, much less name and locate any of the Temple's local officers.

Three hours and fifteen minutes had elapsed since Domokos left them to their own devices and began his hunt. Belasko was quiet, keeping to himself and cleaning his weapons, reloading magazines from the boxes of spare ammunition he carried in one of his black duffel bags. He would be ready when the word came—if it came—and they were suddenly required to move.

Gellar didn't believe the tall American was quite as peaceful as he looked, though. Logic told him that there had to be something happening inside Belasko's mind, perhaps a hypothetical attack plan taking shape. Or maybe he was simply tired of chasing Gerhard Steuben all around two continents, so far in vain. Perhaps he was relieved to have a moment when his life wasn't at risk from flying lead and shrapnel.

Maybe he was thinking of the woman.

It was odd, in Gellar's view, the way Belasko let her tag along. Granted, she hadn't caused them any trouble, but she was a piece of excess baggage, a potential liability—albeit an attractive one—with no apparent benefits to balance out the risk. He didn't care to think of how Belasko would respond if she were injured, much less killed—or, worse, if she should fall into the hands of their opponents. Gellar thought himself a fairly decent judge of character, and while he didn't think Belasko and the woman were in love, or anything approaching such commitment, he could still imagine how the soldier would retaliate if she were placed in jeopardy.

He thought it would be quite a spectacle.

The sudden rapping on the door of their hotel room startled Gellar, and he was embarrassed that he hadn't heard approaching footsteps. What did that mean? Was he simply growing careless and preoccupied, or had the person knocking on the door used conscious stealth on his approach? Was there a raiding party—either uniforms or neo-Nazi jackboots—waiting in the corridor outside?

Gellar scooped up his mini-Uzi as he rose and headed for the door. Behind him, Belasko had his Steyr AUG shouldered and ready, just in case. Gellar leaned in to scan the outer hallway through the peephole's cheap distorting lens, then blinked and checked again, to verify what he had seen.

"Domokos," he informed Belasko. "By himself."

He threw the dead bolt, opened up the door and stood aside, the mini-Uzi ready, just in case his first assessment of the empty hallway was mistaken, someone crouching off to either side and out of view, prepared to burst in once the door was opened. Domokos entered smoking, waited for the door to close behind him, then relaxed a bit and said, "Your man is leaving, maybe gone already. I believe you've missed him."

"Where and when?" Belasko asked.

"My source didn't know times or places, I'm afraid. I pressed him on the matter," said Domokos, "and convinced myself that he was truly ignorant of details."

"So, he's splitting, but we don't know when or where he's going?" There was something dangerously close to anger in Bolan's voice.

"Not so," Domokos said, correcting him. "My source didn't know when Steuben would leave, or from which point his flight takes off. He was, however, fairly confident about the destination."

Gellar frowned. "And that would be?"

"Assuming that my source was not deliberately misled," Domokos said, "your rabbit runs for the Ukraine."

Washington, D.C.

THE TIME-ZONE DIFFERENCE meant Hal Brognola had just come back from lunch, had barely taken off his jacket, when he picked up the receiver for his private line and said, "Hello?"

"It's me," said a deep, familiar voice. "I'm turning on the scrambler now."

"Okay."

Brognola jabbed his index finger at a button near the lower left-hand corner of the chunky telephone and watched a small green light switch off, replaced by winking red. When Bolan spoke again, his voice was crystal clear, but anyone eavesdropping on the line would hear only garbled electronic noise—not far removed, in Hal Brognola's view, from what passed for New Age music these days.

"I'm guessing," Bolan said, "that you already heard about our little shindig over here."

"The presidential thing," the big Fed acknowledged. "You're getting to be a fixture on CNN. They should put you on salary, some kind of commentator for the battle of the week. What's new?"

"We're looking at another change of scene. Heading north and east."

The large wall map mounted immediately to his left didn't console Brognola. Everything north and east of Croatia was former Soviet territory, until you entered Russia itself.

"A bit more detail, if you please," Brognola said.

"Word is, our target wants to see if he can get lost with his neo-Nazi pals in Ukraine. My guess would be that he has more than hiding on his mind."

Brognola couldn't stop the frown that carved deep furrows in his face. Ukraine had been something of a madhouse since it declared independence from the crumbling Soviet Union in August 1991. Organized crime—the so-called Russian *Mafiya*—was rampant in the new republic, and a 1994 agreement to destroy Ukraine's nuclear arsenal, allegedly completed with removal of the last strategic warhead two years later, hadn't prevented Ukrainian dealers from scoring big in the post-Soviet nuclear black market. That deadly trade continued to the present day, serving both terrorists and nations that could never whip a nuke up on their own. Meanwhile, recurring financial crises and political unrest kept the pot simmering in Kiev, with frequent violence reported from the hinterlands.

"You want to let him go?" Brognola asked, dead serious.

If Bolan was surprised, it didn't come through in his tone as he replied. "We've come this far," he said. "It seems a shame to scrub the mission if he's almost on the ropes."

"Does Stevens know he's on the ropes?" Hal asked.

"Four times we've checked him now," Bolan replied. "He isn't beaten yet. I won't say that. But we went into this with the awareness that he had a global network. Day by day, it's being whittled down."

"I understand the theory, but the days have got me worried," Brognola frankly admitted. "Every time you fry one tentacle, another one starts flailing, and it's worse than ever. Now you've got a wild man running around nuke central with his ass on fire, looking for a major score to even up the game. It could get serious."

There was a moment of dead air before the Executioner reminded him, "It's always serious."

"But this clown wants the world," Brognola said. "In fact, I wouldn't be surprised to hear he wants the freaking universe, okay? He isn't in it for the money—he's a true believer. And he strikes me as the jealous type. If *he* can't have the world, I wouldn't be surprised to see him try and fix it up so no one else can have it, either. Scorched earth, right? With what some of the traders in Ukraine supposedly have stashed away for sale, this guy could make Chernobyl look like Friday night around the campfire at a Boy Scout jamboree."

"That's why we need to stop him," Bolan said.

Brognola nodded to the empty room, as if someone were there to see it. "Okay," he said at last. "It's your call. Tell me what you need."

The list was relatively short, all things considered, but Brognola wasn't certain that he could deliver. Still, he put a brave face on it, telling his old friend,

"I'll see what I can do. We'll have to try and work through CIA with some of it."

"Whatever," Bolan said. "Our friend from Tel Aviv apparently has some connections we can use, but I'd prefer to have a backup system ready, so we don't get some kind of a nasty surprise."

"I have a couple folks who owe me favors at the Company," Brognola said. "I'll call in the markers and do my best."

"That's all we ask," Bolan said with a chuckle.

"Thank you, Mother. Now, if you don't need me to reserve a battleship or aircraft carrier..."

"I think that's it for now."

"Oh, hey!" Brognola said. "About the woman..."

"What about her?" Bolan asked.

"Nothing special. I was just wondering if she was going with you on the next leg of your trip."

"We haven't talked about it yet. It's next up on my list."

Another frown tugged at the corners of his mouth as Brognola replied, "Good luck with that."

"I'll be in touch," the Executioner replied, and he was gone.

"I hope so," the big Fed responded, talking to the dial tone. "I really do."

Croatia

"OKAY, WHY NOT?" Marilyn Crouder said. "I've never been to the Ukraine."

"I think it's just 'Ukraine,' now," Bolan said. "And there's no reason I can think of why you ought to break your record."

She frowned and said, "Oh, no, you don't. We've

had this conversation, and I don't like to repeat myself.''

"Neither do I," Bolan replied, "but I can think of things I like a whole lot less.''

"Uh-huh. And this is where you tell me it's too dangerous, I'm excess baggage, a distraction. I should go on home and beg to get my old job back—or maybe meet a nice rich doctor, settle down and have some kids. Is that about the size of it?''

"The going-home part doesn't sound unreasonable," Bolan said. "As for the rest of it, that's up to you.''

"And leaving isn't up to me?" She bristled, clenched fists knuckling her denim-clad hips. "Is this where you try pulling rank? Should I remind you that you're not my boss—that I don't have a boss, in fact? I dumped my job to stick with you.''

"That doesn't make us Hope and Crosby," Bolan told her gruffly. "If you think it's been an ugly trip to this point, you should brace yourself, because the ugly's only getting started.''

"So what?" she challenged him. "No more five-star hotels?''

He stared at her and let the silence stretch between them, tense and simmering.

"Come on," she said at last. "You've run out of excuses, Mike, so face it. You can't say I butted in this time. You can't claim I was in your way, distracting you. We've hardly spoken since you dropped me off here yesterday. There's nothing you can say to change my mind. Get over it.''

The hell of it, Bolan considered, was that she was right. She had refrained from pushing any envelopes or stepping over any boundaries this time. She had been good, and she had still been on his mind, though it didn't prevent his functioning at peak capacity.

"It's different in Ukraine," he told her, playing his last card. "Staying out of the way may not be good enough."

Crouder studied Bolan's face for several seconds, then her eyes went wide. "Oh, God!" she said. "You think he's going nuclear?"

"I think it's possible," Bolan replied. "We won't be sure until we're on the ground. It may not be containable."

Her sudden smile took Bolan absolutely by surprise. "I guess you can't afford to ditch me, then," she said.

"How's that?"

"This time," Crouder said, "there's a good chance that I can help you. And I don't mean chilling out in some fleabag hotel, while you and Gellar go play cops-and-robbers."

"Marilyn—"

"I've met him," Crouder announced before Bolan could frame a discouraging word. "This time, I know the guy."

"Which guy would that be?" Bolan asked suspiciously.

"Oh, just the top man for the Temple of the Nordic Covenant in Ukraine," she said. "That's all."

"You know him." Bolan's tone was frankly skeptical.

"I didn't say we're bosom friends, okay?" she said. "We met one time at Freedom Home, in Oregon. It was about a month before you pulled me out of there. They had some kind of an exchange deal going on, something like that. I wasn't privy to the details, but I met the dude. No doubt about it."

"And his name is…?"

"Hedeon Onoprienko," she replied. "Check it through Gellar's people, if you don't believe me."

"I'm ahead of you on that one," Bolan said. "You got the name, all right, but that still doesn't mean—"

"That I can help you out?" she challenged. "Think about it, Mike. He met me in the States. I'm hanging with the Temple goons at Freedom Home. He splits. As far as this guy knows, I'm still a Hitler groupie in good standing."

"Meaning what, exactly? That you stroll into his office unannounced and ask him if he needs another hand?"

"As I recall," she said, "when we were introduced, he wasn't concentrating on my hands."

"No good," Bolan said in a firm, uncompromising tone.

"That wouldn't be a little green-eyed monster talking, would it?" Teasing him, but serious at the same time.

"Have you forgotten Stevens?" Bolan asked her pointedly. "It doesn't matter whether the Ukrainian's been briefed on your defection, or he hasn't. If Stevens gets one look at you, he blows the whistle, and you wind up in a body bag. That's if you're lucky."

"Maybe not," she said. "The way it looks to me, my plan works out *because* of Stevens, not in spite of him."

"Oh, really? How does that work on the drawing board?" he asked.

"Just think about it, Mike. The führer shows up with this string of massacres behind him, like some kind of Typhoid Gary. He's the freaking kiss of death, for God's sake. He was never wrapped that tightly to begin with, and I have to think he's on the shaky side of gone by now.''

''So what? His whole cult's out to lunch, between the master-race nonsense, the end-time prophecies and thinking any group that size could touch off Armageddon, much less win the fight and wind up ruling Earth. You ask me, it's a wonder that straitjackets aren't the standard party uniform.''

''Nobody ever said these guys were rational,'' Crouder said. ''It's zealotry that makes them dangerous. If Stevens was a well man, he'd have quit by now and done a major fade to parts unknown. If his lieutenants didn't have a few screws loose, they'd drop him in a hole somewhere and concentrate on getting out of this alive, by any means available.''

''So, we agree,'' Bolan said.

''Not so fast. I'm trusting Onoprienko to be more than a little bit paranoid.''

''That sounds like a safe bet to me.''

''Which means,'' she forged ahead, ''that if an emissary from the States showed up to warn him that the führer needs a checkup from the neck up, that he's throwing lives away and jeopardizing everything the Temple loyalists have worked for through the years, it might just strike a spark.''

''Too risky,'' Bolan told her. ''Stevens picked these goons, remember. They're birds of a feather.''

''They're buzzards who'll turn on their own for the cause,'' she replied, ''or maybe for personal reasons, if it comes down to that.''

''I still don't like it.''

''But it's worth a listen, yes? A little look-see? If

we get there, and you still don't think it's feasible, all right. I'll sit in the hotel and knit a shawl, okay? But even if I don't go in, I did pick up a feel for the Ukrainian, the short time we were hanging out. I still think I can help you.''

Maybe, Bolan thought, and maybe not.

''We'll talk about it on the plane,'' he said at last.

* * * * *

The heart-stopping action
concludes with
A DYING EVIL
Book III of
THE TYRANNY FILES,
available in September

When all is lost, there's always the future...

JAMES AXLER

DEATHLANDS®

THE SKYDARK CHRONICLES Book III

Shadow Fortress

The Marshall Islands are now the kingdom of the grotesque Lord Baron Kinnison. Here in this world of slavery and brutality, the companions have fought a fierce war for survival, on land and sea—yet the crafty baron still conspires to destroy these interlopers. They cunningly escape to the neighboring pirate-ruled Forbidden Island, with the baron's sec men in hot pursuit...and become trapped in a war for total supremacy of this water world.

Available in September 2001 at your favorite retail outlet.

James Axler

OUTLANDERS®

SARGASSO PLUNDER

An enforcer turned renegade, Kane and his group
learn of a mother lode of tech hidden deep within
the ocean of the western territories, a place once
known as Seattle. The booty is luring tech traders and
gangs, but Kane and Grant dare to infiltrate the
salvage operation, knowing that getting in is a life-
and-death risk....

*In the Outlands, the shocking truth
is humanity's last hope.*